Edgar Fawcett

An Ambitious Woman

A Novel

Edgar Fawcett

An Ambitious Woman
A Novel

ISBN/EAN: 9783337000844

Printed in Europe, USA, Canada, Australia, Japan

Cover: Foto ©Andreas Hilbeck / pixelio.de

More available books at **www.hansebooks.com**

AN AMBITIOUS WOMAN

A Novel

BY

EDGAR FAWCETT

AUTHOR OF "A GENTLEMAN OF LEISURE," "A HOPELESS
CASE," ETC.

BOSTON
HOUGHTON, MIFFLIN AND COMPANY
New York: 11 East Seventeenth Street
The Riverside Press, Cambridge
1884

AN AMBITIOUS WOMAN.

I.

IF any spot on the globe can be found where even
Spring has lost the sweet trick of making herself
charming, a cynic in search of an opportunity for
some such morose discovery might thank his baleful
stars were chance to drift him upon Greenpoint.
Whoever named the place in past days must have
done so with a double satire ; for Greenpoint is not a
point, nor is it ever green. Years ago it began by
being the sluggish suburb of a thriftier and smarter
suburb, Brooklyn. By degrees the latter broad-
ened into a huge city, and soon its neighbor village
stretched out to it arms of straggling huts and
swampy river-line, in doleful welcome. To-day the
affiliation is complete. Man has said let it all be
Brooklyn, and it is all Brooklyn. But the sovereign
dreariness of Greenpoint, like an unpropitiated god,
still remains. Its melancholy, its ugliness, its torpor,
its neglect, all preserve an unimpaired novelty. It
is very near New York, and yet in atmosphere, suggestion, vitality, it is leagues away. Our noble city,
with its magnificent maritime approaches, its mast-
thronged docks, its lordly encircling rivers, its majesty of traffic, its gallant avenues of edifices, its loud

1

assertion of life, and its fine promise of riper culture, fades into a dim memory when you have touched, after only a brief voyage, upon this forlorn opposite shore.

No Charon rows you across, though your short trip has too often the most funereal associations. You take passage in a squat little steamboat at either of two eastern ferries, and are lucky if a hearse with its satellite coaches should fail to embark in your company; for, curiously, the one enlivening fact associable with Greenpoint is its close nearness to a famed Roman Catholic cemetery. It is doubtful if the unkempt child wading in the muddy gutter ever turns his frowzy head when these dismal retinues stream past him. They are always streaming past him; they are as much a part of this lazy environ as the big, ghostly geese that saunter across its ill-tended cobblestones, the dirty goats that nibble at the placards on its many dingy fences, or the dull-faced Germans that plod its semi-paven streets. Death, that is always so bitter a commonplace, has here become a glaring triteness. Watched, along the main thoroughfare, from porches of liquor-shops and windows of tenement-houses, death has perhaps gained a sombre popularity with not a few shabby gazers. It rides in state, at a dignified pace; it has followers, too, riding deferentially behind it. Sometimes it has martial music, and the pomp of military escort. Life seldom has any of this, in Greenpoint. It cannot ride, or rarely. It must walk, and strain to keep its strength even for that. One part of it drudges with the needle, fumes over the smoky stove, sighs at the unappeasable baby; another part takes by dawn the little-dwarfish ferry-boat, and hies to the great metropolis across the river, returning jaded from labor by nightfall. No wonder, here, if death should seem to possess not merely a mournful importance but a gloomy advantage as well, or if for these toilful townsfolk philosophy had reversed itself, and instead of the paths of glory leading to the grave, it should look as if the grave were forever leading to some sort of peculiar and comfortable glory.

But Greenpoint, like a hardened conscience, still has her repentant surprises. She is not quite a thing of sloth and penury. True, the broad street that leads from steamboat to cemetery is lined with squalid homes, and the mourners who are so incessantly borne along to Calvary must see little else than beer-sellers standing slippered and coatless beside their doorways, or thin, pinched women haggling with the venders of sickly groceries. But elsewhere one may find by-streets lined with low wooden dwellings that hint of neatness and suggest a better grade of living. A yellowish drab prevails as the hue of these houses; they seem all to partake of one period, like certain homogeneous fossils. But they do not breathe of antiquity; they are fanciful with trellised piazzas and other modern embellishments of carpentry; sometimes they possess miniature Corinthian pillars, faded by the trickle of rain between their tawny flutings, as if stirred with the dumb desire to be white and ·classic. Scant gardens front them, edged with a few yards of ornamental fence. Their high basement windows stare at you from a foundation of brick. They are very prosaic, chiefly from their lame effort to be picturesque; and when you look down toward the river, expecting to feel refreshed by its gleam, you are disheartened at the

way in which lumber-yards and sloop-wharves have
quite shut any glimpse of it from your eyes.

In one of these two-storied wooden houses, not
many years ago, dwelt a family of three people, — a
Mr. Francis Twining, his wife, and their only child,
a girl, named Claire. Mr. Twining was an English-
man by birth; many years had passed since he first
landed on these shores. He had come here nearly
penniless, but with proud hopes. He was then only
three-and-twenty. He had sprung from a good
country family, had been fitted at Eton for Oxford,
and had seen one year at the famed University.
Then sharp financial disaster had overtaken his father, whose death soon followed. Francis was a
younger son, but even to the heir had fallen a shattered patrimony, and to himself merely a slender
legacy. With this, confident and undaunted as
though it were the purse of Fortunio, Francis had
taken voyage for New York. At first he had shown
a really splendid energy. Slim of figure, with a pale,
womanish face lit by large, soft blue eyes, he gave
slight physical sign of force or even will. But
though possessed of both, he proved one of those ill-
fated beings whom failure never tires of rebuffing.
His mental ability was unquestioned; he shrank with
sensitive disgust from all vice; he had plenty of ambition, and the instinct of solid industry. Yet, as years
passed on, both secured him but meagre recompense
for struggle. He had begun his career with a clerkship; now, at fifty-three, he was a clerk still. All his
hope had fled; he had undergone bitter heart-burn-
ings; he had striven to solve the problem of his own
defeat. Meanwhile its explanation was not difficult.
He had a boyish trust in his fellow-creatures that no

amount of stern experience seemed to weaken. Chicanery had made him its sport. Five separate times he had been swindled mercilessly by men in whom he had reposed implicit faith. There had lain his rock of ruin: he was always reposing implicit faith in everybody. His life had been one long pathos of over-credulity. He could think, reason, reflect, analyze, but he was incapable of doubting. A fool could have deceived him, and naturally, on repeated occasions, knaves had not found it difficult. At fifty-three his last hard-earned savings had been wormed from him by the last plausible scamp. And now he had accepted himself as the favorite of misfortune; over the glow of his spirit disappointment had cast its dulling spell, like the deep film of ash that sheathes a spent ember. He had now one aim — to keep his wife and child from indigence while he lived, and one despair — that he could not keep them from indigence after he was dead. But his really lovely optimism still remained. He had been essentially amiable and complaisant in all intercourse with his kind, and this quality had not lost a ray of its fine former lustre. With ample excuse for the worst cynic feeling, he continued a gentle yet unconscious philanthropist. There was something piteously sweet in the obstinacy with which he still saw only the bright side of humanity. His delicate person had grown more slim; his rusty clothes hung about him with a mournful looseness; his oval face, worn by worriment, had taken keener lines; but his large blue eyes still kept their liquid sparkle, and kindled in prompt unison with his alert smile. The flaxen growth that had always fringed his lips and chin with cloudy lightness, had now become of a frosty gray. Seen passingly, no one would have called him, as the current phrase goes, a gentleman. His wearied mien forbade the suggestion of leisure, while his broadcloth spoke of long wear and speedy purchase. But a close gaze might have caught the unperished refinement that still clung to him with sad persistence, and was evident in such minor effects of personal detail as a glimpse of cleanly linen about throat and wrist, a cheap yet careful lustre of the often jaded boot, a culture and purity of the hand, or even a choice nicety of the finger-nail.

He had married after reaching these shores, and his marriage had proved another instance of misplaced confidence. His wife had been handsome when a young woman, and she had become Mrs. Twining at about the age of five-and-twenty. She was personally quite the opposite of her bridegroom; she was an inch taller than he, and had an aquiline face, splendid with a pair of very black eyes that she had rolled and flashed at the other sex since early girlhood. She had rolled and flashed them at her present husband, and so conquered him. She was a good inch taller than he, and lapse of time had not diminished the difference since their union. She had been extremely vulgar as Miss Jane Wray, when Twining had married her, and she was extremely vulgar still. She had first met him in a boarding-house in East Broadway, where Twining had secured a room on his arrival from England. At this period East Broadway wore only a waning grace of gentility; some few conservative nabobs still lingered there, obstinately defying plebeian inroads. Its roomy brick mansions, with their arched, antique doorways devoid of any vestibule; their prim-railed stoops that

guessed not of ornate balusters; and their many-
paned, thin-sashed windows where plate-glass had
never glittered, were already invaded by inmates
whose Teuton names and convex noses prophesied
the social decline that must soon grasp this once select purlieu. Jane Wray was neither German nor
Hebrew; she was American in the least pleasant
sense of that word, both as regarded parentage and
breeding. She was an orphan, and the recipient
of surly charity from unprosperous relatives. She
wanted very greatly to marry, and Twining had
seemed to her a golden chance. There was much
about her from which he shrank; but she contrived
to rouse his pity, and then to lure from him a promise
which he would have despised himself not to keep.

The succeeding years had brought bitter mutual
disappointments. Mrs. Twining had believed firmly
in her husband's powers to sound the horn of luck
and slay the giant of adversity. But he had done
neither, and it now looked as if his bones were one
day to bleach along the roadway to success. She
became an austere grumbler, forever pricking her
sweet-tempered lord with a tireless little bodkin of reproach. Her vulgarities had sharpened; her wit, always cruel and acute, had tipped itself with a harsher
venom and fledged itself with a swifter feather; her
bright, coarse beauty had dimmed and soured; she
was at present a gaunt, elderly female, with square
shoulders and hard, dark eyes, who flung sarcasms
broadcast with a baleful liberality, and seemed forever standing toward her own destiny in the attitude
of a person who has some large unsettled claim against
a nefarious government.

Claire Twining, the one child who had been born

of this ill-assorted marriage, was now nineteen years old. She bore a striking likeness to her father; she possessed his blue eyes, a trifle darker in shade, his broad white forehead, his sloping delicacy of visage, and his erect though slender frame. From him, too, had come the sunny quality of her smile, the gold tints in her chestnut hair, the fine symmetry of hands and feet. Rather from association than heredity she had caught his kindly warmth of manner; but in Claire the cordial impulse was far less spontaneous; she had her black list of dislikes, and she took people on trust with wary prudence. Here spoke her mother's share in the girl's being, as it spoke also in a certain distinct chiseling of every feature, that suggested a softened memento of Miss Jane Wray's girlish countenance, though Claire's coloring no more resembled her mother's of past time than wild-rose is like peony, or pastel like chromo. But there was one more maternal imprint set deep within this girl's nature, not to be thinned or marred by any stress of events, and productive of a trait whose development for good or ill is the chief cause that her life has here been chronicled. The birthright was a perilous one; it was a heritage of discontent; its tendency was perpetual longings for better environment, for ampler share in the world's good gifts, for higher place in its esteem and stronger claim to its heed. But what in her mother had been ambition almost as crudely eager as a boorish elbow-thrust, was in Claire more decorous and interesting, like the push of a fragile yet determined hand through a sullen crowd. In both cases the dissatisfaction was something that is peculiar to the woman of our land and time — a desire not to try and adorn the sphere in which she is

born, but to try and reach a new sphere held as more
suited for her own adornment. Yet Claire's restless
yearning lacked the homely grossness of her mother's; it reflected a finer flash; it was not all cut from
one piece; it had its subtlety, its enthusiasm, even
its justification. It was not a mere stubborn hunger
for advancement; it was a wish to gain advancement
by the passport of proper worthiness. She did not
want the air to lift her away from hated surroundings, but she wanted wings that would turn the air
her willing ally. It was what her father had made
her that touched what her mother had made her with
a truly poetic tenderness. By only a little prouder
curve of the neck and a little happier fullness of the
plume, we part the statuesque swan from considerably more commonplace kindred. Something like
this delightful benison of difference had fallen upon
Claire.

II.

CIRCUMSTANCE, too, had fed the potency of this difference. Claire had not been reared like her mother. When she was nine years old her parents were living in a tiny brick house near the East River, among New York suburbs. But Claire had been sent to a small school near by, kept by a dim, worn lady, with an opulent past and a most precarious present. She had studied for three years under this lady's capable care, and had lost nothing by the opportunity. Her swift, apt mind had delighted her instructress, whose name was Mrs. Carmichael. Claire was remarkably receptive; she had acquired without seeming effort. Mrs. Carmichael was one of the many ladies who attempt the education of youth without either system or equipment for so serious a task. Her slight body, doubtless attenuated by recurring memories of a cherished past, would sometimes invisibly quake before Claire's precocious questionings. She knew all that she knew superficially, and she soon became fearful lest Claire should pierce, by a sort of adroit ignorance, her veneer of academic sham. She had a narrow little peaked face, of a prevailing pink hue, as though it were being always bathed in some kind of sunset light, like the rosy afterglow of her own perished respectability. Her nervous, alert head was set on a pair of sloping shoul-

ders, and she wore its sparse tresses shaped into rou-
lades and bandeaus which had an amateurish look,
and seemed to imitate the deft handiwork of some
long-departed tirewoman. She carried her small
frame with erect importance. She was always referring to vanished friendships with this or that notability, but time and place were so ignored in these volun-
teered reminiscences as to make her allusions acquire
a tender mythic grandeur. Claire had watched well
her teacher's real and native elegance, and she had
set this down as a solid fact. Perhaps the child had
probed her many harmless falsities with equal skill.
As for Mrs. Carmichael, she would sometimes pat
her pupil on the cheek and praise her in no weak
terms. " I wish that I had only known you a long
time ago, my little lady," she would say, in her
serene treble voice. " I would have brought you up
as my own dear child, for I never had a child of
my own. I would have given you a place in the
world to be proud of, and have watched with interest the growth of your fine mental abilities, surrounded by those poor lost friends of mine who
would have delighted in so clever a girl as you are."

" When you speak of your friends as lost, Mrs.
Carmichael," Claire had once replied, " do you mean
that they are all dead now ? "

At this question the lady slowly shook her head,
with just enough emphasis not to imperil the modish
architecture of her locks.

" Some of them are dead, my dear," she murmured, with the least droop of each pink eyelid, " but
the rest are much too grand for me at present. They
have quite forgotten me." Here Mrs. Carmichael
gave a quick, fluttered cough, and then put the tips

of her close-pressed fingers to the edges of her close-pressed lips.

Claire privately thought them very churlish friends to have forgotten anybody so high-bred and winsome as Mrs. Carmichael. And she publicly expressed this thought at supper the same evening, while she sat with her parents in a small lower room opening directly off the kitchen. A weary maid, whose face flamed from the meal she had just cooked, was patiently serving it. Mrs. Twining, who had lent no light hand toward the Monday's washing, was in the act of distributing a somewhat meagre beefsteak, which fate and an incompetent range had conspired to cover on both sides with a layer of thick, sooty black. Mr. Twining was waiting to get a piece of the beefsteak; he did not yet know of its disastrous condition, for a large set of pewter casters reared its uncouth pyramid between himself and the maltreated viand; but although such calamities of cookery were not rare to his board, he was putting confidence, as usual, in the favors of fortune, and preparing himself blandly for a fresh little stroke of chagrin.

Outside it was midwinter dusk, and a bleak wind was blowing from the ice-choked river, pale and dull under the sharp stars. One-Hundred-and-Twelfth Street was in those years a much wilder spot than now; its buildings, like its flag-stones, were capricious incidents; its boon of the elevated railroad was yet undreamed of by capitalists; you rode to it in languid horse-cars from the remote centres of commerce, upward past parapets of virgin rock where perched the hut of the squatter, or wastes of houseless highway where even the aspiring tavern had not dared to pioneer. Mr. Twining had just ridden hither by this laggard means, and he was tired and hungry; he wanted his supper, a little valued chat with his beloved Claire, and a caress or two from the child as well. After these he wanted a few hours of rest before to-morrow re-dawned, with its humdrum austerities. One other thing he desired, and this was a blessing more often desired than attained. He had the wish for a peaceful domestic interval, as regarded his wife's deportment, between home-coming and departure.

But to-night it had been otherwise decreed. Mrs. Twining's faint spark of innate warmth was never roused by the contact of suds. Monday was her day of wrath; you might almost have fancied that she had used a bit of her superfluous soap in vainly trying to rub the rust from her already tarnished hopes.

The small room where the trio sat was void of any real cheer. A pygmy stove, at one side of it, stood fuel-choked and nearly florid in hue. From this a strong volume of heat engulfed Mrs. Twining in its oppressive spell, but lost vigor before it reached her husband or Claire, and left the corners of the apartment so frigid that a gaunt sofa, off where the light of the big oil-lamp could only vaguely touch it, took upon its slippery hair-cloth surface the easy semblance of ice. Two windows, not fashioned to thwart the unwonted bitterness of the weather, were draped with nothing more resistant than a pair of canvas shades, gorgeously pictorial in the full light of day, when seen by the passer who seldom passed. These shades were of similar designs; in justice to Mrs. Twining it must be told that they had been rented with the house. On each a plumed gentleman in a gondola held fond converse with a disheveled lady in a balcony. The conception was no less Venetian in meaning than vicious in execution ; but to-night, for any observant wayfarer, such present-ments of sunny Italy, while viewed between blotches of wan frost that crusted the intervening panes, must have appeared doubly counterfeit. Still, the chief discomfort of the chamber, just at present, was a layer of brooding cold that lay along its floor, dog-gedly inexterminable, and the sole approach to regu-larity of temperature that its four walls contained.

It had made Claire gather up her feet toward the top rung of her chair, and shiver once or twice, but it had not chilled the pretty gayety of her childish talk, all of which had thus far been addressed to her father.

"And so you like Mrs. Carmichael, my dear?" Twining had said, in his smooth, cheerful voice. "Well, I am glad of that."

"Oh yes, I like her," replied Claire, with a slight, wise nod of her head, where the clear gold of youth had not yet given way to the brown-gold of maiden-hood. "But I think it strange that all her fine friends have dropped off from her. That's what she told me to-day, Father ; truly, she did ! Why don't they care for her any more? Is it because she's poor and has to teach little dunces like me ? "

Twining's feminine blue eyes scanned the rather dingy tablecloth for a moment. "I am afraid it is," he said, in a low voice, pressing between his fingers a bit of ill-baked bread that grew doughy at a touch.

Mrs. Twining ceased to carve the obdurate beef-steak, though still retaining her hold on the horn-handled knife and fork. She lifted her head so that it quite towered above the formidable group of cas-ters, and looked straight at her husband.

"Don't put false notions into the child, Francis," she said, each word seeming to strike the next with a steely click. "You're always doing it. *You* know nothing of where that woman came from, or who she is."

Twining looked at his wife. His gaze was very mild. "I only know what she has told me, Jane," he said.

Mrs. Twining laughed and resumed the carving. Her laugh never went with a smile; it never had the least concern with mirth; it was nearly always a presage of irony, as an east wind will blow news of storm.

"Oh, certainly; what she's told you! That's you, all over! Suppose she'd told you she'd been Lady of the White House once. You wouldn't have believed her, not you! Of course not!"

"What is a Lady of the White House?" asked Claire, appealing to her father. She was perfectly accustomed to these satiric outbursts on her mother's part; they belonged to the home-circle; she would have missed them if they had ceased; it would have been like a removal of the hair-cloth sofa, or an accident to one of the lovers on the window-shades.

Twining disregarded this simple question, which was a rare act with him; he usually heard and heeded whatever Claire had to say.

"Please don't speak hard things of Mrs. Carmichael," he answered his wife. "She's really a person who has seen better days."

"Better days!" echoed Mrs. Twining. "Well, then, we ought to shake hands. *I* think she's just *the* plainest humbug I ever saw, with her continual brag about altered circumstances. But I'll take

your word for it, Francis. The next time I see her
I'll tell her we're fellow-unfortunates. We'll compare our 'better days' together, and calc'late who's
seen the most."

Twining gave a faint sigh, and looked down. Then
he raised his eyes again, and a new spark lit their
mildness. Something to-night had made him lack
his old patient tolerance.

"I'm afraid Mrs. Carmichael would have much
the longer list," he said.

"Oh, you think so!"

"I know so."

Mrs. Twining tossed her head. The gloss was
still on her dark hair, whose gray threads had yet to
come, later, in the Greenpoint days. She was still,
as the phrase goes, a fine figure of a woman. Her
black eyes had not lost their fire, nor her form its imposing fullness. She raised herself a little from her
chair, as she now spoke, and in her voice there was
the harshness that well fitted her bristling, aggressive
mien.

"Oh! you *know* so, do you?" she said, in hostile
undertone. Then her next words were considerably
louder. "But *I* happen to know, Francis Twining,
*E*squire, who and what *I* was when you took me
from a comfortable home to land me up here at the
end of the world, where I'm lucky if I can get hold
of yesterday's newspaper to-morrow, and cross over
to the cars without leaving a shoe behind me in the
mud!"

The least flush had tinged Twining's pale cheeks.
He had looked very steadily at his wife all through
this speech. And when he now spoke, his voice made
Claire start. It did not seem his.

" You were a poor girl in a third-rate boarding-house, when I married you," he said. " And the boarding-house was kept by relatives who disliked and wanted to be rid of you. I don't see how you have fallen one degree lower since you became my wife. But if you think that you have so fallen, I beg that you will not forever taunt me with idle sneers, of which I am sick to the soul!"

Mrs. Twining rose from her chair. Her dress was of some dark-red stuff, and as the stronger light struck its woof the wrath of her knit brows seemed to gain a lurid augment. She had grown pale, and a little mole, just an inch or so to the left of her assertive nose, had got a new clearness from this cause. She did not speak, at first, to her husband. She addressed the fatigued and heated maid, who waited to hand Twining his share of the doleful beefsteak — in this case a true burnt-offering.

" You can go into the kitchen, Mary Ann," she said, with tones that had a kind of rumble, like the beginning of a large thunder-peal, before its threat has become fury. " See to the range, you know. Dump all the coal out, and then sift it."

Mary Ann went uneasily toward the door. She understood that this order thinly masked a bluff command for her absence. Mrs. Twining slowly turned her head, and followed the poor factotum with her kindled black eyes till she had quitted the room. Then she looked with stern directness at her husband.

" I've stood a good deal from you," she said, pitching her voice in a much shriller key, " but I ain't going to stand *this*, Francis Twining, and it's time I told you so."

2

Twining rose. He did not look at all angry. There was a weary distress on his face, mixed with an unhabitual firmness.

" What have you stood?" he asked.

" Being browbeat by you, sir, because I see fit to talk out my mind, and ain't the weak-spirited goose you 'd like to have me!" retorted Mrs. Twining, all rage and outcry.

" I don't want a quarrel," said Twining, calm as marble. " God knows I don't, Jane! But the time has come for me to speak plainly. I have never browbeaten you. It has been quite the opposite. I have already borne too much from you for the sake of peace. But no peace springs from that course. So now I mean to try another. You and I must live apart, since we can't agree." He turned to Claire, at this point, and reached out one hand, resting it on the girl's head. " Let our child choose which of us she will go with," he added.

Claire started up, sprang to her father's side, and nestled herself against him, catching one of his hands in both her own and drawing his arm about her neck. She was trembling with what seemed sudden fear as she looked up into his face.

" Father," she cried, " I 'll go with *you!* I could n't live alone with Mother. If *you* go, take me with you! Promise — please promise! Mother is n't good to me a bit. I could n't live alone with her! She is cross nearly all the time, when you 're not here, and she struck me yesterday, and she often does it, and I did n't ever tell you before, because I knew it would trouble you so to know!"

These words were spoken in a high, pleading, plaintive voice. The child's sad little secret had been wrung from her by sheer terror of desertion. There was no accusative resentment in her tones; she might have gone on for a long time hiding the truth; it had leapt to her lips now only in the shape of an impetuous argument against the dreaded chance of being left behind, should her father's menace of departure become fact. Mrs. Twining moved from her own side of the table to where her husband and daughter stood. She looked persistently at Claire, during this action, and had soon drawn very close to her.

" You sly young vixen !" she exclaimed. Her cry had a husky note, and she raised one hand. It was plain that she meant wicked work to Claire. Twining pushed Claire behind him, quick as thought, and seized his wife's hand while it fell. He had grown white to the lips. His clasp was not weak about the wrist which he still retained. He did not appear at all like a man in a passion, but rather like one filled with the resolve which gets new sinew from excitement.

" You shall never strike that child again." Then he released his wife's wrist, and half turned, putting his arms round Claire, while she again nestled at his side. " I will do all I can for you," he went on, " but neither she nor I shall live with you after to-morrow. It was bad enough to have you make things hard for me, but you shan't spoil her with your own coarseness." The next moment he turned to Claire, wrapped her still more fervently in both arms, and kissed her twice or thrice on the uplifted forehead.

Mrs. Twining stood quite still, for a short while. She was watching her husband intently. Something new in him had revealed itself to her; it blunted the edge of her anger; she was unprepared for it. Personal defiance in Twining might merely have quickened her own long-petted sense of grievance, which had grown morbidly dear, as we know. But a fresh experience fronted her; she found herself repelled, so to speak, by the revolt of an insulted fatherhood.

It was a very serious rebellion, and she felt its force. Past concessions from her husband gave the measure of his present mutiny. He had never been humble to her, but he had yielded, and she had grown more used than she realized to his pliant complaisance. This abrupt change shocked her with an actual fright. Her ready little body-guard of taunts and innuendoes fled her usual summons. The despot stood deserted; not a janizary was left. She saw, in quick, startled perspective, her own future, uncompanioned by the man whose supporting nearness her bitter gibes had so often slighted. But apart from merely selfish causes, a thrill of human regard for her child and the father of her child lent fresh accent to alarm. It was like the tremor wrought in a slack harp-string, or one rusty with disuse, but it was still a definite vibration.

She succumbed awkwardly, like most overthrown tyrants. Tears would have looked incongruous had they left the chill black of her eyes, just as there are climes of so fixed a rigor that thaws rank in them as phenomena. But her brows met in a perplexed frown that had no trace of ire, and she made a flurried upward gesture with both hands, receding several steps. When she spoke, which she promptly did, her native idiom forgot the slight garb of change that marriage and nicer association had lent it, and stood forth, stripped by agitation, in graceless nudity.

"Mercy me, Francis!" she exclaimed, "you ain't talking as if you was a sane man at all! You'll quit your lawful wife, sir, 'cause she's boxed her own young one's ears? Why, that child can put on the airs of any six, when she's a mind to. I ain't punished her half enough. Do set down and eat your supper and stop bein' a fool!"

These chronicled words have the effect of rather bald commonplace it is true; but to the man and the child who heard them an apprehensive whimper, a timorous dilation of the eyeball and a flurried quiver about the severe mouth were accompaniments that held piercing significance. Such tokens from their domestic autocrat meant surrender, and surrender was hard for both Twining and Claire to join with past impressions of rule and sway, of command and observance, from the very source which now gave forth their direct opposites.

Both father and daughter still remained silent. Claire's head was still nestling against his breast; Twining's arms still clasped her slight frame, as before. Neither spoke. But Mrs. Twining soon spoke again, and she moved toward the door as she did so.

"Oh, you won't set down, eh?" she inquired; and there was now a sullen fright both in her manner and tone. "Very well. P'raps you'll eat your supper when I'm gone. I've always heard crazy people must be humored. Besides 't is n't safe, with so many knives and forks round."

After that she left the room, going up stairs into the little hall above the basement, where she could have seen her breath freeze if economic reasons had not kept the lank, pendant gas-burner still unlighted.

She had beaten a positive retreat. Her exit had

been a distinct concession. Twining turned his gaze toward the vacant threshold after she had passed it, as if he could not just realize the unwonted humility of her leave-taking.

"Claire," he said, again kissing the child, while she yet clung to him, "you should have told me before that your mother struck you. You should have told me the first time she did it." He embraced her still more closely. Since she was a baby he had always treasured her, and now that defeat and disappointment dealt him such persistent strokes, his love grew deeper with each disastrous year. Claire's presence in his life had gained a precious worth from trouble ; it was the star that brightened with sweeter force against a deepening gloom.

He leaned down and slowly passed his lips along her silky hair, just where its folds flowed off from one pale temple. "Oh, my little girl," he said, in a voice whose volume and feeling had both plainly strengthened, "I hope that happy days are in store for you! I shall do my best, darling, but if I fail don't blame me. Don't blame me!"

He appeared no longer to be addressing Claire. He had lifted his head. Both his arms engirt her as previously, but his eyes, looking straight before him, were sombre with meditation.

Claire gazed up into his face. "Father," she cried, "I shall be happy if I am always with you! Don't look like that. Please don't. What does it mean? I have never seen you so sad before. It frightens me. Father, you are so strange and different." He smiled down at the child as her high, pained appeal ended ; but the smile soon fled again ; a gloomy agitation replaced it. She felt his clasping arms tremble.

" You cannot always have me," he answered. " I love you very much, my little one, but some day I must leave you ; my time will have come, and it may come while your life is yet in its first flower. Then I want you to be wiser than I. Listen to what I say. I am in a dark humor now, but it will soon pass, for I can't help being cheerful, as you know ; there 's a good deal more sun than shadow in me. But just now I am all shadow. I feel as if I should never be successful, Claire. That is a queer word to your young ears. Do you recollect, when I took you for that one day to the country, last summer, how we set out to climb the large hill, and were sure, at starting, that we should reach its top ? But half way up we grew tired and hot ; there was no breeze, and the way was rough ; so we sat down, did n't we, and rested, and then went home ? You have not forgotten ? Well, success means to do what you set out for, darling. It means to climb the hill — not to get tired and go home. That is what everybody is trying to do. But only a few of us ever reach the top. And to reach the top means to have many good things — to be like the grand people who were once Mrs. Carmichael's friends. Do you understand, Claire ? "

" Yes," said the child. Her lips were parted. A gloom had clouded the blue of her eyes ; they seemed almost black, and two unwonted gleams pierced them. She was alarmed yet fascinated by the real sorrow in her father's look, and by his unfamiliar speech, with its fervent speed and bitter ring.

" I shall never gain the top of the hill, Claire ! " Twining went on. " Something tells me so now — to-night. To-morrow I shall be changed. I shall turn hopeful again. I shall go climbing along, and pick myself up stoutly if I stumble. But remember what I tell you to-night. In my heart, little girl, there is a great fear. I am afraid I must leave you, when I do die, poor and helpless. We are always helpless when we are poor. But you must not lose courage. There is one thing a girl can always do if she has beauty and wit, and you will have both. She can marry. In the years of life left to me, I shall strain hard to make you a lady. I am a gentleman. My father, and his father, and his father, too, were all gentlemen. It is in your blood to be a lady, and a lady you shall be. But your mother "— Here he paused. Even his raw sense of wrong, and the precipitate reasoning native to all passion, forbade his completing the last sentence.

"I know what you mean, Father," said Claire, who had not lost the significance of a word, and whose mind would have grasped subtler discourse than the present. She spoke falteringly, and turned her eyes toward the deserted table; and then, with her shaken, tragic little voice, she lapsed into the prose of things, slipping over that edge between the emotional and the ordinary whose unwilling junction makes the clash that we like to call comedy.

"Father," she said, "please sit down and eat your supper. It 's getting cold. Please do!"

This is not at all an index of Claire's thoughts, for they were then in a storm of dread and misgiving; but she shrank from the changed aspect of one known and loved in moods widely different. She seized, as if by a fond instinct, the most ready means of re-securing her father as she had at first found him and had always afterward prized him.

But her attempt was vain. Twining's arms only tightened about her frail form. Like all with whom outburst is rare, his perturbation worked toward a climax; it would brook no repression. There are craters that keep the peace for many decades, but in spite of that their stored lava will not be cheated of the eruptive chance.

So it was with Twining. He trembled more than ever, and his cheeks were now quite hueless. "I want you to do all that I shall leave undone, Claire!" he exclaimed, with voluble swiftness. "I want you to conquer a high place among men and women. Be cool and wary, my daughter. Don't live to serve self only, but push your claims, enforce your rights, refuse to be thrust back, never make false steps, put faith in the few and doubt the many. Remember what I am saying. You will need to recall it, for you must start (God help you, little one!) with all the world against you! Yes, all the world against you" . . .

A sudden gasp ended Twining's words. His embrace of Claire relaxed, and he staggered toward the sofa, which was just behind him. As he sank upon it, his eyes closed and his head fell sideways. One hand fluttered about his throat, and he seemed in straits for breath. Claire was greatly terrified. She thought that to be death which was merely a transient pause of vitality. The rough gust will bow the frailer tree, and Twining, weary in mind and body, had made too abrupt drafts upon a temperament far from robust.

The child uttered a piercing cry. It summoned the proscribed Mary Ann from exile in the neighboring kitchen; it was heard and heeded by Mrs. Twin-

ing, aloof in some remoter chamber. Yet, before
either had reached the scene of Claire's disquietude,
her father had already pressed the warm hand which
sought his cold one, and had looked at her with a
gaze that wore the glow of recognition.

"Claire," he soon said, brokenly, and with faint
utterance, "I — I was unwell for a moment — that is
all. Here, little girl, kiss me, and then give me a
glass of water."

"Yes, Father," said Claire. Her response showed
a joyous relief. She knelt beside him, and put her
lips to his. It was like the good-night kiss she always gave him, except that she made it longer than
of old. And then she rose to get the glass of water,
hearing footsteps approach.

As she poured the liquid, with unsteady fingers, a
partial echo of her father's impetuous enjoinder swept
through her mind. "I shall never forget this night,"
she told herself. Her silent prophecy proved true.
She never did forget.

III.

TWINING'S menace was not carried out. There was no actual reconciliation between husband and wife, and yet matters slowly rearranged themselves. The domestic machinery, being again set moving, went at first in a lame, spasmodic way, as though jarred and strained through all its wheel-work. But by degrees the old order of things returned. And yet a marked change, in one respect at least, was always afterward evident. Mrs. Twining had received a clear admonition, and she was discreet enough permanently to regard it. She still dealt in her former slurs and innuendoes ; the leopard could not change its spots ; no such radical reformation was naturally to be expected. But Twining had put forth his protest ; he had shown very plainly that his endurance had its limits, and through all the years that followed, his wife never lost sight of this vivid little fact. She had been seriously frightened, and the fright left its vibration of warning as long as she and her husband dwelt under the same roof. Her sting had by no means been extracted, but its point was blunter and its poison less irritant. She never again struck Claire. She was sometimes very imperious to her daughter, and very acrimonious as well. But in her conduct there was now a sombre acknowledgment of curtailed authority, — an under-current of

concession, occasionally rather faint, it is true, yet
always operative.

During the next year the family deserted One-
Hundred - and - Twelfth Street for a new place of
abode. Twining received a few extra hundreds as
earnest of shadowy thousands promised him by a
glib-tongued rogue who was to appall the medical
world with a wondrous compound that must soon
rob half the diseases known to pathology of their
last terrors. The elixir was to be " placed handsomely on the market," and toward this elegant enterprise poor Twining gave serious aid. For the
lump of savings that went from him, however, he
was paid only a tithe of his rash investment. One
day he learned that the humane chemist had fled
from the scene of his proposed benignities, and a little later came the drear discovery that his miraculous potion was merely an unskillful blending of two
or three common specifics with as many popular
nervines.

Meanwhile the halcyon promise of bettered fortunes had induced Twining to secure easier quarters.
For several months he set his household gods within
apartments on the second floor of a shapely brown-
stone residence in a central side - street. This was
really a decisive move toward greater social importance. The very tone of his upholstery bespoke a
distinct rise in life. There was not a hair-cloth sofa
in his pretty suite of chambers. The furniture was
tufted and modish ; one or two glowing grates replaced the dark awkwardness of stoves ; draughts
were an abolished evil ; to sup on burnt beefsteak
had grown a shunned memory, since the family now
dined at six o'clock each evening in a lower room,

where they had a small table all to themselves, and ate a repast served in courses with a distinct air of fashion, if not always cooked after the loftier methods. Here they met other groups at other small tables, and bowed to them with the bland nod of co-sharers in worldly comfort: It was all a most noteworthy change for the Twinings, and its effect upon Mrs. Twining was no less obvious than acute. She seemed to clutch the new favors of fate with a mingled greed and distrust. She was like one who crushes thirstily between his lips a luscious fruit, won by theft, and thought to be watched with the intent of quick seizure.

She had already quite lost faith in anything like the permanence of her husband's good fortune. "I'd better make hay while the sun shines," she would exclaim, with a burst of laughter that had, as usual, no touch of mirth in it. "Lord knows when it'll end. I'm sure I hope never. Don't think I'm croaking. Gracious me, no! But even the Five Points won't seem so bad, after this. They say every dog has his day, don't they, Francis? So, all right; if mine's a short day, I'll be up and doing while it lasts."

She was undoubtedly up and doing. She carried her large frame with a more assertive majesty; she aired one or two fresh gowns with a loud ostentation; she had a little quarrel with a fellow-lodger of her own sex about the prevailing fashion in bonnets, and said so many personal things during the contest that her adversary, who was a person with nerves, retired in tearful disarray. On more than one Sunday morning she induced her husband to walk with her along Fifth Avenue and "see the churches come out." At such times she would lean upon his arm, grandly indifferent to the fact that her stature over- topped his own, and stare with her severe black eyes at all the passing phases of costume. It is probable that the pair made a very grotesque picture on these occasions, since all that implied refinement in the man's face and demeanor must have acquired a fatal stamp of insignificance beside the woman's preten- sion of carriage and raw spruceness of apparel. But Mrs. Twining was making her hay. as she has told us, while the sun shone, and it is hardly strange that she should not be critical as to the exact quality of her crop. A good deal of rough experience in the woes of dearth and drouth had, naturally, not made her a fastidious harvester.

Claire, meanwhile, had begun to feel as if she dwelt on quite a new sort of planet. Her environ- ment had lost every trace of its former dullness. Its neutral shades had freshened into brilliant and excit- ing tints. Little Mrs. Carmichael, with her hoard of memories stowed away like old brocades in a scented chest, had herself faded off into a memory as dim as these. Claire had of late become one of the pupils in a large, well-reputed school, where she met girls of all ages and characters, but seemingly of only a single social rank. The academy was superin- tended by a magnificent lady in chronic black corded- silk, whose rich rustle was heard for a half minute before she entered each of her various class-rooms and held bits of whispered converse with the in- structresses under her serene sway. Her name was Mrs. Arcularius, and its fine rhythmical polysyllable seemed to symbolize the dignity of its owner's slow walk, the majesty of her arched nose and gold eye-glasses, and the white breadth of her forehead, from which the gray tresses were rolled backward in high solidness, with quite a regal effect of hair-dressing. This lady was the direct contra-type of Mrs. Carmichael. It was widely recorded of her that she had once been a gentlewoman of independent wealth, had chanced upon adverse times, and had for this reason become the proprietress of a school. But she had made her grand friends pay the penalty of her misfortunes; she had acquired the skill of using them as an advertisement of her venture at self-support. She had not gone up to One-Hundred-and-Twelfth Street and mourned their loss; she had stayed in Twenty-Third Street, and suffered their children, little and big, to come unto her. She had at first graciously allowed herself to be pitied for her reverses, but she had always possessed the art of handing back their patronage to those who proffered it, in the wholly altered form of a gracious condescension from herself. This is a very clever thing to do; it is a thing which they alone know how to do who know how to fall from high places with a self-saving rebound; and Mrs. Arcularius, who was a decidedly ignorant woman, was also a marvelously clever one. She knew rather less, in a strictly educational sense, than poor, unsuccessful Mrs. Carmichael. She had been a friend of Mrs. Carmichael's in the latter's gladsome days, but she was now not even aware that her old associate was teaching school anywhere. Everybody was aware, on the other hand, that Mrs. Arcularius was teaching school, and just where she was teaching it. Poverty had crushed one; it had stimulated the other. Mrs. Arcularius was now exceedingly particular as regarded her visiting-book.

She was a conspicuous figure at the most select receptions. Whether the fact that she presided over a fashionable school had made her lose caste or no, she chose secretly to believe that it had, and for this reason let her voluminous black silk robes rustle only in the most irreproachable assemblages.

She greatly desired that her pupils should all bear the sacred sign of aristocratic parentage. She did not object to the offspring of struggling plutocrats; for she was wise in her generation, and had seen more than one costly-laden camel squeeze itself through a needle's eye straight into the kingdom of the blessed. But she had strong objections to having her school lose tone. Above all things, this was her dread and abhorrence.

And therefore she had been covertly distressed by the application of Twining for his daughter's admission. She had "placed" him before he had spoken three words to her. She always "placed" with equal speed everybody whom she met for the first time. He was a decayed foreigner, and she abominated decayed foreigners. He was a person who wanted to make his common little daughter profit by the prestige of her establishment, and she had a like distaste for all persons of this class. She looked at Claire's attire, and inwardly shivered. The girl had on a frock cut and trimmed in a way that struck her observer as positively satanic. The lovely natural wave of her hair had been tortured by her mother into long ringlets, made sleek and firm under the stiffening spell of sugar-and-water, and pendant about her shoulders with a graceless vertical primness. But the head and front of the poor child's offending was, in the sight of her new critic, a hat which Mrs. Twining esteemed a triumph of taste, which she had bought as a great bargain the day before, and which was half-smothered, from crown to brim, in small white roses, each bearing a little movable glass bead that was meant to imitate a dew-drop.

Mrs. Arcularius decided, however, to receive Claire as one of her pupils. There had been a falling-off, of late, in their list. A good many sweet girl-graduates had gone off at her last commencement day. Besides, it was absurd to suppose that any flock could be kept from an incidental black sheep or so. More than this, there was a fascinating intelligence about Claire's face, with its two dark-blue stars of eyes, and a musical sorcery in the child's timid tones when she spoke, that no *diablerie* of millinery could dispel.

It soon proved that Claire's fellow-scholars were far from sharing this latter opinion. She was received among them with haughty coolness, varied by incidental giggles. She suffered three days of silent torture, and at their end told her father, in a passion of tears, that he must take her away from Mrs. Arcularius's school. The girls there all despised her and laughed at her; hardly one of them had yet even spoken to her; they seemed to think her beneath them; it was horrible; she could not stand it; it was just as if she had some disease and they were all afraid of catching it from her.

"There is one girl," sobbed Claire, with her arms round her father's neck and her head on his dear, kindly breast, "that I know I shall slap or throw something at if I stay. She has red hair and very white skin, with little freckles all over it, and she is quite fat. She wears a different dress every day, and it's always something handsome but queer to look

3

at. . . . I heard her tell another girl that all her clothes came from Paris. She brings two bananas for lunch, and long cakes spread over with chocolate, that spirt out something soft and yellow, like custard, when she bites into them, and soil her fingers. . . . Well, Father, that girl sits near me, and she is always making fun of me behind my back, and whispering things about me to the others that make them burst out laughing and watch me from the corners of their eyes. . . . Of course this is only at recess, but at all times, Father, I can feel how they are thinking that I have no right, no business among them. . . . And perhaps I haven't. Oh, Father, I want to be a lady as much as you want me to be one, but . . . isn't there some other way of learning how? If you'll only take me from that dreadful place, I'll . . . I'll go anywhere else you please!"

Indignant, yet pierced with sympathy for his darling, Twining promised her that she should go back no more to Mrs. Arcularius's.

Claire kissed him, and then put her wet cheek against his. But an instant later she lifted her head. She had thought of her mother, who was paying one of their fellow-boarders a visit that evening, and at this very moment was stating to her hostess, with a sort of saturnine braggadocio, that Claire's new school "ought to be a regular first-class one, and no mistake, for it was going to cost a regular first-class kind of a price."

"But Mother?" said Claire, in anxious query, "what will *she* say, Father?"

"Never mind what your mother will say, my dear," answered Twining, in his gentle undertone. And Claire remembered a certain night in One-Hundred-

and-Twelfth Street, — a night which she had never really forgotten, as we know, and whose incident was fated sharply to revisit her through many an eventful year yet unlived.

But Claire's tears were scarcely dried before she regretted the promise won from her father, and asked him to revoke it. Her young face looked pale and resolute as she did so. Her brief burst of weakness had passed. The ambition to seize and hold any near means of advancement was already no weak impulse in her youthful being. As it afterward struck the great key-note of her life, and became the source of every discord or harmony which that life was to contain, so now its force had begun to stir secret centres and to prelude the steady influence which must soon impel and sway her.

"Let me try a little while longer, Father," she said, standing near him and holding his hand. · Her head was slightly thrown backward; her mouth was grave and firm. She was so slender and fragile that this solemn mood might have made one think, as he regarded her, of a lily that had found some art to cast aside its droop, while all its lightsome traits of stem or petal still remained.

"Yes, I mean it, Father," she continued, with a very deep seriousness. "I have begun to climb the hill, and I shan't get tired so soon and sit down to rest. You told me I must not, and I won't. I do not want to sit down at all until I shall reach the top. . . . But you can help me, if you will; you can make it easier for me." She pressed his hand. "*Will* you make it easier, Father?" she said.

"Yes!" he answered. He spoke the word without knowing what she meant. He could have spoken no other at this moment, with her eyes fixed on him like that, and her clinging hand tense about his own. He loved her so well that he would have faced any peril to save her from any harm. She was his cheer, his pride, his hope, his happiness. He thought her the most beautiful little girl in all the world. He had forgotten to tell himself that her mother made her look a guy in seeking to make her more pretty. To him she was always his innocent, blameless idol — his Claire, whom he had named after his own dead mother, known only in the idealizing years of early childhood. He never looked into her face without feeling his heart beat a trifle quicker. He had been in love with her from the time when he first held her, a new-born baby, and he was in love with her still. It was a love which had the best glow and thrill of those dramatic passions that make our tales, our tragedies, and our epics, only that by absence of the one fevered sentiment knit and kinned with these, it so gained in purity and unselfishness as to strip from all hint of over-praise the holier epithet of divine.

Naturally enough came Twining's afterthought.

"What is it that I can do for you, Claire?" he asked. "How *can* I make it easier?"

"In this way, Father. Listen. I want to dress differently at school. I want to wear another frock — I know which one — I am afraid you would n't recollect which it is if I told you. But it is not the pink merino which I have on now. Pink merino is not nice. And my new hat with the white roses is not nice, either. I did n't think of this till I noticed how the other girls dressed at Mrs. Arcularius's. Then I remembered that mine was something very like the style in which Mrs. Halloran used to dress her little

girl, Bridget, every Sunday. You do recollect Mrs.
Halloran, don't you Father? Her husband used to
work on one of the Harlem boats, and they lived
down near the river in that small red house, and
there was a bee-hive in the garden, and a horrid bull-
dog that used to jump out of his kennel if he heard
the least noise, and bark so, and try to break his
chain. But little Bridget used to have pink kid shoes,
though, to match her dress, and very proud they
made her. And her hair was curled in that stiff
way, just as Mother curls mine. Now, Father, I
want you to let me brush all the curl out of my hair
except what it has of its own free choice, and to let
me just tie it in a bunch behind with a dark ribbon,
and to let me wear my brown bonnet, which is rather
shabby, perhaps, though I don't mind that. And if
Mother cares to buy me anything new, I want you to
go with us — say some Saturday evening when the
stores keep open — and to let me use my own taste
in choosing quiet and pretty things. But that will
be afterward. I'd like you to think, just now, only
about to-morrow, you know. I'd like" — But there
Twining stopped her with a kiss. He was smiling,
but his eyes were moist.

"You shan't dress like little Bridget Halloran any
longer, Claire, darling," he said. "I'll see to it as
soon as your mother returns."

He kept his word. When Mrs. Twining reap-
peared he sent Claire out of the room. She knew a
storm was coming; she was glad to be away while it
broke and raged. She went as far away as possible,
into her own bedroom, two chambers off, closing the
intermediate doors. Once, while waiting here, she
heard the smothered sound of a high, wrathful voice.

It was ner mother's, no doubt. But she knew that however hot the conflict, her father had made up his mind to be victor.

And he was. The next day Claire went to Mrs. Arcularius's without her white roses or her pink merino.

"You look for all the world like a charity-child," her mother said to her, in gruff leave-taking. "Still, I don't s'pose it matters any. You might as well practice for a short spell beforehand."

Claire's altered raiment produced an immense sensation among her classmates. Even several of the teachers showed signs of surprise. The new plainness of her attire brought out her unquestioned beauty, as gaudier and ill-blended vestments had before marred and obscured it. The back-drawn effect of her chestnut tresses, which were still streaked here and there with sunny threads, could not be doubted as charming even by the most prejudiced caviler. Her brow and temples were shown in their full purity of moulding, and the eyes beneath them gained poetic tenderness from this lovely exposure. She was not yet a girl clothed at all after the dainty manner of the girls about her, but she was at least no longer spoiled and hampered by unbecoming and vulgar garments. Everybody felt this promptly, and Claire herself soon recognized, by an intuition which always stood vassal to her singularly quick perceptions, that everybody had felt it.

This was to be a memorable day with her. It may seem trivial to employ so august a term when dealing with one yet on the threshold of our truly vital episodes, but, after all, there is a reality about the chagrins and victories of childhood which is none the less

potent while both exist because both must shortly
drop into shadow before harsher pangs and warmer
transports.   Claire had resolved to be a kind of miniature heroine if occasion should ask her to play that
part; and she had a conviction, based on very fair
grounds of reasoning, that some such demand might
be made of her before the school-exercises for that
day should reach their end.

Nor was she wrong.   The recitations began, and
were continued under various teachers until the
twelve o'clock recess.   Claire had suffered hitherto
from the embarrassments of her surroundings, as regarded any frank assertion of what she knew and just
how she knew it.   But to-day she had conquered embarrassment; she was on her mettle, as the phrase
goes; it was the main aim of her meditated plan to
let herself be browbeaten in no particular, and the
excitement born of this resolve had put her best faculties into nimble readiness.

Her understanding was of the quality beloved by
instructors; it had a prehensile trait; it seized things
and clung to them.   The alarm of Mrs. Carmichael
lest her pupil should unmask her elegant deficiencies
had been no unfounded one.   This lady's tuition of
Claire had been but a series of suggestions, each of
which the girl had rapidly tracked to its lair of remoter truth.   Mrs. Carmichael had pointed her the
path — quite often, it must be owned, with a somewhat faltering finger — and she had glided whither it
led at a pace no less swift than secure.   This was
especially true of the French language, for which her
aptitude was phenomenal, and which, under new conditions of instruction, she soon almost mastered.   As
a matter of mere fact, she had been placed, at pres-

ent, among her inferiors in knowledge. She was
much more advanced than the class of superb young
misses who had wounded her with their callow disdain. And to-day she made this tellingly evident.
Her answers came placid, self-assured, unhesitating.
She sat, all through the morning, with hands folded
together in her lap, and with looks that paid no seeming heed to any of her associates. Some of them
were extremely stupid. They gave stammering re-
sponses, or rattled off the wrong thing with fatal
glibness, or preserved that stolid silence which is the
most naked candor of ignorance. The freckled girl,
who ate bananas, cut an especially dull figure.
Through some novel freak of parental indulgence she
had been permitted to wear, this morning, a ring of
clustered sapphires and diamonds, very beautiful and
precious; and this she turned and re-turned, while
puckering her forehead, whenever a question was put
to her, as though the fair bauble might prove talis-
manic and show her some royal road out of learning's
tangled mazes. No one appeared to think her replies
particularly blundering or fatuous. Her ring, and
her last new Parisian gown, and the luxurious prospect of her approaching lunch, seemed to invest even
her weak wit with prestige. Claire felt it to be somehow in the air that this maiden's mental poverty
should receive nothing except respectful sympathy
from her fellows. Fortune does not shower every
known gift on one favorite; that seemed to be tacitly
understood. When she floundered in a French verb,
or came to dire grief in compound fractions, the imbe-
cility provoked no laughter; it bore a sort of gilded
pardonableness, like the peccadillo of a princess.

When recess came, Claire had distinguished herself. Everybody was convinced that her powers of mind were much above the common. Two of the teachers, both ladies of gentle bearing and kindly disposition, came to her side, and cheered her with a few words of complimentary encouragement. The grand Mrs. Arcularius did not come; she was elsewhere, in her elegant little reception-room; she had not yet heard of her new pupil's handsome exploits. But if she had already heard of them she would have paid Claire no congratulations. Good scholarship, she would have argued, with splendid egotism, was in this case a form of gratitude to which she was of course amply entitled, since she had allowed Twining the honor of seeing her autograph on his daughter's future receipted bills.

During the first portion of the recess hour Claire ate her modest lunch, choking it down with strong reluctance. But one teacher now remained in the large class-room, and she was closely occupied in the examination of some written exercises. The girls were gathered here and there, among the files of desks, in whispering groups. They were all discussing Claire; she herself knew it; an instinct told her so. She was very much excited, but outwardly quite calm. The girls no longer stared at her; not a single giggle now broke the air; they had been impressed, startled, and perhaps a little awed as well; their pariah had turned out a sort of notability; she had clad herself in a sudden armor of cool defiance against impudence. They might have regarded her lately-revealed endowments as a queerness collateral with the eccentric quality of her clothing. But the pink robe, the brittle-looking curls, the beflowered hat, had vanished and left them no chance for such associative ridicule.

There had been a transformation, abrupt and baffling. Claire was not going to be their butt; of this there was no doubt; she must either be accepted as an equal, or avoided as an inferior; she could no longer hold the position of a target for their covert raillery.

The freckled girl, of the sumptuous mid-day meal, however, preserved opposite opinions. Her name was Ada Gerrard, and her family was one of great wealth and distinction. Her elder sister, a mindless blonde with creamy skin and exuberant figure, had made a notable English marriage, having wedded no less a potentate than the young Marquis of Monogram, heir of a renowned ducal house. Miss Ada was a leader in her way, and she felt keenly disappointed by the unforeseen turn of affairs. She had anticipated prodigious fun out of the new scholar. She was by nature cruel and arrogant, and she was now affected as some feline creature that has been cheated of the prey it has meant to maul and maim.

Her reddish-hazel eyes, that showed so little white as to look like two large beads of clouded amber, and were fringed with scant lashes of lighter red, kept up a persistent scrutiny of Claire. She was sitting not far away from the latter, who caught, now and then, a waft of the delicate violet perfume which exhaled from her fine foreign apparel. She was occupied with her epicurean repast, whose dainties she devoured with a solemn gluttony; but this did not prevent her from keeping up a little fusillade of whispers to a friend on whom she had bestowed one or two bites of luscious cake as a mark of peculiar clemency.

The converse was at first low-toned. Claire had finished her brief refreshment. She had opened a book, and maintained at least the semblance of being engaged in its contents. Suddenly she heard Ada Gerrard speak these words, in a voice lifted above her former key, though doubtless meant solely for her companion's ears :

"I don't care *how* much she knows. She's a common little thing, and *I* would n't notice her if she got on her knees and begged me to."

Claire waited a few seconds, with head lowered above her book. She trembled while she so waited. The tremor was half from anger, half from intimidation. She felt, in every fibre of her being, the coarseness of this speech, but through her sensitive soul had shot a pang of false shame, dealt by the piercing sense of contrast between her own humble state and the probable grandeur and comfort of life which had fed Ada Gerrard's present superciliousness. But anger conquered. She ceased to tremble, and closed her book. Then she rose, quietly, and faced her classmate. It may have been that the generations of gentlewomen from which, on her father's side, she had sprung, helped to nerve and steady her now; since the primal source of all aristocracy is a cogent self-assertion, and those races alone gain heights over-browing their kind whose first founders have had the will and vigor to push forward resisted claims.

Everybody saw her rise. It flashed through the little throng, in an instant, that something had spurred her into a course of retaliation. At least fifteen pairs of eager eyes were leveled upon her pale face. But she regarded Ada Gerrard only ; and when she spoke, with enough clearness to be heard in all parts of the room, her first words were addressed strictly to that special offender.

" You say that you will not notice me," Claire began, " and yet you say it so loudly that I can hear you, and thus you very plainly contradict yourself ; or, in other words, you try to attract my attention by speaking a falsehood."

Here she paused. A dead silence ensued. Many bewildered looks were exchanged. The presiding teacher stopped her task, and sat with a gaze of puzzled alarm fixed upon this resolute young combatant. Ada Gerrard flushed crimson, and ceased to discuss her savory confections.

Claire's voice quivered as she now proceeded, but she quickly controlled this perturbed sign : " I do not think there is much chance of my begging you on my knees to notice me," she said. " But I might be tempted to take such a way of begging that you would try and help me to forget, as long as I remain here, how I have had the ill-luck of being thrown near anyone so unkind, so impudent, and so vulgar as yourself."

Ada Gerrard sprang to her feet as the last calm word sounded from Claire's lips. She had clenched both of her plump hands, and there was a wrathful scowl on her face. Several titters were heard from her companions ; they seemed to sting her ; it was impossible for her to fail in perceiving that she had met an adversary of twice her own prowess. She knew to which side the sympathy had veered ; all her imposing superiority in the way of dress, of diet, of home-splendor, of titled kindred, were momentarily as nothing beside Claire's placid antagonism. She was only an ugly girl in an ugly rage, who had behaved insolently and been rebuked with justice ; while Claire, pale, unflinching, wholly in the right and wholly aware of it, her drawbacks of uncouth costume no longer present, her beauty a fact beyond dispute, her intelligence a recent discovery and a sharp surprise, stood clad with the dignity of easy and complete conquest.

Ada Gerrard suddenly burst into tears. They were very irate tears; there was not the least tincture of remorse or shame in them. She flung herself back into her chair, and covered her face for several minutes while she wept.

Claire watched her, tranquilly, for a little while. Then she sat down again and reopened her book. An intense silence reigned, broken by the sobs of Ada Gerrard. Claire leaned her head on her hand, feigning abrupt absorption in the page that she regarded, and feigning it very well. But her mind was in a secret whirl, now. She was mutely, but impetuously asking herself: " Will they think I was right? Will they take my part? Will they treat me any more kindly, or just as before? "

These silent, pathetic queries were fated to receive a speedy answer. Before the school hours of that same day had ended, the ostracism which had so wrung poor Claire's spirit was in a measure ended likewise. Less than a week had elapsed before she was on friendly terms with a number of her classmates. A little adverse clique soon shaped itself against her. Ada Gerrard, fiercely unforgiving, headed this hostile faction; its remaining members were a few stanch personal adherents who had never been able to resist the dazzling fascination of Miss Gerrard's toilets and lunches. But this opposing element was not actively inimical. Claire's party had the strength of multitude and the courage of its opinions. Still, its members were by no means ardent devotees; they sometimes hurt her with the sly stab of patronage, and they often gave her furtively to understand that her claims upon their favor were of a sort which they practically recognized without theoretically approving.

It would be hard to define just how they conveyed this impression. And yet Claire frequently felt its weight, like that of some vague tyranny which offers no tangible excuse for revolt. She could neither realize nor estimate the force with which she had been thrown into contact. Her years were yet too few, her experience was yet too limited; nor was the force manifest in active strength at Mrs. Arcularius's school, a narrow enough theatre for its exercise, and one where its full-grown momentum must of necessity dwindle into something like mere juvenile parody. Claire was yet to learn with how much rank haste its evil growth had sprung up in the big metropolis outside, thwarting and clogging any pure development of what has been called the republican idea, and making us sometimes bitterly wonder if the great dead philosophers were not tricked, after all, by wills-o'-the-wisp no less lovely than elusive.

But there were a few girls who met Claire on a perfectly equal footing, and left from their intercourse, at all times, the least frosty sparkle of condescension. Some of these may or may not consciously have undertaken their rôles. But with one, past doubt, and for excellent reasons, the kindly impulse was in every way spontaneous. The name of this pupil was Sophia Bergemann. She professed a deep fondness for Claire, and it was evidently sincere. She belonged among Mrs. Arcularius's tolerated plutocrats. Her father was a German brewer who had made a very large fortune out of lager-beer, and who dwelt in Hoboken, where he had built an immense house on spacious grounds. It was said that the lawns were adorned with statues in bronze and marble, and that the main drawing-room of the mansion was frescoed with a design representing Germany offering a tankard of foaming beer to Columbia, in colossal sociability. But the latter statement may have been only the caustic invention of Sophia's foes. She was stoutly disapproved by the conservative element, and this fact had helped to make her so warm a supporter of Claire. Being at daggers drawn with Ada Gerrard, she naturally hailed Claire's public rebuke with rapture, and immediately became her stanch ally.

"I was afraid you'd stay meek and mild right straight along, just as you began," she afterward confessed. "Somehow you looked as if you hadn't got any spunk. And I do like spunk. I believe in it." This article of faith Sophia had several times frankly verified. She had once pulled the ear of her fellow-pupil, and again narrowly escaped expulsion by slapping another's face. She had a buxom figure, a broad-blown countenance, nearly as round as a moon at the full, solid cheeks of constant vivid coloring, and hair so yellow that its keen tint blent with her brilliant complexion in producing the effect of an expensive wax doll enlarged and animated. She was drearily stupid at all her lessons, rivaling Ada Gerrard as the regnant ignoramus of the academy. Her gestures were painfully awkward; her walk was a cumbrous prance; she seemed incapable of seating herself without an elastic bounce. She grew very fond of Claire, as weeks went on, and gave her re-peated invitations to pass a portion of the summer holidays at the grand Hoboken abode.

But before the summer holidays arrived, Claire had left Mrs. Arcularius's school for good. Twining had awakened to one more dismayed perception of having been grossly duped ; the reed on which he had leaned had snapped beneath him ; prompt re-trenchments became inevitable ; his poor ventured thousands were dissolved, as a last ironical sort of ingredient, in the worthless elixir.

For a long time his affairs stood miserably in-volved. His innocent share in a matter of impos-ture and chicanery was misconstrued and sharply censured by his employers. He was discharged from his clerkship, and put face to face with the worst threats of need. Mrs. Twining, forced to resign her briefly-worn robes of ease for the old garb of drudg-ery, spared no zeal in proving herself not to have been a false prophetess of disaster.

"I ain't a bit surprised," she would declare, with one of her thin, acid laughs. "Mercy, no! Don't mind *me*. I was prepared for it, Francis. So here we are over in Jersey City, and a pretty shabby part of it, too ! Oh, well, it's better 'n keeping a peanut-stand, anyhow. You'll bring me there, some day ; you're bound to. I ain't eaten a peanut in ever so long. I'm saving my taste for 'em."

Twining secretly writhed under these thrusts. His meagre stock of money was slipping from him daily. But he was still cheerful. The tough tex-ture of his optimism still refused to be rent. A few more years, and its severance must come, warp and woof, but as yet the sturdy fibres held good against every strain.

He secured another position at last. The salary, smaller than before, was at least regular. But the quarters in Jersey City, though humble and restricted, made too strong an annual drain upon his impoverished purse. After two years of pitiful struggle, the family removed to Greenpoint. Claire was then sixteen. But before this new change occurred, Twining's evil genius had again tempted him, and with the usual malign result. He trusted a fellow-man once more, and once more he was confounded. This time it was of necessity a much smaller hazard. Only three hundred dollars went, though millions were of course to be ultimately realized. One day a sallow, elderly man, with eyes bleared from dissipation and clothes that hung glazed round a bony figure, fell in with poor Twining, and talked to him glibly about a miraculous patent. It concerned the giving of signals on railroads by an electrical process. It was to effect a sublime security against all future accidents of travel by land. A few primary steps were to be taken before this marvel should obtain the indorsements of eager capitalists. The sallow little man, in three interviews, during which he cleverly contrived not to smell too strongly of liquor, convinced Twining that he was a neglected genius. The money was given him, and a receipt for it was signed with a hand whose insecurity passed for grateful emotion. But this origin might have been ascribed with more truth to the rheumy moisture that filled the recipient's eyes when he placed a plump roll of bills within his threadbare waistcoat-pocket. Twining never saw him after that eventful conference. He died about three weeks later of delirium tremens in a city hospital. It was his seventh attack.

4

This fresh blow leveled Twining. Neither his wife nor his child ever knew of it. But it struck into him a sort of terror at himself from which he never recovered. He had trusted humanity for the last time. He still remained amiable, genial, gentle. But despair had turned his heart to lead. Both Claire and Mrs. Twining saw the change, though ignorant of its cause. The Greenpoint epoch had now begun.

In Jersey City Claire had been sent to a public school. Here she had met genuine daughters of the people. Some of them were almost in rags; others represented thrifty home-surroundings; all were very different from the sleek children of wealth and caste whom she had known at Mrs. Arcularius's. At first she suffered torments of disgust. But by degrees the slow, continual pressure of habit wore away the edge of her distaste, as a constant sea-wash will blunt the rim of a shell. She absorbed herself in study, made rapid progress, and learned much that a fashionable school would have left untaught.

Her fastidiousness in a measure vanished. A good deal of the old acquired nicety stayed, but her age was impressionable, and ceaseless contact with rough manners and crude opinions wrought its certain effect She was now rubbing against taffetas, and before it had been against silk. She was hearing the boorish laugh and the slovenly idiom to-day, when yesterday she had heard the mirth of culture and the phrase of decorum. Her young life had thus far been a strange discord of opposing influences. She felt this in periods of half-bewildered retrospect, and sometimes with moods of passionate melancholy as well. The intense contrast of the changes through which she had passed, disheartened while it stimulated her. She meant to try her best; she wanted with all her energy to gain secure and permanent elevation; she had no intent of sitting down and resting before she reached the top of the hill, for her father's heated words of admonition and entreaty yet swept their insistent echo through her spirit.

But the hill seemed a sheer steep, defiant of any foothold. If she was eager to ascend, loath to rest, full of splendid activity, what mattered these favoring conditions when circumstances turned them to mockery?

They were at Greenpoint, now. They had been there three years. Claire was nineteen. Her school days had ended. They could no longer afford to keep a servant; she had to help her mother in all menial domestic offices. She had to bake, to sweep, to wash, to sew. She hated the place; she hated the life. But she saw her father's hidden despair, and so hid her own. More than this, she trembled at certain signs that his health was failing. He would have seizures of sudden weakness at morning or night; she feared to ask him whether they also occurred when he was absent at his business, lest he might suspect the acute nature of her anxiety, and so acquire new cause for worriment.

She loved him more than ever. The dread of his loss would steal with ghastly intrusion along her dreams at night. She thought of her grim, acrimonious mother, and said to herself: 'If he should die! It would be terrible! I should be worse than alone!' Every kiss that she gave him took a more clinging fondness.

He never spoke of his future. He never spoke of

hers. She understood why. Each always met the other with a smile. There was something beautiful in their reciprocal deceit. They heard the dead leaves crackle under their footsteps, but they strove to talk as if the boughs were in bud.

And so the weeks went on. The bitterness of their second winter in Greenpoint had now yielded to the mildness of a second spring. But the vernal change brought no cheer to Claire. In the little yellowish-drab wooden house where they dwelt, with lumber-yards and sloop-wharves blocking all view of the river, with stupid, haggling neighbors on either side of them, with ugliness and stagnation and poverty at arm's-reach, was a girl so weighed upon and crushed by the stern arbitraments of want, that she often felt herself as much a captive as if she could not have moved a limb without hearing the clank of a chain.

IV.

ONE afternoon Claire said to her mother: "I intend to take a little holiday. I am going out for a walk." Mrs. Twining and her daughter were in the kitchen when this very novel announcement was made. The elder lady had just taken her preliminary steps toward the getting of supper. She let her big knife remain bedded in the side of a large, soggy potato that she was peeling, and glanced up at Claire with her quick black eye. A long spiral of skin hung from the half-pared vegetable. It seemed to denote with peculiar aptness the paralyzing effect of Mrs. Twining's astonishment.

"Going to take a holiday, are you?" she exclaimed, with the favorite jerky, joyless laugh. "And what am *I* going to do, if you please? Stay at home, no doubt, and slave over this stove till supper's cooked. Hey?"

"I cooked the supper yesterday," said Claire, "and you vowed that everything I had done was bad, and that I should never make myself so smart again. I recollect your exact words — 'make myself so smart,'" continued Claire, with cutting fidelity of quotation. "I would readily do the whole cooking every afternoon, on Father's account. For he likes the food I prepare better than he likes what you prepare. There's no doubt about that."

"Oh, not a bit," returned Mrs. Twining, who could never cow her daughter nowadays, and avoided all open skirmishes with Claire, preferring to fire her volleys under cover of ambiguous sneers, being sure of rout in any fair-fought engagement. "Not a bit, certainly. When he knows you 've pottered away at anything, he 'll eat it and smack his lips over it whether it 's roasted to a cinder, or as raw as a fresh clam."

"I 'm very glad to hear you say so," returned Claire, with a weary little smile. "It 's pleasant to think Father loves me like that."

Mrs. Twining vigorously resumed work on her potato, speaking at the same time. "Pity about both o' you two, I *do* declare," she retorted, lapsing into the vernacular with which she loved to accompany her worst gibes. "'Pears to me that if he 's so fond o' *you* he might n't have made you the poor mean fag at nineteen that he 's made o' me at forty-four; and if you are so fond o' *him*, why, you might try and catch a decent husband, with a few dollars in his pocket, to raise up the family out o' the mud and muck Francis Twining 's got it in."

Claire's eyes flashed a little; but she was not specially angered; she was so used to this kind of verbal savagery.

"Father never meant anything but good to either of us," she said, "and you know it. I don't want to hear you speak against him when he is away and can't defend himself. *I* am able to defend him, if I choose. I think you know that, Mother, by this time. I 'm going out, as I told you. I shall be back rather soon, I suppose."

She left the kitchen, and presently the house as

well. She might have stayed to wrangle; but she knew that would be for no purpose. She had stood up for her loved father so often, and always with the same results. Her wit was quicker than her mother's; it could thrust deeper and parry more dexterously; but she was very tired of this aimless warfare, where she got wounds that she hid and gave wounds that it cost her only pain to deal. She had no definite idea whither she would go, on quitting the house. At first she took her way through the cheap and vulgar main street of Greenpoint. It was the first real day of Spring; the air was bland; something had called her forth to breathe it, even here in this dreary spot. She did not quite know whence the silent summons had come. She was by no means sure if it were her own youth that had called her, conspiring in some subtile way with the push of leaves and grasses out toward the strengthened sunshine. She had felt old and tired, of late; the monotony of toil had dulled her spirits; her mother's arrowy slurs had pierced and hurt her more than she guessed. But the mild atmosphere, stirred by tender breezes, made it pleasant to be abroad, even in this malodorous thoroughfare.

Everything was dull and common. It seemed a sort of beautiful outrage that the pure, misty blue of the afternoon sky should arch so contentedly over these slimy gutters, shabby tenements, dirty children, and neglected sidewalks. A German woman jostled against her as she pressed onward; the woman carried a pail of liquid refuse, and issued from a near doorway. She had a tawdry red bow at her throat, one or two smaller bows to match it in her tossed blonde hair, and an immense flat water-curl glued against either temple, with the effect of some old hieroglyph. She was a beer-seller's wife, and she was about to empty her vessel of stale malt upon the neighboring cobble-stones. But the random speed of her gait caused her to collide abruptly with Claire's passing figure, and some of the contents of her pail shot out upon the latter's dress, making an instant stain. Claire paused, and looked at the woman with a slight annoyed motion of the head. The offender was a high-tempered person; it was currently whispered by members of their special Teuton clique that her husband was a rank socialist who had been forced to fly the police of his native town overseas, and that she shared in secret his rebellious opinions. This may or may not have been truth; but the woman flung her pailful fiercely into the street, and then as fiercely confronted Claire.

"Vell, vat you got to say?" she cried, shrilly. "You looks at me as if I vass to blame for you running against me, ain't it? I see you before. You ain't much, annerhow. You got a big lot uf airs; you valks shust like a grant laty." Here the virago dropped her pail, set a hand on either hip, and attempted, with sad lack of success, while two long, tarnished ear-rings oscillated in her big, flushed ears, to imitate Claire's really graceful walk. "Sho," she continued, in sarcastic explanation of her parody. "You valks jush sho! Bud you ain't much. You ain't no laty. You better stop ride avay treing to be one. Dot's too thin, dot iss. Aha, you're off. I t'ought I'd freiden you!"

Claire was indeed "off," and moving somewhat briskly, too. She had grown rather white. This rude encounter left a harsh memory behind it. For some time she could not dissipate the recollection of the German jade's insolence.

"Perhaps she was right," her set lips at length murmured. "I am *not* a lady. I *had* better stop right away trying to be one."

A little later she had quitted the main street of the town, and gained an open expanse at whose verge the houses stood with wide gaps between them, as though a forlorn effort had been made to conquer vacancy by ugliness. But vacancy had won the fight; space never resisted time with more complete conquest. An immense drab plain, shorn of the least green feature, now stretched before Claire's gaze. On one hand, like a slow, interminable snake, wound a black thread of slimy creek, flanked by ragged embankments of crumbling clay. On the other hand was a dull, bare sweep, unrelieved by even a single hut. Far to the eastward, facing Claire, gleamed a wide assemblage of cottages; this was a settlement that some wag or optimist, whichever he may have been, had long ago named Blissville.

Claire had a fanciful thought, now, as she walked along the hard macadamized road which the incessant trains of funerals took toward Calvary, that Blissville, seen so distantly at the end of this treeless, herbless waste, was like the mirage glimpsed by a wanderer on a desert. But she might more aptly have compared the lonely desolation which encompassed her to those classic fields where the Greek and Roman dead found their reputed bourne. The shocking creek would have made an excellent Styx, and even the most barren imagination could have traced ready analogy between these monotonous levels of sun-baked mud and the flowerless lands where disconsolate shades were supposed to wander.

The tender amethyst sky, arching over this hideous spot, alone saved it, to-day, from the last sort of infernal suggestiveness. An enormous funeral presently appeared in sight, just as Claire reached a certain uncouth bridge that spanned a curve of the impure current. The slow procession of dark carriages uncoiled itself, so to speak, from the massed habitations of Greenpoint, and drew gradually nearer without yet revealing its final vehicle. It was a mortuary cavalcade of phenomenal length, even for the present place, where New York quite often sends some of her worst reprobates to their graves under conditions of the most imposing solemnity. The whole retinue was at last unfurled upon the smooth roadway, along which it crawled with something of the same serpentine stealthiness as that of the almost parallel creek. A sombre rivalry seemed evident, now, between the two differing streams. This blank tract of repulsive land, so strangely dedicated to death, had lost every hint of Lethean likeness. The arrival of the funeral had wrought striking change. Here we had the modern mode of dealing with death. It seemed to make paganism wither and vanish. An old, half-rotten barge, moored in a slushy cove, might have served for an emblem of the decay and contempt now fallen upon antique legend. Was this the melancholy boat that once ferried the ghosts to Hades? Ah! but if so, the oars were lost, the planks leaked wofully, and the grim pilot had gone permanently away into the great shadow-land of all the dead gods! Claire looked toward the coming funeral, and shuddered in silence. There seemed so unholy a contrast between her own fresh, vital maidenhood and this ghastly, morbid domain. How had her healthful young spirit ever courted death, that it should thus force upon her its continual grisly fellowship? She placed both elbows on the rough balustrade of the bridge, leaned her fair girlish chin against both hands, and stared straight before her across the bleak heath. Not far off several venturesome swine were waddling; they were near enough for their absurd grunts now and then to reach her, and for her to see the pink flush of their cumbrous bodies between coarse, soiled hairs, and the earthward thrust of their long, gray, cylindrical noses. But a moment later a flock of pigeons suddenly lighted just at the foot of the bridge, on a little loamy flat. The sight gave her a thrill of pleasure. It was so odd to get any bit of beauty here, and each bird was a true bit of beauty, with its flexible irised neck, its rounded sleekness, and its rosy feet. Presently the flock began their rich peculiar coo, and the sound fascinated Claire as much as their shapes had done. She quite forgot the advancing funeral; here were color, grace, and a sort of music. They had fallen to her, as might be said, from the skies. In a dumb, unformulated way she wished that more of all three charms would so fall to her. It was such a wretched doom to dwell in this abominable suburb. All her youth was being wasted here. She was already getting rather old. She was already nearly twenty — four months of her twentieth year had gone — and she had been accustomed to think people quite old when they were twenty. Would it last years longer? Ah! to fly as those lovely birds could! Why had they come hither, of all places in the world? If she were a green-and-purple thing, with strong wings, like any of them, she would soar away to the window of some rich lady's house on Fifth Avenue, and be taken inside some handsome chamber, perhaps, and fed and petted —yes, even put into a cage, if the lady chose. A cage there would be better than one's full freedom here, where the dead were always going to their graves.

From a reverie which may or may not have resembled this if it had been made into actual language, the sudden spontaneous flight of the whole charming flock roused poor ruminative Claire. She now perceived that the funeral train had drawn much nearer. A sort of metallic resonance sounded from the many horse-hooves on the hard surface of the road. But another sound, at this point, turned her attention elsewhere. It was a cracked, thin, piping voice, and its utterances were delivered only a short distance from her side. She discovered that an old man had joined her on the bridge during her absorbed preoccupation with the pigeons. He was a very old man; he leant on a staff, and was clad in an evident holiday-attire of black, whose rusty broadcloth hung about his shrunken shape with tell-tale looseness; it had too evidently been cut for a far more portly person. He had a wrinkled face, and yet one of rubicund plumpness; a spot of red flushed each cheek, centring in a little crimson net-work of veins there, while the same peculiarity cropped out a third time, as it were, on the ball-like lump at the end of his irregular nose. Claire had a feeling, as she looked at him, that he was a reformed toper. Everything about him told of present sobriety, but he was like a colored lantern seen without the illuminative candle; you had a latent certainty, as you regarded him, that only a few glasses of sufficiently bad liquor were needed to warm up those three red spots into their old auroral splendor. While speaking, he put forth a brown hand that trembled a good deal. The tremor came, no doubt, from senile feebleness, and the hand was so gnarled and knotty that it might almost have been one of those rough excrescences which sometimes bulge from tree-trunks, instead of the sad rheumatic member that it really was. The new-comer spoke with an extremely strong Irish accent, and in a hollow, husky voice that implied, on first hearing it, a kind of elfin and subterranean origin.

"Begorra, ma'am, here it is, ma'am! I 'm alludin' to the funeral, ma'am. Shure I made th' ould woman dresh me up in mee besht clothes thish day, ma'am, so I did. Fur it 's Mishter Bairned McCafferty that 's to be buried thish day, I sez, ma'am, sez I to th' ould woman, I sez, an' sez I, ever since I haird he was n't expected, I sez, it 's his wake I wants to be goin' to. An' if I wus too ould, I sez, to crossh over an' pay mee respechts when they waked him in the city, sez I, it 'll be meeself, I sez, that 'll shtand here an' watch 'em parade 'im to Calvary, ma'am, sez I."

Claire had a pity for the old man, at first. But before his speech ended he had roused in her a repulsion. He appeared quietly hilarious; he had produced several distinct chuckles, and his watery, peering eyes, which one of his misshapen hands soon shaded, revealed an actually gay twinkle.

"I don't see why you wanted to come out and watch the person go to his grave," said Claire. "What pleasure can that possibly give you?"

"Pleasure, ma'am, is it, ma'am?" was the startled response. "Why, shure, ma'am, it 's the foinest funeral that's been seen in these parts, ma'am, fur manny a day! An' it's mee own son, Larry, that's drivin' the hairse, ye'll understand, ma'am, an' it's a proud day for Larry, so it is. Excuse me, ma'am, but do ye take sight o' the hairse yet?"

"Oh, yes: very well," said Claire. "It has a number of wooden ornaments along its top, that are gilded and look like large black cabbages." She gave a little burst of weary laughter as she finished the last sentence, whose irony was quite lost on her dim-sighted companion. "And its sides are glass," she continued, "and you can see the large coffin within quite plainly, and there are four horses with white and black plumes."

"An' — an' — the carriages, ma'am, if ye plaise, ma'am?" eagerly questioned the old man. "Shure there should be forty if there's wan, ma'am, an' a few loight wagons thrown in behoind as well. How's that, ma'am?"

"I think there must be forty," said Claire, turning a curious look on the questioner, as he bent excitedly forward to hear her answer. "And there are several light wagons, also."

The old man rubbed his weird hands together in gleeful ecstasy, nearly toppling over as he did so, because the act necessitated a transient disregard of the needful prop lent by his staff. "Shure I towld th' ould woman jusht that!" he cried, in great triumph. "Shure I sez to her, sez I, Barney McCafferty's too daicent a man, I sez, to go to his grave, sez I, anny less daicenter nor that, I sez. It'll be forty carriages, I sez, if it's wan. An' there'll be a shport or so, sez I to her, ma'am (bee thish shtick in mee hand, ma'am, I sed it, ma'am!) there'll be a shport

or so that 'll bring a buggy or so, sez I, for a woind
up at the end, I sez, like the laugh that comes, ye
mind, at the tail of a joke, I sez. An' it 's you I 'm
thankful to, ma'am, fur the loan o' your two broight
eyes, ma'am, that lets me see the soight that God 's
denied me, ma'am : an' I mean, wid a blessin' to yer,
the shtyle o' the hairse an' the gineral natur o' the
intertainmint altogether, ma'am, the Lord love yer
fur yer frindly assistance ! "

"Perhaps you can see the funeral better when it
gets in front of the bridge," said Claire, somewhat
kindly, but with a shocked sense still remaining.
Her varied past, that had shown her so many differing human phases, had not till now presented to her
the extraordinary fact of how positively festal are
the associations with which the Irish, as our shores
find them, are wont to accompany death. At the
same time, she felt interested, and rather curious.
She could always manage, on brief notice, to feel interested and curious regarding any fellow-creature ;
and this trait (one that has grown historic among the
most noted charmers of her own sex) was now tested
to perhaps its last limits.

"Does your son always drive hearses ? " she continued, unconsciously looking at the old man as if he
were something in a museum, to be marveled at for
antiquity and strangeness, but not, on pain of expulsion, to be touched.

"Oh, no, ma'am. Larry 's wan o' the hands to a
livery shtable, ma'am ; but yer see, ma'am, he 's tim-
perance, an' so they gives 'im the hairse at mosht o'
the high-toned funerals, bekase they 're shure, then,
that there 'll be no dishrespect showed to the corpse,
y' undershtand. An' it 's always the behavior o' the

hairse that's mosht cruticized, fur if that goes an'
comes quiet, wid no singin' nur shkylarkin' on the
part o' him that drives it, d' y' undershtand, why
there's lesh talk nur if all the mourners an' rela-
shuns should come home shtavin' drunk, ma'am, d'
ye mind?"

"And who is this Bernard McCafferty?" asked
Claire.

"Is it Barney McCafferty that ye 're ashkin'
about?" was the old man's amazed response, a
sharp falsetto note piercing through his usual huski-
ness. "Why, shure, ma'am, he run six places acrosh
in the city fur tin year all to wanst, so he did, an'
that ain't countin' the wan he kep' in Harlem, nay-
thur."

This explanation was delivered with an air of as-
tonished rebuke, as though one should enumerate the
possessions of some slighted prince.

"What sorts of places do you mean?" inquired
Claire.

The old man put his head on one side and looked
at her with uneasy suspicion, as though he feared she
was making sport of him.

"Places? Why, liquor-sthores, to be sure."

"Oh," said Claire. "And what did he die of?
Drink?"

Her companion brightened noticeably, and seemed
to gain confidence in his questioner. He scratched
one cheek, where the unshorn beard showed in white,
bristly patches along the fleshless jaw, and winked
at Claire as though she had at once put the matter
upon a basis of mutual and intimate comprehension.

"I guess it *was* the drink ash laid 'im out at lasht,
ma'am. Manny is the good glass I had wid Barney

afore he went into politics an' got shut of his besht frinds, bad luck to 'im. But he shtood well up to his liquor fur nigh forty year, though I 'm thinkin' it fetched 'im in the end, ma'am."

This was said with the manner and tone of a person who might have alluded to some rather genteel foible in the deceased, like a fondness for chess or whist. Claire found herself confronting another fact in the lower Irish nature, hitherto but half surmised: the enormous indulgence and sympathetic tolerance with which this unique race regards every form and feature of drunkenness.

" If he sold liquor all his life and died of it himself," she exclaimed, with heat and force, " he does n't deserve to have half so large a funeral. And I think it's dreadful," she went on, with a little angry stamp of the foot, while she lifted one finger and shook it at the old man in a way with which her sex had doubtless familiarized him at an earlier stage in his long career — " yes, I think it's perfectly horrible that you people should ever dare to get drunk at funerals as you do ! I often see the carriage-loads come back from the cemetery through Greenpoint, laughing and smoking, and sometimes yelling and swearing as well ! Oh, I don't know how you *can* do it ! There is something so grand, so terrible about death ! You ought to be ashamed, all of you ! Such actions make this place more sad and wretched than it really is. It is a miserable place enough, Heaven knows ! "

She moved away from the old man as she spoke the last sentence. Going forth upon the road, she retraced her steps in the direction of the town, and **thus met each separate vehicle of the long funeral as**

5

it stole laggingly onward. First came the black-and-gilt hearse, flaunting its interior coffin with horrid ostentation, as though it wanted you to see how many wreaths and crosses had been lavished upon the remains of Mr. McCafferty by his bereaved constituents. Then followed a carriage to whose driver had been confided a capacious wooden box which would doubtless receive the coffin before its interment, and into which the driver, having placed its glaring unpainted mass on a line with the dashboard, had thrust his feet, and by the act engulfed, as it were, nearly half his person. He was a man of sallow, cadaverous visage and very gaunt frame; he looked as if he might possess some eerie fellowship with the corpse itself; he seemed to alter the popular phrase about having a foot in the grave, and to make it quite thinkable that life could exist under still more moribund conditions. In the conveyance which he drove was a group of four people. Two of them were stout Irishwomen, swathed in crape, and two were middle-aged Irishmen, dressed with a holiday smartness. In this vehicle silence appeared to reign; its occupants, all four, sat with lowered eyes. But in the other carriages, as one by one passed Claire, not a sign of grief was manifest. There was a good deal of audible conversation; there was considerable leaning of heads out of windows; there were not a few querulous children of various ages, some of whom had been given oranges to suck or sticks of striped candy to munch; there were buxom women and spare women, massive men and slim men, little girls and little boys, all huddled together, quite often three or even more on a seat. But in the whole long panorama of human visages, as it glided past her, Claire could not discern a single trace of solemnity. The impression of mere hollow and senseless form was produced, by this crude *cortège*, with complete and dismal success. Nobody — with the slight exceptions recorded — seemed to be sorry that Mr. McCafferty had made a permanent departure from the liquor-business.

"I wonder why they come, if they are not sorry," Claire said to herself, as she reëntered the town, leaving the great serpentine funeral behind her. "I suppose it is because of the ride. They seize on even this grim excuse for getting a little pastime." . . . Then her thoughts took a new, self-questioning turn. "And what reason have I to pity them and call them 'poor'? They come here only in the way of holiday, but I never get a glimpse of anything better or worse, month after month. I dare say there *are* worse places than this. I should like to see one, if there really are, just for the change."

Passing back through the unlovely streets again, Claire had a desire to be near the water before she returned in-doors. She now regretted not having gone thither at first, instead of taking her dolorous inland walk. It was nearly sunset; the twilight had not yet learned to loiter, as it does in maturer Spring, and a gloom had already crept, with purplish effect, into the sweet pale azure of the heavens. Claire made as short a cut toward one special place at the water's edge as her regretted familiarity with Greenpoint would permit, and presently stood on a raised spot close beside the river. It was a bare scarp of earth, touched faintly, here and there, with the most meagre intervals of struggling green. Its site commanded the delightful view beyond, and now,

at the ruddy but transient advent of evening, this
view was peculiarly delightful. You saw the wrinkled river, drab and tremulous, under a stretch of
sky which the sinking sun had made from verge to
zenith a turmoil of little rosy and feathery clouds.
Each cloud had the damask glow, without its fleet-
ness, that we see in the scales of a darting trout.
The whole ember-colored array arched over the wide
stream in brief, unusual brilliancy, and stole now
and then from the gray waves beneath it a slight
gleam, no larger than the bud of a carnation, but
quite as rich-hued. Just beneath Claire was a low,
uncouth, many - patched hut, near to the muddy
strand, and looking not unlike something that had
drifted up from aqueous recesses with the intent of
making itself habitable for men. A ragged contigu-
ous wharf had been built here, at whose edge, when
summer came, small boats would be grouped to let.
A little northward, great yellowish piles of lumber
loomed, tier after tier, with big sloops moored beside
them, and with one acute red pennon, on one slim
mast, blown out bright against the darkening air.
Steamboats and sail - boats were slipping over the
ruffled river, these urged by their steady mechanic
push, those winning the capricious breeze to favor
their full - stretched canvas. Beyond, in dusky, irregular semicircle, lay the opposite city. Its many
church-spires pierced the dimness, but all its other
traits of architecture, viewed at this distance, had a
flat, massed look. There was something symbolic in
the isolated saliency of these spires ; they seemed to
typify the permanence of a faith which had already
defied centuries. But still more, their vague group
merged every detail of creed into one pictorial whole;

you forgot, as you gazed, what various paths toward
salvation this or that steeple might be supposed to
point. The whole effect was simply and powerfully
Christian.

Claire fixed her eyes upon the shadowy city. A
few early lights already dotted its expanse with gold,
as if to outspeed the tardier stars overhead. It
spread away, for the gaze that watched it, like a
huge realm of fascinating mystery. Claire forgot
how much sin it hid; perhaps she scarcely knew if
it hid any. She thought only of the diversions, re-
laxations, festivities that would soon hold sway there.
Odd memories of her old school-fellows crossed her
mind. Doubtless Ada Gerrard was there now, thinking of some new robe in which she would show her
plump white neck with the little freckles on it, that
very evening. It should be a pale-blue dress, Claire
decided; that would suit Ada's red hair the best.
How full was the big city, yonder, of happy, handsome, prosperous people! And so many of them
were saying, now that the nightfall had begun, " I
shall go to this ball to-night," or " I shall go to that
theatre." They were getting the theatres ready for
the plays, now; the entrances were being lighted.
She could see Wallack's and the Union Square, each
with its small court and the baize doors beyond. Oh,
how pleasant it would be to do something, to look at
something, to hear something, to-night, that she had
not done and looked at and heard, again and again,
for weeks and months past! The girl's blood and
bone hungered for a holiday. She must go back
home, soon. And there was only one thought to
make the prospect of return endurable; that thought
was meeting her father. But he would be tired; he

was always more tired nowadays than in other times. When he lay upon the lounge in the basement, and she got the stool and sat down beside him, he would smile to have her put both arms round his neck and press her cheek up close to his, but he would go to sleep very soon afterward; he would be so tired that he would forget even to ask her if she had had a hard time with her mother that day. And then her mother would grumble a hint that the dishes were yet to be washed, and she would take her arms away from the beloved neck, and scrape and clean for quite a long time; and then she would get sleepy, more because she remembered how early she must rise to-morrow than because a very little diversion would not have made the alert young lids loath to shade her eyes for hours to come.

It would all be the same as on other nights. It was always, every new night, the same as on that which went before. There was the dull burden of it. When would the burden be shifted? Would it ever be shifted? Would it not merely grow heavier, and slowly crush her down, till her back should get the crook of age, and so bear it with better ease?

She went nearer to the edge of the hillock, and set her eyes once more upon the city, as if for a farewell view. Its lights had become more numerous; the tips of its spires were lost in tender vapor. Above, the tiny scraps of luminous cloud had begun to fade; the river had roughened and grown dull, and there was a damp keenness in the freshening breeze. That exquisite melancholy which is sure to breathe from evening when it sheds a spell over the triple charm of blended sky, land, and water, was now in the full tide of its lovely power.

Claire lifted her hand to her lips, and waved a kiss toward the glooming city. It was a pretty gesture, and so furtive and stealthy that it might have fled the notice of any one who stood quite close at her side. And the low words that now succeeded it, too, were just low enough to escape such heed, though their sense might easily have met a possible listener with the effect of broken and half-audible speech.

" Good-night," she said to the city. " Good-night, and be merry for hours to come. You seem just like something alive and breathing, but I know that if you had one mind and one heart to think and to feel with, instead of the thousands and thousands that you have got, you would pity me because I'm so sorry that this big, cold river is always between us!"

Claire nearly broke into a laugh at her own soft and quaint little apostrophe. Like most lonely people who dislike their solitude, she often felt the temptation to soliloquize; especially since her imagination was vigorous, and sometimes loved, as well, to let mount from its wrist the agile falcon of fancy. But a practical bent, as we call it, and a rather sharp sense of the humor of things besides, usually mingled to repress this volatile impulse. As it was, she gave a strong, tired sigh instead of a laugh, and turned her face homeward, though not her steps quite yet, for she still remained standing on the mound beside the water.

" My holiday," she thought, " is over." She did not know that it was just beginning.

Her last action had brought her into abrupt contact with a girlish figure, whose countenance she might have recognized had not the dusk so deepened.

V.

"I was mos' sure 't was you, Miss Twining," said
the new-comer, holding out a hand to Claire, "so I
run a little further up the hill, jus' to make reel certain sure."

"Well, you were not wrong, Josie," said Claire,
giving her own hand. It did not occur to her that
she had been called "Miss Twining" and had answered by "Josie." In this case she took her rights
of superiority without thinking; she did not stop to
consider their soundness; it had always been to her
an accepted fact that she was an alien and an exile,
here in Greenpoint, and that the few residents whom
she knew must of necessity admit her claim to having existed under better previous conditions. There
was no taint of arrogance in this unargued assumption.

"You ain't often out 's late 's this, Miss Twining,"
said Josie, with a little burst of laughter. "Are you,
now?"

"No, indeed," answered Claire. "I am not often
out at all." She sighed again, quite unconsciously.
"Well, Josie," she went on, "I must be getting back
home. I 've been away too long, as it is. You seem
to be dressed in your very finest. Does it mean that
you are going to enjoy yourself somewhere?"

Josie gave another laugh. "I expect so, Miss

Twining," she said, with a touch of mysterious piquancy in her manner. She turned herself quickly about, looking over her shoulder all the while with the air of waiting for some one to appear. Claire watched her closely during the unconscious but significant by-play.

The name of this young girl was Josephine Morley. She was of Irish parents, but felt ashamed of the fact. Perhaps consciously, perhaps not, she had banished from her speech all hereditary traces. She spoke in a rattling way, and every now and then she would heap massive emphasis on one special word. Her talk made you think of a railway that is all broken up with *dépôts*, none of which the engine discountenances. Her widowed mother kept a grocery store, not amply patronized, and of moderate prices. By pre-arrangement with the Twinings on a basis of the most severe economy, Josie would bring them their needed supply of vegetables thrice a week. She was not so jaunty-looking on those occasions as she now appeared. Then she would be clad in any flotsam and jetsam of apparel that charity might have drifted toward her. But to-night she was smartly dressed. Now that Claire scanned her closer in the dimness, it was plain that she wore very unusual gear. Josie was not much over twenty. She was extremely thin, but still rather shapely, and endowed with a good deal of grace. Her face would have been pretty but for its high cheek-bones and the hectic blotch of color that was wont to flush them, in sharp contrast with her remaining pallor. She had had several sisters who had died of a speedy consumption. Her eyes were black, and would glitter as she moved them; she was always moving her

eyes; like herself, they never seemed at rest. She
constantly smiled, and the smile would have had a
charm of its own if it had failed to reveal somewhat
ruinous teeth. Claire had always liked her vivacity,
though it had seemed to possess a spur that came
from an unhealthy impulse, like the heat of internal
fever. She wore a wide-brimmed hat of dark straw,
with a great crimson feather, and a costume of some
cheap maroon stuff, violently relieved by trimmings
of broad white braid. The *ensemble* was very far
from ugly. She had copied its effect from a popular
weekly journal, whose harrowing fiction would sometimes be supplemented by prints of the latest fash-
ions, " given away " to its devoted patrons.

Claire, having drawn nearer to Josie, took in all
her details of costume with ready swiftness. This
fleet sort of observation was always an easy matter
for Claire. In most cases of a like sort, she would
both see and judge before others had accomplished
even the first process.

" You seem to be waiting for somebody, Josie,"
she now said.

" Yes, I am," returned Josie, with another laugh.
She put one slim hand to her mouth as she laughed;
she nearly always employed this gesture at such a
time; it came, no doubt, from a consciousness of
dental deficiencies. "I ain't goin' to be *shy*, Miss
Twining," she pursued. " Why *should* I ? I'm ex-
pectin' a gent'man friend o' mine. We was goin'
over t' the city together. We was goin' to *Niblo's*.
There's an el'gant play there, they *say*." . . . Here
Josie paused, drew backward for an instant, and then
impulsively seized one of Claire's hands in both of
her own. " Oh, Miss Twining ! " she suddenly ex-

claimed, " I know I had n't ought to ask you if *you'd*
come along, too, but I do wish you just *would!* You
ain't the same kind as me a bit, and there's more 'n
me in Greenpoint — now, 'pon my word there is —
that's said when they see you that you *was* a reel
lady. But still, you might come with me and my
friend, Mr. MacNab, and just get a spell of *'musement*. I know you ain't had any 'musement in goodness sakes *how* long! It's a reel el'gant play! *Do*
say you will! Now I ain't a bit *soft* on Mr. Mac-
Nab. P'aps he 'd *like* me to be, but I *ain't*. So
three won't spoil comp'ny. Now, *do!* Oh, Miss
Twining, I 'd be awful glad if you *would!*"

Josie's tones, like her words, were warmly persuasive. She still retained Claire's hand. Nor did
Claire withdraw it. She was tempted. She turned
her head toward the darkling city, in whose realm
of deepened shadow many new lights had begun to
burn.

" Ah, Josie," she said, " you are very kind to ask
me. But I 'm quite shabby beside you, you know."

" Pshaw!" flatly objected Josie ; " you look fust
rate. That ain't *no* sort of reason. . . . Do! Now,
do!"

Claire laughed nervously. She was thinking how
pleasant it would be to hear an orchestra play, to see
a curtain rise, to watch a drama roll its story out, behind vivid footlights, between painted scenes.

" I am sure Mr. MacNab would n't like," she said.
And then she thought of how her father would soon
come home and miss her, and have to be told, when
they next met, that she had been to the theatre over
in New York with the girl who brought them vegetables thrice a week. She seemed quite to have

made up her mind, presently. She withdrew her hand from Josie's with a good deal of placid force.

"No, Josie, I can't," she said.

"Yes, you *can!*" was the fervid reply. "Yes, you just *shall*, Miss Twining; now *there!* I ain't goin' t' let you *off!* When I get my mind set right *onto* anything, I'm as stubb'n as ever I can *be!* An' I'm sure you'd *like* to come. There ain't no doubt of 't — not one single *grain!*"

Josie was laughing while she thus spoke, and had again caught Claire's unwilling hand with more of entreaty than boldness.

"What makes you sure?" Claire asked. She smiled now, though the smile was sad.

Josie's laughter became a high treble ripple. She put both feet, visible beneath her short skirt, suddenly very close together, and curved her lithe body in an abrupt burlesque bow. The trick was graceful, though vulgar; it savored of the cheaper variety entertainments, where Josie had no doubt found it. She still held Claire's hand, and she was looking straight into the eyes of her companion with her own dark, brisk eyes.

"What *makes* me sure you'd like to go?" she said. "Why, sakes alive, Miss Twining, I can see the need of a little fun oozin' right out of your *face* — now, 'pon my word and sacred honor I just *can!* Oh, pshaw! We'll be home early 'nough. It won't be *much* more 'n quarter past 'leven, I guess. B'sides, who'll *know?* 'Tain't anybody's business but *ours.*"

'Father would know. It would be his business,' Claire thought. But she did not answer aloud, as yet. She permitted Josie to retain her hand, while she turned and gave another glance toward the city across the river.

The rapid darkness had thickened. Where New York had lain, dim as a mirage, hundreds of lights had clustered; their yellow galaxy more than rivaled the pale specks of fire now crowding with silent speed into the heavens domed so remotely above them.

She faced Josie again. She trembled, though imperceptibly. Drooping her eyes, at first, she then raised them. "Well," she said, "I will let you persuade me. I will go with you, Josie."

It was the first time she had ever made a resolve whose fulfillment she felt sure would displease her father. The certainty that he would not sanction her going in companionship of this proposed sort made Claire's decision a sacrilege to herself, even while she perversely took it. She trampled on her own filial loyalty, and she seemed to feel it tremble in pained protest under the outrage. It was in vain that a troop of self-excusing pleas sprang to battle against her shamed afterthought. She knew that remorse was already whetting for her its poniard. The gloom of her father's future rebuke had already made itself a part of the increasing nightfall.

"Oh, *ain't* I glad, though!" Josie broke forth, gleefully. Her triumph was one of pure good-natured impulse, but at the same time she had a flattered sense that her evening's amusement would now gain a stamp of distinction. One or two girls in Greenpoint had derided her for encouraging Mr. MacNab as a devotee. She herself secretly derided the young man in that same tender office. For this reason she had arranged that they should meet here to-night at the foot of the little hillock near the river, and invest their purposed trip with enough clandestine association to defeat the couchant raillery of certain unsparing neighbors.

Almost immediately Mr. MacNab made his appearance below, and Josie tripped lightly down toward him, followed by Claire at a much more sober pace. The introduction promptly followed, and Josie's glib, matter - of - course explanation soon succeeded that. The reason of Claire's presence was given Mr. Mac-Nab by Josie with a handsome, off-hand patronage. "It's awful nice o' Miss Twining to *consent* to go along with us," she ended. "*Aint* it, now?"

"Oh, yes, indeed," said Mr. MacNab.

The young man was inwardly tortured by this abrupt announcement. He was very much in love with Josie, and he had felt deeper and deeper thrills of anticipation all day long, as the hour of their rendezvous drew near. He was a youth of about two-and-twenty. His stature was so low as to be almost dwarfish; both Claire's and Josie's well overtopped it. He was very stout, however; the breadth of his shoulders and the solid girth of his limbs might have suited six feet of clean height. He had a large, smooth, moon-like face, a pair of little black eyes, and a pair of huge red ears. He was immoderately ugly, but with an expression so simply amiable as quite to escape repulsiveness. You felt that his ready smile possessed vast hidden funds of geniality; there was no telling what supple resources that long slit of big-lipped mouth might draw upon, at a really mirthful emergency. One glance at his abnormal hands, where every joint was an uncouth protuberance and every nail a line of inky darkness, left it certain that they held no dainty share of the world's manual requirements. Mr. James MacNab was an oyster-opener for about eight months in the year, and a clam-opener through the remaining four. The nar-

row window of his employer's shop looked upon
Greenpoint Avenue, wedged between the stores of
a butcher and a candy-seller. Like Josie Morley,
James was of Irish parentage; like her, he abjured
the accent of his ancestors, having been born here,
and having breathed into his being at an early age
that peculiar shame of Celtic origin which belongs
among our curiosities of immigration. His wages
were meagre, and his hours of work numerous. . To-
night was a precious interval of relaxation. He had
been released at three o'clock that afternoon, and had
gone heavy-lidded to a tiny cot in a garret-room,
where he had slept the exhausted sleep of one who
is always in arrears to the drowsy god. Not long
ago he had waked, highly refreshed, and pierced
with the expectation of soon meeting his beloved
Josie. He had four dollars and seventy-five cents in
his pocket, and the possession of this sum gave him
a firm sense of pecuniary security. The strong faith
that he was finely dressed, too, increased his confidence. He had a little low hat of black felt, tipped
sideways on his ungainly head; an overcoat of muddy
cinnamon-brown, with broad black binding along its
lappels and edges; and a pair of boots so capably
polished that their lustre dissuaded you from too
close scrutiny of the toe-joint bulging from either
clumsy foot. He was entirely satisfied with his general effect. He knew that nature had not made him
comely, but he felt complete repose of conscience in
the matter of having atoned artistically for this personal slight.

Josie's tidings left him almost speechless. In a
trice his glowing hopes had crumbled to ashes. He
had long known Claire by sight. He had, in a way,

admired her. But she was not of his *monde*, and he saw with woe and dismay that for this reason her company would prove all the more burdensome. As a matter of expense, too, it presented the most painful objections. New drafts must be made upon his limited capital. All his past calculations were suddenly rendered null. Who could say what financial disaster might overtake him, if he should now aspire to three oyster-stews after three seats at the theatre? Would his four dollars and seventy-five cents not pass its powers of elasticity if subjected to this unforeseen stretching-process? Claire, meanwhile, was wholly unconscious of his distress. It was not till they had embarked on the ferry-boat that the thought of her escort's possible poverty occurred to her flurried mind. "Oh, Josie," she soon found a chance to whisper, "I am afraid I shall be a great expense to your friend! I would have thought of it sooner if you had not pressed me so, without any warning beforehand. And I have only a little change in my pocket, so I can't" —

But here Josie interrupted her with a magnificent murmured fiction to the effect that they were under the protection of a young man who "jus' made money hand over fist"; and Claire, believing this handsome falsehood, let Josie talk with her gallant while she relapsed into silence.

They were all on the forward deck of the steamboat, close against its wooden railing. Claire was a little apart from her companions; she had instinctively withdrawn from them. The night had now woven its web to the full. Overhead the stars beamed more richly; below, the black river shimmered with glassy lustre where it met the sides of

the speeding vessel, and then rolled off again into
darkness with great swollen waves. Long points of
light pierced the gloom below the opposite shore,
like golden plummets that were slowly fathoming its
opaque tide. Here and there scarlet or green lights
moved over the waters, given by the viewless barks
that bore them the look of weird, wandering jack-o'-
lanterns. These were simply fantastic; they held no
human analogies. A sloop, thus brilliantly decked,
hove on a sudden into sight, not many yards from
Claire's peering gaze. Its expanse of canvas, tense
in the sharp breeze, caught a momentary unearthly
pallor; it slipped into view like a monstrous phantom, and like a phantom it vanished again. This,
too, was a merely elfin and quaint apparition; no
sense of vital reality lay behind it. But the journey-
ing ferry-boats, that voyaged to their several goals
on either side the river, took, with their curved lines
of small, keen-lit windows and their illuminations at
various other points, the likeness of stately galleys
gliding after nightfall to some opulent port. All
their horrors of nautical architecture were deadened
by merciful shadow. Claire felt the quiet splendor
of the suggestion. Her varied educational past made
this fully possible. But the whole effect of transformation, of magic, of mystery, and of beauty, which
follows the advent of night along all the watery en-
virons of our great metropolis, appealed to her with
deep force.

She had a fancy that the hard prose had left her
life forever; that she was now being softly swept into
luxurious and romantic surroundings; that the festal
and poetic look of city and river symbolized a fairer
and kindlier future. The indulgence of this fancy

6

thrilled her delightfully; it was a sort of intoxication; she no longer felt culpable, unfilial; she leaned
her graceful young head far over the boat-rail, as
though to gain by this act a stronger intimacy with
the sweet, drowsy sorceries that encompassed her.

"*My!* ain't it *reel* chilly out here, though?" said
Josie. "We'd ought to 'a stayed inside, *had n't* we,
Miss Twining?"

This half broke the spell with Claire. "I like it
so much better out here," she answered. "The air
is n't too sharp for me, and then everything is so
beautiful and strange." She slightly waved one hand
toward the brilliant city as she spoke.

Josie did not understand at all. How could there
be anything beautiful in a lot of boats screaming to
each other after dark with steam-whistles? But she
said "yes," and cast a glance at Mr. MacNab, which
was meant to veto in him the first symptom of surprise. Claire's superiority must not have the least
slight cast upon it. It would never do to encourage
Mr. MacNab in undervaluing the compliment of her
companionship.

The boat soon landed, and all Claire's lovely illu-
sions fled. Still, here was the city, noisy, populous,
alluring. After disembarking at the ferry they were
yet far away from Niblo's, and a long ride ensued, in
a car crowded and of ill odor. Then came a walk
of considerable length, fleetly taken, for they were a
little late by Mr. MacNab's silver time-piece, which
afterward proved to be fast.

Mr. MacNab was meanwhile in a sort of nervous
trance. He had made what for him was a *tour de
force* in mental arithmetic, though he still remained
insecure about the exactitude of his calculation.

However, he felt confident of one thing : three seats, of a certain kind, would cost three dollars. A dollar would solidly remain to him, though the precise amount of surplus change now in his pocket defied all his mathematical modes of discovery. Pride forbade that he should take out the silver bits and count them. But his residual dollar could at least pay the homeward fares. Cold as this comfort may have been, it took, no doubt, a certain relative warmth when contrasted with dire pecuniary exposure.

They at length reached the theatre, and easily procured upstairs seats that commanded an excellent view of the stage. The curtain had not yet risen. Claire was glad of that ; she had the desire not to miss a single detail of the coming performance. She was intently examining her play-bill, when, on a sudden, a man's voice, close at her right, spoke to this effect : —

" Hello, Jimmy, is that yerself ? "

The next moment Claire perceived a hand and arm to have been unceremoniously thrust in front of her, while a young man leaned his body very much sideways indeed. She receded, herself, not without annoyance.

Josie sat next to her, and then came Mr. MacNab, who now permitted himself to be shaken hands with across the laps of the two girls.

" Hello, Jack," he responded, at the same time. " What you doin' here ? "

" Come t' see the show," said the person called Jack.

" Is that so ? "

" 'Course. Nuthin' strange 'bout it, is there ? "

" That's all right."

" S'pose you 're on the same racket yerself. Hey ? "

" You bet, ole boy."

All these utterances were exchanged in tones of the most easy cordiality. The two young men had ceased to shake hands, but were leaning each toward the other, apparently quite unconscious of the inconvenience which they inflicted upon both Josie and Claire.

" I got sold t' night," Jack continued, with a blended wink and giggle.

" How 's that ? "

Jack gave a demonstrative jerk of the elbow, meant to indicate a vacant seat on his further side. " Me an' my gal was comin' t'gether, but she gimme the slip after I 'd got mer seats. Sent word she had the headache. Well, I dunno how 't is, but I reckon I 'll have to punch some feller's head, 'fore long. Hey, Jimmy ? "

This hostile prophecy was hailed by Jimmy with a laugh whose repressed enjoyment took the semblance of a goose's hiss, except that its tone was more guttural and its volume more massive.

" I guess that 's 'bout the size of it, Jack," he replied. The next moment he straightened himself in his seat, having received an exasperated nudge from Josie.

Mr. MacNab's friend followed his example. Claire felt relieved. She examined her programme again. She had already managed to see quite as much as she wished of the person seated next her.

His name was Slocumb. He had a cousin in Greenpoint, an undertaker's son, whom he would occasionally visit of a Sunday, bringing across the river to the doleful quarters of his kinsfolk a de-

meanor of high condescension and patronage. He
was in reality a loafer of very vicious sort, feeding
his idleness upon the alms of an infatuated woman,
whose devotion he did not repay with even the saving grace of fidelity. He had contrived to hide his
real badness of life and lowness of repute from both
uncle and cousin, and had won the latter to believe
him a superior kind of metropolitan product. Together MacNab and he had partaken of refreshment
at the shop of the former's employer, and from such
events had sprung an intimacy with the oyster-opener
which had found its most active development in a
near drinking-shop. Mr. John Slocumb had a dull,
brownish complexion, a light-brown eye, and a faint
brown mustache. His face was not ugly, judged by
line and feature, but it had a hardness that resembled bronze ; you fancied that you might touch its
cheek and meet no resistance. There was a look of
vice and depravity about it that was not to be explained ; the repulsive element was there, but it
eluded direct proof ; it was no more in eyelid than
in nostril, but it was as much in forehead and chin
as in either. Claire felt the repelling force almost
instantly. Mr. Slocumb's dress was not designed in
a fashion to decrease its effect. He wore a suit of
green-and-blue plaid, each tint being happily moderated, like evil that prefers to lurk in ambush. The
collar of his shirt sloped down at the breast, leaving
an unwonted glimpse of his neck visible. But you
saw a good deal of his cravat, which was green,
barred with broad yellow stripes, and pierced by a
pin that appeared to be a hand of pink coral clutch-
ing a golden dumb - bell. His figure was slender
almost to litheness, but his shoulders outspread two

such long and bulky ridges that you at once placed
their athletic proportions among the most courageous
frauds of tailoring.

The orchestra had now begun to play a lively and
rather clangorous prelude. And meanwhile Claire
was gradually made to learn that Mr. John Slocumb
was keeping up a cool, persistent stare at her half-
averted face. She soon became troubled by this
unrelaxing scrutiny, as minutes slipped by. Mr. Slocumb had a slim black cane that looked like a polished and rounded whalebone and ended in the head
of a bull-dog, with two white specks of ivory for its
eyes. Holding this between his knees, he flung it
from one hand to another in nervous oscillation, while
continuing his stare.

He had decided that Claire was a damned good-
looking girl. He had a secret contempt for her escort, Mr. MacNab. He judged all men by the capa-
bilities of their muscle, and he had practical reasons
for feeling sure that his own wiry frame held easy
resources for the annihilation of "poor little Jimmy."
'She looks putty high-toned,' he was reflecting, 'but
I guess that's on'y a put-up job to tease a feller. She
can't be much if she's along with that young un.
I'll say somepn.'

He was on the verge of carrying out this resolve
and addressing Claire, when an event occurred which
had the effect of thwarting his meditated impertinence.

The mind of James MacNab was dull and sluggish.
But he had seen a way of perhaps securing for himself the undivided attention of Josie. He did not
wait for the latter to sanction his design; he feared
her opposition to it, and suddenly spoke, leaning forward again with his look directed full upon Claire.

"Miss Twinin'," he said, "'low me t' intrerdooce a friend o' mine, Mr. Slocumb. Mr. Slocumb, Miss Twinin'; Miss Twinin', Mr. Slocumb."

During this ponderous formula of presentation Claire had started, colored, turned toward the neighbor thus pointedly named, and finally bowed with extreme coldness, at once re-averting her face after doing so.

She seized the chance of whispering to Josie: "Why did he do that? I don't want to meet any strangers to-night. I hoped he would understand."

"He'd *ought* to," replied Josie, in swift aside. "I do declare it's *too* bad!"

The next moment she addressed Mr. MacNab. Claire could not hear what she said to him, but her brisk asperity of gesture somewhat plainly denoted reprimand. Her remarks, whatever their nature, were met in stolid silence. He who received them rather enjoyed being scolded by Josie. Her wrath had the charm of exclusiveness; for the time, at least, it vouchsafed to him her unshared heed.

Slocumb made prompt use of his new opportunity. "I guess we'll have a putty decent show to-night," he said. "They say it lays over most ev'rything that's been here fur a year or two."

Claire was now forced to turn and look at the speaker. To ignore him was no longer to preserve dignity. He had received his right of way beyond the barriers of her disregard; he had become an authorized nuisance; civility from herself had taken the instant shape of a debt, due her present escort.

"I shall be glad if it is a good play," she said. Her tones were chill and forced; her manner was repellent because so restrained. Immediately after speaking she looked at the stage. The orchestra had just stopped its brassy tumults. The green width of curtain was slowly rolling upward.

The play began. It was one of those melodramas that are the despair of reformatory critics, yet reach the protective approval of the populace through scenic novelty, swift action, and vivid, if coarse-lined, portraitures. Claire was too infrequent a theatre-goer not promptly to fall under the spell wrought by a playwright deft enough for the capture of others far more experienced than she in tricks of climax, dialogue, and situation.

Occasionally, during the progress of this act, she would murmur pleased comments to Josie. She betrayed an interest that was childish; she had forgotten the proximity of Slocumb. He still stared at her; he had not been effectually repulsed by her suppressed, colorless demeanor. Her refined accent and the musical quality inseparable at all times from her voice had affected him like a new sensation. He failed to follow the actors while they diligently stored up material for future agony. He had enormous confidence in his own powers of fascination with women, It did not occur to him that Claire might be a lady. He knew nothing of ladies. He had met some women who disliked him at sight, who would have none of him, whose fortresses of prejudice he could not storm. But these incidents of disfavor were rare; his list of conquests far outnumbered them.

"She's playin' off," sped his further reflections, once more shaped in the vernacular of actual speech. "I'll let up on her fur a spell. When the fust act's through I'll tackle her agin. *She* aint's offish as she looks. Bet she ain't!"

The act progressed, and at length ended. Its *finale* foretold a plentitude of woe and disaster; a great deal of pipe, so to speak, had been laid for future calamity; everything promised to be inclement and tempestuous. The audience exchanged murmurs of grim approbation; it was going to get its money's worth of horror.

But now an event abruptly took place which for lurid reality far eclipsed all within the limits of canvas and calcium. Just as the drop-curtain had reached half-way in its descent, a sudden burst of flame was seen to issue from one of the wings. It may at once be said that the fire was completely extinguished soon after the curtain had touched the boards, and that nothing more serious had caused it than the momentary conflagration of some gauze side-scene which was to serve in a coming effect of misty moonlight.

But the large mass of people who witnessed the blaze, and who saw and smelt the smoke as it curled and eddied in black spirts forth from behind the edges of the fallen curtain, had no knowledge of their own slight peril. Here, in the upper tiers, they rose impetuously; it was a prompt and general panic. Dashes were made on every hand toward the staircases. Cries of "fire" sounded from many throats. Claire felt herself swept by sheer bodily pressure at least twenty yards. A few seconds before this she had heard a sort of whimpering shriek from Josie Morley, and then had seen a sidelong wedge of close-packed humanity pry itself between her own form and that of the girl. Josie was clinging with both hands to the arm of James MacNab at the moment of her disappearance.

Claire was more shocked than frightened. She had never before found herself in physical danger; to-night was a crucial test for her nerve and coolness. Both stood the test well. John Slocumb, who had kept close at her side, with his stout arm firmly clasped about her waist, now felt a thrill of admiration as she turned to him and quietly said, while they stood jammed together in the panting throng, whose very fierceness of impetus had produced for it a brief, terrible calm, " I wish you would not hold me like that, please. There's no need of it."

We sometimes hear of the ruling passion that is strong in death. Claire knew there was danger of her being crushed. But she had not lost her head, as the phrase goes. She could still prefer solitary extinction to the fate of being annihilated while in the embrace of Mr. John Slocumb.

He removed his arm. " All right," he muttered, " if you'd rather go it alone."

" I would, thank you," said Claire.

VI

BUT, as it happened. they were not separated. The crowd, pouring down either staircase, soon thinned. There was better breathing-space, and a fairer chance as well, for the more demoralized to push and struggle. Slocumb kept close behind Claire. He warded off from her a number of desperate thrusts. She was not aware of these defensive tactics; she paid no further heed to her former champion; as her sense of danger lessened, the idea of re-meeting Josie took shape and strength. When the first step of the staircase was reached, she stumbled, and then regained herself. She had no suspicion, at this moment, what actually doughty work Slocumb was doing, just in her rear. He was a man of unusual muscular power, and, like not a few of his rough, pugnacious species, endowed with dogged physical courage. At sight Claire had keenly attracted him ; her recent aversion had piqued him into liking her still more. If the occasion had grown one of sharper immediate jeopardy, it is by no means doubtful that he might have shown intrepid heroism as her rescuer. He was gross, coarse, unprincipled, but he had that quality of stubbornly defending what he liked which we often see in the finest of brutes and sometimes in the least fine of men.

Up to this time the prevailing affright had meant

bitter ill to all whom it had seized. The threat of
a hideous destruction had by no means passed when
the crowd about Claire grew less dense; for not far
behind her were two opposite streams of life that had
met and were each destroying the other's progress by
their very madness of encounter. Below stairs, and
at one of the intermediate landings, numerous people had already been severely hurt; limbs had been
broken, and acute injuries of other kinds had been
dealt. The cries heard here and there were made
as much by pain as fear.

But powers of good were working with ardor
among the lower quarters of the building. A man
had sprung forth upon the stage, and was imploring
order amid the smoke which partly enveloped him,
while at the same time he shouted to the multitude
that the fire was now under perfect control. Two
policemen and two ushers were abetting him further
on, where neither his entreaties nor explanations
could reach. Suddenly, with the same speed shown
by the panic at its origin, an orderly lull was manifest in its haphazard turmoil. A few caught the
sense of the cheering intelligence, and these spread it
swiftly from tongue to tongue. At the moment when
this change began to be clearly assertive, Claire and
Slocumb had almost gained the last landing of the
stairs. By the time they were in the lower part of
the theatre, not a few persons who desired to air their
bravery, now that safety seemed certain, were returning to their seats in dress-circle or parquette. "It's
on'y a hoax, after all," said Slocumb. "There's a
heap more scared nor hurt. S'pose we git upstairs
again? Hey? What d' yer think?"

Claire shook her head. "No, I want to find Josie,"

she answered. "I don't care to go back. I think she will not, either."

"All right," said Slocumb; "jus' take my hook, an' we'll git out o' here, an' watch fur Jim an' her where they're mos' likely to be."

He extended an arm to Claire as he spoke, and pointed at the same time toward a spacious outer hallway, in which the terrified multitude had already become much more tractable. But Claire resolutely refused to see the offered arm. She had begun to tremble; now that the cause for fright had passed, she was made to realize with how strong a wrench she had screwed her nerves to the sticking-point. A touch of giddiness came upon her; then a knot rose in her throat, and she fought transiently, but with silent success, against a novel sensation that only slight self-surrender might have encouraged into turbid hysteria. Still, she preserved her repugnance, as it were. She would not accept Slocumb's arm. She had made up her mind that he was a vulgar and worthless creature, and moreover she had a distressing instinct that he had thus stayed at her side because of some new-born personal enticement.

He saw plainly her rebuff, though she did not put it in any salient way, choosing to let him suppose it a mere unconscious omission. But he preferred not to let it pass unnoticed.

"Oho," he said, with surly force, while still keeping his arm crooked, and shoving it so prominently toward her that no further subterfuge was possible. "So y' ain't goin' to ketch on, hey? W'at's the reason? We can git 'long better. Come, now, *let's.*"

"No," said Claire, driven to bay. "I am very much obliged to you, but I don't need any help."

"Oh! You'll go it alone. All right."

But Mr. Slocumb did not look as if he thought it by any means right. His hard, brown face had clouded with sulky disapprobation. A little gleam of teeth had stolen out under his crisp, short mustache, with an effect not unlike what we see when an angry dog snarls. He felt offended, and this meant that he should either sting with his tongue or smite with his fists. But in the present case a fresh glance at Claire, whose profile was turned to him, made his spleen swiftly perish. Her cheek had got a deep tint of rose; he saw the liquid sparkle of one dark-blue eye, and the dense, rippling hair, chestnut threaded with gold, flowing above one faint-veined temple.

'*Ain't* she a stunner!' he thought. After that he forgot to be offended. They were now in a spacious hallway leading directly to the street. The panic had quite subsided. Knots of people were standing here and there, loudly discussing their late alarms. Some of the women looked and acted as if they were midway between mirth and tears. Most of the men seemed grave; a few were laughing, but in a nervous, furtive way. Along the centre of the broad passage pressed a line of people whom the shock had left too dispirited for further sojourn in the house.

Claire, with her adherent, was among these latter. In quest of Josie, she scanned every face within her field of vision. She had already caught sight of more than one injured unfortunate, further back, where the rush on the lower floor had been most disastrous, and just before she and Slocumb had gained their present open quarters. On this account, rather than because of the wild stampede itself, she had quite lost desire to wait through the rest of the play. It was now her fixed design to regain Josie and urge the plan of an immediate return to Greenpoint. Her sense of having met her father's known wishes with overt disrespect had become an assailant self-reproach. The very harshness of the event which had so rudely broken in upon her enjoyment seemed to have borrowed its disrelish from the rebuke that she had known as waiting all along to shame her. Providence, for the time, had gone with her father; it had abetted him; it had been telling her, in stern terms of personal threat, how flagrant was her filial disloyalty.

She searched for Josie, but found her nowhere visible. She had soon reached the limit of the large passage. A gate now confronted her, where a man waited, ready to give those who sought egress a strip of cardboard insuring their readmission.

Claire took this guarantee of further diversion unconsciously. The man had stood at his post through all the furor that had just ended. He was a sort of new Horatius at the bridge, though possibly with less sublime motive, his wage being a permanent annuity, and his position one of easy proximity to Broadway.

Claire stood in the vestibule of the theatre, and felt the breeze from the street blow on her heated face, before she was well aware just what vantage of exit she had secured. Still she had not seen Josie. And she now began to realize that there was a very strong chance of not seeing Josie. True, the girl might have returned with Mr. MacNab to their former seats in the second gallery of the theatre. But Claire's reluctance to place herself again within the walls of the building had by this time grown a fierce distaste. Meanwhile, Slocumb had maintained an unrelenting nearness to her. She knew this perfectly well. If possible, a more meagre means than the extreme corner of each eye had told her of it; for so great was her repugnance that she had thus far grudged him even the knowledge of receiving the most minute regard. But now she was forced to turn and look at him.

" Do you think Josie can have gone back into the theatre? " she asked, not being herself aware just what frost and distance she had put into voice and manner.

" Dunno," said Slocumb. " Guess she ain't, though. Guess her an' him 's out there in the crowd." The crowd to which he referred was already dense, and every moment increasing. It flooded the flag-stones and a portion of the middle street. Three or four policemen were stirring it to the needful sense of decorum, no less by application than menace of their clubs.

" I am afraid I should never find her there," Claire said, hopelessly.

" That's so," quickly returned Slocumb. " You 'd better come inside agin. The scare 'll be over in a minnit. The piece 'll go on, 'fore long, certain sure."

" I don't care for the piece," replied Claire, with a little toss of the head, more anxious than imperious. " I don't want to see the rest of it. I want to find Josie, and have her take me home at once."

" All right. Jus' step inside an' wait fur 'em both."

Claire looked straight at the speaker. She did not know of the droop in each full-fringed lid of her beautiful eyes. It was an unconscious token of her abhorrence.

"Suppose that they should not return," she said.

"All right," replied Slocumb, brutally impervious. "*I 'll* take yer home, if they don't."

"Thank you," faltered Claire. This view of the question gave her a new shock. It was like hearing that the ferry-boats between New York and Greenpoint had stopped running for the night. "But I won't trouble you," she added, trying to make her voice and mien indifferently calm. "I will wait here a little while, and then, if I don't find Josie, I will go home alone."

"Go home alone?" repeated Slocumb, with a sort of sympathetic interrogation that was detestable to her. "Why, how far is it?"

"Oh, not very far," she replied, turning her back on him, and feeling that in another moment she might treat his offensive persistence with the blunt rigor it deserved.

"I thought you was livin' over to Greenpoint," said Slocumb, shifting with tough pertinacity round to her side.

What a man of cleaner life and thought would simply have praised as sweet and chaste about her fired in this corrupt oaf his one gross substitute for sentiment. She could no more appeal to him by her fineness of line, coloring, or movement than the field-flower when cropped by the brute mouth whose appetite its very grace and perfume may perhaps whet. And Claire divined this. Pure things know impure ones, all through the large scheme of nature. There are nicer grades of intelligence, of course, as we move along the upward scale of such antagonisms. The milk will not cloud till we dilute it with

7

the ink-drop, but a white soul can usually note a black one by earlier and wiser signals of alarm.

"Why should I not go home alone?" Claire had been saying to herself. "No one would know me — I could reach the Tenth Street Ferry — I could ask some one, and get the right car — Yes, I will try no more to find Josie — I will break away from this low creature — I have enough money to bring me safely home — I don't care; I will take my chances and slip off — he will not follow me when he sees me shun him like that."

She ignored his last remark. She did not even glance at him where he now stood. Her gaze was fixed on the crowd, and she was watching to find a brief break in its edge, through which she might flit and be lost. The next instant such a chance came. Claire seized it. She made an oblique dart through the large doorway, slanted her nimble steps across the pavement, and was soon breasting the adverse tide, so to speak, of a little human sea. Each man or woman stood in the place of a choppy, obstructive wave. At every moment poor Claire found herself gently buffeting a new impediment, male or female, as the case might be. Since she wanted to move in a course different from that of nearly every one before or beside her, the carrying out of her object involved a good amount of determined propulsion. But she at length gained the open, as it were. She had now only to strike along in a northerly direction until she reached the point at which a certain line of small cars crossed Broadway. She was not sure at just what street this intersection occurred; she knew that it was by no means near by. A cumbrous omnibus rolled clamorously toward her, and for a mo-

ment she was inclined to hail it; but a swift look
into its lighted space, well freighted with passengers,
made her shrink from the concentration of stares that
her sex and loneliness must equally provoke. The
publicity of the long, lamp-fringed sidewalk, with its
incidents of potential if not always tangible policemen, expressed, after all, a more secure privacy.
When she took one of the little trundling cars which
would bring her eastward to the ferry, she would not
be forced to clamber and stoop and stagger before
getting a seat. Their mode of conveyance, too, would
be somehow more safely plebeian; they would hold
their last fragments of the work-a-day world going
back to Greenpoint; in case of insult, she might have
her final appeal to some reputable occupant bound
for the same destination as herself.

Meanwhile, the big-bodied omnibus clattered by.
Claire had resolved to walk. The high-perched
driver had not seen her pause, hurry to the curb-
stone, and then lift a hand which was straightway
dropped at the bidding of her changed mood. But
this action, while it wrought delay in her progress,
rendered somewhat earlier her meeting with one who
still obstinately pursued her. Just as she had again
started, with slightly quickened pace, the inexterminable Slocumb appeared at her side. He seemed to
have used no effort in catching up with her. There
was a terrible ease in the way his length of limb ac-
commodated its free stride to Claire's more repressed
motions. He had not immediately given chase. She
had got rather deep into the crowd about the theatre-
doors before his impudence, positive as it always was,
had trumped up sufficient real nerve to follow her.
Claire continued walking; but she looked at him

with fixity as she said, "I suppose you saw that I wanted to go alone."

"'T aint right, nohow," he replied, peering into her face with his bad, hard eyes. "A putty gal like you had n't ought t' walk the streets all by herself after dark. You lemme go along. Don' look scared; I would n't hurt ye fur a cent."

"Oh, I am not afraid of you," said Claire, between her teeth. "Why should I be?"

"That 's the ticket. W'y should ye be?"

"I don't want your company. I have shown this to you, and now I tell it to you."

Slocumb laughed. It seemed to Claire that his laugh had the cold of ice and the thrust of steel in it. His lowered arm touched hers with intentional pressure, but she swerved sideways, at once thwarting the contact. He, however, promptly narrowed the distance thus made between them.

"Say!" he now broke forth, in peculiar, confidential undertone, as though a third party were listening. "W'at ye mad fur, hey? You was along with Jimmy MacNab, was n't ye? An' was n't we intrerdooced all reg'lar? I 'm a better feller 'n Jim, any day in the year. Jus' gimme a show. Won't ye? Say, now, *won't* ye? I took a dead shine to you the minnit I clapped eyes on them two nice pink cheeks — blowed if I did n't! I sez to myself, 'She can walk round any gal I 've seen fur a devil of a time,' I sez."

Claire looked straight ahead. She still went quickly along. Her feet and limbs felt light, almost void of sense. Fear had to do with this, and she was keenly frightened. For the first time in her life she knew the terror that feminine honesty has when fronted with the close chance of physical insult.

Slocumb justified her dread. He had no more regard for common laws of restraint than the majority
of untamed brutes, when conscious, as in his case, of
firm thews and active bulk. As for moral bravery,
his nature harbored no concern with such nicer elements. The only vices he did not possess were those
for which he had never known an hour of temptation.
His father had drank himself to death, and he inherited what was perhaps an embryo taste in the
same direction. He got drunk once a fortnight, now,
in his twenty-seventh year, whereas, two years ago,
these diversions had been much rarer; in a decade,
under his uncontrolled conditions, there was a fair
chance of his becoming a sot. To speak more generally, the vast social momentum of heredity, which
seems to be so plainly understood and so ill appreci-
ated in our golden century, had Slocumb well in its
stern grip. There were no outward incident forces, as
the philosophic phrase goes, to make his case in any
way a hopeful one. He had seen Claire; he had exchanged a word with her; he had liked her. If his
liking were put in the baldest form of explanation it
would have to deal with rather darksome realisms.
And it is always preferable that the pursuant satyr
and the unwilling nymph be treated wholly from the
poetic and picturesque point of view.

Claire would not speak. She was very frightened,
as before has been recorded: she seemed to see, between the gloomy interspaces of the lamps, a phantasmal semblance of her father, looking untold rebuke at her, and then vanishing only to reappear.
She walked onward with fl et energy. An idea shot
through her mind that she might call a policeman to
rid her of this incubus. But she dismissed the idea

at once. It was too savagely desperate even for the confronting dilemma.

By this time Slocumb had begun to see plainly that Claire was proof against all his known methods of conquest. But she was unprotected, and he had a dogged dislike of giving up the siege. The silence continued for nearly five blocks. During this time his eyes scarcely once left her face, gleaming distinct or dim as the lamplight waxed or waned.

"Say!" he at length re-addressed her. "Ain't ye hungry? I was thinkin' a stew would go putty good, just now, or a dish o' ice-cream. P'r'aps ye 'd rather tackle sumpn sweet. Hey?"

She made no answer. He peered closer into her face, and repeated the last odious little interrogative monosyllable a good many times. But Claire remained as mute and irresponsive as though it had fallen on stone-deaf ears.

This lure suddenly held out to appetite was his last persuasive stroke. It sprang naturally enough from the man who dealt it. It expressed in the most exhaustive terms just how narrow and barren his conception was of Claire's reasons for shunning him. He stood as the hideous result of a hideous phase of society; and he could no more divine or imagine higher and richer levels of life than if to know of these had meant to be familiar with the soil and climates of a remote star.

He was disappointed and chagrined, but not angry. Anger could not consort with his present state; another kind of heat already filled his veins; one flush kept the other aloof. He had now decided that Claire was not to be conciliated, and yet the perfect lawlessness of his past made him in a manner unable to snap the bond of attraction and leave her. Self-control was a sealed book to him; he had not even opened its cover, apart from learning its rudimentary lessons.

When they had gone five or six blocks further, and the street at which Claire would take the cross-town car was by no means far away, he abruptly caught her arm and drew it close to his side, so holding it with an exertion of purely muscular strength, beside which her own resistance counted for little more than the flutter of a bird.

Even at this most trying juncture she still moved on. He continued to walk, as well. She veered her face toward his, however, forced out of all her previous pitiful disdain, and he saw that she had grown pale as death.

"Let me go," she said. "Don't dare to hold me like this!"

"Look here!" he returned, his tones taking a nasal whisper, and his breath sweeping so close to her nostrils that she caught in it a stale taint, as of liquor drank some time ago. "I would n't harm a hair o' your head; you can jus' bet on that. I 've took a likin' to you, an' I 'll treat ye good. If you wus a lady livin' up t' Fifth Avenyer, ye would n't git more respectfuller behaved to nur I 'll do."

"If you don't let me go," said Claire, gasping a little as she got out the words, "I 'll complain to the first policeman we meet."

He dropped her arm at once, stopping short. "D' ye mean it?" he asked, with great show of reproach. "Say! d' ye mean it?"

But Claire hurried on. She had a wild momentary hope that she had hit at random upon a blessed source

of deliverance. Here, however, she had quite mis-
calculated. Slocumb's outburst had merely formed
a bit of the cheap sentimentality which one of his
race and stamp would select as the lame makeshift in
a forlorn cause.

It chanced that when Claire reached the desired
corner a car was opportunely passing. She signaled
to it; the driver saw her; it stopped, and she entered
it. Meanwhile Slocumb had kept at her side, though
with the distance between them materially widened.
She paid no heed to the question of whether or not
he entered with her. The car was entirely empty as
she took her seat. A little later she slipped a five-
cent piece into the small glass repository for passengers' fares — that touching proof of the confidence
reposed in drivers by those who employ them.
Shortly afterward she saw Slocumb standing on the
outer platform. Her heart and courage almost failed
her, then. He presently walked inside the car, and
paid his fare, as she had done. She expected him to
sit down and resume his persecutions, but he did
neither. He went out again and stood on the platform.

The little car jingled along Eighth Street. It
passed the grim, bastard architecture of the Mercantile Library, once, long ago, an opera house, in which
Steffenone sang to assemblages where a gentleman
in evening-dress or a lady without her bonnet was
a rare enough incident, and nothing prophesied the
horse-shoe of resplendent boxes before which Patti
and Nilsson have since revealed their vocal charms.
Soon afterward it came to Third Avenue, easily betrayed by the flare of gaslight in beer-saloon or liquor-
shop, and a thoroughfare in which night revelry seems

to have claimed especial stronghold.   Near at hand, that hideous monument of philanthropy, the Cooper Union, frowns its unavailing displeasure upon the malt of Schneider and the alcohol of Moriarty, both of which project their noxious forces southward through the Bowery to the City Hall, and northward across many reputable side streets on to the shabby vulgarity of Harlem.

But Claire was naturally unprepared, just now, either to recognize or ponder the importance of this great popular boulevard which we call Third Avenue; how it blends our ruling Irish and German elements in one huge strand of commercial interests, each petty by itself, yet all, when massed together, of enormous metropolitan note; how its very name is pronounced with a mild sneer by our so-called better classes; how it is held common and of ill repute; how one must not speak of it in a Fifth Avenue drawing-room, lest he shall be suspected of having trodden its tainted pavements; and yet how there pulses through its big, tough artery nearly all the hot, impure political blood that feeds the venality of our elective systems, making it for this reason a fact to be always deplored but never lightly dismissed.   Should the sombre growl against that sin of over-possession which we term monopoly ever grow into a revolutionary roar, it is very thinkable that the Robespierre of such an event would be born in Third Avenue; but if not, he might safely be depended on for having near relations there.   The little car presently crossed Second Avenue, at its most quiet portion.   All the garish brilliance had now quite vanished.   Once beloved of respectability, this broad street, here in what we designate its lower portion, has preserved abundant souvenirs of perished fame. Many of the roomy old mansions that line it may be dispeopled of their pristine Knickerbockers, but even these retain much of their old stately repose. Up beyond, the tenement-house thrives, and the tavern flaunts a bottle-decked casement; but here, within generous limits, it remains a quarter full of decent though not dismal gloom, and touched with an occasional solid grandeur.

The car soon advanced into a very different region. It had reached one of the two long if not deep river-edges which skirt the central domain of our wealth and thrift. That squalor which dogs the heel of poverty was everywhere manifest. The very street-lamps seemed to burn with a dejected flicker. Night, however, was kind, and spared from view much unsightly soilure. The high brick houses, thronged with inmates whom all degrees of want and all modes of toil oppressed, lost themselves in shadow; but now and then you caught glimpses of the liquid filth clogging the gutters, and perhaps of a half-submerged cabbage-leaf or a more buoyant egg-shell, to fleck its slime with baleful color. Here spoke a crying municipal disgrace. The prosperous part of our city has its streets kept cleanly throughout the year, but dread injustice is wreaked upon those that are skirted by abodes of penury and need. Fat appropriations are of no avail; the tax-money slips into fingers that are deft in legerdemain; fraud and mismanagement meet as friends; it is not enough that our beautiful island must crowd her shores with all the disfeaturing accompaniments of commerce; she is forced, as well, to see them polluted, far inland, by the foulness born of bad legislation. This is one of the too frequent cases where, in our enlightened polity, democracy plays wantonly into the hands of monarchism.

A little later the car came into a wide, airy expanse, along two of whose sides it journeyed for a considerable distance. Here was Tompkins Square, now lighted with innumerable lamps, but only a few years ago a dark horror to all decent citizens living near it. By day set aside as a parade-ground for the city militia, which paraded there scarcely twice a year, its lampless lapse of earth was by night at least four good acres of brooding gloom, which he who ventured to cross stood the risk of thievish assault, if nothing more harmful. What added to the unique repulsiveness of the place for peace-loving denizens of its near streets, was an occasional concourse of growling and saturnine German socialists, held with stormy harangues and blood-thirsty diatribes under. moon or star, and amid the congenial environing shadow, which was relieved, on these lurid occasions, by torches whose fitful flames typified the feverish theories disclosed.

But the car now passed a very different Tompkins Square from that of old. The grim blank has become, since then, a bright-lit realm where the tramp may fall prone on some of its many neat - built benches, but where the highwayman will find slim chance to ply his fell trade. When this region had been passed there remained only a brief space to be traversed before the ferry was reached. The avenues by this time had ceased to be numerically named ; they had become alphabetical. But Avenues A, B, C, and D are all quite homogeneous as regards dolorous discomfort. The city here hides some of its worst lairs, and many a desperado infests them. After a little journey, such as Claire now took, you gain the small, dull-looking ferry.

Meanwhile seven or eight new passengers had entered the car. They were mostly Germans, and of
both sexes. Claire felt a sense of protection. One
stout woman, of truly colossal build, with a sleeping
baby in her arms and an evident husband so hollow-
cheeked and slight that it seemed wrong for him even
to assume the responsibility of paying their double
fare, especially reassured her. The rest were commonplace people enough. One was a weary work-
girl; one was a collier, grimy with his trade and
drowsy from drink ; one was a dapper, bejeweled
Hebrew, with oily amber whiskers and large, loose
red lips ; still another was a handsome young woman,
smartly geared, who had said good-night, on entering,
to a male escort, and who now glanced uneasily about
her at intervals, as though fearful of being known. All
this while Slocumb remained on the outer platform.

Presently the car stopped. Everybody alighted.
The Tenth Street Ferry was close at hand. Claire
knew that her hateful adherent was close at hand
also. She paid her toll to the ferryman and glided
through the narrow bit of passage-way forth upon
the long dark dock beyond. She expected, at every
new step, to be re-accosted by Slocumb. A boat
had landed, and was soon to disembark again. From
the opposite dimness came an ominous clank of
chains, made by the men at either of the two wheels,
and a sudden " All aboard ! " flung out in gruff tones
as a stimulating monition. The other passengers all
hastened forward. Claire was among them, though
in the rear of the hurry. The foremost had gained
the boat, when she felt a strong clutch upon her arm.
Compelled by sheer force to pause, now, she turned,
meeting Slocumb's face quite near her own. He at

once spoke, in the same intimate sort of whisper that she had before found so distressing.

"Say! 'Tain't right t' shake me like this. I ain't goin' t' stand it, either. Come, change your mind. Treat me square. Will ye?"

Claire, driven to bay, did what her sex is sometimes held by a few renowned cynics as having a special talent for doing; she employed stratagem.

Her voice shook as she said: "Very well. What is it you wish me to do?"

She could feel the tense grasp upon her arm relax a little. This was just the kind of result she had aimed for.

"I want ye t' stay this side the river a spell yet, an' we'll eat somepn somewhere. Hey?"

The fingers about her arm had acquired a fondling laxity that half sickened her. But she waited a little. They were a good ten yards from the boat. It was possible that both their figures were too shadowed for the men at the chains to see them. Perhaps, on the other hand, these wardens did not care to shout a final notice that the boat was now unmoored.

Claire still chose to temporize. Her heart beat so that it seemed about to burst through her side; but she nevertheless kept her brain clear enough to maintain a subtlety of intent in strange contrast to her deep fear.

She had determined to get free if she could, and find refuge among the passengers on the boat. Here, in the lonely dusk of the dock, she was at a sad disadvantage; but once within the lighted cabin of the boat, she could find the same silent protection of mere surrounding that the car had afforded. She had a latent resolve, also, of future appeal to some of

those whom she knew had preceded her, though this
formed no real part of her present quick - formed
scheme.

"Suppose that I do go with you," she said. "At
what time would I be able to get home?"

Slocumb's grasp materially loosened. "Why, any
time at all!" he exclaimed. "The boats run till
'bout two o'clock or so, an'" —

His sentence was cut short in its valuable explanation by a sudden disengaging spring on the part of
Claire. She ran with her best speed toward the
boat. She now perceived that it was just leaving
the pier. By the time that she had gained almost
the extreme edge of the latter, a voice from the receding boat itself cried out to her, "Don't jump!"

She saw, then, that a long, curved crevice was
widening in a very rapid way at a slight space beyond the spot where she had abruptly halted. A
few more seconds would make the leap a mere madness; now it needed nerve, agility, and was indeed
a venture. But Slocumb stood behind her. The
risk was worth the prize. Claire waited perhaps ten
seconds; the crevice had grown a fissure; she saw
the murky water give a dull flash or two, far below
it. Then she jumped.

The space had not been more than three feet. She
cleared it well. But *what she had cleared* sent a
sharp terror through her the instant after both feet
had touched the firm bourne of the deck. For a little while she stood quite still, shivering, with her
back to the dock thus boldly quitted. Her mind was
wholly in a whirl. She did not hear the half-growled
words of one of the men who had lately unloosed the
boat, chiding her upon her folly, in gruff contempt of
syntax.

But very soon this access of intense alarm lessened. She partly ceased to fix her thought upon what she had done, recalling instead, why she had done it. She turned, giving two flurried looks to right and left, doubtless from a sense that the abhorred one might have breasted the same peril as herself — in his case far lighter, of course.

Her gaze swept the opposite pier. It gleamed drowsy and obscure, with the effect of some grave marine monster just risen from the muddy tides below it. Strangely, also, the lights at either side gave it the semblance of two malign blazing eyes. And in the glimmer thus made Claire saw Slocumb.

He had not taken the leap. At first amazement had wrought in him its brief yet telling effect. Then he had dashed to the end of the pier, momentarily furious at thus being balked. But in a second his fury had cooled. And something had cooled it, very new to him, though very forcible. This was pity. He might easily have cleared the interspace. But he forbore to do so. He thrust both hands into his pockets, and with lowered head moved away. In an instant more it was too late for him to have changed his novel resolve, even had he so wished.

By the time that Claire's look lighted upon the pier he was nowhere visible. He had disappeared from her sight forever, as also from her life. He had been a dread though brief experience — a glimpse given her into the melancholy darkness of human wrong. The shadows had seemed to take him back among themselves, where he rightly belonged. Perhaps the episode of his insolence wrought some sort of effect upon her future acts; it is certain that she never quite forgot the miserable dismay he had roused ; and when the struggle for worldly success afterward spurred her with so keen a goad, some vague remembrance of to-night may have quickened her aspiring impulses and made what we call the socially best gain fresh worth in her eyes by contrast with such foul deeps as lie below it.

Once confident that Slocumb had not followed her, she managed, with unsteady pace, to reach the outer rail of the deck and lean against it while the boat traversed the river. She was trembling a good deal, and felt an extreme weakness as well. But a glow of triumph upbore her. She had escaped at last !

The ugly boat, as it sped along, seemed a sentient accomplice of her final good fortune. She had a fancy that its thick wooden rail dumbly throbbed beneath her grasp. Her posture was a half-cowering one ; the spell of her poignant fears had not yet passed. Her head leaned itself peeringly from stooped shoulders in such a way that its slim neck took the sort of curve we see in a frightened deer's.

A somewhat late moon had recently risen, whose advent had altered the whole face of the heavens, flooding it with a spectral, yellowish light. But borne rapidly across the moon's blurred disk, on some high, fleet rush of air, scudded volumes of rolling and mutable vapor. They constantly soared above the great dusky city, at first in dense black masses, then thinning and lengthening as they came midway between zenith and horizon. While Claire watched these strange and volatile clouds, so incessant in their motion and so swift in their continual upward stream, they took, for her confused fancy, the semblance of pursuant phantom shapes. They formed themselves into visages and bodies ; they stretched forth uncouth yet life-like arms; they clenched hands of misty gloom, and shook them far above her, with ghostly, imminent defiance. Her former transit across the river had been fraught with sweet, poetic mystery; her present voyage was one touched with a kind of allegoric terror.

But the boat soon found its second wharfage. Claire sped out through the two cabins in time to join the crowd of disembarking passengers. Once more back in Greenpoint, she hurried along certain familiar streets until she arrived at her own dwelling. It was now a little after ten o'clock. She had an instinct that it was about this time. Above the high piazza, both parlor-windows were dark, but below it the windows of the basement portion were brightly lit. She passed into the scant space of garden and sought the lower door; she pulled the bell, set in the woodwork at her right, and waited.

No answer came, and she rang again. One of the side-lights gave her a good view into the hall beyond. She presently saw her mother appear. Mrs. Twining opened the door. It was not till she and her daughter stood face to face that the latter made a certain sharp, abrupt discovery.

"Mother!" she said, "you're pale — you look very strange. Is it because I staid away so long?"

"No," replied Mrs. Twining.

Claire grasped her mother's arm with both hands. "Then what is it?" she questioned. "You don't mean that — that Father's sick? *Do* you?"

Mrs. Twining was white as death, and had dark rings round her fine black eyes. She laughed with great bitterness as she closed the door.

8

"Oh, no," she said. "Your father ain't sick, Claire."

These few words teemed, somehow, with a frightful irony. Claire knew her mother's moods so well that she now staggered backward a little as the two faced each other in this narrow hallway.

"Mother," she said, with a gasp, "what do you mean? Has anything *happened* to Father?"

"Yes," said Mrs. Twining with a cruelty that Claire never forgot and never forgave. "Your father's dead. He died at nine o'clock. The doctor's here now. He says it's heart-disease. You're a nice gadabout, to be off for hours, nobody knows where, and come home to find" . . .

Mrs. Twining ended her sentence at just this point, for Claire had dropped in a swoon before the next word could be spoken, upon the oil-cloth of the little hall which her own hands had so often swept.

VII.

THAT night was one of anguish and horror. As soon as enough strength had come to her with the return of consciousness, Claire insisted upon being taken to where her father lay. Not a tear left her eyes as she knelt beside his body. She was very white, and seemed perfectly calm. She kissed the dead man, now and then, on forehead and cheek. Once she rose, went to the window, and set both arms lengthwise upon its sash, propping her chin against her clasped hands. In this attitude she stared forth at the heaven, still full of moony light and still alive with its black pageantry of hurrying clouds. But their motion was more quick, now; the wind had grown stronger and colder; all touch of mildness was rapidly vanishing from the atmosphere. Claire felt the panes shake, and heard them rattle, as she leaned thus. There seemed an awful sympathy between this wild phase of nature and her own tumultuous, distraught sensations.

Grief and alarm clashed within her soul. She could not simply and passionately regret her father's loss, for the thought of her own friendless and penurious state would thrust itself into her consciousness. Her feelings of pure bereavement, of standing face to face with a vast and stern solitude, of having had something torn from her heart by the roots, were terrible enough. But none the less, on this account, could she fail to think with inward thrills of fright on the subject of her merely material future. In an hour or two something solidly defensive had been shattered and swept away. Her father's protection had kept aloof, so to speak, the huge, merciless forces of society. Now these forces were rushing upon her like yonder stream of antic-shaped clouds.

"What is to become of me?" she murmured aloud, not knowing that she spoke at all. "Who will help me? Where shall I turn? I am so alone — so fearfully alone!"

Mrs. Twining had come into the room, as it chanced, a moment before the utterance of Claire's first words. It was now a little before midnight; she had entered this chamber of death twice before, and had looked at her daughter's kneeling figure, there beside the corpse, but had retired again in silence. Now she spoke, as Claire finished speaking. The girl turned instantly as she began.

"Yes," she said, in her most hard and curt way. "I s'pose you *are* alone, now *he's* gone! You ain't got any mother, of course not! She's a cipher; she always was. You're going to quit her, I dare say; you're going to leave her in the lurch. P'raps you'll find some of those you was with to-night that'll see you don't come to grief. Well, 't ain't for me to complain at this late day. I've had chance enough to take your measure, Miss, long ago!"

There was a look of dreary fatigue on Claire's white face as she slowly answered: "Mother, I will not leave you. I don't wish to leave you."

"Oh, you don't, eh? Then why did you say you was *alone?*"

"Did I say it?" returned Claire. She put one hand to her forehead. "I — I must have spoken aloud without knowing it." . . . Immediately afterward she crossed the room, going very close to her mother's side, and looking with eager meaning into the cold, austere, aquiline face.

"Don't be unkind to-night," she went on. "Remember this dreadful thing that has happened. It — it ought to — to soften you, Mother. It has nearly crazed *me*. I cannot reason ; I can scarcely think. I — I can only suffer ! "

Mrs. Twining curled her mouth in bitter dissent. "Oh, you did n't know the poor man was sick when you ran off and staid for hours. No, indeed! If you had, you would n't 'a' worried him as you did when he come home to tea and found you gone. He fell like a log, just as he got up from the table. But he had n't eaten hardly a thing, and I guess you know why he did n't."

Claire uttered a quick, flurried cry. She grasped her mother's arm. "You — you don't mean," she exclaimed, in a piteously fierce way, "that *I* killed Father — or — or hastened his death by — by not being home? Oh, say, Mother, that you don't mean this! It would drive me mad if I believed so! Please say it is n't true ! "

Claire's aspect breathed such desperation that it wrought havoc even with so stolid a perversity as that of the harsh, unpropitiable being whom she confronted.

"Well, no, I don't say *that*," murmured Mrs. Twining, with sullen alteration of mien and tone. "But I *do* say, Claire, that you was off somewhere, and *he* was fretted and pestered because you was, and " . . .

Here the peculiar nature of this most tormenting woman suddenly revealed a change. Her grim mouth twitched; her nostrils produced a kind of catarrhal sniff; her cold black eyes winked, as if tears were lurking to assail them. The next words that she spoke were in a high, querulous key.

"Oh! so you're the only one that's fit to mourn for that poor dead one, hey? I, his lawful wedded wife, and your own mother, ain't got any right to grieve! Oh, very well! I'm nobody at all, here. I'd better get away. You're chief mourner. There's nobody but you. I s'pose you'll pay all the expenses of the funeral, since you're so dreadful stuck-up about it!"

Claire shook her head, in a pathetic, conciliating way. She lifted one finger, at the same time. Her face was still white, and her dark-blue eyes were burning feverishly.

"No, no, Mother!" she said. "This is all wrong. You mustn't speak like that, here. If you didn't love him, I did. There's a little money yet. It's yours, but you'll give it; you've told me of it; it will be enough to bury Father decently. I promise you that if you *do* give it I will try very hard to get some work that will support us both."

Mrs. Twining put a hand on either hip. She stared at Claire for a moment. Then she answered her.

"No," she said. "I won't give a cent of it. It's only about a hundred dollars. He ain't led me such a nice life that I should be so awful grateful to him now he's gone. There's ways of burying that don't cost money. Yes, there's ways. . . . Let 'em come and take him. I ain't going to beggar myself because he wants a rosewood coffin, and"—

"Mother!" cried Claire, pointing toward the dead, "he is *here!*"

"Oh, well!" said Mrs. Twining. She spoke the two brief words in a sort of abrupt whimper, taking a step or two toward the calm sheeted form of her dead husband. "S'pose he *is* here. I can't use that money, and I won't!"

Claire felt the hideous taste of those words. They who have thus far read this chronicle must have read it ill if they are not sure that no love for a mother so ceaselessly froward and hostile could now survive in her daughter's heart. But though she knew her mother capable of dread acts if occasion favored, Claire was thunderstruck by this last announcement.

It appeared to her monstrous and barbarous, as it indeed was. She clenched both hands, for an instant, and her eyes flashed.

"Say what you mean!" she retorted, not raising her voice, because of that piteous reverence which the still, prone shape inspired. "*Can* you mean that you will let charity bury our dead for us? *Can* you mean that?"

Mrs. Twining gave a quick, grim nod. "Yes, I do mean it," she returned. "And if you was n't a fool you 'd see why."

Claire folded her arms. Her next words came with grave, measured composure from white, set lips. "I may be a fool," she said, "but thank God I have n't your kind of wisdom! Keep your money, Mother. Do as you threaten. But when Potter's Field takes poor Father's body, that will be the end of everything between you and me. Remember that I said this. I will never speak to you, never notice you again, if you do so shameful a thing. If you spend

that money as duty and as decency should both
prompt, I will work for you, slave for you, cling to
you always. But if not, we are no longer mother
and daughter. You see, I don't speak with heat or
with haste. I am perfectly calm. Now choose which
course you will take. But never say that I did not
fully warn you, when it will be too late for retrac-
tion!"

There was a splendidly quiet impressiveness in this
speech of Claire's. She went and knelt once more
beside her father's body after she had finished it.
She had resolved upon no further entreaty or argument. The very atrocity of her mother's proposed
design seemed to place continued discussion of it beyond the pale of all womanly dignity.

Mrs. Twining was too coarse a soul to see the
matter as Claire saw it. She preferred to take the
chances that her daughter would relent when the
ignoble interment was over.

To-morrow came, and she gave no sign of altering
her purpose. Claire scarcely addressed a word to
her during this day. A few of the Greenpoint folk
called at the house. Among these was Josie Morley,
distressed at the tidings of death, and prepared to
utter voluble regrets for having lost Claire in the
crowd during the previous night.

But Claire would see no one. She remained with
her father's body in the little room upstairs, locking
its door when she thought there was any chance of a
a visitor being brought thither.

Now and then she wondered, with a dumb misery,
whether her mother had made any attempt to bring
about the loathed burial. She herself had a few dollars in her possession. This sum she meant to use in

seeking employment after the earth had closed over her father's corpse. Once or twice a passionate impulse had seized her to go and seek help from those under whom her father had lately served in his drudging clerkship. But she repressed this feeling — or rather shame at the thought of possible refusal, mixed with a natural proud reluctance to own the sad need in which she stood, repressed it for her.

The next day she learned the full, torturing truth. Mrs. Twining had carried out her threat. Two shabby men came with a pine box. They placed the corpse herein. Claire had already paid it all the final reverential rites which her sex and her grief would allow. It was dressed in the same rusty outward garments which it had worn when death came. The men held a little discussion below stairs with Mrs. Twining. They afterward departed and remained away two good hours. When they returned they brought a dark wagon with an arched top. In the interval Claire still watched. She was quite silent. Perhaps if she had deigned now to plead with her mother, the latter, already a little frightened at the girl's stony, unvaried calmness, might have relented and agreed to more seemly obsequies. But except one glance of immeasurable reproach, during a brief visit which Mrs. Twining paid to the chamber, Claire gave no further sign of revolt.

When the men returned, she chanced to be looking from the window. She saw the wagon. She shuddered, and went back to her father. No one saw her bid him the last farewells. She showed no trace of tears when the men presently reëntered the room, but her dark-blue eyes shone from her hueless face with a dry, glassy glitter. Her mother now appeared.

She looked at Claire in a covert, uneasy way, though there was much dogged obstinacy about the lines of her mouth. A moment later she spoke to the men. It seemed to Claire like the refinement of hypocrisy that she should set her voice in a mournful key.

"I s'pose you want to get it through right away," she said.

"Yes, ma'am," replied one of the men. "Those is always the orders."

Claire went to the window again. It was a raw, misty, drizzling day. She stared out into the dreary street. She did not want to see that pitiful box closed and sealed. She presently heard a grating sound which told her just what the men were doing.

And then she heard another sound that was quite as harsh. It was her mother's voice, lowered, and with a sort of whine in it.

"It 's true enough that the dead ought to be buried properly, Claire, but that ain't any reason why the living should n't live — the best way they can. You take it hard now, but after a while you 'll see you ain't got any real right to blame me. You 'll see " —

"Don't touch me, please," interrupted Claire. Her mother had laid a hand on her arm, and she had receded instantly. Then she said, while steadying her voice, though not caring whether the men heard or no: "Did you intend going to — to the grave with him ?"

Mrs. Twining gave a great elegiac sigh. "Oh, no, I could n't stand it. I should break right down long before I got there."

"Very well," said Claire, "I am going."

One of the men looked up at her. He had a small, round face, an odd blond tuft of beard, and a pair of

mild blue eyes. He held his screw-driver thrust into
a screw while he spoke. His voice was very respectful. He had noticed Claire's look and mien before ;
he had a wife and children at home. Scarcely ever,
in his experience, had he known a burial of this sort
to take place from a dwelling as apparently thrifty
as the present one.

" Excuse me, Miss," the man said, " but you
could n't ride in the wagon. There's just room for
him and me." He indicated his companion by a little motion of the head. " And there's three other
bodies. We're takin' 'em to the almshouse."

" Where is the almshouse ? " asked Claire. She
could not help giving her mother one shocked sidelong glance while this question left her lips.

" It's over in Flatbush," the man said.

Claire went close up to his side. If he had not
seen the white distress in her face before, he must
plainly have seen it now. " I know where that is,"
she said. " I could go there. The cars would take
me." She put her hand on the rough wood of the
box. The touch was so light that it resembled a caress. " Would they let me go to — to the almshouse
and wait . . . near *him* . . . till he is buried ? "

Mrs. Twining at once began to weep. Or rather,
she spoke in a wailing tone that indicated tears, even
if no tears really either gathered or fell.

" Claire, you must n't think of going ! No, you
must n't ! Things are bad enough, as it is. Now,
promise me that you won't take any such notion !
Do promise ! "

Claire paid no heed to this outburst. She was
looking with eager fixity at the man. She had already roused his sympathy ; she felt certain of it ;

his big, mild eye seemed to tell her so. "They won't all be buried till about two o'clock," he said. "There'll be five or six bodies to-day, I guess. If you start from here in about an hour, Miss, you can get to the buryin'-ground by just the right time. I'll see to it you do." The speaker here turned and winked one mild eye at his companion. The latter was staring rather lifelessly at Claire. He had a long, pale, tired-looking face.

"All right," he muttered, apathetically, as if he had not at all comprehended, but was willing to take matters on trust.

"I'll see to it that he ain't got in till you come," pursued Claire's new friend. "The Potter's Field ain't far from the County Buildings, as they call 'em. I s'pose you know how to get to Flatbush?" He scratched his sandy shock of hair for an instant, and told her just what cars to take.

Claire put faith in him. Something made her do so. When the pine box had been carried down stairs, placed inside the dark wagon, and driven away, she went to her own room and made a small, neat brown-paper parcel. Her clothes were few enough, and she left all of these except what seemed to her of vital necessity. "I don't want to look like a tramp," she told herself, with a darksome pleasantry. "I shall not, either. I shall only be a poor, shabby girl with a bundle."

When she emerged from her room her mother met her in the hall. Claire wore her bonnet. Mrs. Twining gave a frightened whimper as she saw this and the parcel.

"Oh, Claire," she said, "you ain't really going to the — the grave?"

"Yes, I am," she said. Her tones were so frigid and so melancholy that they caused a palpable start in her who heard them.

"Oh, Claire," moaned her mother, "if you go, *I* can't! I can't see him buried that way! Of course *you* can, if you want!"

"I do want," said Claire.

"But you'll come back! you'll come home again!"

As she was passing her mother, there in the hall, Claire turned and faced her. "I shall never come home again," she said, scarcely raising her voice above a whisper. "You remember what I told you."

Mrs. Twining was no longer merely frightened; she was terrified. "Claire!" she burst forth, "I ain't done right, perhaps. But don't be headstrong —now, don't! if you'd spoke to me yesterday — if you'd even spoke to me this morning, I might, . . . well, I might, after all, have given the money. But it's too late now, and " . . .

"Yes, it is too late now," Claire interrupted, and somehow with the effect of a shaft, shot noiselessly, and tellingly aimed.

After that she hurried straight down stairs, passed along the lower hall, and made rapid exit from the house.

A number of heads had been thrust from neighboring windows while the body was being borne away. Claire, who endured what was thus far the supreme humiliation of her life, wondered whether any one was watching now, but she kept her eyes drooped toward the pavement as she moved along, and never once looked to left or right. She despised these possible watchers, and yet she remembered what her dead had been — how kindly, how pure,

how noble; and it was to her sense an infamy that
his ignominious burial should be made a theme of
vulgar gossip.

"He is to be put in Potter's Field," she told her
own aching, bursting heart, while she still hurried
along. "Yes, *he!* And he was so good, so fine, so
much a gentleman! He is to be put in Potter's
Field! . . . But I will see the last sod placed over
him. . . . That man *will* keep his word. . . . I shall
stand by poor Father, his only mourner. He will be
glad if he knows. What a slight thing it is to do for
him, after all the love he gave me! But it is all I
can do. All, and yet so little!"

A dreary ride in the cars at last brought her to
Flatbush. After alighting she had quite a long walk
through the gray, foggy atmosphere of a region
which the sweetest mood of spring or summer finds
no spell to beautify. It was now as hideous and
lonesome as that hateful tract just beyond Greenpoint. The immense gloomy structures of the alms-
houses loomed beside the path she took. The con-
ductor on the car had told her just how to reach the
pauper graveyard. It lay at some distance from the
grim buildings that she was obliged to pass, and
within whose walls were prisoned the sin, the sickness and the madness of a great city.

Nothing could be more common, more neglectful,
more wretchedly melancholy, than the place she at
length gained. It was scarcely an acre in extent;
it did not contain a single tree or shrub; it was en-
closed by a fence of coarse, careless boarding. Its
graves were so thick that you could scarcely pass
between them. In each grave had been laid four
bodies, and excepting a pathetic half-dozen or so of

simple wooden crosses, there were no signs to tell who slept here, except rough, low stakes, each bearing four numbers. Never was the oblivion of death more sternly typified; never was its dark mockery more dolefully accentuated!

A little group of men stood near an open grave as Claire reached the gate. She saw them, and recognized one of them, who advanced toward her. She felt herself grow slightly faint as she perceived a box placed just at the rim of the earthy cavity.

"Was I in time?" she asked of the man, as they walked together inside the enclosure.

"Yes," he said, with a very kind voice. "You was just in time, Miss. All the others is turned in except him. I saved him on purpose."

VIII

THIS same afternoon, about two hours later, Claire was in New York. She had crossed thither, spurred by an idea born of her desperation. It was a forlorn hope; it was like the straw clutched by the sinking hand; and yet it formed a comforting preventive against complete despair. She had remembered her old friend at Mrs. Arcularius's school, the plump-cheeked and yellow-haired Sophia Bergemann. She had determined to seek her out and ask her aid in obtaining work. Years had elapsed since Claire and Sophia had met; but if the buxom young creature had preserved even half of her old amiable friendship, there was excellent chance of cordial welcome and kindly assistance.

'I only hope that she still lives in Hoboken,' Claire thought, while taking the journey across town. 'Suppose the family have left there. Suppose I cannot find Sophia. Suppose that she is married and has gone to live elsewhere — in Europe, perhaps. Suppose that she is dead.'

More than once, before she had reached the central part of the city, Claire felt herself grow weak with dread. Night would soon approach. She had money enough to get lodgment, but in her ignorance and her loneliness how could she secure it? Her mother's face, clothed with the old mocking smile, repeatedly rose before her fancy. She seemed to see the hard, bitter mouth frame certain sentences. " Oh, you 'll come back," it seemed to say. " You 've got to. You can't go gallivanting round New York after dark. I ain't afraid. Oh, you 'll come back to Greenpoint, *sure!*"

' I will never go back,' Claire said to her own thoughts, answering this phantasmal sort of taunt. ' No, not if I walk the streets to-night and many another night. Not if I have to beg for food. Not if I die of hunger. I will never go back *there!* No, no, no !'

There was nothing theatrically fervid about this silent resolve. The girl was quite capable of confronting any sharp ill rather than remeet the woman who had so pitilessly outraged her most sacred instincts. She knew well enough that her mother confidently counted upon her return. She knew well enough that her mother would undergo wild alarm on finding herself permanently deserted. Yet Claire, with a grim desire of inflicting punishment for the insult flung at her beloved dead, silently exulted in what she could not help but deem a just and rightful vengeance. True, her own act may have dealt the vengeance; but did it not really spring from that departed soul whose corpse had met the lash of so undeserved an indignity ? When Claire had reached the centre of the city she suddenly determined to seek Mrs. Arcularius's establishment. The school might either have changed its locality or else ceased to exist. Still, she would apply at the old quarters. There she would inquire for Sophia Bergemann. They might know nothing concerning the girl. But if this resulted, she would still have all Hoboken left,

9

in which the dwelling-place of so prominent a resident — even though one of past time — would most probably be known on inquiry. A throng of memories beset her as she rang the bell of Mrs. Arcularius's abode. The name of that august lady gleamed on a large silver-plated square, affixed to the second door, beyond the marble-paved vestibule. A smartly - dressed maid answered her summons. Claire stated in brief, civil terms what information she desired to gain. The maid left her standing in the well-known hall for several minutes, and at length returned with the tidings, apparently fresh from the lips of Mrs. Arcularius herself, that Miss Bergemann was then living at No. — Fifth Avenue, only a slight distance away.

Claire felt a thrill of relief as she thanked the maid and resought the street. This intelligence seemed a most happy stroke of luck. It augured well for the success of her sad little enterprise.

The Fifth Avenue dwelling proved to be a mansion of imposing dimensions. It stood on a corner, and had a wide window at one side of its spacious entrance, and two at the other. From either panel of its polished walnut door jutted a griffon's head of bronze, holding a ring pendant from its tense lips. Beyond the glossy plate-glass of the casements gleamed misty folds of lace, and still further beyond these you caught a charming glimpse of large-leaved tropic plants in rich-hued vases. Claire pulled a bronze bell-handle that was wrought in the likeness of some close-folded flower. A dull yet distinct peal ensued, having in its sound a trim directness that suggested prompt and capable attendance from interior quarters. While Claire waited for admission she cast her look downward upon the middle street, and across at the line of opposite residences, all marked by a calm uniformity of elegance. The sight was very new to her after Greenpoint, but at the same time it stirred certain sources of youthful recollection. Many carriages were passing. One or two were shaped with fashionable oddity, having only a single pair of huge wheels and a booted and cockaded flunkey, who sat in cramped, oblique posture, with his back to the other occupants, a lady and a gentleman, and who seemed forever taking a resigned plunge off the vehicle, with stoically folded arms. Another was a heavy, sombre family coach, with two men on the box, both clad in dark, dignified livery. Still another was the so-called dog-cart, borne along by a team of responsible silver-trapped bays, and having on its second seat a footman graciously permitted, in this instance, to face the horses whose lustrous flanks his own hands had doubtless groomed into their present brilliance. The two parallel yet contrary streams of vehicles made an incessant subdued clatter; numerous pedestrians were also passing to and fro along either sidewalk; the weather had changed again from harsh to clement; the strip of clear, blue sky above the massive housetops wore a shining delicacy and airiness of tint; even Claire's new wound, that still bled unseen, could not distract her from a buoyant congeniality with the prosperous and festal tumult so amply manifest. She understood then, and perhaps with a qualm of shame as well, that no grief could quite repress, however transiently, her love for life, action, and refined social intercourse. The old desire to win a noted place among those of her own kind who were themselves notable, quickened within her, too, as she gazed upon the bright bustle and the palatial importance which were both so near at hand.

'Near,' she mused, 'and yet so far! Shall I ever do what *he* bade me to do on that night long ago? Shall I ever climb the hill? Shall I not grow tired and sit down to rest? What chance have I *now* of ever reaching the top? Where is the hand to help me even ever so little? Will Sophia Bergemann do it? Yes; if the ways of the world have n't changed her since we met at school.'

A man-servant, in what is termed full-dress, soon opened the door, and Claire asked if Miss Sophia Bergemann was at home. The man appeared to be a very majestic person. Claire felt a good deal of secret awe in his presence. He had a superb development of the chest, a sort of senatorial nose, and two oblong tufts of sorrel whisker, growing with a mossy density close to either ear.

But he was very civil, notwithstanding his grandeur. He told Claire, in a rich voice that would have deepened her veneration if it had not been blent with a valiant North-of-Ireland brogue, that Miss Bergemann was at home but about to leave the house for a drive.

The hall in which this announcement was made glowed with sumptuous yet tasteful decorations. A dark curve of heavy-balustered staircase, which four or five persons might have ascended abreast, met the eye only a short space away. From the lofty ceiling depended a costly lamp of illumined glass. Soft, thick tapestries of Turkish design drooped from several near doorways. A fleet remembrance of the old school-room sarcasms about the Bergemanns' vulgar Hoboken home flashed through Claire's mind.

" Will you tell Miss Sophia, please," she said, in as firm and calm a tone as she could manage, "that Miss Twining, whom she knew some years ago, would like to speak with her?"

The butler was about to reply, when a loud feminine voice suddenly pealed from upper regions. In reality it was the voice of a lady who had already descended several steps of the broad, winding staircase; but the lady was still in obscurity, and therefore the liberal size of the house caused her tones to sound as if they had come from a still greater distance. " Michael," shrilled the voice, " I see the carriage is n't here yet. It 's nearly a quarter of an hour behind time. Thomas has done this twice before in one week. Now, you just send Robert straight round to the stable, and let him say that we 're very angry about it, and that Ma won't put up with such behavior if it ever happens again!"

The butler had left Claire before the end of the final belligerent sentence, and had moved, with a certain military briskness, toward the first wide step of the staircase.

" Yes, Miss Sophia," he said, employing his fine sonorous voice so that it somehow had the effect of not being unduly raised, though still strongly audible. The next moment he turned toward Claire, with a mien in which his natural official gravity gave sign of being cruelly fluttered.

" Miss Sophia is coming downstairs, Miss," he said.

Claire had a swift feeling of gratitude for that single word " Miss." She knew that she was dingily clothed; she had fancied that all her claims to the nicer grades of gentility lived solely within her mental wish and hope; but she failed to perceive that her face was filled with those tender and sweet charms which we term patrician, and that her least gesture carried with it a grace which previous conditions of culture alone have the art to bestow. It was indeed true, as Michael had said, that Miss Sophia was coming downstairs. Claire soon heard a decisive rustle of robes, and presently a descendent shape dawned upon her view, arrayed in very modish costume.

But the instant that Claire caught sight of Sophia she recognized the plump, rubicund face, grown only a trifle more womanly beneath its low-arranged floss of yellow hair. She went forward to meet her old friend. Just as Sophia left the last step of the staircase, Claire had so managed that they stood very near to each other.

She did not put forth a hand. Her pale, beautiful face had grown paler, through fear of some possibly haughty reception. But she spoke the moment that Sophia's round blue eyes had fairly met her own.

"I hope you know me," she said. "I hope you have not forgotten me."

A blank, dismayed look possessed Sophia for a few seconds, and then she put forth two hands which were sheathed half-way up to the elbow in dull-brown gloves, seizing both of Claire's hands the next instant.

"Forgotten you!" she cried. "Why, you 're Claire Twining! Of course you are! And as pretty as a picture, just as you always were! Why, you dear old thing! Give me a kiss!"

Claire felt the lips of the speaker forcibly touch each of her cheeks. Sophia still held her hands. The welcome had been too abruptly cordial. A mist slipped before her sight and clouded her brain. She staggered backward. . . .

Perhaps she would have fallen, if the magnificent Michael had not been near enough to place a muscular arm between herself and the floor. But she rallied almost at once. And while clearness was returning to her mind, she heard Sophia say, in imperious yet hearty tones, —

"Michael, take her into the reception-room! Now, don't look so stupid! Do as I say!"

Claire's attack, though more than partly past, still left her weak. She allowed herself to be led, and indeed half supported, by Michael. A little later she was seated on a big, yielding lounge, with the sense of a big, yielding pillow at her back. And presently, close beside her, she saw the ruddy, broad-blown face of Sophia, surmounted by a Parisian bonnet of the most deft and dainty millinery.

"Sophia," she said, breaking into a tremulous, pathetic little laugh, "please don't — *please* don't think I 've lost my senses! But it — it was so good of you to — remember me, after we had n't met for such a long time, that — that I " —

Here Claire burst into an actual tempest of tears and sobs, and immediately afterward felt Sophia's hands again clasp both her own.

"Michael!" cried her new hostess at the same moment, in tones of imperative command, "for Heaven's sake, don't stand staring there, but *do* leave the room!"

"Yes, Miss," came the nicely decorous reply. Faultless servant as he was, it must still be set to the credit of Michael that he closed a sliding door of solid rosewood, which worked on easy grooves between the double *portière* of the apartment, just after crossing its threshold. His act was wholly unneces-

sary, considering the nature of the command his
young mistress had given; and when we note the
obstructing force of the door itself, it implies a sublime abstinence from the fascinations of eavesdrop-
ping.

"Now, don't cry so!" exclaimed Sophia, with great
sympathy and a strong suspicion of active emotion as
well. "I suppose something dreadful has happened
to you, dear old Claire. What is it? Just tell me,
and I'll see what I can do. You're not dressed as if
you were very well off. Is it poverty? Oh, pshaw!
I'll soon fix things all right if you want help that
way. I'll" —

Here Sophia abruptly paused, and withdrew her
hands. She stood facing Claire, who still struggled
to master the sobs that shook her. Sophia seemed
sternly troubled: her full cheeks had reddened; this
was her one invariable way of showing agitation;
she never turned pale, like other people. "Claire!"
she broke forth, in solemn undertone. "I do hope it
is n't one *thing!* I do hope you have n't been . . .
been *going wrong!* You know what I mean. I
would n't mind anything but that, and that I could
n't forgive — or even excuse!"

Claire sprang to her feet as the last word passed
Sophia's lips. Wrath had calmed her, and with a
wondrous speed. The tears were still glittering on
her cheeks, however, as she spoke, with eyes that
flashed and a lip that curled.

"Sophia!" she said; "how dare you insult me like
this!"

The distressed frown on Sophia's face instantly
vanished. "Oh, Claire," she cried, "I'm so glad it
is n't true! Don't be angry. You see, my dear, we

had n't met for so long, and you looked as if — as if something horrible had happened, and it 's such a funny, topsy-turvy world. So many queer things do happen in it. *Don't* be angry, please ! ''

" I am angry," said Claire. In her shabby dress she gave, notwithstanding, a noble portrayal of disdain. She had taken several steps toward the door, though Sophia, having caught her arm, endeavored, with a mien contrite and even supplicating, to detain her within the chamber. " Why should I not be angry ? " Claire went on, her voice dry and bitter. " Allow that I do look as if I were miserable. Is misery another name for sin ? . . . No, Sophia, let me go, please. . . . Perhaps you may learn, some day, as I 've learned already, that the unhappy people in life are not always the bad ones ! "

But Sophia, whose impulsive and explosive nature had not altered very markedly since we last heard of her childish escapades, now replied by a most excited outburst of appeal. Her exuberant figure, which no dexterity of dressmaking and no splendor of combined satins and velvets could turn less unwieldy and cumbrous, bowed and swayed till you almost heard the seams of its rich garb crack their stitches under the fleshly disturbance to which she subjected them.

"Claire! Claire! " she ejaculated; " I *have* insulted you. . . . But you 'll forgive me — I know you will. I 've never forgotten you. You stood up against that horrid Ada Gerrard and her set so finely, years ago! You were good then — yes, just as good as gold, — and I 'm sure you 're just exactly as good still. Now, Claire, don't look that way! I was talking to Ma about you only a few days since. Pa 's dead,

you know — but I suppose you don't. Yes, I said to
Ma that I'd give anything to find out what had become of you. Ma and I are dreadfully rich — I
mean well off. Poor Pa left ever so much money.
He's been dead nearly three years. There's nobody
but Ma and I left. I hate Hoboken. I made her
buy this house. Now, Claire, just stop! You shan't
go. You're going to tell me all about your troubles.
Yes, you shall! I'll be your friend. There, let me
kiss you. . . . Do, Claire! . . . You know I was always awfully fond of you. I never knew any girl I
was half so fond of as you. I've asked your pardon.
You were always a lady. I remember about that
dreadful dress you came to school in, first. But that
did n't matter. You were a lady born, and you
showed it afterward. Every girl thought so, too.
Even those hateful snobs had to own it — I'm sure
they did. I see some of them quite often. Ada
Gerrard's a great swell, as they say, now. She gives
me a little nod when I meet her, driving in the
Park or on the Avenue. But you're twice the lady
she is. Yes, Claire, I mean it. Kiss me, now, won't
you? Kiss me, and be friends!"

Claire had succumbed several minutes before this
eager tirade was ended. Her anger had fled. She
let Sophia put both arms about her. She returned
Sophia's kiss. Then she leaned her head upon the
shoulder of her companion, and gave way to another
access of tears. But they were quiet tears, this time.
The hysteric impulse had wholly passed. A little
later she told Sophia, with as much placid directness
as she could manage, every important detail of the
hard, dreary life lived since they two had last met.

While she thus spoke, the extraordinary charm of

her manner and the distinct loveliness of her delicate
yet notable beauty more than once thrilled her listener. Sophia's old worship, if the term be not too
strong, returned in full force. She had sworn by
Claire, as the phrase goes, in earlier days. She was
prepared to swear by her still. The story of Mr.
Twining's death and the disloyal deportment of his
wife roused her vehement contempt. By the time
that Claire had finished her gloomy recital, the two
girls were seated close together. Sophia's large fat
hand, in its fashionable glove, was fervidly clasping
Claire's.

"You did perfectly right!" Sophia at length exclaimed, after the pause had come, and while her
visitor sat with drooped head and pale, compressed
lips. "Your poor father! To bury him that way!
It was frightful! And you told her you'd do anything on earth for her if she only would n't! And
I know how you loved your father. Don't you recollect telling me about him, one recess, when I gave
you half my sardine-sandwich? You said he was a
gentleman by birth, and had come of a fine family in
England. That's where you get your swell looks
from, Claire. Yes, you *are* a swell, even though
you've got on a frock that did n't cost, altogether,
as much as one yard of mine. . . . Why, just look
at me! I'm awkward and clumsy, exactly as I was
at Mrs. Arcularius's. I'll never be any different.
And yet I spend loads and loads of money on my
things. I do, really! But gracious goodness! there
you sit, with your sweet, pure face, shaped like a
heart, and your hair that's got the same bright
sparkle through its brown that it used to have, and
those long eyelashes over those black-blue kind of

eyes, and that cunning little dimple in your chin, and those long, slender, ladylike hands " —

Here Claire stopped her, with a sad smile and a shake of the head. She spread open one hand, holding it up for scrutiny at the same moment.

"Don't talk of my hands, Sophia," she said. "They've been doing hard work since you saw them last."

Sophia gazed down at the inner portion of her friend's hand, for a moment, and then suddenly exclaimed, —

"Work! Why, they're not hard a bit. Oh, Claire, you've worn gloves all the time you worked. Come, own up, now!"

Claire smiled in a furtive way. But she spoke with simple frankness the next instant. "Well, yes, Sophia," she said, "I *have* worn gloves as often as I could. I wanted to save my hands. Some of the girls at Mrs. Arcularius's used to call them pretty. I wanted them to stay pretty — if I could manage it. I don't mind telling you so. But I thought they must have lost every trace of nice looks by this time."

Sophia bent over the hand that she still held, and whose palm was turned upward to the light, so that all its inner details, from wrist to finger-tips, could not possibly escape notice.

"Why, there's a pink flush all round the edge, inside there," commented Sophia. "It's funny, Claire. I never saw it in any other girl's hand before. It's just like the rose-color at the edge of a shell. Upon my word it is! I don't care a straw what work you've been doing; you've got hands like — well, I was going to say like a queen. But I don't doubt a

good many queens have awful hands, so I 'll say like
a lady. . . . There, kiss me again. . . . Here 's Ma.
Don't mind Ma. She 'll be nice. She always *is* nice
when I want her to be. Isn't that so, Ma ? "

A lady had just entered the small, brilliantly-ap-
pointed room in which Claire and Sophia had thus
far held their rather noteworthy converse. The lady
was Mrs. Bergemann.

She was exceedingly stout; both in visage and
form she looked like a matured and intensified Sophia. As far as features went, she wonderfully resembled her daughter. Every undue trait of plumpness in Sophia's countenance was reproduced by Mrs.
Bergemann with a sort of facial compound interest.
Flesh seemed to have besieged her, like a comic mal-
ady. Her good-natured eyes sparkled between two
creases of it; her loose, full chin revealed more than
one fold of it. She was by no means attired like a
widow of recent bereavement. She wore a bonnet
in which there was no violence of coloring; it was
purple and brown, but at the same time so severely
à la mode that if any symbol lurked behind its decorative fantasies this must have signified the soothing influences of resignation and consolation.

She had heard her daughter's last words. She was
devoted to Sophia; it was an allegiance wed with
pride. She had been a poor German girl, years ago,
and had drifted, through the chance of matrimony,
into her present opulent place. She was by nature
meek and conciliatory; all Sophia's temper and te-
merity had come from her father, who had combined
large superficial good-humor with a notorious intolerance of the least fancied wrong. Sophia's last words
had embarrassed her. She had no idea who Claire

was, but the evident cordiality of her daughter's deportment produced the effect of a gentle mandate.

"I shan't go driving, Ma!" Sophia exclaimed, after she had made Claire and her mother acquainted. "I'll stay at home and talk of old times with Claire Twining. Poor Claire's in trouble, Ma. I won't tell you about it yet. You go off in the carriage — that is, if it ever comes; but I'm afraid we'll have to discharge Thomas; he's always behind time."

"The carriage is here, Sophia," said Mrs. Bergemann. She spoke without the slightest German accent; this had perished long ago. She was looking at Claire with the manner of one who has been deeply attracted. "I've often heard you mention Miss Twining." she went on. " You was talking of her only the other day, was n't you, Sophia ? "

" Yes," said Sophia, rising. She went to her mother, and spoke a few low words, which Claire quite failed to hear. The prompt result of this intercourse was Mrs. Bergemann's exit from the room. Sophia followed her to the door, with one hand laid upon her shoulder.

"All right, Ma," she said, pausing a moment on the threshold. "You go and take your drive. I'll stay and chat with Claire."

A little while afterward Sophia had reseated herself at Claire's side. " Ma likes you," she at once began, in her voluble, oddly frank way. " She told me she did. She's very funny about liking and disliking people. She takes fancies — or she does n't. Ma is n't a swell. She's what they call vulgar. But she's ever so nice. She never had much education, but she has a large, warm heart. I would n't have her one bit different from what she is. I would n't

give Ma for Queen Victoria. She and I are the
dearest friends in the world. I know you'll like her,
Claire. She likes you, as I said. And Claire, look
here, now; I want to say something. It may surprise you. I hope, though, that it will please you,
too. You're going to stay here in this house. You're
going to live here as my friend. Yes, you are. You
were always as smart as a steel trap. We'll read
together, every morning. Yes, we will. You know
what a perfect fool I used to be at Mrs. Arcularius's.
Well, I'm the same fool still. But *you* know a lot;
you always did. And you shall help me to be less of
an ignoramus than I am. We've got a library upstairs. Oh, there are a crowd of books. I got Mr.
Thurston to buy them for me. He's a gentleman
friend of ours, and he knows a tremendous amount.
He just filled all the book-shelves for us. I'm sure
he bought the right kind of books, too; he knows
pretty much everything in that line. Now, Claire,
if you'll do as I say, we'll get along splendidly together. And as for . . . well, as for salary, you
know, I'll " —

Here Claire rose, placing a hand on Sophia's arm.
"No," she said, " I couldn't accept such a place as
that. I'm not able to fill it. I have been living a
life of hard work for three or four years past. I've
scarcely looked into a book, Sophia, in all that time.
I came here to ask you if you would get me work.
I can sew very well; I was always clever with my
needle. If you will give me something of that sort
to do, I will gladly and thankfully remain. But
otherwise, I can't."

IX.

Sophia consented to this plan, but only as a strategical manœuvre. She had determined that Claire should fill precisely the position just proffered her, and no other. By seeming to yield she at length won her cause. She was quite in earnest about her wish for mental improvement. Nor was Claire, in spite of latter years passed under the gloom of toil, half as much at sea among the many smart-bound volumes of the library as she herself had expected. She had been, in her day, a diligent student; she found that she remembered this or that famous writer, as she examined book after book. Now and then a celebrated name recurred to her with sharp appeal of recollection; again she had a vivid sense of forgetfulness, and of ignorance as well. But she was of the kind who read swiftly and retain with force. It was not long before she had discovered certain volumes which guided and at the same time instructed her in just that literary direction needful for the task required by her would-be pupil. A great deal of her old intellectual method and industry soon came back to her. She turned the pages of the many good books stored on the shelves near by with a hand more composed and deliberate; she began to see just what Sophia wanted her to do, and realize her full capability of doing it.

Meanwhile a week or more had passed. She was now clad in appropriate mourning. She was one of the family. Sophia, devoted and affectionate, was constantly at her side.

Now and then Claire said, with a nervous laugh, "I'm afraid I have never learned enough to be of the least use to you, Sophia, in the way you've proposed."

But Sophia would smile, and answer, "Oh, I'm not afraid, Claire dear. You'll get it all back again, pretty soon."

She rapidly got it all back again, and a great deal more besides. The morning readings began. Sophia soon expressed herself as in raptures; but it was the teacher that charmed her far more than the teaching.

Claire's life was now one of easy luxury. She walked or drove with Sophia every afternoon; she ate delicate food; she slept in a spacious bed-chamber that possessed every detail of comfort; all things moved along on oiled wheels; the machinery of her life had lost all its clogging rust. Greenpoint began to fade from her thoughts; it grew a dim, detested memory. Scarcely a day passed, however, without she definitely recalled some incident connected with her father. Now that this softness and daintiness surrounded her, the refinement which no adverse years could alienate from his personality became for her a more distinct conception. She realized how complete a gentleman he had been. At the same time, under these altered conditions, her own taste for the superfine niceties of cultivation increased with much speed. She was like a plant that has been **borne back** to its native soil and clime from some

10

land where it has hitherto lived but as a dwarfed
and partial growth ; the foliage was expanding, the
fibre was strengthening, the flowers were taking a
warmer tint and a richer scent.

She soon perceived that the Bergemanns moved in
a set of almost uniformly vulgar people. Many of
them seemed very wealthy. Nearly all of them
dressed handsomely and drove about in their private
carriages. Not a few of them lived in fine adjacent
houses on "the Avenue," as it is called. Sophia
had a number of intimate friends, maidens of her
own age, who constantly visited her. She had admirers, too, of the other sex, who would sometimes call
for her of an evening, and take her to a party, unat-
tended by any chaperone. She went, during the
winter months, to numerous parties. She belonged
to an organization which she always spoke of as
"our sociable," and which met at the various homes
of its female members. One evening a "sociable"
was given at the Bergemann mansion. The music
and dancing were kept up till two o'clock in the
morning, and the house was effectively adorned with
flowers. Claire, because of her mourning, abstained
from this and all similar gayety. But as a matter
of course she met many of Sophia's and Mrs. Bergemann's friends. Only one of all the throng had
power pleasurably to interest her.

This exceptional person was Mr. Beverley Thurston, whom we have already heard Sophia mention as
having selected the volumes of her mother's library.
He was a man about forty years old, who had never
married. His figure was tall and shapely ; his face,
usually grave, was capable of much geniality. He
had traveled, read, thought, and observed. He stood

somewhat high in the legal profession, and came, on the maternal side, of a somewhat noted family. He managed the large estate of Mrs. Bergemann and her daughter, and solely on this account was a frequent guest at their house. He had one widowed sister, of very exclusive views, who possessed large means, and who placed great value upon her position as a fashionable leader. For several years this lady (still called by courtesy Mrs. Winthrop Van Horn) had haughtily refused her brother's urgent request that she should leave a card upon Mrs. Bergemann, though several thousand a year resulted from his connection with the deceased brewer's property. But Mr. Thurston, while he succumbed to the arrogant obstinacy of his sister, had employed great tact in blinding his profitable patrons to the awkward truth of her disdain. He had been bored for three years past by his politic intimacy with Sophia and her mother, and he had always felt a lurking dread lest they should make a sudden appeal for his aid in the way of social advancement. But here he had committed a marked error. Mrs. Bergemann and Sophia understood nothing whatever about social advancement. They were both magnificently contented with their present places in society. The inner patrician mysteries were quite unknown to them. Their ignorance, in this respect, was a serene bliss. They believed themselves valuably important. They saw no new heights to gain.

Mr. Thurston had long secretly smiled at their self-confidence. He was a clever observer; he had seen the world; the Bergemanns were sometimes a delicious joke to him, when he felt in an appreciative mood. At other times the bouncing, coltish manners

of Sophia, and the educational deficiencies of her
mother, grated harshly upon his nerves. But when
Claire entered the household he at once experienced
a new sensation. He watched her in quiet wonder.
No points of her beauty escaped his trained eye.
What he had learned of her past career made her
seem to him remarkable, even phenomenal. By degrees an intimacy was established between them.
At first it concerned literary subjects; Claire con-
sulted him about the books appropriate for her readings with Sophia. But they soon talked of other
things, and occasionally these chats took the form of
very private *tête-à-têtes*. Claire was perfectly loyal
to her new friends, but she could not crush a spirit of
inquiry, of investigation and of valuation, so far as
concerned the people with whom they associated.

The gentlemen distressed her more than the ladies.
The latter were often so full of grace and prettiness
that their loud talk, shrill laughter, and faulty gram-
mar could not wholly rid them of charm. But the
gentlemen had no grace, and slight good looks as an
offset to their haphazard manners. Some of them
appeared to be quite uneducated; others would blend
ignorance with conceit; still others were ungallant
and ungracious, and not seldom pompously boastful
of their wealth.

Mr. Thurston was at first cautious in his answers
to Claire's rather searching questions. But by degrees he threw aside restraint; he grew to understand just why he was thus interrogated.

He had a slow yet significant mode of talk that
was nearly sure of entertaining any listener. Shallow people had called him a cynic, but not a few
clever ones had strongly denied this charge. Claire

began to look upon him as one who was forever opening doors for her, and showing her glimpses of discovery that either surprised or impressed the gazer.

On the evening of Sophia's "sociable" Claire remained in a large chamber that was approached from the second hall of the house, and appointed with that admirable taste which clearly indicated that the Bergemanns had once confided devoutly in their upholsterer, just as they now did in their milliner. She was quite alone; she held a book open in her lap, but was not reading it; her black dress became her charmingly; it seemed to win a richer shade from the chestnut-and-gold of her tresses, and to increase the delightful fragility of her oval, soft-tinted face. The music below stairs kept her thoughts away from her book; it pealed up to her with a dulcet, provocative melody; it made her feel that she would love to go down and join the merry-makers. But this was only a kind of abstract emotion; there was nobody in the bright-lit, flower-decked drawing-rooms whom she would have cared to meet, with the possible exception of Mr. Thurston, although what she then considered his advanced age made him seem more suitable as a companion of less jubilant hours.

But it chanced that a knock presently sounded at the half-closed door, and that Mr. Thurston soon afterward presented himself. He sat down beside her. His evening dress had a felicity of cut and fit that gave his naturally stately figure an added distinction, even to the inexperienced eye of Claire. She thought how the white tie at his throat became him — how different he was, in spite of the gray at his temples and the crow's-feet under his hazel eyes, from the younger men clad in similar vesture, whom she had seen pass through the upper hall a little earlier in the evening.

By this time Mr. Thurston's acquaintance with Claire had grown to be a facile and agreeable intimacy. He had learned from Sophia that she was here alone, and he had sought her with the freedom of one wont to make himself wholly at home in the mansions of his clients. At the same time, as it happened, he came with a vastly fatigued feeling toward the guests below.

"I did n't want to leave," he began, with his nice, social smile, "until I had seen you for a few moments."

"Ah," said Claire, pleased at his coming, and with a little sweet-toned laugh, "I'm afraid you came up here only because it was too early to go just yet."

Mr. Thurston put his head on one side, and his eyes twinkled quizzically. "Oh, come, now," he said; "are you going to talk badly about the party? You have n't seen it. I'm sure you'd like to be down there, dancing and romping among all those young people."

Claire shook her head; she looked rather serious as she did so. "No," she answered; "I should n't like it at all. I think you know why. There is nobody there — that is, among the guests — whom I like. Some of them I've never met. But I don't doubt that they are all much the same. Now, please don't look as if you did n't understand me. I am sure that you do, perfectly. Remember, we have talked on these subjects before."

Mr. Thurston stroked his thick gray mustache, whose ends slightly curved against cheeks which somehow looked as if they still wore the sun-tan of travel in remote sultry climates.

"Of course we have, Miss Claire," he gently exclaimed. "It's wonderful what an inquiring turn you possess. We've settled that there's no treachery to Sophia and her mamma in all these dreadful things that you and I say; haven't we?"

"Certainly we have settled it," returned Claire, still looking serious. "But I'm not by any means sure that we do say dreadful things. I ask the truth, and you tell it me." Here Claire's expression suddenly changed. She looked at her companion archly, and each cheek dimpled. "At least I hope you do."

Mr. Thurston shifted in his seat, and crossed his legs. "I do. I speak by the card when you ask questions. I'm compelled to. There's an enormous earnestness about you. You make me think of a person with a purpose. I'm sure you have a purpose. I haven't yet fathomed it, but I'm sure it's there."

"I have a purpose," Claire said.

"Very well. What is it?"

"To know about the world I live in. I mean New York, of course. That is my world, now. I think it a very nice world. At least, I've never seen a better one."

"Yes; I understand. And you want to explore it. You want to examine it in detail. You want to know its bad, worse, worst, and its good, better, best."

"I want to know its good, better, best."

Mr. Thurston laughed again. "Do you know," he said, "that the more I see of you the more you amuse me? No; I won't say 'amuse'; I'll say 'interest.' You are such a tremendous type. You are so characteristic. I called you a person with a purpose, just now, and I pretended not to know what

your purpose was. That was an intentional hypocrisy on my part. I comprehend your purpose thoroughly. You wish to find out what New York society
means. You're making a mental social dictionary.
And you desire that I shall supply you with defini-
tions to the best extent of my ability. Isn't that
true ? Pray confess, now."

Claire looked at him steadily for several seconds.
There was a mild yet bright spark in her dusky-blue
eyes, and a faint smile on her lips.

" You say less than you mean," she answered. " I
think that I guess what is behind your words. I
think that you suspect me of wishing to make my
dictionary from motives of future personal preference. That is, you believe that I am a girl with
strong ambitions — that I want to rise, thrive, succeed. . . . Well, you're not wrong. I do want to
rise, thrive, succeed. It's in me, as the saying goes.
I can't help the impulse."

Mr. Thurston lifted both hands and slightly waved
them. " The impulse is enough — with you," he
said.

Claire started. " What do you mean ?" she asked.

Mr. Thurston looked at the floor, for a moment,
then raised his eyes. They dwelt on Claire's very
forcefully.

" I mean," he said, " that you are too beautiful
and charming not to gain your object."

Claire laughed, lightly and yet a little consciously.
" That is very kind of you. If a young man had
only said it ! How delighted I would have been !"

" Then you think me so very old ?" Thurston replied, watching her face with intentness.

" Oh, no," Claire at once said, growing serious

again. "Not that, of course. But still . . . well, it would be idle for me to declare that I think you young."

"Perhaps I am younger than you think," he said, with low, peculiar emphasis on each word. "Mind, I only say 'perhaps.' . . . But do not let us talk of that. As I told you, I am sure you will gain your object. You will succeed. That is, you will find a higher level than these poor Bergemanns. There is a restless fire in your soul that will goad you on. And in the end you must win."

"Tell me by what means, please."

"Marriage will be your first stepping-stone."

"To what?"

"Success."

"Success in what form?"

"Social success. I assume that your aim lies there. You want men and women of a certain grade to pay you courtesy and deference."

Claire seemed to muse, for a brief time. "Yes, I do," she then said. "You are quite right. But you speak of my gaining all this by marriage. How shall I meet the man who is to lend me such important help?"

There was a daring candor about this question — a simplicity of worldliness, in fact — which startled her hearer. But his usual gravity betrayed no signs of dismay.

"You will meet him," he said, tranquilly. "Oh, yes; you will meet him. It is your fate. He will drop to you from the skies. But after you have secured through matrimony this desired end, will you be contented with what you have secured? So much depends on that — the success of your success, as one might say."

Claire raised her brows in demure perplexity. "I don't understand," she murmured.

Thurston slowly shook his head. A smile was on his lips, but it held sadness, and a hint of pity as well. "If I read you rightly," he answered, "you *will* understand, some day."

Claire made an impatient gesture. "Please don't talk in riddles," she exclaimed. "Do you mean that the prize will turn out worthless after I have got it? I have not found this true in my reading. I have not found many kings or queens who wearied so much of their thrones that they were ready to resign them." An eagerness now possessed her manner; she leaned slightly forward; her nostril dilated a little; her color deepened. "Power and place are what I want, and never to have them will be never to have contentment. This sounds cold to you. I 'm sure of it."

"Yes," he said, softly; "it sounds very cold. But I don't know that such a coldness as that will not prove for you a tough safeguard. It is very protective to a woman — if it lasts."

"Mine will last, such as it is."

"I neither affirm nor deny that it will. Time will show."

She broke into a laugh, full of sportive irony. "You mean that I may fall in love with somebody. But I have little fear of that." . . . Her face suddenly grew very sober, and her voice trembled somewhat as she next said: "I loved my poor dead father dearly. I shall never love any one else half so much again. No mere words could tell you of my firm certainty on this subject. But the certainty remains. I don't mean that I wish to live a loveless life. Far from that! I wish to have friends in abundance. And I shall not be disloyal to them in any case. But they must be friends of influence, standing, importance. They must not be like the Bergemanns, though I mean never to falter for an instant in my grateful fidelity toward Sophia and her mother."

" Your frankness," said Thurston, with one of his calm, wise smiles, " has a positive prodigality. What another woman would hide with the most jealous care, you openly speak. It is easy to see that your experience is yet limited."

" I should not talk to every one as I talk to you," Claire quickly answered.

He took one of her hands in his for a few moments. He held it, and she let him do so. He looked into her face with great fixity.

" My poor child," he said, " you have a hard road before you. But I know you mean to tread it with determined feet. In many women there would be something repellent about such resolves as those you have just confessed. In you they are charming. I suppose that is easily explained: you are charming yourself. I shall watch your career with the deepest concern. You will not mind if I watch it? Am I wrong, here ? "

Claire, still letting him keep her hand, swiftly replied : " Oh, no ; of course I shall not mind. You belong to that other world. You are one of the people whom I wish to have for my adherents — my clients, as it were. I hope we shall always be friends. I like you very greatly. You remember we have talked it all over before now. You have told me of the people whom I wish to meet. You have even told me some of their names. I have forgotten nothing of what you have said. I count you as my first conquest. If others follow — as I firmly believe that they will — we will have talks together, and laugh over the old times when I was obscure and a nobody. Yes, if I ever get to be that great lady you prophesy that I shall become, we will discuss, in little intimate chats, every detail of my progress toward grandeur and distinction. It will be very pleasant, will it not? But now I must say something that I have never said before. I must ask you to help me. Why should you not do so? You have means of doing so. And you like me; we are excellent friends. If you give me some real aid I will never forget it. I 'm not ungrateful. I 'm cold, if you choose, in a certain way, but I always recollect a service. Don't think I am begging any favor of you. I 'm rather requiring one. Yes, requiring. You 've told me that you think I have . . . well that I 'm not ugly. You know just what I want to do. And you 've said that I have . . . well that I 'm very far from a fool. . . . Now let us strike a compact. Shall we? Put me into some path where I may reach your fine, grand world, in which I should like to shine and be a power!"

The audacity of this whole speech was exquisite. In plain substance it belonged to what we call by harsh names. It was the sort of thing that in ordinary dealing we denounce and even contemn, as the effort of unsolicited pretension to thrust itself against barred gates with immodest vigor. But in Claire's case there was no question of ordinary dealing. Her impetuosity was so lovely. her youth, her beauty, and her freshness were so entirely delightful, that the unreserved freedom with which she spoke of aims in their essence purely selfish acquired a charming picturesqueness. Her ambition, thus openly expressed, lost every trace of gross worldly meaning. She became, to the eyes of him who watched her, a fascinating zealot. She seemed to demand what was merely her just due. It was indeed as though she had been robbed by some hostile fate of a royalty that she now declared her stolen right, and proudly reclaimed. All this time she had let Thurston retain her hand. Once or twice her slight fingers pressed against his palm, with unconscious warmth. Her face, meanwhile, lifted above the darkness of her mourning robes, was sweet and brilliant as some early dew-washed flower.

Thurston fixed his gaze upon her eyes, whose dark-blue depths were full of a rich, liquid light. His clasp tightened about her hand.

"I will give you my help," he said, with a new note in his voice that was a sort of husky throb; "I will give it to you gladly. But I am afraid you will not accept it when it is offered."

"Yes," returned Claire, still not guessing the truth, "I will accept it most willingly, since it comes from one whom I know to be my friend and well-wisher."

"That is not what I mean," Thurston objected. He rose as he spoke, still holding Claire's hand.

She looked at him wonderingly. She perceived his changed manner. "Explain," she said. "How do you mean that you will help me?"

"I will help you as my wife," Thurston replied. He looked as grave, as gray, as bronzed, as always; but his voice was in a hoarse flurry. "I will help you, as my wife, to be something more than a great lady. You shall be that, if you choose, but you shall be more. Your ambition is made of finer stuff than you know. I will help you to see just how fine it is."

The instant that he began to speak thus Claire had drawn away her hand. She did not rise. But she now looked up at him, and shook her head with negative vehemence.

" No, no! " she said. The words rang sharply.

X.

Not long afterward Claire found herself alone. Thurston had gone. She felt her cheeks burn as she sat and stared at the floor. His declaration had strangely shocked her, at first, for the entire man, as it were, had undergone a transformation so abrupt and radical as to wear a hue of actual miracle; and it is only across a comfortable lapse of centuries that the human mind can regard such manifestations with anything like complacency. Balaam could not have been more bewildered and disturbed when the Ass spoke. Claire had never thought of Thurston as capable of a live sentiment toward any woman. She had taken it for granted that all this part of his nature was in dignified decay, like his hair and complexion. She had drifted unconsciously, somehow, into the conviction that his passions, if he had ever felt them, were now like the lavendered relics that we shut away in chests. She had warmed to him with a truly filial ardor, and this sudden ruin of their mutual relations now gave her acute stings of regret.

But Thurston, who had managed to depart from her with a good deal of nice repose of visage and demeanor, also contrived, with that skill born of wide social experience, to make their next meeting by far less awkward than Claire herself had nervously anticipated. Sophia and Mrs. Bergemann were both present on this occasion. He looked at Claire in so ordinary a way, and spoke with so much apparent ease and serenity, that her self-possession was fed by his, and her dread swiftly became thankful relief.

Through the days that followed, Claire and Thurston gradually yet firmly resumed their past agreeable converse. Of course matters could never be the same between them. He stood toward her, inevitably, in a new light; a cloak had fallen from him; she was not quite sure whether she liked him less or more, now that she knew him as the man who had asked her to be his wife; but in reality she did like him much more, and this was because, being a woman, she constantly divined his admiration beneath the intimate yet always guarded courtesy of his manner.

Their former chats were resumed, steadily interrogative on her side, complaisantly responsive on his. As Winter softened into Spring, the dissipations of Sophia decreased. She had more evenings at home, and not a few of her devotees would pay her visits during the hours of nine and eleven. It frequently happened that Thurston would enter the drawing-room at such times. He always talked with Claire, who would often emerge from back recesses on his arrival. Both Sophia and her mother would occasionally deliver themselves of comments upon the evident preference of their legal adviser. But Mrs. Bergemann was much more outspoken than her daughter. Sophia could not bring herself to believe that there was "anything in it," as her own phrase repeatedly went. She thought Beverly Thurston "just as nice as he could be"; but the slender and blooming beauty of Claire made to her young eyes anomalous contrast with Thurston's *fade* though attractive appearance.

"Good gracious, Ma!" she once asseverated, in private debate, "Claire would n't ever think of marrying a man old enough to be her father!"

"She might do worse, now, Sophia," protested Mrs. Bergemann, with the coolly formulated style of talk and thought which marks so many matrons when they discuss matrimonial subjects. "You just leave Claire alone. Wait and see what she 'll do. He 's taken a shine to her. Recollect, she ain't got a cent, poor dear girl. He 'd make a splendid husband. I guess he 'll propose soon. I hope he will, too. He 's a real ellergant gentleman. Just think how we trust him with rents and mortgages and things. I declare I don't scarcely know half what he does with my own property."

"Pshaw, Ma," responded Sophia, with vast contempt. "Claire would n't look at him that way. She 's young, like me. She may be as poor as a church-mouse, but she is n't going to sell herself like that. Now do be quiet."

Mrs. Bergemann became obediently quiet. But she continued to have her private opinions. Meanwhile Claire and Thurston held their brief or long interviews, as chance favored.

Matters had rearranged themselves between them on the old basis. There was a change, and yet not a change. Claire spoke with all her former freedom. Thurston listened and replied with all his former concession.

A certain admirer of Sophia's had of late deserted her, and sought the attention of Claire whenever occasion permitted. His name was Brady. His father was the owner of a large and popular emporium on Sixth Avenue. He was an only child, and supplied

11

with a liberal allowance. The mercantile success of his father had been comparatively recent. He was now three-and-twenty; his early education had been one long, persistent neglect. After the money had begun to flow into the paternal coffers, Brady had gone abroad, and seen vice and little else in the various European capitals, and finally, coming home again, had slipped, by a most natural and facile process, into just that ill-bred, wealthy, low-toned set of which poor, rich Sophia Bergemann was one of the leading spirits.

Claire could hardly endure the attentions of Brady. She was civil to him because of her two hostesses, whose perception in all matters of social degree seemed hopelessly obtuse. But Brady had fallen in love with her, severely and effusively, and she soon had good cause to know it. He was very tall and slim of figure, with a face whose utter smoothness would have been the despair of a mercenary barber. His large ears, jutting from a bullet-shaped head, gave to this head, at a little distance away, the look of some odd, unclassic amphora. He spoke very indifferent English, and always kept the last caprice of slang in glib readiness, as a tradesman will keep his newest goods where he can soonest reach them. He was excessively purse-proud, and liked to tell you the price of the big sunken diamond worn on his little finger; of the suite of rooms at his expensive hotel; of the special deep-olive cigars, dotted with a lighter yellow speck, which lined his ivory cigar-case. He possessed, in truth, all the cardinal vulgarities. He was lavishly conceited; he paid no deference to age; he had not a vestige of gallantry in his deportment toward women; his self-possession was so fran-

gible that a blow could shatter it, but his coarse
wrath would at once rise from the ruin, like the foul
aroma from a broken phial. At such times he would
scowl and be insolent, quite regardless of sex, years,
or general superiority on the part of the offender.
Indeed, he admitted no superiority. The shadow of
the Sixth Avenue emporium hedged him, in his own
shallow esteem, with impregnable divinity.

"I think," said Thurston, speaking of him one
day to Claire, "that he is truly an abominable creature. The ancients used to believe that monsters
were created by the union of two commingling elements, such as earth and heaven. But to-day in
America we have a horrid progeny growing up about
us, resultant from two forces, each dangerous enough
by itself, but both deadly when they meet. I mean
Wealth and Ignorance. This Brady is their child.
If he were merely a poor man, his illiteracy would be
endurable. If he were merely illiterate, we could
stand his opulence. But he is both very uneducated
and very rich. The combination is a horror. He
is our modern way of being devoured by dragons,
minotaurs, and giants."

Claire laughed, and presently shook her head in
gentle argumentative protest. "I think there is a
flaw in your theory," she said, "and I'll tell you
why. There are the Bergemanns. Sophia, I admit,
is not precisely uncultivated — that is, she has had
good chances of instruction and not profited by them.
This may mean little, yet it is surely better than having had no chances at all. But Mrs. Bergemann —
she is both rich and ignorant, poor dear woman.
And yet she is very far from a monster. She is a
sweet, comfortable, motherly person. She would not

harm a fly." Claire put her head a little sideways, and looked with winsome challenge at her companion ; she assumed pretty airs and graces with him, nowadays, which she had never dealt in before the occurrence of a certain momentous episode. " What have you to say," she went on, " in answer to my rather shrewd objection ? Does n't it send you quite into a corner."

" Well, I confess that it rather floors me to have Mrs. Bergemann cited against me," he said, smiling. " I am afraid that I must yield. I am afraid that my theory is torn in tatters. I must congratulate you on your destructive instincts."

He spoke these words with his usual robust sort of languor, in which there was never a single trace of affectation or frivolity. At the same time a secret feeling of wonder possessed him ; he was thinking how swiftly active had been the change in Claire since their first acquaintance. She had told him every particular of her past life, so far as concerned its opportunities of instruction. He marveled now, as he had repeatedly done on recent occasions, at her remarkable power to grasp new phrases, new forms of thought, new methods of inquiry. She had never, from the first, shown a gleam of coarseness. But she had often been timid of speech and falteringly insecure of expression. Yet latterly all this was altered. Thurston had a sense of how phenomenal was the improvement. It was plain that the books in the library, and Claire's power of fleet reading, had wrought this benefit upon a mind which past study and training had already rendered flexibly receptive. And yet all of the explanation did not lie here ; at least half of it lurked in the fact that she had quitted drudgery, need, and depression. Her mental shutters had been flung open, and the sunshine let to stream in through the casements. A few days later she had suspected the existence of Brady's passion. He made no attempt, on his own side, to conceal his preference for her society. Claire saw love in his prominent, slate-colored eyes; she saw it in the increased awkwardness of his motions when he either walked or sat near her; she saw it in his bluff yet repressed bravado of manner, as though he were at surly odds with himself for having been suddenly cut off in the flower of his vainglorious bachelorhood. She had grown sharper-sighted for the detection of these tender signs. And even in Brady their tenderness was unmistakable. His clownish crudity had softened, in all its raw lines. The effect might be compared to those graceful disguises in which we have seen moonlight clothe things that repel us under the glare of day.

One morning when Claire came down to breakfast she found a huge basket of Jacqueminot roses awaiting her, with Brady's card attached to it. She flushed, for a moment, almost as red as the florid, velvety petals themselves. Then she said, equally addressing Mrs. Bergemann and Sophia:

"How strange that he sent them to *me!* There may have been some mistake."

"Oh, not a bit of it!" Sophia exclaimed. "He's dead gone about you, Claire. I've seen it lately. So has Ma." Here the young lady turned toward her mother, and lifted an admonishing finger. "Now, Ma, don't you say a thing!"

But Mrs. Bergemann would say a number of things. Her amiability was so expansive, and made

such a radius of glow and warmth all about her, that
she rarely found it possible to dislike anybody. She
had failed to realize that Brady was an offensive
clod. In her matrimonial concern for Claire, the
fact that he would one day, as the only child of his
father, inherit a vast fortune, reared itself before her
with irresistible temptation.

"Upon my word," she declared, "I don't know as
any girl *had* ought to refuse a fellow as awful well-
off as he is. Sophia's always talking of his great
big ears, and his boastful ways, and his style of getting into tantrums about nothin' whatever. But
still, I guess he might make a good husband. He
might be just the kind that'll tame down and behave 'emselves after marriage. And they say he
ain't a bit mean; he ain't got *that* fault, anyhow.
And I guess he'd buy a manshun on the Avenu for
any girl he took, and just make her shine like a
light-house with di'monds, and roll round in her carriage, and be high an' mighty as you can find. *I'd*
think twice, Claire, if *I* was you, before I let him
slip. That is, I mean if you don't decide you'd
rather have Mr. Thurston, who *does* seem fond o'
you, though I ain't said so before in your hearing,
dear, and who's an ellergant gentleman, of course,
even if he *is* a bit too old for a fresh young thing
like yourself."

Claire laughed, in a high key, trying to conceal
her nervousness. "Oh, Mr. Thurston is quite too
old, Mrs. Bergemann," she said. "Please be sure of
that."

The rich hue of the roses haunted her all day,
even when she was not near them. Their splendid
crimson seemed like a symbol of the luxury that she

might be called upon to refuse. She had heard about the emporium on Sixth Avenue. It made her bosom flutter when she thought of being the mistress of a great mansion, and wearing diamonds and rolling about in her carriage. Then she remembered Thurston's words concerning this man who had sent her the roses. Was he so much of a monster, after all? Might she not be able to humanize him? For a long time she was in a very perturbed state. During this interval it almost seemed to her that if he should ask her to marry him she would nerve herself and answer 'yes.'

That afternoon she did not go to drive with Sophia. Mrs. Bergemann went in her place. Claire sat beside one of the big plate-glass windows of her delightful chamber, and watched the clattering streams of carriages pass below. Some of these she had now grown to remember and recognize ; a few of them possessed a dignity of contour and equipment that pleased her greatly. She would have liked to lean back upon the cushions of some such vehicle, and have its footman jauntily touch his hat while he received her order from within, after he had shut the shining door with a hollow little clang. The door should have arms and crest upon it ; she would strongly prefer a door with arms and crest.

Suddenly, while watching from the window, she saw a flashy brougham, with yellow wheels, a light-liveried coachman and a large, high-stepping horse in gilded harness, pause before the Bergemanns' stoop. The next instant Brady sprang out, and soon a mellow bell-peal sounded below. Claire sat and wondered whether he who had sent her the roses would now solicit her company. It even occurred to her that he might have passed Sophia and Mrs. Bergemann on the avenue, and hence have drawn the conclusion that she would be at home alone.

She was quite right in this assumption. The grand Michael presently brought up Mr. Brady's card. Claire hesitated for an instant, and then said that she would see the gentleman.

She found Brady in the reception-room. He was dressed with an almost gaudy smartness, which brought all his misfortunes of face and figure into bolder relief. He wore a suit of clothes that might have been quiet as a piece of tapestry, but was surely assertive in its pattern when used for coat and trousers; his cravat was of scarlet and blue satin, and a pin was thrust into it which flashed and glittered so that you could not at first perceive it to be a cock's head wrought of diamonds, with a little carcanet of rubies for the red comb. He had a number of brilliant rings on his big-knuckled hands, and the sleeve-buttons that secured his low, full wristbands were a blaze of close-bedded gems at every chance recession of his sleeve. As he greeted Claire it struck her that his expression was unwontedly sulky, even for him. He appeared like a person who had been put darkly out of humor by some aggravating event.

"How are you, Miss Twining?" he said, holding Claire's hand till she herself withdrew it. "I hope you're well. I hope you're as well as they make 'em."

Claire sat down while she answered: "I am very well, Mr. Brady." Her visitor at once seated himself beside her, leaning his face toward her own. "I am sorry that both Mrs. Bergemann and Sophia are out," she went on, with the desire to bridge an awkward interspace of silence.

"Oh, *I* ain't, not a bit," said Brady, ardently contradictory. "I'm glad of it, Miss Twining. I wanted to have a little chin with you." He laughed at his own slang, crossed his long legs, and leaned back on the lounge which Claire was also occupying. At the same time he turned his face toward his companion.

Claire felt that decency now compelled her to offer a certain acknowledgment. "I want to thank you for those lovely flowers," she said. "They were beautiful, and it was very kind of you to send them."

He began to sway his head slightly from side to side. It was his way of showing nearly every emotion, whether embarrassment, perplexity, chagrin, or even mollification.

"Come, now," he began, "you did n't really think a lot about 'em, did you?"

"I liked them very much," returned Claire. She was watching him, in all his unpleasant details, though very covertly. She was asking herself, in the dispassionate reflectiveness born of her calculating yet feverish ambition, whether she could possibly consent to be his wife if he should ever ask her. The remembrance of his great prospective wealth dealt her more than one thrilling stroke, and yet feelings of self-distrustful dread visited her also. She feared lest she might commit some irreparable mistake. She was still very ignorant of the world in which she desired to achieve note and place. But she had, at the same time, a tolerably definite understanding of some things that she aimed to do. Her talks with Thurston had let in a good deal of light upon her mind. She had not lost a single point in all his explanatory discourse.

"I'm glad you *did* like 'em," said Brady, examining his radiant rings for an instant. "They cost a heap of stamps," he added, suddenly lifting his head and giving her an intent look. "But I don't mind that. I ain't a close-fisted chap, especially when I'm fond of anybody. I guess you've seen that I think a deal about *you*. I can't talk flowery, like some chaps, but that don't matter." . . . At this point he suddenly took Claire's hand; his face had acquired a still more sulky gloom; it was clouded by an actual scowl. "Look here, now, Miss Twining," he said, "I never expected to get married. I've had some pretty nice girls make regular dead sets at me — yes, I have — but none of 'em ever took my fancy. You did, though. I stuck it out for two or three weeks, and I daresay I kept giving myself clean away all the time. But I saw 't was n't any use; I'm caught, sure; there ain't any mistake about it. We'll be married whenever you say. I'll do the handsome thing — that is, Father will. Father's crazy to have me settle down. He's worth a lot o' money — I s'pose you know that. He'll like you when he sees you — I ain't afraid he won't. We can have a slam-bang stylish wedding, or a plain, quiet one, just as you choose. And don't you be alarmed about too big a difference between you and I. Father may kick a little at first, but he'll come round when you've met once or twice. He'll see you're a good, sound girl, even if you ain't as high up, quite, as he'd want me to go for. There, now, I've broken the ice, and I s'pose it's all fixed, ain't it?"

Claire had been trying to withdraw her hand, for several moments, from the very firm grasp of this remarkable suitor. But as Brady ended, she literally snatched the hand away, and rose, facing him, contemptuous, and yet calm because her contempt was so deep.

" It is impertinent for you to address me like this," she said, in haughty undertone. " You have no right to take for granted that I will marry you. In the first place, I do not like you ; in the second place, I think myself by no means your inferior, but greatly above you as regards breeding, education, and intelligence ; and in the third place, I would never consent to be the wife of one whom I do not consider a gentleman."

She at once left the room, after thus speaking, and saw, as she did so, that Brady's face was pale with rage and consternation. His insolent patronage had wounded her more than she knew. On reaching her own room, she had a fit of indignant weeping. But by the time that Sophia and Mrs. Bergemann returned from their drive, she was sufficiently tranquil to betray no sign of past perturbation.

That evening Sophia went to one of her "sociables." A male friend called for her, and they were driven together to the entertainment in question, with superb yet innocent defiance of those stricter proprieties advocated in higher social realms. Mrs. Bergemann retired somewhat early, and Claire was left alone, as it happened, with Thurston, who chanced to drop in a little after nine o'clock. Just before Mrs. Bergemann left the drawing-room, she contrived to whisper, in garrulous aside, with her plump face quite close to Claire's, and all her genial, harmless vulgarity at a sort of momentary boiling-point: " I should n't be surprised, dear, if he should pop tonight. And if he does, I ain't sure that you had n't better have him than Brady, for he's ever so rich, though the other 'll get that Sixth Avenu store and two or three millions o' money behind it. Still, please yourself, Claire, and don't forget to leave the hall gas burnin' for Sophia when you go upstairs."

Claire was in a very interrogative mood to-night. "I should like to have Mr. Brady explained a little more fully," she said, when Thurston and herself were again seated side by side.

Her companion gave a soft laugh. "I thought that we had exhausted that subject," he said. "It's not a very rich one, you know."

"I don't want you to tell me anything about his character as a man," Claire quickly replied. "But I want to find out his standing in society."

"He has no standing in society," said Thurston, with instant decisiveness.

"Do the people of whom you have spoken repeatedly — those whom you term the best class, I mean — entirely refuse to know him?"

"Not at all. They have never been called upon to know or not to know him. The best class is in a different world altogether. Perhaps Brady is aware of their existence; he may have read of their entertainments in the newspapers, or he may have seen them occasionally at watering-places. But that is all. His self-importance prevents him from realizing that they are above him. He is essentially and utterly common. He is surrounded by a little horde of sycophants who worship him for his money, and who are, in nearly all respects, as common as himself."

"You mean the set of people with whom Sophia associates?"

"Yes. I mean the rich, vulgar set of which you have so frequently seen specimens in this very room."

Claire seemed to muse for a short while. "But the others?" she soon asked. "Those people who hold themselves above the Bergemanns—are they all refined and cultured? That is, are there any Bradys among them? Are there any Mrs. Bergemanns or Sophias?"

"I should emphatically say not. One may meet people among them who are by no means models of propriety or of high - breeding, but only as exceptional cases. They are generally found to be ladies and gentlemen; I don't know two more comprehensive words than those for just what I desire to express. Of course I have no large moral meaning, now. I would merely imply that in outward actions, at least, they preserve the niceties. Their occasional deeds of darkness may be as solidly bad as anything of the kind elsewhere. I should be very loth to describe them as saintly. But they are usually polished. Quite often they are rank snobs. Still oftener they are stupid. Their virtues might best be explained negatively, perhaps. They don't shock you; they are not crude; they haven't forgotten that a verb agrees with its nominative in number and person; they don't overdress themselves; they very rarely shout instead of talking, and . . . well, for a final negative, they never tell the truth when its utterance might wound or annoy."

Claire had seemed to be listening very earnestly. She did not respond with her usual promptness. Her tones were slow and thoughtful when she at length said: "And they are what you would call an aristocracy?"

" I don't know why they are not. They are incessantly being compared, to their own disadvantage,
with the aristocracies of foreign lands. But I have
traveled considerably, in my time, and on the whole
I prefer them to all similar bodies. There is less
sham about them, and quite as much reason for
existence. They point a very sad moral, perhaps ;
they illustrate what certain austere critics like to call
the failure of republican ideas. But I 've had so
many good friends among them that I can't consider
any institution a failure which is responsible for their
development."

" And it is very hard to become one of their number," Claire said, after another little pause. She did
not put the words as a question.

" You seem to think it hard," Thurston answered.
Rare as was any impulsive order of speech with him,
this slight yet meaning sentence had nevertheless
found utterance, almost against his will.

It was his first reference to the episode which both
vividly remembered, though in far different ways, and
which had cast round their subsequent intercourse,
even when directed upon the most mundane topics, a
delicate glamour of sentiment plainly perceptible to
each. Claire dropped her eyes, for a moment, then
suddenly lifted them, while the pink was yet deepening in her cheeks.

" Let us suppose that I am not speaking of myself," she said. " Indeed," she went on, with a soft,
peculiar smile that had hardly lighted her lips before it fled, "you have told me that *my* gate into
the kingdom of the elect is through — well, through
matrimony." She now looked at her companion
with so subtle a blending of the arch and the grave

that Thurston, in all the solidity of his veteran experience, was baffled how to explain it. "Suppose," she suddenly announced to him, "that I should marry Mr. Brady. He is your abhorrence, I know. But if he put his millions at my disposal, could I become the great lady you and I have talked about?" .

Thurston was stroking his mustache, and he now seemed to speak under it, a trifle gruffly, as he answered her.

"Yes," he said, "I think you could — provided Brady quitted the world after marrying you."

Claire gave a little rippling laugh. "They would never allow him to be one of them?" she asked, in tones whose precise import her hearer still failed to define, and which impressed him as midway between raillery and seriousness.

"No, never. If he has proposed to you, my poor child, don't for an instant flatter yourself that you could use him as a ladder by which to climb up into your coveted distinction."

These words were spoken with a commiserating ridicule. Tried a man of the world as he was, Thurston had of late been so deeply wounded that he now felt his wound bleed afresh, at an instant's notice, and deal him a severe pang as well. But Claire, quite forgetting to make allowances, flushed hotly, and at once said: —

"I never told you that Mr. Brady had proposed to me. And I do not think it proper or civil for you to throw in my face what I have put to you in the shape of a confidence."

"Marry Brady. By all means marry him," said Thurston. He had not been so bitterly affronted in years.

Claire felt conscience-stricken by the recollection of her own thoughts just previous to Brady's offer. She had permitted herself to weigh the question of whether or not marriage with such a man might be possible. Then had come the sharp sense that it would be degrading. For this reason she was now humiliated beyond measure, and hence keenly angry.

"I shall not marry him," she said, her lip faintly quivering. " Why do you speak to me like this?" Tears of shame now gathered to her eyes, and her voice notably faltered. She found no more words to utter. She felt that she was in a false, miserable position. She felt that she deserved Thurston's contempt, too, since she had given him, stupidly and rashly, a hint of what had passed between herself and the man whom they both despised.

Thurston rose and placidly faced her. He was so angry that he had just enough control left to preserve tranquillity.

"I don't know that I have said anything very hard to you," he began.

"Yes, you have," retorted Claire, her voice in wretched case. She knotted both hands together while she spoke. She was still seated.

Thurston went on as if there had been no interruption. "But if I tell you the plain truth, I don't doubt you will think me hard. I will tell it because you need it. You are still a mere girl, and very foolish. I am profoundly sorry for you. You have no possible regard for that frightful young millionaire, and yet you have permitted yourself to think of marrying him. Such a marriage would be madness. You would not accept me because you thought me old, but it would be better if you married a decent man of ninety than a gross cad and ruffian of twenty-three. But whether you do sell yourself in this horrid way or no, it is a plain fact that you are in danger of committing some terrible folly. I see by your face that you do not mean to heed my words. But perhaps if you listen to them now, you will recall them and heed them hereafter."

"No," cried Claire, tingling with mortification, and seizing on satire as a last defensive resort against this deserved rebuke, whose very justice revealed her own culpability in a clearer light; "no, if you please, I won't listen! I shall ask, instead, that you will kindly grant me the liberty of purchasing my own sackcloth and of collecting my own ashes."

She half turned away from him, with glowing face, as she spoke; it was her intent to beat a prompt retreat; but Thurston's firm, even tones detained her.

"I warn you against yourself," he went on. His anger had cooled now, and melancholy had replaced it. "You have some fine traits, but there is an actual curse hanging over you, and as a curse it will surely fall, unless by the act of your own will you change it into a blessing. It is more than half the consequence of your land and your time, but it is due in part, also, to your special nature. In other countries the women whom fate has placed as it has placed you, are never stung by ambition like yours. They are born *bourgeoises*, and such they are contented to remain. If they possess any ambition, it is to adorn the sphere in which their destinies have set them, and this alone. They long for no new worlds to conquer; their small world is enough, but it is not too small to hold a large store of honest pride. All over Europe

12

one finds it thus. But in America the affair is quite
different. Here, both women and men have what is
called 'push.' Not seldom it is a really noble discontent; I am not finding fault with it in all cases.
But in yours, Claire Twining, I maintain that it will
turn out a dowry of bitter risk if not woful disaster.
I exhort you to be careful, to be very careful, lest
it prove the latter. Don't let your American 'push'
impel you into swamps and quicksands. Don't let it
thrust you away from what is true and sterling in
yourself. Be loyal to it as a good impulse, and it
will not betray and confound you like a bad one.
You can do something so much better than to wreck
your life; you can make it a force, a guidance, a
standard, a leadership. You can keep conscience and
self-respect clean, and yet shine with a far surer and
more lasting brilliancy on this account. . . . Think
of my counsel; I shall not besiege you with any more;
no doubt I have given you too much, and with too
slight a warrant, already. . . . Good-by. If I should
never see you again, I shall always hope for you
until I hear ill news of you. And if bright news
reaches me, I shall be vain enough to tell myself that
we have not met, talked, argued — even quarreled,
perhaps — without the gain on your own side of
happy and valued results." . . .

Thurston passed from the room, swiftly, and yet
not seeming to use the least haste, before Claire,
strongly impressed and with her wrath at a vanishing point, could collect herself for the effort of any
coherent sort of reply.

She had caught one very clear glimpse of his face
just as he disappeared. His hazel eyes, troubled, yet
quiet, had momentarily dwelt with great fixity on

her own. As she afterward recalled this parting vision of a face grown so familiar through recent weeks, it appeared to her solely in imaginative terms. It ceased to be a face ; it became a reproach, a remonstrance, an advice, an entreaty.

Immediately after his exit she sank into a chair, feeling his late words ring through mind and heart. She had never liked him so much as at that moment.

She had a sense that he meant to avoid seeing her again. But she did not realize through how much vivid novelty of experience she must pass before they once more met. If any such prescience had reached her, she would have gone out into the hall and plucked him by the sleeve, begging him to return, filled with conciliatory designs, eager that he should abandon all thought of permanent farewell.

But as it was, she let the hall-door close behind him, and sat staring at the floor and saying within her own thoughts : " He is right. I am in danger. I can save myself if I choose. And I *will* save myself in time !"

She clenched both hands as they drooped at either side, and her eyes flashed softly below their shading lids.

XI

SHE was wholly unprepared for the intelligence, a few days later, that Thurston had gone, in the most sudden manner, to Europe. The Bergemanns, mother and daughter, were both amazed by the departure of their legal adviser, without a premonitory word from him on the subject and apparently at such brief notice. Claire, in the midst of her own consternation, sharply dreaded lest some suspicion should dawn upon them that she was concerned in this precipitate change. But if Mrs. Bergemann let fall any hint that such was her belief, it was made in the hearing of Sophia alone; and the latter had scouted from the first, as we know, all idea that Thurston's regard for her friend could partake of lover-like tenderness. The letter which he had written to his client, announcing that he had sailed, gave no reason for this abrupt course. It was a letter somewhat copious in other respects, however, and made thoroughly plain the fact that the partner of him who wrote it would in every way defend and supervise the interests of Mrs. Bergemann. "I shall probably be abroad a number of months," ran Thurston's written words, "but during that time rest sure that all details of the slightest importance with respect to your affairs shall be safely communicated through Mr. Chadwick."

Mr. Chadwick soon afterward presented himself. He was a lank man, of bloodless complexion and irreproachable manners. "I think he's a reg'lar wet blanket," said Mrs. Bergemann, with critical cruelty, " after dear, high-toned Mr. Thurston. He *was* high-toned, Claire, was n't he, now?" she persevered, with a sidelong, timorous look toward Sophia, who chanced, besides Claire, to be present at the time.

" Now, Ma!" broke in Sophia, accompanying this vocative with a tart gesture of remonstrance, " Claire does n't know a bit better than you or I do whether he was high-toned or not. *Do* you, Claire?"

" I think almost everybody who ever met him," said Claire, answering the appeal, "must have seen it very clearly."

She spoke this with nice composure. But she was inwardly dismayed, wounded, almost tortured. For many succeeding days she contrived to absent herself from all Sophia's guests. Brady had totally disappeared from her experience ; he no longer presented himself at the house. He was secretly fearful lest Claire might publish the fact of his proposal broadcast among the adherents with whom he stood supreme as their moneyed and autocratic leader. He suffered those torments of humiliation which only a small soul, with small views of things and an immoderate vanity, has learned the petty trick of suffering. It is by no means hyperbole to state that he inwardly cursed Claire for being the girl within whose power he had put it to say that she had actually repelled his superb matrimonial advances. Longer concern with so unwholesome a creature would be idle for the chronicler, especially since henceforth he drops out of our record somewhat as

Slocumb did, and with a scarcely more chivalrous exit.

Claire now passed through a period of extreme repentance. Her old longings had vanished; she silently planned for herself, with ascetic enthusiasm, a future of humility and obscurity. She was a zealot in a totally new way; she had abandoned all thought of marrying, and had conceived the idea of mentally fitting herself to become a governess. With this end, she spent hours in the library. Incapable of doing anything by halves, she now bent the full force of her strong will and capable intellect toward obtaining a proper educational competence. She swam far out, so to speak, into the blue waters of knowledge, and breasted them with good, vigorous strokes. She was, for the time at least, passionately in earnest. Thurston's farewell words rang incessantly through her memory. She would crush down all that American "push," once and forever. She would steer from the perils against which he had warned her, by one broad, divergent swerve. Her remorse and her resignation held a poetic ardor of kinship. Her past longings had indeed been a folly, and as such she would unvaryingly treat them. She would be consistent henceforward, and seek only what lay within her lawful scope of action. She was like the convert to a new faith, and she had all a convert's intensity of fervor.

From her two friends, however, she chose to guard with caution the secret of this change. It was now the early portion of June, and the fierce heat of summer had literally leapt down on the city after several weeks of raw, inclement May weather. The judgment long ago passed upon our climate, that it has a summer, an autumn, a winter, but no spring, had never been more fully confirmed. The city was wrapt all day in a torrid drowse; the pavements lay either in bleak glare or breathless shadow. On the benches of the parks, where spots of dusk were wrought by overbrowing branches, groups of jaded citizens huddled together in moist discomfort. The cars tinkled sleepily; the omnibuses lagged in rumbling sloth; foul smells beset the nostrils, even from genteel gutters or the door-ways of high-priced restaurants. People looked up at the wool-like pallor of the sky, and wished that it would darken into the cooling gloom of a thunderstorm.

But Claire scarcely minded the heat. She had known the fetid miseries of a Greenpoint summer. Those spacious chambers and halls of the Bergemanns' solid-built mansion were delicious indeed by contrast. Striped awnings had been affixed to each window, whose scalloped edges would flap in chance waftures of breeze, while the stout bunting above them changed the sunny rigors outside to a continual soothing gloom. It was true that she had no sympathy with hot weather; she liked an atmosphere in which quick movement was pleasantly possible. But she was nevertheless very much at her ease here and now. She read; she studied; the library, bathed in a tender dimness, pleased her with its vague rows of books, its rough rich carpeting, its dark massive wood-work. She had, for a time, that exquisite feeling of the scholar who clothes himself with silence, solitude, and repose, and who lets the outer world touch him through soft, impersonal yet cogent mediums. During this interval she was completely happy. It was the old self-surrender of the *dévote*.

Literature was henceforth to be her cult, her idolatry. The mere process of reading had always been one of ease and speed with her. Past training helped her now in the way of method and system. She had learned how to learn. Her French readings were frequent. Sophia had a French maid with whom she often conversed. Her proficiency in the language soon became marked and thorough.

But suddenly her new contentment was shattered, and by a rude stroke. Mrs. Bergemann began to talk of leaving town. Claire almost felt, at first, as if the ground were giving way beneath her feet. She could only accompany her friends to a watering-place in the position of a dependent and pensioner. Her salary must stop, because her relations with Sophia must of necessity lose all their instructive character. " You would never continue our readings, Sophia," she said, " in a crowded hotel, where you would have countless distractions."

" Oh, yes, I would, Claire," was the alert reply. " We 'll keep it up just the same. You 'll pack a few books in one of the trunks, and I 'll promise to be a good girl; you need n't feel a bit afraid. Ma 's decided on Coney Island. Now, don't look so glum, as if you did n't have a friend in all the world. You 've been sort of queer, lately; you talk slower, somehow, and you stick up there in the library nearly all the time. But you 're still my own nice Claire. I swear by you, dear girl, just as I always did. If there 's anything on your mind I won't ask you what it is."

" There *is* something on my mind, Sophia," Claire said. " But you must not ask me what it is, just yet. I will tell you soon. Yes, I hope to tell you quite soon."

She went with them to Coney Island. They engaged rooms at the Manhattan Beach Hotel. The books had been packed and brought, but very few of them were ever opened.

"It's not a bit of use, Claire!" Sophia affirmed, after the lapse of about five days. "We can't manage it. There's always something happening, as you see. Besides, nobody works here. Everybody idles. It's in the air. Let's take a vacation."

"Why, yes, girls," said Mrs. Bergemann, at this point, with motherly persuasion. "You better just lay up some health for next winter, and quit the books till we get home. Or p'raps we may get tired of this place 'fore the summer's through, an' go somewheres where it ain't so lively — I mean some lazy place like Lake George or the White Mountains. Then books and reading will fit in kinder natural. But I don't think *I'll* care to leave here for a good big while. I ain't ever seen anything like it before. If we could only go driving here, now, and them horses was n't eating their heads off over in the city, why 't would be a reg'lar paradise. Sophia, I've just rec'lected that I came to this very spot twenty years ago if it's a day, with poor Pa! We was quite a young couple, then . . . that girl was n't more 'n a baby, Claire. We took her along. Pa carried you, Sophia. The Brewery was n't started in them times, an' . . . well, I guess we got along with about five hundred dollars a year, over at the small saloon at Hoboken."

"Now, Ma, you need n't go into such very close particulars, please!" chided Sophia, whose large, warm heart was not democratic enough always to stand the intense humility of certain maternal reminiscences.

"Pshaw!" said Mrs. Bergemann, with a good-humored laugh; "we don't mind Claire. She's one of us. Besides, we're up here in the bedroom, not down on that crowded piazzer. Well, girls, as I was saying, Pa and me came here that day, an' I declare to goodness, the place was only a bare strip o' sand with a few little shanties here and there, that they called hotels. And just look at it now! Three monstrous palaces, and all New York streaming down every decent afternoon. It's like enchantment. I can't believe I'm where I was twenty years ago. I'm afraid I must be dreaming. But if I am, I don't want to wake up; I want to keep right on till the first o' September."

"Only a few years ago the island was very much the same as you describe it twenty years ago," said Claire, who had dipped into a small descriptive hand-book telling about the marvelous growth of this unique and phenomenal watering-place.

"I s'pose I ought to find it a little bit too *gay*," pursued Mrs. Bergemann, presently, in reflective afterthought. "Poor Pa's been gone such a short time." Here the lady heaved an imposing sigh which her massive bust made no less visible than audible. "But I can grieve just as well by mixing in with folks as if I was hung round with crape an' stuck off alone somewheres. Everybody's got their own ways o' grieving, an' I ain't goin' to forget poor Pa merely 'cause I look about a little and make my second-mourning kinder stylish. Not a bit of it!"

Mrs. Bergemann certainly showed the courage of her opinions, as regarded the sort of grief due her departed spouse. Her laugh was loud in hall, in dining-room, or on piazza. Her costumes tinkled with black bugles, or rustled and crackled in sombre yet ornamented grandeur. It is probable that grief may have dealt her real pangs, and yet that the irrepressible glow and warmth of her spirits kept always at bay the gloom and chill of grief. Her nature was not a shallow one; she could feel with depth and force, but she could not mope or even muse; solitude was hateful to her; she was gregarious; she wanted to hear the voices and look into the faces of her kind. In spite of her German origin she was excessively representative, from a purely American stand-point. Her very vulgarities — and they were certainly profuse — possessed a wide, healthful sincerity. Her enormous benevolence stood for her in the place of refinement; it was indeed a certain code of manners by itself; she was always so good to you that you might pardonably forget to remark the unconventionalism of her goodness. She was precisely the sort of person whom Coney Island must have pleased.

But it pleased Claire in a totally different way. The immense concourse of people who flocked thither, by such easy modes of travel, from New York and Brooklyn and elsewhere, were an incessant source of interest. Their numbers, their activities, their enjoyments, kept her blood in a soft tingle. This brilliant and picturesque city by the sea appeared to her in the light of a delicious reparation. It was a long, splendid festivity, compensating her for those years of dire dullness passed but a few miles away. All her recent resolutions to spend a life of lowly quietude, had melted into thin air. The ambition to climb, to shine, and to rule was once more a dominant force within her being. It seemed to her as if she had flung away some sort of irksome disguise, and now beheld it lie like an ugly heap near at hand, while wondering, in the exhilaration of regained freedom, how she had ever chosen to shroud herself with its clogging folds.

She bathed every day in the ocean, and acquired a richer fund of health on this account. Either with Sophia or alone, though more often the latter, she explored the whole wondrous little life-crowded island, in which every grade of human society, from lowest to highest, held for her its distinct representation. The two huge Iron Piers, jutting out into the surf and assailed by continual salty breezes, charmed her with their streams of coming and departing people, with their noonday lunchers, with their *table d'hôte* diners, seated over cigarettes or coffee in the sweet marine dusk. She loved West Brighton, with its beer-bibbers, its gaudy booths, its preposterous exhibited fat woman, its amazing Irish giant, its games of strength or skill, and its whirling *carrousels*, where delighted children span round on wooden horses, cows, lions, or dragons, to the clamors of a shameless brass band. But Brighton Beach, Manhattan Beach, and the Oriental each afforded a steadier satisfaction. The delicate and lightsome architecture of these three hotels, with their myriads of windows, their *chârlet*-like patterns of roof, gable, and chimney, and their noble outlooks upon the sea, grew dearer to her as the structures themselves became more familiar. She loved the fine sonorous music that pealed forth from the big deft-built pavilions, where troups of well-trained minstrels set many a brazen instrument to their capable lips, and would often find assembled thousands for their listeners, either in the long, salubrious afternoons, or in the breezy starlight and moonlight of those exquisite seaside evenings. Her observant eyes were never weary of watching, and they forever found something to watch. She soon acquired an extraordinary keenness in the matter of "placing" people at sight. Few points of manner, costume, or visage escaped her. She found herself classifying and arranging the vast crowds that she daily encountered. She became familiar with the faces of many who frequently disembarked from the loaded cars. Nor was her own face in turn unnoticed. Augmented health had freshened its tender tints, and lent to its lines a choicer symmetry. Many an eye dwelt upon her with admiration. Almost instinctively she had learned the art of disposing her black garments to dainty advantage, and of heightening their effect with little subdued touches of maidenly tastefulness.

Sophia's diversions increased with each fresh day. Many of the male devotees with whom she had romped during "sociables" of the previous winter, sought her in these new surroundings. Claire was compelled to acknowledge former introductions, and sometimes to assume a conversational attitude with the friends of her friend. But they all seemed to her alike; they all reminded her of Brady, though in a mercifully moderated way. She was invariably civil to them, though they wearied and tried her. They made her recall Thurston, whose remembered comments fleeted through her mind, while his grave, manly image appealed to it in retrospective vision. She was on the verge of a novel and important experience; but, of this unborn fact her longing for better companionship alone gave monition, and addressed her by the imaginative stimulus which we sometimes carelessly term presentiment.

One evening, as she joined Mrs. Bergemann and Sophia upon that portion of the hotel piazza which was usually set aside for its regular patrons, she found the two ladies in conversation with two gentlemen, of whom she knew only one, ranking him as not by any means the most ill-bred of Sophia's friends. He was a young man named Trask, of canary-colored eyebrows and a cloudy complexion, who had made himself a favorite with both sexes of his particular set through rousing no jealousies by superior personal and mental gifts, yet winning golden repute as one whose complaisant good - will would wince under nothing short of positive imposition. The second gentleman was presented to Claire as Mr. Hollister, and her look had scarcely lit on his face before she felt convinced that he was quite of another world from his companions. Even while he was seated she could see that he was tall and of shapely build. His head was small, and covered with glossy blond curls; his blond mustache fringed a lip of sensitive cut, though the smooth chin beneath it fell away a little, leaving his large, frank blue eyes, broad forehead, and well-formed nose to fail of implying the strength they would otherwise have easily told. He wore a suit of some thin, dark stuff that clung tightly about his athletic arms and chest, and contrasted with the light silken tie knotted at his wide, solid throat. Every detail of his dress was what Claire soon decided to be in the best fashion; she had already learned a good deal about the correct reigning mode in men's dress. The extraordinary nicety and com-

prehensiveness of her observation had made this one
of the sure results of her present sojourn.

She liked Mr. Hollister at sight, and she liked him
more after she had heard him speak. His voice was
full and rich, like the voice of a man used to the
shout that often goes with the out-door game; he
could not be more than five-and-twenty, at the most,
she decided; he seemed a trifle bashful, too, but
bashful with a virile grace that pleased her better,
in so robust and engaging a person, than the most
trained self-possession could have done.

Sophia had always felt a liking for the yellow-eye-
browed young gentleman; they were the firmest of
friends. The coming of Claire appeared to relieve
her from the responsibility of " entertaining " Mr.
Hollister, whom she had never met till this evening.
She soon drifted away arm-in-arm with her preferred
companion, among the dark throngs beyond the huge
bright-lit piazza. Mrs. Bergemann, perhaps from an
instinctive perception of how matters lay with Claire,
presently rose and sought the society of a matronly
friend, seated not many yards distant, whom she had
known in anterior Hoboken days, and who had
reached nearly as fat a prosperity as her own, from
possibly similar causes.

Claire was glad to be alone with her new acquaintance. He had roused her curiosity; she wanted to
find out about him, to account for him. Thus far
they had said the most impersonal and ordinary
things to each other. She remembered afterward
that they had used the old meteorological method
which has so often served as the plain, dull path into
fervent friendships or still warmer human relations;
they had talked of the weather.

" I 'm really surprised to hear that it has been so very hot in the city," Claire said, breaking the pause that followed Mrs. Bergemann's departure.

" Oh, it has been dreadful, I assure you," said Mr. Hollister. " Ninety in the shade at four o'clock."

" Why, we have had a lovely breeze here, all day, straight from the ocean," Claire resumed, with a pretty little proprietary wave of one hand seaward, as though she were commending the atmospheric virtues of her own special domain. " Once or twice I have felt actually chilly." He looked incredulous at this, then broke into a soft, bass laugh ; laughter was frequent with him, and made his blue eyes sparkle whenever it came.

" I 've forgotten how it feels to be chilly," he said. " I wonder if I could stand any chance of reviving the sensation down on the shore yonder."

He spoke the words in the manner of an invitation, and doubtless seeing prompt acquiescence in Claire's face, at once leaned forward to ask " Will you go ?" Claire straightway rose, answering " With pleasure." She took his offered arm, and thought while she did so how strong and firm it was, as if bronze or stone were beneath its flimsy vestment, instead of muscular mortality. The band in the illuminated pavilion near by had lately paused, but it now struck up a waltz rich in long mellow-pealing cadences. " Is this your first visit here ?" said Claire, as they descended the broad piazza steps, down toward the smooth, trim levels of grass and the massive, rounded beds of geranium, whose scarlets and greens now looked vague in the starlight. " Or have you been here many times before," she went on, " during past seasons, and so lost all your enthusiasm for this charming place ?"

"I've been here about six times in all," he answered, "but my enthusiasm is still in fine order.
It's ready to break forth at any minute. If you
want, Miss Twining, we can have a combined erup-
tion this evening."

Claire thought this clever; it had so fresh a sound
after the blunt fun she had long heard; it made her
think a little of the way Beverley Thurston phrased
his ideas, though any resemblance between the two
men could only exist for her in the large generic
sense that they were both gentlemen. She laughed,
with a note of real glee among the liquid trebles of
her mirth. It seemed to her that she had already
got to know Mr. Hollister quite well. And yet they
were still such strangers! She had still so much to
learn regarding him!

"I'm glad you've nothing to say against this delightful island," she declared, as if mildly jubilant
over the discovery. "I heard a man on the sands
talking about it to a friend only a few mornings ago.
He was a shabby man who wanted shaving, and I'm
not sure that he had on any collar. I think he must
have been a kind of philosopher. He said that
Coney Island was an immense fact. There is just
my opinion — that it is an immense fact." They
were now but a slight distance from the foamy, rolling plash of the dark sea-waves. The music came
to them in bursts of softer richness. With her arm
still in that of her companion, Claire half turned toward the hotel, starred with countless lights, and
looking, as it rose above the vague throngs beneath
it, like some palace of dreamy legend, lit for festival.

"I often think that this mere strip of sand must
be so surprised," she continued, "to find itself grown

13

suddenly important and famous after it has lain here lonely, almost unnoticed, for long centuries. I sometimes fancy that I can hear the waves talk to it as they break on its shore, and ask it what is meant by this wonderful change."

" That 's a very pretty way of looking at the matter," replied Hollister, while he gazed down into her face from his considerably taller height with a keener expression of interest and charm than he himself guessed. " Perhaps the waves congratulate Coney Island on its final success in life, and gently quote to it the old proverb about everything coming to those who know how to wait."

Claire started. " Do you believe that ? " she said. " *Does* everything come to those who know how to wait ? "

Hollister laughed again. " You talk as if *you* had been waiting. But I 'm sure it can't have been for very long."

This last sentence was put at least half in the form of a question. But she evaded it, saying with a light little toss of the head : " Has n't everybody always something to wait for, between youth and old age ? "

" Tell me something about your expectations, won't you ? " he asked, with the non-committal tenderness of a man whose acquaintanceship has been too brief for any serious depth to accompany his words. " You can't think how much I wish that I was one of them."

" One of my expectations? You ? "

" Decidedly."

" But how could I answer you on that point ? " she returned, letting him catch in the gloom a glimpse of her sly smile. " You 're only a name to

me. If you'll not think my candor rude, I have n't
an idea who you are."

"I don't believe I should think you rude if you
really were so," he said, smiling, and yet seeming to
mean with much quiet force each word that he
spoke. "So you want me to give an account of myself? Well, I'm a rather obscure fellow. That is,
I don't believe I know more than ten people in New
York at all well. I lead a quiet life; I'm what they
call a Wall Street man, but I mingle with the big
throng there only in a sort of business way. I was
graduated at Dartmouth two years ago, and spent a
year in Europe afterward. Then I came back, and
began hard work. There were reasons why I should
do so — I mean financial reasons. I'm not a New
Yorker; I was born and reared in Providence. Do
you know Providence?"

"No," said Claire. "I know only New York."

She was looking at him interestedly at short intervals; they had resumed their stroll again; her arm
was still within his; he had continued to please her,
though she felt no thrill of warm attraction toward
him, however mild in degree. She had a sense of
friendship, of easy familiarity. But apart from this,
she was conscious, as a woman sometimes not merely
will but must be, that she had won him to like her by
a very easy and rapid victory. Already she was not
sure but that she had won him to like her strongly
as well. Her few recent words of reply had carried
with them a subtle persuasion of which Hollister
himself was oddly and most pleasurably conscious.
He yielded to their effect, and became somewhat
more free in his personal confidences.

"My father had been a Dartmouth man," he went

on. " That was the reason of my going there. Father and Mother have both passed away, now. It 's a lovely old college, and it gained me some strong friendships. But I find that all my favorite classmates have drifted into other cities. They sometimes write to me, even yet, after my year in Europe. But, of course, the old good feeling will shortly cease . . . how can it fail to cease ? . . . I 'm a good deal alone, just now. I know a number of men there in Wall Street, but I feel a little afraid of making friends with them. I don't just know why, but I do. Perhaps it 's because of getting into bad habits. Some of them, I 've noticed have very bad habits. And I 've made up my mind . . . that is, I — I half promised my poor dear mother just before she . . . Well, Miss Twining, the plain truth is that I keep regular hours and live straight, as they say. I like to take a sail down here while the weather is hot, but I nearly always take it quite by myself. To-night I happened to meet Trask on the boat. I 'd nearly forgotten Trask. He was in my Freshman year with me, but he dropped off after that. It was he who introduced me to — to the Miss — excuse me, but I really forget your friend's name."

" Miss Bergemann," said Claire.

" Oh, yes — Miss Bergemann." He paused, at this point, gently forcing Claire to pause also. They were still beside the sea; the music still came to them in its modulated sweetness. Hollister bent his head quite low, looking straight down into her upturned face.

" I 've told you ever so much about myself," he said. " I wish, now, that you 'd give me a little knowledge also. Will you ? "

" About *my*self ? " asked Claire. "About just who I am ? "

" Well, yes, if you don't mind."

She reflected for a short space. Then she began to speak. She told him, as she went on, more than she had at first intended to tell. He listened intently while they slowly walked on, beside the dark, harmonious billows.

Before she had ended, he had realized that he was in love with her. He had never known anything of such love till now. His heart was fluttering in a new, wild way; he could scarcely find voice to answer her when she at length ceased to speak. But she had not told him all her past life. She had reserved certain facts. And her own feelings were entirely tranquil. Not the least responsive tremor disturbed her.

XII.

HOLLISTER nearly missed the last boat back to the city, that evening. His night was partially sleepless, and morning brought with it a mental preoccupation that was surely perilous to what tasks lay before him. Like most men who have escaped the stress of any important sentiment until the age of five-and-twenty, he was in excellent condition for just such a leveling seizure as that to which he had now made complete surrender. He was what we call a weak nature, judged by those small and ordinary affairs of life which so largely predominate in almost every human career. If some great event were ever fated to rouse within him an especial strength, this summons had not yet sounded, and he still remained, for those who had found cause to test the fibre of his general traits, a person in whom conciliating kindliness laid soft spell upon them all. His friends at college had been mostly of tough calibre, of unyielding will; he seemed unconsciously to have selected them in order that they might receive his concessions. But they were never encouraged in fostering the least contempt for him. The spark of his anger always leapt out with the true fire, prompt to resent any definite disrespect. Yet the anger sometimes cooled too quickly toward those whom he liked; there had been cases where he would waive his own claims to be indignant, with too humble a repentance of past heat. Necessarily such qualities made him popular, and this result was not lessened by the fact of his being almost rashly generous besides. His mental gifts had never been called powerful, but he had cut no sorry sort of figure as a student ; and he possessed an airy humor that seldom deserted for a long time either his language or thought.

During the week that followed his introduction to Claire, he visited the hotel where she was a guest on every evening but two. One of those evenings chanced to be fiercely rainy ; he could not have come to Coney Island without having his appearance there savor markedly of the ludicrous. The other evening was the last of the week. He had asked Claire to marry him the night before. She had not consented, neither had she refused : she had demurred. He was piqued by her hesitation, and affrighted by the thought of her possible coming refusal. He passed a night and a day of simple torture. Then, his suspense becoming insupportable, he appeared once more within her presence. His aspect shocked her ; a few hours had made him actually haggard. His hand trembled so when she placed her own within it that she feared the perturbation might be noticed by others besides herself, there on the crowded piazza where they met.

"I 've come to get your answer," he began, doggedly, under his breath. " You said last night that you were not sure if you — you cared enough for me. Have you found out, by this time, whether you do or no ? "

" There are two empty seats, yonder, near the railing of the piazza. Shall we sit there ? " She said this almost in a whisper.

"If you choose. But I — I'd rather be down on the sands. I'd rather listen to it there, whatever it is."

But Claire feigned not to hear him. It was her caprice to remain among the throng. She moved toward the empty seats that she had indicated, he following. In all such minor matters she had already become the one who dictated and he the one who acquiesced.

The night, lying beyond them, was cool but beautifully calm. An immature moon hung in the heavens, and tinged the smooth sea with vapory silver, so that its outward spaces took an unspeakable softness, as though Nature were putting the idea of infinity in her very tenderest terms.

There was no music to-night, for some reason. The buzz of voices all about them soon produced for each a sense of privacy in the midst of publicity.

"You asked me to be your wife last night," Claire began, looking at him steadily a little while after they were both seated, and not using any special moderation of tone because certain of her own vantage in the prompt detection of a would-be listener. "Before I give you any final answer to that request — which I, of course, feel to be a great honor — it is only just and fair that I should make you know one or two facts of my past life, hitherto left untold."

This was not the language of passion. Perhaps he saw but too plainly its entire lack of fervor. Yet it seemed to point toward future consent, and he felt his bosom swell with hope.

"If it is anything you would rather leave untold," he said, with a magnanimity not wholly born of his deep love, "I have not the least desire to learn it."

Claire shook her head. "You must know it," she
returned. "I prefer, I demand that you shall know
it."

He felt too choked for any answer to leave him.
If she imposed this condition, what was meant by its
sweet imperiousness except the happy future truce
for which he so strongly yearned? On some men
might have flashed the dread suspicion that her words
carried portent of an unpardonable fault, about to be
confessed there and then. But Hollister's love clad
its object in a sanctifying purity. Apart from this,
moreover, his mind could give none of that grim welcome which certain dark fears easily gain elsewhere.
The sun had long ago knit so many wholesome
gleams into his being that he had no morbid hospitality for the entertainment of shadows.

"I want to tell you of how my father died," Claire
went on, with her face so grave in every line that
it won a new, unwonted beauty from the change.
"And I want to tell you, also, of something that was
done to me after his death, and of something that I
myself did, not in personal revenge for my own sense
of injury, but with the desire to assert my great respect for his loved memory, and to deal justice where
I thought justice was deserved."

Then in somewhat faltering tones, because she had
deliberately pressed backward among recollections
so holy that she seemed to herself like one treading
on a place filled with sacred tombs, she recounted
the whole bitter story of her mother's avarice, of
her father's ignoble burial, and of her own resultant
flight. The tears stood in her eyes before she had
ended, though they did not fall. As her voice ceased
she saw that Hollister had grown very pale, and that

his brows met in a stern frown. At the same moment his lip trembled; and as he leaned forward, took her hand into his own, pressed it once, briefly but forcibly, and then released it, she caught within his gaze a light of profound and unmistakable sympathy.

" I think your mother's course was infamous," he said. " Did you suppose that I could possibly blame you for leaving her ? "

Claire had dropped her head, now, so that he could see only the white curve of her forehead beneath its floss of waved and gold-tinted hair. And she spoke so low that he could just hear her, and no more.

" Yes, I thought you might blame me. . . . I was not sure. . . . Or, if not this, I feared that the way in which poor Father was buried might . . . might make you feel as if I bore a stain — or at least that the disgrace of such a burial, and of having a mother who could commit so hard and bad an act, must reflect in shame upon myself."

If they had been alone together, Hollister would have answered this faint-voiced, hesitant speech by simply clasping Claire within his arms. But the place forbade any such fondly demonstrative course. He was forced to keep his glad impetuosity within conventional bounds; yet the glow on his face and the tremulous ardor of his tones betrayed how cogent a surge of feeling was threatening to sweep him, poor fellow, past all barriers of propriety.

As it was, he spoke some words which he afterward failed to remember. except in the sense that they were filled with fond, precipitate denial of all that Claire had said. He felt so dazed by the bliss that had rushed upon him as to fail, also, of recall-

ing just how he and Claire left the populous piazza,
and just how they reached the lonelier dusk of the
shore. But the waves brought him rare music as he
paced the sands a little later. His was the divine
intoxication that may drug the warder, memory, but
that wakes to no remorseful morrow. . . .

Claire wondered to herself when she was alone,
that night, at the suddenness of the whole rapid
event. She had given her pledge to become Herbert Hollister's wife in the autumn. While she
viewed her promise in every sort of light, it seemed
to her sensible, discreet, even creditable. He was a
gentleman, and she liked him very much. She had
no belief, no premonition that she would ever like
any one else better. She was far from telling herself
that she did not love him. We have heard her call
herself cold, and it had grown a fixed creed with her
that she was exempted by some difference of temperament from the usual throes and fervors. He
suited her admirably, in person, in disposition, in
manners. She need never be ashamed of him ; she
might indeed be well proud of so gallant and handsome a husband. Her influence over him was great ;
she could doubtless sway, even mould him, just as
she desired. And she would bear clearly in mind
those warning words of Beverley Thurston's : she
would use her power to good ends, though they
might be ambitious ones. From a worldly stand-
point, he was comfortably well off; his income was
several thousands a year ; he had told her so. With
his youth and energy he might gain much more.
She would stimulate, abet, encourage him toward the
accomplishment of this purpose. He should always
be glad of having chosen her. She would hold it

constantly to heart that he should find in her a guide, a help, a devoted friend. And he, on his side, should aid her to win the place that she coveted, loving her all the better because she had achieved it.

When these rather curious meditations had ceased, she fell into a placid sleep. She had been wholly un. conscious of the selfish pivot on which they turned. It had quite escaped her realization that they were singularly unsuited to the night of her betrothal. She had no conception of how little she was giving and how much she was demanding. She fell asleep with a perfectly good conscience, and a secret amused expectancy on the subject of Sophia's and Mrs. Bergemann's surprise when to-morrow should bring them the momentous tidings of her engagement.

But they were not so much surprised as she had anticipated. The attentions of Hollister had been brief, yet of telling earnestness. Sophia hugged her friend, and cried a little. "You mean old thing," she exclaimed, "to go and get engaged! Now, of course, you'll be getting married and leaving us."

"I'm afraid that's the natural consequence," said Claire, with a smile. Mrs. Bergemann pressed her to the portly bosom, and whispered confidentially, just after the kiss of congratulation: "He's a real ellergant gentleman. I think I know one when I see one, Claire. And don't you let Sophia set you against him. She better try and do half as well herself. *She'll* marry some adventuring pauper, if she ain't careful, I just do believe."

Claire felt a great inward amusement at the thought of Hollister being depreciated in her eyes by any light value which Sophia might set upon him. As it proved, however, Sophia soon learned to

forgive him for the engagement, and to treat him
very graciously. Before the summer had grown much
older Claire and her lover began to be pointed out by
the few other permanent boarders of the hotel, with
that interest which clings like a rosy nimbus about
the doings of all betrothed young people. They certainly made a very handsome couple, as they strolled
hither and thither. But Claire's interest, on her own
side, had been roused by certain little côteries that
would often group at one end of the monster piazza.
The ladies of these small assemblages were mostly
very refined-looking persons, and many of the gentlemen reminded her of Hollister, though their coats,
trousers, boots, and neck-ties not seldom bore an elab-
orated smartness unpossessed by his. They looked,
in current idiom, as though they had come out of
band-boxes, with their high, stiff collars, their silver-
topped walking sticks, and their general air of polite
indolence. The ladies, clad in lace-trimmed muslins
and wearing long gloves that reached above their elbows, would hold chats with their gallants under the
shade of big, cool-colored parasols. Claire was often
pierced by a sense of their remarkable exclusiveness
when she watched their dainty gatherings; and she
watched them with a good deal of covert concern.
Hollister could not even tell her any of the gentlemen's names. This caused her a sting of regret. She
wanted him to be at least important enough for that.
His ignorance argued him too unknown, too unnoted.
One day, to her surprise, Claire perceived Mrs. Arcu·
larius, her former august schoolmistress, seated amid
a group of this select description. Mrs. Arcularius
had lost none of her old majesty. It was still there,
and it was an older majesty, by many new gray hairs,

many acquired wrinkles. She was a stouter person,
but the stoutness did not impair her dignity; she bore
her flesh well.

Claire determined to address her. She waited the
chance, and carried out her project. Mrs. Arcularius
was just rising, with two or three other ladies, for
the purpose of going inside to luncheon, when Claire
decided to make the approach.

She looked very charming as she did so. Hollister
had brought her a bunch of roses the evening before,
and she had kept them fresh with good care until
now. They were fixed, at present, in the bosom of
her simple white muslin dress, and they became her
perfectly. She went quite close to Mrs. Arcularius,
and boldly held out her hand.

"I am very glad to meet you again," she said,
"and I hope you have not forgotten me."

Mrs. Arcularius took her hand. Under the circumstances she could not have done otherwise without
committing a harsh rudeness. And she was a woman
whose rudenesses were never harsh.

With her disengaged hand she put up a pair of
gold eye-glasses. "Oh, yes, surely yes," she said,
while softly dropping Claire's hand; "you were one
of my pupils?"

Claire did not like this at all. But she would not
have shown a trace of chagrin, just then, for a heavy
reward. She smiled, knowing how sweet her smile
was, and promptly answered:

"I'm sorry that you only remember me as one of
your pupils. I should like you to remember my
name also. Are you quite certain that it has escaped
you? Does not my face recall it?"

"Your face is a very pretty one, my dear," said

Mrs. Arcularius. She looked, while speaking, toward her recent companions, who were moving away, with light touches of their disarranged draperies and side-long glances at Claire. Her tones were impenetrably civil, but her wandering eye, and the slight averted turn of her large frame, made their civility bear the value, no less, of an impromptu veneer.

Claire divined all this, with rapid insight. Her wit began to work, in a sudden defensive way. She preserved her smile, looking straight at Mrs. Arcularius while she said, in a voice pitched so that the other ladies must of necessity hear it:

" I was so obscure a little girl among all the grand little girls who went to your school in my time, that I don't at all blame you for finding it inconvenient to recall me. I fear I have been mistaken in addressing you as the woman of business, my dear madam, when you find the great lady alone to your humor. But you have played both parts with so much success that perhaps you will pardon me for alluding to one at the expense of the other."

There was nothing pert in Claire's little speech. The few seconds that it took her to make it were epical in her life; they showed her the quality of her own powers to strike back with a sure aim and a calm nerve; she was trying those powers as we try the temper of a new blade.

She moved away at once, with tranquil grace, and not a hint of added color or disconcerted demeanor. It was really very well done, in the sense that we call things well done which depend upon their manner, their felicity, their *chic* of method. The ladies looked at each other and smiled, as though they would rather have kept their lips grave through politeness to Mrs.

Arcularius; and she, on her own side, did not smile at all, but revealed that disarray of manner which we can best express in the case of some large fluttered bird by noting its ruffled plumage.

Nothing in Claire's past had qualified her for this deft nicety of rebuke. Those stands made against her mother's coarse onsets had surely offered but a clumsy training-school for such delicate defiance. And yet her history has thus far been followed ill if what she said and did on a certain day in Mrs. Arcularius's school-room has not foreshadowed in some measure the line of her present action. Perhaps it was all purely instinctive, and there had been, back in the gentility of her father's ancestry, some dame of nimble repartee and impregnable self-possession, who had won antique repute as dangerous to bandy speech with.

But Claire's tranquillity soon fled. She was scarcely out of Mrs. Arcularius's sight before an angry agitation assailed her. When, a little later, she met Sophia in one of the halls, it was with sharp difficulty that she hid her distress.

Still, however, she did hide it, sure of no sympathy, in this quarter, of a sort that could help to heal her fresh wound. That evening, however, a little after the arrival of Hollister, and while they walked the sea-fronting lawns and listened to the distant band, as had now grown a nightly and accepted event with them, she narrated the whole circumstance of the morning.

"Do you think I did right, Herbert?" she finished, sure of his answer before it came.

"Perfectly, my darling," he said, looking down into her dim, uplifted face. "I would n't have had you do anything else. You must cut that old Gorgon if you ever meet her again. You must cut her dead, before she has a chance to serve the same trick on you."

"I don't know about that," returned Claire, as if his words had set her thoughts into a new groove. "Perhaps she may be of use to me afterward. I may need her if we ever meet in . . . society." She slightly paused before speaking the last word. "If she hasn't left by to-morrow I shan't see her, you know. I won't cut her; I simply shan't see her. It will be better."

Hollister laughed. What he would have disliked in another woman fascinated him in Claire. "You little ambitious vixen," he said, in his mellow undertone. "I suppose you will lead me a fine dance, after we are married. I suppose you will make me strain and struggle to put you high up, on the top rung of the ladder."

"I should like to be on the top rung of the ladder," said Claire, with that supreme frankness a woman sometimes employs when sure that the man who listens to her will clothe each word she speaks in an ideal halo.

At the same time, she had an honest impulse toward Hollister which should be recorded to her credit. She had not planned for him any thrilling discoveries of her worldliness after their marriage; she candidly saved him all peril of disappointment. But he, on the other hand, could see neither rock nor shoal ahead. If she pointed toward them, he looked only at the hand which pointed, and not at the object it so gracefully signaled.

She did not see Mrs. Arcularius again. That

14

lady's visit had doubtless been for a day only. The dainty groups still assembled, mornings and afternoons, just as before. Now and then she thought that some of their members — those who had witnessed the little scene with her former schoolmistress — gave her a look of placid attention which seemed to say: "There you are. We remember you. You are the young person who asserted yourself."

She wanted them to address her, to strike an acquaintance with her. But they never did. This piqued her, as they were all permanent residents at the hotel. She made no concealment of her wish to Hollister.

"It is too bad you do not know some of their male friends," she said. "If you did, I should get you to introduce them."

He fired a little at this, mildly jealous. "Do you really mean it?" he asked, with doleful reproach.

Claire did not understand his jealousy, at first; then it flashed upon her, through a sudden realization of his great fondness.

"Oh, I should merely like to know them for one reason," she said, laughing. "They would introduce me in turn, perhaps, to those charming looking ladies, who belong to another world. I like their world — that is, the little I have seen of it. I want to see more. I want to have them find out that I am quite suited to be one of them."

His jealousy was appeased. He softened in a moment. It was only her pretty little foible, after all — her delightfully droll longing to be ranked among the lofty aristocrats.

"I wish I did know some of the men you mean," he said, with apologetic concern, as though she had asked him for some gift which he could not manage to secure. " I think that I have seen two or three of them in Wall Street; but we have never met on speaking-terms."

More than once he pointed out to her a gentleman in the throng whom he did know, or told her the name of such an acquaintance, after transiently bowing to him. But Claire, with a fleet glance that was decisively critical, never expressed a desire to meet the individuals thus designated. Something in their mien or attire always displeased her. She dismissed them from her consciousness with the speed born of total indifference.

And now a most unforeseen thing happened. Mr. Trask, of the yellow eyebrows, had made repeated visits to Sophia, but Claire, because of the novel change in her own life, had failed to observe what to Mrs. Bergemann had become glaringly evident. One day, in the middle of August, Claire entered the latter's room, and found Sophia weeping and her mother briskly loquacious.

"I don't know what she's crying about, Claire," Mrs. Bergemann at once proceeded to explain, with an aggrieved look toward her tearful daughter. " She don't want to go with me home to Germany; I s'pose that's it. And there's my own flesh and blood, Katrina Hoffmann, who's written me a letter, and begged me in it to come and pay her a visit before she dies. And because I want to go across in September — after you're married, Claire, of course — Sophia behaves like a baby."

"Katrina Hoffmann!" now exclaimed Sophia, with plaintive contempt. "She's Ma's second-cousin, **Claire.** And what does Ma care about Germany?

She was a child of ten when she left it. I don't want to go, and I won't go, and there's all about it!"

But Sophia, for the first time in her life, had found a master in the mother who had so incessantly yielded to her least whim. The letter from Germany, as Claire soon discovered, was a mere pretext for flight. And Trask, of the yellow eyebrows, had caused this fugitive impulse in Mrs. Bergemann. She had learned about Trask; he was a clerk in an insurance company, on seven hundred a year. Sophia was the heiress of three millions. It would never do. All Mrs. Bergemann's rich fund of good nature shrank into arid disapproval of so one-sided a match. She developed a monstrous obstinacy. It was the old maternal instinct; she was protecting her young. They went to Germany in spite of all Sophia's lamentations. They went in the middle of September, and poor Trask was left to mourn his lost opportunities. Certain threats or entreaties, declaimed in private to Sophia by her affrighted parent, may have laid a veto upon the maiden's possible elopement. Or it may have been Trask's own timid fault that she did not fly with him. For she was very fond of Trask, and might have lent a thrilled ear to any ardent proposition from so beloved a source. But Trask had not a romantic soul; he accepted his fate with prosaic resignation. Moreover, his tendency to be obliging, to grant favors, to make himself of high value in an emergency, may have come forth in heroic brilliancy at the private request of Mrs. Bergemann herself.

Wherever the real truth of the matter may have lain, Mrs. Bergemann and Sophia, as a plain fact, went to Europe in September, leaving the bereaved

Trask behind them. But both, before their departure, were present at the marriage of Claire and Herbert Hollister.

It was a very quiet wedding. It occurred on an exceedingly hot day. Sophia and her mother were to sail the day after. They both gave effusive good-byes to Claire as she left the Fifth Avenue mansion in her traveling-dress at Hollister's side.

"I feel as if I should never, never see you again!" Sophia said, in a sort of pathetic gurgle, with both arms round Claire's neck.

It was indeed true that they never met again. Sophia afterward forgot Trask, and married in Europe. Her husband, as a few ill-spelled letters would from time to time inform Claire, was a Baron. Up to the period when these letters ceased, Sophia had repeatedly declared herself to be very happy. Claire occasionally wondered whether Mrs. Bergemann had approved of the Baron. But Mrs. Bergemann did not come back to tell, which, after all, seemed like a good omen.

On that sultry September day of their marriage, Claire and Hollister started for Niagara, where they remained but a brief while. They then returned to Manhattan Beach by mutual consent. The weather still remained very hot. It was what we call a late season.

They found at the hotel a moderate number of guests, who were waiting for the first sharp gust of autumn to make them scurry in droves from the seaside.

Hollister resumed his business. He went and came every day in the train or boat.

Claire did not feel at all like a bride. But she and her husband had talked together about their future, and she had the sense of a great, vital, prosperous change. She felt like a wife.

XIII.

A LONG chain of days followed, each in every way like the other. One steady yet lazy wind pulsed from the south; the skies were clad with an 'unaltering blue haze from dawn till dark, except that a rosy flush, like a kind of languid aurora, would steal into the full round of the horizon with each new sunset, and stay until evening had first empurpled it, then darkened it completely. Afterward the stars would come forth, golden, globular, and rayless, while the same unchanged southerly wind would get a damp sharpness that made at least a light wrap needful if one remained out of doors. The great piazza would be almost vacant an hour or so after nightfall, and the whole shore quite lonely. As regarded all after-dark visitors, the island had virtually closed its season. But Claire and Hollister haunted the piazza a good deal when the early autumnal darkness had emptied it of occupants. After they had dined he would light his cigar, and then select a certain hundred yards or so of the firm wooden flooring, over which they passed and repassed, arm-in-arm, more times than perhaps both their healthful young frames realized. The other guests of the hotel doubtless conjectured that they were saying all sorts of tender trifles to each other, according to the immemorial mode of those from whom the honeymoon has not

yet withdrawn her witching spells. But in reality
there was very little between them of what we term
lover-like discourse. Claire discouraged it in her husband, who obeyed the tacit mandate.

She was prosaic and practical on these occasions.
It amused and charmed Hollister to find her so. In
any guise that it chose to wear, her personality was
an enchantment. Claire planned just how they were
to live on their return to town, and he thought her
irresistible in this rôle of domestic anticipation.

" We shall have to find apartments," she told him.
" We cannot afford to rent a house of our own. But
apartments are very nice and respectable. They are
quite different from a boarding-house, you know. I
should be very sorry if we were compelled to board."

" So should I," declared Hollister. " Are you sure
that we have not enough to let us rent a small
house ? "

Claire's eyes glistened, as though the chance of
their income being made to stretch thus far suggested charming possibilities. But she soon gave a
sad shake of the head. " No," she decided. " We
should only find ourselves running into debt. We
had better take no rash risks. Your business is full
of them, as it is, Herbert. Besides, a year or two
may make the change easy for us."

She amazed him by the speed with which she
learned just how his affairs stood. Her quick mastery of facts that with most women baffle both memory and understanding, was no less rare than thorough. It had always been thus with her. Whatever
she wanted to comprehend became her mental possession after slight and brief effort. It was not long
before she read the price-list of stocks in the morning

papers with nearly as lucid a perception of just what it meant as Hollister himself. She made her husband explain as well as he could — and this was by no means ill, — both the theory and practice of Wall Street speculation. She soon began to know all his important investments, and talk of them with facile glibness.

Her control over Hollister daily strengthened. She would have swayed a man of much firmer will, and it is certain that he grew steadily more deferent to her judgment, her counsel, or even her caprices. The desire that she so plainly laid bare to him he had already estimated as a most right and natural development. In his eyes it was touched with no shade of selfishness; its egotism was to be readily enough condoned; one liked self-assertion in those whom nature had wrought of finer stature, from better clay. The queen pined for throne and sceptre; they were a debt owed her by the world; she could not help being born royal.

It irritated him that those people in the hotel whom she had expressed a wish to know, should not have sought her acquaintance and society. She must have struck them as a creature of great beauty and grace. Why had they not been won into paying her tribute? This was Hollister's fond way of putting the matter to his own thoughts. A few of these same people still remained. They formed a little clique among themselves; they, too, were waiting for the drowsy and torpid weather to wake up and send them townward. They saw Claire daily, almost hourly, and yet they never showed a sign of caring to do more than see her. Hollister secretly resented their indifference. His pride perhaps conspired with his love in making him bring Claire a fresh supply of flowers every evening, that she might wear them brilliantly knotted in the bosom of her dress. She remonstrated with him on the extravagance of this little devoted act, but for once he overruled her protest by a reference to the cheapness of flowers at that especial season. She always wore the flowers. Jutting forth in a rich mass from the delicate symmetry of her breast, they became her to perfection, as their lovely contact becomes all save the most ill-favored of women. She allowed Hollister to continue his pleasant, flattering gift. The mirror in her dressing-room was of generous proportions.

By day she liked to stroll the shore, or to sit with a book on one of the many benches, and watch, when not reading, the pale blue sweep of ocean, smooth as oil, and flecked with a few white-winged ships. Some of the sails were so faint and far away to the eye that they made her think of blossoms blown by a random breeze clear out into the misty offing. But now and then a boat would move past, hugging the shore, and wearing on its breadth of canvas huge black letters that advertised a soap, a washing powder or perhaps a quack medicine. The tender poetry in sky or sea gave these relentless merchantmen (if the term be not inapt) a most glaring oddity. But Claire did not wholly dislike, after all, the busy push of life and traffic which they so harshly indicated. If she had been less capable of understanding just how vulgar a note they struck, she might have disapproved of them more stoutly. As it was, she accepted their intrusion with full recognition of its ugliness, yet with a latent and peculiar sympathy. It reminded her of the vast mercantile city that lay so near — the city where her young husband was seeking to augment his gains, and by a process of slight essential difference.

But curiously in contrast with this feeling was Claire's mode of now and then speaking to the shabby people who frequented the shore, and repeatedly giving them alms when this or that woful story of want would meet her ears. Past experiences made her singularly keen in detecting all the sham tales of beggars. She had learned the real dialect of poverty, and her sense was quick to perceive any suspicious flaw in its melancholy syntax. More than once she would engage little dingy-clad children in converse, and nearly always a coin would be slipped into their hands at parting. But one day it happened that a child of smart gear, a little girl about five years old, came up to her side and began prattling on the subject of a sandy structure which the plump, tiny hands had just erected, a few yards away. The child had a fat, stupid face which was shaded by a big, costly-looking hat, along whose brim coiled a fashionable white plume. Every other detail of her dress implied wealthy parentage. Her little form exhaled a soft perfume, as of violets. She looked up into Claire's face with dull, unintelligent eyes, but with a droll assumption of intimacy, while chattering her fluent nonsense regarding the product of her recent sportive toil. Claire was not prepossessed, but at the same time she took the little creature's hand very socially, and listened to her brisk confidences with amiable heed.

But a French *bonne*, in a fluted cap, suddenly appeared upon the scene, and cut short the child's further overtures of friendship by drawing her away with swift force and a gust of voluble French reprimand. The child broke into peevish screams, and was at once lifted by the strong arms of the *bonne*, just as a lady abruptly joined them. The lady shook her forefinger at the child, while she was being borne away with passionate clamor.

"Tu as été très méchante," exclaimed the newcomer, remaining stationary, but following with a turn of the head and unrelaxed finger this tragic departure. "Nous avions peur que tu ne fus tombée dans la mer. Tais-toi, Louise, et sois bon enfant!"

Distance soon drowned the lamentations of little Louise, and the lady now addressed herself to Claire.

"I hope my bad little girl has n't been troubling you," she said. "It is really the nurse's fault that she strayed away in this wild style. Aline is horridly careless. I've already discharged her, and that makes her more so. Last week at Newport the poor child nearly fell over the cliffs because of that woman's outrageous neglect."

"Your little girl was in no danger here, I think," said Claire, smiling.

"Oh, no; of course not," returned the lady. She gave Claire a direct, scanning look, and then dropped upon the bench beside her. "Coney Island is very different from Newport. We had a cottage there all summer. Do you know Newport?"

"No," said Claire. "It is a very delightful place, is it not?"

"Well, yes," returned the lady, with a covert dissent in her admission. "It 's nice, but it 's awfully stiff."

"Do you mean ceremonious?" asked Claire.

"Yes. I got frightfully tired of it. I always do.

My husband likes it, and so I go on his account. I'd much rather go to Narragansett or Mount Desert. They're more like real country, don't you know? You have n't got to button your gloves all the time, and pose your parasol. You're not bothered with thinking whom you shall know and whom you shan't. You can let yourself loose. I love to let myself loose. But you can't do it in Newport. Everybody there is on a kind of high horse. Now I like to come down, once in a while, and ride a pony."

The lady gave a shrill, short laugh as she ended these words. Claire had already noted all her personal details. She was tall of figure and extremely slender. She had a sharp-cut face which would have gained by not being of so chill a pallor. Her black eyes were full of restless brilliancy; her lips were thin, and marked at their rims by a narrow bluish line. She carried herself with an air of importance, but her manner was very far from the least supercilious display. She promptly impressed you as a woman whose general definition was a democratic one, though aristocracy might also be among her minor meanings. She had no claims to beauty; she was too meagre in point of flesh, too severe in general contour, too acute in her angles. She lacked all the charm of feminine curves; she was a living conspiracy of straight lines. You could not closely observe her without remarking the saliency of her joints; she seemed put together on a plan of cruel keenness. At the same time, her motions were not awkward; she managed her rectilinear body with a surprising ease and pliancy. Her health appeared excellent, notwithstanding her slim frame and chalky color. The warmth, speed, and geniality of her speech, evidently springing from high animal spirits, no doubt enforced this inference.

Claire felt not a little puzzled by her, and had an immediate wish to find out just who she was. On the afternoon of yesterday she had once or twice joined the patrician group and had chatted with this or that member of it, apparently on the most familiar terms. Claire already knew, having thus observed her, that she was a recent arrival. But past experiences made it seem quite probable that she was merely a tolerated nobody. 'Would she join me like this and address me so affably,' Claire asked herself, 'if she were some one of real note?'

At the same time, any trace of such self-depreciation was far enough from showing itself in Claire's spoken answer.

"Everything is tiresome, I suppose," she said, "if there is too great a supply of it. For my own part I think that I like the conventionalities, as they are called. I haven't seen enough of them in my life to be wearied by them. I have known what poverty is in other years, and now, when I contrast it with the little ceremonies and forms that accompany prosperity, I find myself rather glad that these exist."

Her companion looked surprised for a moment. She put her thin face rather close to Claire's. The candor of the latter was a novelty. Claire had used it with a somewhat subtle intent. Her feet had told her that it was best frankly to count herself outside of the social pale behind which she more than suspected that this garrulous matron belonged.

"Oh, so you've been poor?" came the somewhat rambling response. "But of course you're not so now, or you wouldn't speak of it. Poverty must be

so perfectly awful. I mean when one is born different from the people who . . . well, don't you know,
the people who live in tenement-houses, and all that."
The speaker here paused, while arranging the long
mousquetaire gloves that reached in baggy wrinkles
far up either sharp arm. "Well," she suddenly re-
commenced, "I dare say I ought to care more for
style and form and fashion. I was brought up right
in the midst of it. All my relations are perfectly
devoted to it. They look on me as a kind of black
sheep, don't you know? They say I'm always going into the highways and hedges to pick up my
friends. But I don't mind them: I laugh at them.
They're here now in full force. There are two of
the Hackensacks and two of the Van Corlears, and
two of the Van Kortlandts — all cousins of mine,
more or less removed. I was a Van Kortlandt before
I married. I'm Mrs. Manhattan Diggs now, and I
have been for five years. The best of the joke is
that my husband, whom I perfectly dote on, by the
way, and who's the dearest in all Christendom, dis-
approves of me as much as my relations do. The
other day he called me a Red Republican, because I
said society in New York was all trash. So it *is*
trash. It's money, money, and nothing else. When
he makes me dreadfully mad I throw his name at
him. *Diggs*, you know. Isn't it frightful? His
mother was a Manhattan — one of the real old stock,
and she married a man of that name — an English-
man with a fortune. If he hadn't been rich I'd
have pitied my poor husband. He'd never have
made a dollar. I tell him that all he can do is to sit
in the club-window, and drive, and bet, and play
cards. But he's just as lovely to me as he can be,

so I don't mind. I worship him, and he worships me, so we get on splendidly together, of course. . . . And now I've told you my name, you must tell me yours. I hope it's prettier than mine. It ought to be, you're so immensely pretty yourself."

"My name is Mrs. Hollister," said Claire. "Mrs. Herbert Hollister. I have been married only a few weeks."

"A bride! Really? How delightful! Do you actually mean it? I dote on brides. I'm sure we shall be friends."

They rapidly became so. Claire was by no means averse to the arrangement. Mrs. Diggs was violent, explosive, precipitate, but she was not vulgar. Besides, her roots, so to speak, were in the soil that Claire liked. They lunched together that day at one of the little tables in the vast, airy dining-room. While they were seated at the meal, several of the elegant ladies passed on their way toward other tables. Mrs. Diggs nodded to each of them familiarly, and her nods were distinctly returned. Claire took special note of this latter point.

"Your relations will think you have deserted them," she said.

Mrs. Diggs laughed. "They think I'm always deserting them," she exclaimed. "I don't believe my absence is a great affliction; they manage to endure it. . . . Oh, by the way, here comes Cousin Cornelia Van Horn. She must have arrived to-day. Excuse me for a moment. I'll have to go and speak to her."

Mrs. Diggs hastily rose and went toward a lady who was herself in act of crossing the room, but who paused on seeing her approach. The meeting took place not far from where Claire was seated. She saw Mrs. Diggs give her kinswoman a kiss on each cheek like the quick peck of a bird. They were cheeks that time had faded a little, but the face to which they belonged had a haughty loveliness all its own. At least five-and-thirty years had rounded her figure into soft exuberance, mellowing but scarcely marring its past harmonies. She was very blonde; her eyebrows, each a perfect arch, and the plenteous hair worn in a dry, crisp matwork low over her white forehead, were just saved from too pale a flaxen by the least yellow tinge. Her features were cut like those of a cameo, but they were too small and too near together for positive beauty, while her eyelids had too deep a droop, and her nose, by nature lifted too high at the extreme tip, lost nothing of the pride, even the arrogance it bespoke, from the exquisite poise of her head above a long throat and sloping shoulders. Claire decided that she had never seen a woman so stately and yet so lightsome, or one who could so clearly suggest the serenity and repose of great self-esteem without thrusting its offensive scorn into harsh evidence.

Mrs. Diggs remained with her new companion several minutes. Her severe back, in all its rather trying outlines, was presented to Claire during this interval, though once she slightly turned, making a little gesture with her bony hand that seemed to indicate either the table she had just quitted or the figure still seated there. And soon afterward Claire saw that the person whom she had heard named by Mrs. Diggs was looking steadily at her with a pair of cold, light-blue eyes. While she returned this look it struck her that a change of color touched the

15

placid face of her observer, though the flush from faint pink into pink only by a shade less dim might easily have passed for a trick of deceptive fancy.

Mrs. Diggs presently came trotting back to the table, with her odd combination of graceful movement and bodily sharpness.

"My dear Mrs. Hollister," she began, while seating herself, "do you know that Cousin Cornelia knows all about you? I happened to mention your name before you were married — Miss Twining, was n't it?"

"Yes," replied Claire.

"Well, the name seemed to strike her, and she at once asked if you had not stayed quite a long time with Mrs. . . . Mrs. . . . Oh, you mentioned her when you spoke of being here several weeks before your marriage."

"Mrs. Bergemann," said Claire, and immediately added, in tones full of quiet interest: "Well, Mrs. Diggs?"

"Why, that was what *placed* you, don't you know, with Cousin Cornelia. Yes, Mrs. Bergemann; that was the name."

"Did your cousin know Mrs. Bergemann?" inquired Claire.

"She did n't say so. But she appeared to know just who *you* were. I think she 's going to make me present you. There seems to be some queer mystery. She acted rather strangely. Are you sure you 've never met before?"

"Yes, I am perfectly sure," answered Claire. "Did you not say that the lady's name was Van Horn?"

"Cousin Cornelia's? Why, yes; of course it is.

She's my second cousin. She's related on the Van Kortlandt side. She was a Miss Thurston."

"Thurston," repeated Claire, not interrogatively, but as though she had caught the sound with recognition the instant it left the speaker's lips. She broke into a smile, now. "That explains everything. She is a sister of Mr. Beverley Thurston, is she not?"

"Cousin Beverley? Of course she is. Do you know *him?*"

"Oh, yes," said Claire. "I knew him very well."

"Why, you don't tell me so!" blithely exclaimed Mrs. Diggs. "I dote on Beverley. I suppose he thinks me dreadful, but I dote on him, just the same. He is so broad, don't you know? He's seen so much, and read so much, and lived so much, generally. And with it all he's so conventional. That is the way I like conventionality — when you find it in some one who makes it a sort of fatigue-dress for liberal views, and not the uniform of narrow ones."

"I approve your description of Mr. Thurston," said Claire, slowly. "It tells me how well you know him."

Mrs. Diggs creased her forehead in puzzled style, and bent her face closer toward Claire's. "What on earth do you suppose it was that made him dart off so suddenly to Europe?" she asked.

Claire stooped, as though to discover some kind of objectionable speck in the cup of chocolate that she was stirring, and then removed what she had found, with much apparent care. "He did go quite unexpectedly, did he not?" she said, lowering her head still more as she put the speck on her saucer and examined it with an excellent counterfeit of the way

we regard such things when uncertain if their origin
be animal or vegetable. She wondered to herself, at
the same time, whether Mrs. Diggs would notice her
increased color, or whether she herself had merely
imagined that her color had undergone any sort of
change. "At some other time," she went on, letting
the words loiter in utterance, with a very neat simu-
lation of preoccupied attention . . . "at some other
time, Mrs. Diggs, I should like to talk more with you
about Mrs. Van Horn's brother. But just now I
want to ask you about Mrs. Van Horn herself."

Here Claire briskly raised her head. The problem
of the aggressive speck had seemingly been solved.
"I have heard Mr. Thurston mention that he had
a sister of that name," she continued, now speaking
with speed, "but he told me almost nothing regarding her. She appears to be a very important person."

Mrs. Diggs glanced toward a distant table at which
she had already seen her cousin seat herself. Then
she turned to Claire again, as though confident of
how safely remote was the lady whom she at once
proceeded to discuss.

"Cornelia *is* a very important person, Mrs. Hollister. As I told you, she's my second cousin. I
used to see a good deal of her before I was married. She's at least ten years older than I am. She
brought me out into society. I was an orphan, don't
you know, and there was nobody else to bring me
out. I *had* to be brought out, for I was eighteen,
and all the rest of the family were either in mourning, or were too old, or else had gone to Europe, or
. . . well, something of that sort. So Cornelia gave
me a great ball. It was splendidly civil of her. But

I don't think she did it from the least benevolence.
No, not at all. She had ended her term of widow-
hood, and wanted to *appear* again, don't you know?
The ball was magnificent, and it gathered all her old
clientèle about her. I remember it so well; it is
only eight years ago. I stood at her side, behind a
towering burden of bouquets which it made my wrist
ache to hold. Cornelia was in white satin, with
knots of violets all over her dress. I shall never
forget that dress. She wore amethysts round her
throat, and in her hair, and on her arms. It was a
kind of jubilant second-mourning, don't you know?
She looked superb; she was eight years younger
than she is now. People gathered about her and
paid their court. She resumed old acquaintances;
she received open or whispered compliments; she
was the event of the evening. *I* was nearly ignored.
And yet it was *my* ball; it had been given for me,
to celebrate my *début* in society. But as the evening progressed I began to discover that I had been
made a mere pretext. Cornelia herself was the real
reason of the ball. She had simply used me as an
excuse for reëmerging. She reëmerged, by the way,
with seventy thousand a year, and a reputation for
having been one of the reigning belles of New York
before she married Winthrop Van Horn. She was
poor when she married Winthrop, and he lived only
a few years afterward. He left her every penny of
his money; there were no children. Cornelia was a
devoted wife; at least, I never heard it contradicted,
and I've somehow always accepted it. I think
everybody has always accepted it, too. He died of
consumption in Bermuda, and it is usually taken for
granted, don't you know, that he died in Cornelia's

arms. For my part, I can't imagine anybody dying
in Cornelia's arms. . . . But that's neither here nor
there. She kept herself as quiet as a mouse for five
years. But mice are nomadic, and they gnaw everything. And Cornelia, during those five years of
bereaved woe, to my certain knowledge, took a peep
at every capital in Europe. After the ball — the
ball that she gave *me*, please understand — she became a great leader. She's a great leader still.
Did n't Beverley tell you *that*, Mrs. Hollister?"

"No," stated Claire, keenly interested by this nimble monologue. "As I said, Mr. Thurston scarcely
did more than mention his sister's name."

Mrs. Diggs applied herself actively to a fragment
of cold chicken, which she had left neglected through
all these elucidating items. Claire watched her,
thinking how clever she was and yet how uncircum-
spect. With what slight incentive had been roused
this actual whirlwind of family confidences!

"She perfectly adores Beverley," Mrs. Diggs presently continued. "I have an idea that she does so
because he's a Thurston — or rather because *she's*
one. She has contrived to make it appear very exceptional to be a Thurston. The Thurstons have never
been anything whatever. Her mother married into
the family, and cast a spell of aristocracy over them.
But Cornelia never alludes to the Van Kortlandt connection. She knows that can take care of itself. I
believe her grandfather, on the other side, was a saddler. But she has managed to have it seriously dis-
puted whether he was a saddler or a landed Knicker-
bocker grandee. The panels of her carriage bear a
Thurston crest. It is a very pretty one; I am quite
sure she invented it. I once told Beverley so, and

he laughed. *He* has never used it, though he has never denounced it as spurious. The joke is that she ignores the Van Horn crest entirely, which is the only one she has any right to air. Cornelia is a great leader, as I said. She has Thursday evenings in the big old house on Washington Square which her late husband left her. Lots of people have struggled to go to Cornelia's Thursdays, and not gone, after all. It's absolutely funny to observe what a vogue she has got. She could make anybody whom she chose to take up a social somebody by merely lifting her finger. But she never lifts her finger. That is why she is so run after. You can't get her to use the power she possesses. It yearly grows more of a power, don't you know, on this very account. It's like a big deposit in a bank, that gets bigger through lying there untouched. She won't spend a penny; she lets it grow. The women of New York are becoming a good deal less flippant, some of them, than they used to be. Clubs and receptions have come into fashion, where intellectual matters are seriously, even capably discussed. Somebody will read a paper on something sensible and literary, and a little debate will follow. At one of these clubs — composed strictly of women — it is forbidden to mention the last ball, though this may have occurred on the preceding night and everybody may have seen everybody else there, talking the usual gay nonsense. The whole thing is a kind of 'movement,' don't you know? It's very picturesque and it's extremely in earnest. It makes one think a little of the old historical French *salons*. It has laid bare some charming and surprising discoveries. It has shown how many women have been reading and

thinking in secret, during those long intervals of
leisure that have occurred between their opportunities for being publicly silly, inane, flirtatious, and
hence of correct form. On the other hand it has led
certain women to cultivate their minds as they would
a new style of dressing their hair. All that we used
to satirize in former entertainments of this kind fails
to exist in those I am describing. Pipe-stem curls
and blue spectacles are replaced by the most Parisian
felicities of costume. A delightful-looking creature
in a Worth dress that fits her like a glove will give
us her 'views' on the Irish land-question or the
persecution of the Jews in Russia. . . . And now I
come to the real object of my digression, as the long-
winded orators say. Cornelia Van Horn frowns upon
all this. She has gathered about her a little faction,
too, which frowns obediently in her defense. You
must not fancy for a moment that Cornelia could not
shine in these assemblies if she chose to favor them.
She has brains enough to *outshine* nearly all their
supporters. But she condemns the intellectual tendency in women when thus openly exhibited. If
they want to read and think, they should do it in
the quiet of their closets, and in the same way that
they write their letters, or glance over their accounts,
or distribute their household orders. There is no objection to philosophy, science, belles-lettres, so long
as these are not made to interfere with the general
dignified commonplace of the higher social life. To
be individual, argumentative, reformatory, is to be
professional. To be professional is not to be 'good
form.' The moment that a drawing-room is made
to resemble a lecture-room or a seminary it becomes
odious from a patrician stand-point. Only queens

and duchesses can afford to paint pictures or to write books, without loss of caste. A consistent aristocracy never discovers new ideas; it accepts old ones. Agitators are the enemies of repose, and repose is the soul of refinement."

Here Mrs. Diggs gave a gleeful trill of laughter that made Claire compare it to her mind as well as her person; it was so clear and sharp. " Oh, you can't imagine," she went on, " how radical Cornelia is in her positively feudal conservatisms. I'm so liberal, don't you know, that I can appreciate her narrowness. I relish it as one does a delicious joke. But it's a very curious sort of bigotry. There's nothing in the least spontaneous about it. I've a conviction that she sweeps her eye more widely over this fine Nineteenth Century than any of the ladies I've been telling you about. She has seen that she can only reign on one kind of a throne, and she sticks there. And I assure you, there isn't the least doubt that she reigns in good earnest. . . . I'm surprised that Beverley Thurston didn't tell you about her. Beverley has got her measure so exactly. He thinks me dreadful, as I said, but he's fond of me. I'm sure we always amuse each other."

" No," said Claire, shaking her head slowly, " he was very reticent on that subject. Perhaps he thought I might want to know her if he painted her portrait as you have done. That would have been awkward for him, provided his sister had declined my acquaintance. And I dare say she would have declined it, as I was not in her exclusive circle."

Mrs. Diggs put her head a little on one side. She was looking at Claire intently. A smile played like a faint flicker of light on her thin lips, whose two bluish lines always kept the same tinge.

"Why are you so candid with me?" she asked.

"Candid?" repeated Claire.

"Yes. Why do you show me that you would like to know Cornelia Van Horn?"

"Why?" still repeated Claire. "Did I show you that?"

"Not openly — not in so many words, don't you know? But I imagine it."

"You are very quick at imagining," said Claire, with a little playful toss of the head. "Well, if you choose, I *should* like to know her. I should like to know any one who ranks herself high, like that, and has a recognized claim. I have a fellow-feeling for ambitious people. I'm ambitious myself."

Mrs. Diggs seemed deeply amused. She lifted a forefinger, and shook it at Claire.

"I'm afraid you're *very* ambitious," she said.

"Well, I am," admitted Claire, not knowing how much rosy and dimpled charm her face had got while she spoke the words. "I am quite willing to concede that I have aims, projects, intentions."

Mrs. Diggs threw back her head, and laughed noisily. But she lowered her voice to a key much graver than her laugh, as she said: —

"You're as clever as Cornelia, in your way. Yes, you are. I shouldn't be surprised if you were a good deal cleverer, too. I suspect there's a nice stock of discreet reserve under your candor."

Claire creased her brows in a slightly piqued manner. "That is not very pleasant to hear," she said.

Mrs. Diggs stretched out her hand across the table so pointedly and cordially that Claire felt forced to take it.

"I like you. You interest me. Forgive me if I've annoyed you."

"You haven't annoyed me," was Claire's reply.

"I want to see those aims, projects, intentions," Mrs. Diggs continued, still holding her hand, and warmly pressing it besides. "Yes, I want to see you *exploiter* them — carry them out. You shall do it, if I can help you. And you will *let* me help you, I hope? You won't think me disagreeably patronizing, will you? I only speak in this way because I 've taken a desperate fancy to you."

"Thanks," said Claire. Her eyes were sparkling; her heart was beating quickly.

XIV.

WHEN Hollister returned that evening, almost the first words that Claire spoke to him were: "Congratulate me, Herbert. I have taken a fine forward step at last."

"What do you mean, my dear?"

"I have got to know somebody of importance. I have launched my ship."

"Oho," laughed Hollister, understanding. "I hope the ship will prove seaworthy, little captain. You must steer with a prudent eye, remember. All sorts of squalls will lie in wait for your canvas, no matter how well you trim it."

"That is just the kind of sailing I like," said Claire. "I've been becalmed long enough."

He laughed at this, in his hearty way, as though it were quite a marvel of wit. "Come and tell me," he proposed, "about the important somebody who has been sensible enough to discover you."

They were alone together, in their wide, cheerful apartment, overlooking the ocean. They were about to go down and dine, and Hollister had just finished a few preparatory details of toilet. Lights had been lit, for the rapid autumn dusk had already thickened into nightfall; but though they could not see the starlit level of waters just beyond their windows, they had a sense of its nearness in the moist, salty breeze, whose tender rush made the drawn shades bulge, and set the loose lawn curtains fluttering buoyantly.

Hollister sank into a chair as he spoke the last sentence, and at the same time put an arm about his wife's waist, drawing her downward until she rested upon his knee. The roses at her bosom brushed his face, and he thrust his head forward with a sigh of comic infatuation, as though rapturously inhaling their perfume. But his free hand soon wandered up along the chestnut ripples of her hair, and he began to smooth them, with a touch creditably dainty for his heavy masculine fingers.

Claire permitted his caresses. She always permitted, and never returned them. He had slight sense that this was a coldly unreciprocal course; it appeared to fit in neatly enough with the general plan of creation that she should receive homage of any sort without further response than its mute recognition. That was the way he had constantly known her to act, or rather not to act; a change would have surprised, perhaps even shocked him; she would have ceased to be his peculiar, accustomed Claire; his revered statue would have lost her pedestal, and he had grown to like the pedestal for no wiser reason than that he had always seen it enthrone her.

"I will tell you all about my discoverer," Claire said, with matter-of-fact directness; and she at once began a swift and succinct little narration.

"Diggs," Hollister suddenly broke in, with one of his fresh laughs. "Oh, look here, now; you've made some big mistake. She can't be one of your adored swells, with such a name. It's—it's . . . cacophonous, positively!"

"Wait, if you please," said Claire, with demure toleration, as though a bulwark of proof made this skeptic assault endurable. "Her husband's name, in the first place, is not *simply* Diggs; it's *Manhattan Diggs.*" She made this announcement with an air of tranquil triumph; but Hollister at once gave another irreverent laugh.

"Oh, of course!" he cried. "I remember, now. I know him. That is, I nod to him on the street, now and then. Is *he* here? Why, he's nearly always tipsy, you know."

"Tipsy!" repeated Claire, rising with an incredulous look. "Oh, Herbert, you must be mistaken. She worships him. She says that he treats her charmingly, and that they get on together with perfect accord."

"It would be rather strange to find two of that name even in such a great place as New York," said Hollister, with a slight shrug of the shoulders. "I don't believe I am mistaken a bit, Claire. He's a tall man, with fat yellow side-whiskers and a face as red as your roses. He's got a lot of money, I'm told. He goes down into the street, and dawdles an hour or so a day at his broker's. But I've never seen him thoroughly sober yet. Upon my word, I haven't."

Claire soon met the husband of Mrs. Diggs. It was after dinner, in one of the spacious, modern-appointed sitting-rooms, now so often half-vacant of occupants, or sometimes wholly vacant, through these lengthened September evenings.

"I want to present my husband," said Mrs. Diggs, preceding a tall man with fat yellow side-whiskers, whom Hollister had before this recognized across the dining-room as his own particular, chronically tipsy Mr. Diggs, beyond all possibility of mistake.

Claire had a little chat with Mr. Diggs, while Hollister, who had claimed acquaintance and shaken hands with him, seated himself at the side of his volatile spouse.

Claire soon became bored. Mr. Diggs was plainly tipsy; Herbert had been right. But he was most uninterestingly tipsy. He had sense enough remaining to conduct himself with a sort of haphazard propriety. He incessantly stroked either one or the other whisker, and kept up a perpetual covert struggle not to appear incoherent. He was at times considerably incoherent; a few of his sentences made the nominative seem as if it were swaggering toward its verb. But he was vastly polite. He told Claire that his wife had fallen in love with her. A little later, however, he spoke of his wife with a certain jolly disparagement.

"Kate is full of a lot of new things. I don't know what I'm going to do with her — really, I don't. She'll be a regular free-thinker before I know it. And I don't like free-thinkers; I think they're a sad lot. Now, don't you?"

Claire gave short, evasive answers to these and a number of similar appeals. Mr. Diggs distressed her; he was not at all the sort of person whom she desired to meet. She soon made herself so intentionally *distraite* that he rose and told her he was going to smoke a cigar, which he would bring into the sitting-room after he had obtained it, provided she did not object. She professed herself wholly sympathetic with this arrangement, and tried not to let her lip curl as she watched the unsteady pace of its proposer across the long sitting-room.

But he had scarcely retired before Mrs. Diggs broke off her converse with Hollister and exclaimed to Claire : —

" Where on earth has dear Manhattan gone ? You don't mean that he has left you ? How shameful of him ! "

" I believe he has gone to get a cigar," Claire said.

" Oh, a cigar," retorted Mrs. Diggs. " Yes, poor Manhattan is an inveterate smoker." She now looked at Hollister and Claire equally, with quick, alternate movements of the head. " I feel sure that tobacco is beginning to injure him, though it is really a very small kind of vice, don't you know ? It saves a man from other worse ones. Manhattan, dear boy, smokes a good deal, and I suppose I should be grateful it 's only that. I hear such dreadful tales from my friends about their husbands *drinking*. I don't know what I should do if dear Manhattan *drank*. I 'm so glad he does n't. If he did, I — well, I actually believe I should get a divorce ! "

Claire felt that her husband's eye, full of merry furtive twinkles, had fixed itself upon her all through this unexpected speech. But she kept her face from the least mirthful betrayal. Mr. Diggs did not come back with his cigar.

Claire now wondered, as she watched her new friend, and entered into conversation with her, whether this unconsciousness of her husband's continual excesses could be real and not feigned. It was hard to suppose that so much shrewd observation and so cunning a recognition of human foibles and follies could by any chance consort with the obtuse lack of perception which her late comments had implied. And yet Claire somehow became conscious that Mrs. Diggs had really meant it all. The anomaly was hard to credit; it was one of those absurd contradictions with which human nature often loves to bewilder us; and yet its element of preposterous self-delusion held at least the merit of being genuine.

Claire had reached a distinct conclusion to this effect, when Mrs. Van Horn, entering the room, paused and looked all about her. There were several other groups scattered here and there, but the lady presently fixed her gaze upon that small one of which Mrs. Diggs was a unit. And very soon afterward she began to move in the direction of her cousin.

Mrs. Diggs was so seated that she could plainly note the approach. She half-turned toward Claire, and said in rapid undertone, seeming only to speak with the extreme edges of her lips : —

"Can I actually trust my senses ? Is it fact or hallucination ? Cornelia is coming this way. I told you she wanted to know you, but I didn't dream that she would condescend to seek anybody, like this, short of a queen, or, at the lowest, a duchess. . . . Yes, here she comes ; there's no mistake."

Mrs. Diggs quitted her chair, a little later. She took a few steps toward her cousin, meeting her. Hollister also rose ; Claire, naturally, did not rise.

"I want to present Mrs. Hollister," said Mrs. Diggs, after a few seconds of low-toned converse with the new-comer. "My cousin, Mrs. Van Horn," she at once added, completing the introduction. It was then Claire's turn to rise also, which she did.

"I think you know my brother," said Mrs. Van

16

Horn to Claire, when all were again seated. "I mean Mr. Beverley Thurston."

"Oh, yes," said Claire.

Her monosyllables were quite intentional. She had not liked the lady's manner. There had been a remote, superb chill about it. She was distinctly conscious of being descended to, as though from an invisible stair. The nearer view that she had gained of Beverley Thurston's sister made her sensible of a new and original personality. Mrs. Van Horn was so blonde, so superfine, so rarely and choicely feminine. Her warmth was so faint and her coolness so moderated. She was like a rose that had in some way blent itself with an icicle, the shape of the flower remaining, and its flush taking a hue that had the tint of life yet the pallor of frost.

Claire determined not to speak again unless Mrs. Van Horn addressed her. This event soon occurred. Hollister and Mrs. Diggs had fallen into conversation. Mrs. Van Horn surveyed them, with her nose a little in the air, and her eyelids a little drooped. She seemed on the point of interrupting their talk, and of ignoring Claire, who had leaned back with a nice semblance of entire unconcern. In a few moments, however, this mode of treatment underwent change.

"I have heard my brother speak of you," she said, fixing her light-blue eyes full on Claire's face. "It was before you were married, I think."

"Yes," replied Claire. "We were very good friends. I missed him after he had gone."

"He went suddenly," said Mrs. Van Horn.

"Very suddenly," responded Claire, with a smile as complaisant as it was inscrutable.

Mrs. Van Horn looked downward; she appeared to be examining one or two of her rings ; they were not numerous, though each of them had an odd individuality of prettiness. " There seemed to be no good reason why he should go," she soon said, lifting her eyes again. " He has been there so often."

" I should think it would be hard to go too often," said Claire.

" You have been, then ? "

" No. But I wish to go very much. . . . Not yet, however."

" Not yet ? " repeated the lady. Claire could not accuse her of staring, in any downright way, but she had an impression that every least detail of her own dress or person was receiving the most critical regard. " I suppose your husband's affairs detain him here, for the present."

" Yes," returned Claire, but at the same time she shook her head negatively. " It isn't that, however. I mean it would not be only that. There is something for me to see, to know, to do, here. I haven't finished with my own country yet," she proceeded, giving a bright smile. " I am not yet ready for Europe."

Mrs. Van Horn laughed. But it was not a laugh with any amusement in it, neither was it one that contained any irony. " My brother thought you very clever," she said. " He told me so repeatedly."

" That was kind of him," Claire answered. She did not decide that Mrs. Van Horn was patronizing her; she decided, on the contrary, that the sister of Thurston was trying to make her disinclination to patronize most plainly apparent. " It is pleasant to hear that he thinks well of me," Claire went on.

"He is a man whose good opinion I shall always highly value."

Mrs. Van Horn leaned forward. She was smiling, now, but it struck Claire that her smile was at best a chilly artifice. "You did not show much regard for his good opinion in one instance," she said, lowering her voice so that Claire just caught it, and no more. "I mean when he asked you to marry him. You see, I know all about that. He told me. It sent him to Europe."

This was, of course, a bombshell to Claire. But even while the color was getting up into her cheeks with no weak flood, she realized that it had been meant for a bombshell, and made swift resolve that its explosion should not deal death to her self-command.

"I am sorry that he told you," she rather promptly managed to say. "I have kept it a secret from everybody. I thought he would do the same."

"Oh, he has no secrets from me," returned Mrs. Van Horn, with what seemed to Claire an extraordinary brightness of tone. The speaker immediately drew out a little jeweled watch and looked at the hour. "It is later than I thought," she now said. "I have two letters to write; I must be going upstairs. Pray come and see me, Mrs. Hollister, when you are back in town," she continued, while putting her watch away again, and calling Claire by her name for the first time since they had met. "Mrs. Diggs will tell you my address. Promise me that you will not forget to come. I leave rather early to-morrow, and may not have a chance of repeating my request." Here she rose and put out her hand. Claire took it, but said nothing. She had lost her self-command, after all; she was almost too embarrassed to utter a word. Mrs. Van Horn had nearly gained one of the doors of the great room before Claire realized what had taken place. A certain splendor of courtesy enveloped the whole departure. It was admirably conducted, notwithstanding its abruptness. It was one of the things that Mrs. Van Horn always did surprisingly well; she could enter or retire from a room with an effect quite her own in its supple graciousness and dignity. But Claire soon felt that both the graciousness and dignity had something mystic about them. It was somehow as if an oracle had pronounced something very oracular indeed. The civility of the invitation had been so totally unforeseen, and it had followed with so keen a suddenness the recent bewildering revelation, that Claire did not know how to explain the whole proceeding, to construe it, to read between its lines.

Hollister, who had received a brief, polite bow of adieu, and risen as he returned it, broke the ensuing silence.

"Did n't she go away quite in a hurry?" he asked. "I hope you have n't offended her," he added, jocosely, to his wife.

"Cornelia did n't look a bit offended," said Mrs. Diggs, regarding Claire, or rather her continued blush. "But that means nothing. You did n't quarrel, now, did you, Mrs. Hollister?"

"Oh, no," said Claire, still dazed and demoralized. "She asked me to visit her in town; she was very urgent that I should do so."

"You don't really tell me such a thing!" exclaimed Mrs. Diggs. "You 've no idea how prodigious an honor she was conferring. It's like decorating you with the order of St. Something — actually it is."

"I 'm afraid I failed to value it in that way," replied Claire, who was recovering herself.

"Of course you did. You have n't yet taken in the full enormity of Cornelia's importance. You can't do it until you see her surrounded by her own proper atmosphere — with her foot on her native heath, so to speak. Then you 'll understand the massive condecension of to-night."

"I think *I* would just as lief not understand it," laughed Hollister, with his characteristic play of gentle humor. "It does n't repay you to climb these *very* big mountains. Everybody says that there 's very little to see after you 've got to the tops of them."

Mrs. Diggs echoed his laugh. She was looking at Claire, however, with her bright, black, restless eyes. "I think your wife may want to climb," she said. "I 'll be her guide, if she 'll let me. There 's a very good view from the summit of cousin Cornelia. You can look down on a lot of smaller peaks."

Claire shook her head. She had got her natural color again, but not her natural manner; she spoke in a tone of preoccupied seriousness that did not harmonize with her light words.

"I should n't like to fall down one of her glaciers and be lost," she said.

"Oh, there 's no fear of that," cried Mrs. Diggs. "You 're too sure-footed."

Somewhat later that evening, when they were alone together, Hollister asked his wife:

"Did that Mrs. Van Horn say anything that hurt you, Claire?"

"Oh, no. What made you think so, Herbert?"

"I . . . Well, perhaps I only fancied it. . . . You had known her brother, had n't you?"

"Yes. He was a good deal at the Bergemanns' last Spring. He went to Europe afterward. I suppose that was why she wanted to know me better."

Claire said this with a fine composure. She was standing before her dressing-table, disengaging the roses from her breast. Hollister stole up behind her and clasped her in his arms, setting his face close beside hers, and looking with a full smile at their twin reflection, which the mirror now gave to both.

"So you've got among the great people at last, little struggler," he said; "you've begun to be a great person yourself." He kissed her on the temple, still keeping his arms about her. " I suppose you'll make quick work of it now. I'm glad, for your sake —you know I am! You're bound to succeed. I shall be awfully proud of you."

This seemed quite in the proper order of things to Claire. Her husband's approval was a matter-of-course; it was like the roses he gave her every day —like the kiss, the embrace, the loving devotion that had each grown accepted synonyms of Herbert himself. She forgot the words and the caress with careless promptitude. But she did not forget what Mrs. Van Horn had said to her, downstairs in the great sitting-room. Her sleep that night was perturbed by the memory of it. "Does that woman like me, or does she hate me?" repeatedly passed through her mind, in the intervals between sleeping and waking. " Does she feel that she owes me a grudge, and long to pay it? Is she angry that I refused her brother? How strange it would be if I should find myself face to face with some hard, bitter enmity just at the threshold of the new life I want to live."

But the bright morning dissipated these brooding

fears. It was a very bright morning, and an unexpectedly cold one. The sea sparkled with the vivid
brilliance of real autumn as Claire looked at it from
her window on rising, and every trace of its former
lazy mist had left the silvery crystal blue of the over-
arching sky. A sharp barometric change had occurred during the night. Claire and Hollister effected
their toilets with numb fingers and not a few audible
shivers. The flimsy architecture of the huge hotel,
reared to court coolness rather than to resist cold,
had suddenly become an abode of agnish discomfort.

Its occupants fled, that day, in startled scores.
Mrs. Diggs was among the earlier departures. She
bade farewell to Claire, wrapped in a formidably
wintry mantle. Her leave-taking was warm enough,
though her teeth almost seemed to chatter while she
gave it. Her husband was at her side, looking as
though the altered weather had incited him to even
a more bacchanal disregard of his complexion than
usual. The chubby-cheeked little girl, her French
bonne, and the maid of Mrs. Diggs, were also near at
hand. They were all five on the piazza, where Hollister and Claire had also gone, both careless, in their
youthful health and vigor, of the rushing ocean wind
that blew out into straight lines every shred of raiment that it could seize. Little Louise was whimpering and contumacious; she wanted to break away
from Aline, and pulled against the latter's tense
clasp of her hand as if the wind and she were in
some hoydenish, fly-away plot together. An admon-
itory stroke of bells had just sounded from the near
dépôt; the train would soon glide off from the big
wooden platform beyond. Mrs. Diggs was in a
flurry, like the weather; her great wrap could not

warm her; she looked more chalky of hue than ever, and the bluish line at her lips had grown purplish. But a defective circulation had not chilled her spirits; she was alive with her wonted vivacity.

She had caught Claire's hand, while turning at very brief intervals toward Aline and the child. Her sentences had become spasmodic, polyglot, and parenthetical; they were half addressed to Claire and half to the recalcitrant Louise.

"Now you *won't* forget just where you're to find me, will you, my dear Mrs. Hollister? . . . *Sois bonne fille, Louise; nous allons à New York toute de suite.* . . . I want so much to see you as soon as you can manage to come. Did you ever know anything like this dreadful gale? I'm so cold that I believe it will take a good month to warm me. . . . *Tais-toi, chérie, tu vas à New York, où il ne fait pas froid du tout.* . . . You're going this afternoon, you say? I don't see how you can wait. There's cousin Jane Van Corlear just going inside — I promised to go along with her. Say good-by, Manhattan; the cold weather has made you as red as a turkey-cock, hasn't it, dear boy? . . . *Aline, prenez garde! Elle est bien méchante, elle veut d'être absollument perdue.* . . . Well, good-by, both of you. I do hope you won't freeze before you get off!"

When the Diggs family had disappeared, Claire and her husband went and finished their packing. That afternoon they left the deserted hotel, reaching New York at about dusk. They had themselves driven to the Everett House; Hollister had occasionally lodged there in bachelor days, and proposed it as a temporary place of sojourn.

It proved less temporary than they had expected.

Apartments were easy and yet hard to procure. A good many sumptuous suites, in haughty and handsome buildings, were offered them at depressing prices. They found other suites, in buildings far less grand, which pleased them less and suited their purse better, but still left a certain margin as regarded proposed rental expenditure. Five or six days were consumed in these monotonous modes of search. They could obtain lodgment that was too dear, and lodgment that was too cheap; but they could not hit the golden mean of adaptability which would combine delectable quarters with moderate rates.

"It is tiresome work," Claire at length said, "and it is keeping you from your business, Herbert, in a most shameful way. I really don't see what we are to do."

"The apartments in West Thirty-Sixth Street, that we saw yesterday," ventured Hollister, genially, "were rather nice, though small, of course."

"Quite too small," affirmed Claire. "Besides, the house itself had a dingy air. It looked so — so economical, Herbert. We don't want to look economical; we want only to *be* it."

Hollister made a blithe grimace. "I am afraid that to be it and to look it are inseparable," he said. "The grain of the rind tells the quality of the fruit." He put his head a little sideways and glanced at his wife with a quizzical eye. "Now, in the way of downright bargains, Claire," he went on, "there is that nice basement house which is for rent entire in Twenty-Eighth Street. The one we drifted into by mistake during our wanderings of yesterday, you remember."

"I'd rather not think of it," said Claire, with a

sort of musing demureness. "I liked it very much. I don't believe there is a furnished house to rent in the whole city that could be had for the same terms. But you know very well that we could not afford to take it, with the need of at least three servants, apart from other expenses."

"True," said Hollister. "That is, unless I get along better — make a hit on the street, you know."

"Oh, well," said Claire, "there is no use in depending upon chance. Of course," she added, slowly, with a grave, affirmative motion of the head, "I should like very much to have the house. You know I should."

"Then, we'll rent it," Hollister struck in, swiftly and with fervor. "It won't be much of a risk, but we'll take what risk there is. The first quarter's rent would be absolutely sure, Claire. Are you agreed?"

He spoke entirely from his loving perception of how much she would like to reign as the ruler of her own establishment. It thrilled him to think of her in this proper, sovereign sort of character.

"It will not be right, Herbert," Claire said. "We made up our minds to spend just so much and no more." . . .

But her tones lacked all imperative disapproval. Perhaps she was thinking how pleasant it would be for Mrs. Diggs to find her handsomely installed as the mistress of her own private dwelling.

On the following day Hollister rented the little basement house in Twenty-Eighth Street. Claire accompanied him while he did so. She was frightened when the terms asked were finally accepted. She was still more frightened when she thought of the steady, draining expenses which must follow. But, after all, her alarm only acted as a sort of undercurrent. Above it was the large, delightful satisfaction of foreseeing herself the reigning head of a distinct establishment. It was an extremely pretty house, no less outside than inside. The occupation by its new tenants had been arranged as immediate, and this notable event soon occurred. Claire went herself to hire the three servants. She found a great supply at a certain dépôt for this sort of demand. She engaged three whom she liked the most, or rather disliked the least. And very soon she and her husband quitted their hotel for good. They became the co-proprietors of the basement house in Twenty-Eighth Street.

Certain new tasks occupied Claire. She quickly performed them. Her administrative faculty now showed itself in clear and striking relief. Her penurious past had taught her unforgotten lessons; she went into her new place with none of a neophyte's unskilled rawness; her fund of domestic, of managerial experience was like an unused yet efficient well; she had only to give a turn of the hand and up came the buckets, moistly and practically laden. True, she worked under the most altered conditions; she was no longer a drudge but a supervisor; and yet the very grimness of that early apprenticeship had held in it a radical value of instruction. She who had known of the prices paid for inferior household goods, could use her knowledge now to fine profit in the purchase of better ones. Having swept with her own toil floors that were clad coarsely, she could in readier way discern uncleanly neglect on the part of underlings who swept floors clad with velvet.

Her responsibility was borne with great lightness. "I think I am a sort of natural housekeeper," she soon told her husband. "It all comes very easy. I find that my daily leisure is increasing at a rapid rate." She directed with so much system, discipline, and keen-sightedness, that speed was a natural result. Her detection of negligence and fraud was prompt and thorough. She discouraged the least familiarity in her servants. On this point she was severely sensitive; she maintained her dignity in all intercourse with them, and sometimes it was a dignity so positive and accentuated that it blent with her personal beauty in giving the effect of a picturesque sternness. The secret of its exercise lay wholly in her former life. She had once been socially low enough for these very employees to have treated her as an equal. All that was dead and in its grave. She wanted to keep it there forever. Instinctively she stamped down the sods, and even held a vigilant foot upon them.

She was soon prepared to seek out Mrs. Diggs and pay her a long, intimate visit. She found her new friend in a small but charming home. The drawing-room into which she was shown displayed a great deal of good taste, and yet it had not a touch of needless grandeur. Its least detail, from the cushion of a sofa to the panel of a screen, suggested permanent and sensible usage. It was a room that shocked you with no inelegance, while it invited you by a sort of generally sympathetic upholstery and appointment.

Mrs. Diggs was delighted to hear of the new Twenty-Eighth Street residence. She took Claire's gloved hand in both of her slim, bony ones, and proffered the most effusive congratulations.

"It's so much nicer, don't you know, to be a real *châtelaine*, like that — to have your own four domiciliary walls, and not live in a honeycomb fashion, like a bee in its cell, with Heaven knows how many other bees buzzing all about you. I'm inexpressibly glad you've done it. Now you are *lancée*, don't you know? You can entertain people. And I'm sure, my dear, that you do want to entertain people."

Claire gave a pretty little trill of a laugh. "I have no people to entertain, yet," she said.

Mrs. Diggs was still holding her hand. "Oh, you sly mouse!" she exclaimed. "You've got great ideas in your head for the coming winter. Don't tell me you haven't. Remember our talks at Coney Island. And you're going straight for the big game. You're not of the sort that will be content with a small, low place. Not you! You want a large and a high one. It's going to be a great fight. Now, don't say it isn't. I know all about you. I dote on you, and I know all about you. You intend to try and be a leader. You've got it in you to be one, too. I believe you'll succeed — I do, honestly! I'll put my money on you, as that dear Manhattan of mine would say of a horse. . . . You're not annoyed at me?"

"Not at all," smiled Claire. "But everything must have a beginning, you know. And I have no beginning, as yet. I have only met yourself and " . . . She paused, then, looking a little serious.

Here Mrs. Diggs dropped Claire's hand, and burst into a loud, hilarious laugh. Her mirth quite convulsed her for several seconds.

"Cornelia Van Horn!" she presently shouted in a riotously gleeful way. "Myself and Cornelia Van

Horn! That is what you mean. Is n't it, now?
Is n't it?"

She was looking at Claire with both hands in her
lap and her angular body bent oddly forward. She
gave the idea of a humorous human interrogation-
mark.

"Well, yes," said Claire, soberly, and a little offendedly; "I do mean that. Pray what is there so
funny about it?"

Mrs. Diggs again became convulsed with laughter: "Funny!" she at length managed to say.
"Why, it's magnificent! It's delicious! You 're
going to tilt against Cornelia! Of course you are!
You don't know a soul yet; you 're quite obscure;
but you have a sublime self-confidence. That is always the armor-bearer of genius; it carries the spear
and shield of the conqueror. My dear, I always
wanted to have somebody beard Cornelia in her den,
don't you know, like the Douglas! I 'm with you
—don't forget that! I 'll help you all I can. And
when you 've shaken the pillars of New York society
to their foundations, please be grateful and recollect
that I set you up to it."

She threw back her head and laughed again, in her
boisterous, vehement, but never ill-bred way.

Claire sat and watched her. She was not even
smiling now; she was biting her lip. She had con-
cluded, some time ago, that she understood Mrs.
Diggs perfectly. But she did not know, at present,
in what spirit to take this noisy paroxysm. Was it
sincere, amiable amusement, or was it pitiless and
impudent mockery?

XV.

BUT Claire's doubts were soon settled. If that visit did not precisely end them, a few succeeding days forever laid the ghost of her spleen. Mrs. Diggs had been jocundly candid, and that was all. No baleful sarcasms had pulsed beneath her vivacious prophecies. She soon convinced Claire that she was a stanch and loyal confederate.

She often dropped into the Twenty-Eighth Street house, and praised its appointments warmly. "Your little reception-room is perfect," she told Claire, "with those dark crimson walls and that furniture so covered with big pink roses. I like it immensely, don't you know? I wouldn't have liked it two or three years ago; I would have thought crimson and pink a weird discord; but fashion gives certain things their stamp; it makes us wake up, some morning, and find our hates turned to loves." About the dining-room, on the same floor, and the drawing-room, on the floor above, she was genially critical. This or that detail she discovered to be "not just quite right, don't you know?" and Claire in nearly all such cases changed dissent into agreement after a little serious reflection. Some of the resultant alterations involved decided expense. This Claire regretted while she would let her husband incur it. Hollister always did so readily enough. Wall Street

had rather smiled upon him, of late. A few of his
ventures had become bolder, but flattering successes
had persistently followed them.

" The theatre is all lit," he said to her one evening,
" but the curtain does n't rise. How is that, Claire? "

She knew perfectly well what he meant, but chose
to feign that she did not know. They had been
surveying together a few decorative improvements,
recently wrought, in mantel, dado, or even table-
cover.

" I don't think I follow your metaphor," said
Claire. There was the tiny outbreak of a smile at
each corner of her mouth. It struck Hollister, who
was standing quite near her, that she looked delightfully prim. He kissed her before he answered, and
then, while he did so, let his lips almost graze her
ear, saying in an absurd guttural semitone, as of
melo-dramatic confidence : —

" I mean that it 's time for Act First. Time for
the lords and ladies to enter, with a grand flourish of
trumpets. Of course, when they do come, they 'll
all kiss the hand of their charming hostess, just like
this."

But she would not let him kiss her hand, though
he caught it and made the attempt.

" There are no lords and ladies in New York," she
said, laughing and receding from him at the same
time. " And if they *should* come, they would never
behave in such an old-fashioned style as that."

But though she treated them lightly, his words fed
the fuel of her deep, keen longing. She had made
up her mind that Mrs. Diggs had been right. She
would never be content to take a low place. Nothing save the highest of all would ever satisfy her.

17

At the same time she clearly understood that great sums of money were needed to accomplish any such end. She spent several days of brooding trouble. She had not great sums of money — or rather, Hollister had not. And there seemed slight chance of her husband ever securing them.

"The season is dreadfully young yet," said Mrs. Diggs to her, the next day, while they sat together. "There is simply nothing going on. There are no teas, no receptions, and, of course, no balls. But we 'll go and take our drive in the Park. Do hurry and dress."

Claire dressed, but not very quickly. She kept Mrs. Diggs waiting at least fifteen minutes. Mrs. Diggs's carriage was also waiting. It was not at all like its owner, this carriage. It was burly and somewhat cumbrous. The silver-harnessed horses that drew it had clipped tails and huge auburn bodies. But the wheels of the vehicle were touched here and there with a tasteful dash of scarlet, as if in pretty chromatic tribute to the violent complexion of "dear Manhattan." When they were being rolled side by side together in this easy-cushioned carriage, Mrs. Diggs said to Claire : —

"You kept me waiting a little eternity. I hate to wait. I suppose it 's because I 'm so nervous. I 've been to three or four different doctors about my nervousness. They nearly all say it 's a kind of dyspepsia. But that seems to me so ridiculous. Dyspepsia means indigestion, and I can digest a pair of tongs — no matter at what hour I should eat it. My dear Claire" (she had got to use this familiar address, of late), "I don't see how you can get on without a maid. That is why you 're so slow with your bonnet and wraps; be sure it is. Oh, a maid is a wonderful comfort."

"So is a carriage like this," said Claire, smiling.

"Yes, a carriage is indispensable, too. At least I find it so. You will also, my dear, when you come to pay visits among a large circle of friends."

"I'm afraid that both the maid and the carriage will be out of my reach for a very long time yet," said Claire. "Our taking the house, you know, was a great act of extravagance."

"Oh, your husband is doing finely in Wall Street. I have heard from Manhattan about his brilliant strokes. Manhattan thinks him intensely clever. His success is creating a good deal of talk, I assure you."

This was true. Hollister would now often laugh and say: "The luck seems to be all on my side, Claire. And I don't take any very fearful risks, either, somehow. The money isn't coming in by hundreds, at present; it is coming in by thousands. I'm getting to be a rather important fellow; upon my word, I am. My own dawning prominence amuses me considerably. But it isn't turning my head the least in the world. A lot of the big men down there are taking me up. A month ago they scarcely knew if I existed."

Then he and Claire would talk together of the real speculative reasons for his success; he would find that she had forgotten hardly an item of past information; her judgments and decisions were sometimes so shrewd that they startled him, considering how purely they were based upon theory and hearsay. Once or twice he permitted her counsels to sway him, though not with her secured sanction. The result turned out notably well. He told her what he had done, and why he had done it, after the triumph had been achieved. She was by no means flattered on discovering the faith he had reposed in her. She even went so far as to markedly chide him for having reposed it.

"Remember, Herbert," she said, "that I am of necessity ignorant regarding these matters, in every practical sense. All my opinions are quite without the value of experience. Please never take me for your guide again. Never sell nor buy a single share because I venture the expression of an idea on sales or purchases. I am proud and glad to think myself the cause of your having made a lucky operation; that, of course, I need not tell you. But I should not forgive myself for ever leading you into disaster."

She reflected, secretly: 'How weak Herbert is! He is no doubt clear and quick of mind, and he is of just the light-hearted, easy temperament that has what he himself calls "nerve on the Street." But how weak he is in his trust of *me!* Does not that show him weak in other ways? Would a man of strong nature let his fondness ever so betray his prudence? I must be guarded hereafter in my talks with him. I really know nothing; I only use his knowledge to build upon. What he is doing is three quarters mere hazard, and the rest cleverness. I see plainly that he has begun a very precarious career. He may win in it; others have won. He may win enormously; I am just beginning to accept his chances of doing so. But there must be no balking and thwarting on my part. He would ruin himself, most probably, if I proposed it. He is so weak where I am concerned! Yes, in all such ways he is so weak!'

She could not dwell upon the fact of this weakness with any tender feeling. She had grown to accept his love as something so natural and ordinary that she could coldly survey as a flaw any point in its devotion which verged upon indiscreet excess. Just at this period in her life it sometimes struck her that she was very cold toward her husband. But no pang of conscience accompanied the realization. She had disguised nothing from Herbert. He knew precisely what she wished to do. He even sympathized with her aim, and desired to abet it. She could not help being cold. Besides, he had never offered the faintest objection to her coldness. He evidently wanted her to be just as she was. And moreover, she was no different at this hour, when the possibility of a great social victory assumed definite outlines — when she was his wife and the mistress of his household — when she was sure of sharing his fortunes until death should end further companionship — than she had been at the hour when he had first asked her to marry him. She had a great sense of duty toward him. She meant to leave no obligation of wifely fealty unfulfilled. And this determination, flinchlessly kept, must stand for him in place of passion. She had no passion to give him. She had given all that to her dear dead father. If he were alive, now, and dwelling with her, what joy she would have in putting her arms about his neck, her lips to his cheek, and telling him how the hopes whose seed he had sown long ago might soon ripen into splendid fruit!

"You tell me that you have new adherents, new friends," she soon said to her husband. "If any of them are people of prominence — of the sort I would wish to know — why do you not ask them here, to our house ? "

" True enough," said Hollister. " That is an idea." And then, with beaming hesitation, he added : " But I thought you would not want them without their wives."

Claire seemed to meditate, for a slight time. " I should not want them without their wives," she presently said, " unless I felt sure that their wives were the kind of women whom I would be very willing to have among my acquaintances."

A few days later Hollister announced to Claire that he had arranged a dinner at which some four gentlemen besides himself were to be present. He had placed the whole affair in the hands of a noted *restaurateur*, who assured him that it should be conducted on the most admirable plan.

" It was intended as a little surprise for you," he said. " The men are all of the kind that I am nearly sure you will approve. I mean they are what is called " in society." You see, I am getting quite wise with regard to these matters. A few weeks have made a world of difference with me. I am waking up to a sense of who is who. Before, it was all stupid treadmill sort of work. I cared very little about associates, connections, influence. I wanted to make both ends meet, and found the process a rather dull one. Now I am in a wholly different frame of mind. I am beginning to amuse myself as much by the study of men as by the study of stocks. I have several distinct adherents, several more distinct supporters, and one or two would-be patrons. I don't think I was ever unpopular on the Street ; I was simply unimportant. But now that I 'm important I have got to be quite popular. . . . I dare say the whole thing is attributable to yourself, Claire. You've pricked me into life. I was torpid till I met and knew you."

She was considerably alarmed about the plan of the dinner-party. She was not at all sure if it would ' be in good style for Hollister to give it with herself as the only lady present. As soon as circumstances permitted, she hastened to consult with Mrs. Diggs.

"Oh, it's all right," decided the oracle. "You are always certain of being correct form if you do anything like that in company with your husband. But, my dear Claire, it is too bad that you could n't find three more ladies besides yourself and me. You see, I invite myself provisionally, so to speak. Is n't it dreadful of me? But then I take such an interest in you that I want to be present, don't you know, at the laying of your corner-stone. Manhattan ought to be asked, too, dear fellow; it's etiquette, don't you know? But then you need not mind, this once."

"I wish that I knew three more ladies," said Claire, thoughtfully.

"Yes . . . that would make a dinner of just ten. A dinner of ten is so charming. Mr. Hollister would n't object, would he?"

Claire quickly shook her head. "Oh," she said, "Herbert never objects."

It was so seriously spoken that Mrs. Diggs broke into one of her most mutinous laughs. "How delicious!" she exclaimed. "What a superb conjugal truth you condense in one demure little epigram! . . . Well, if 'Herbert,' as you say, 'never objects,' there is . . . let me see . . . there is Cornelia Van Horn."

"Would she come if I asked her?" said Claire.

"You have n't asked her, so of course you don't know. Nobody can ever predicate anything about Cornelia. But considering how grand was her amiability at Coney Island, I should say that . . . Well, yes, I should say that Cornelia *would* come." Here Mrs. Diggs raised one thin finger, and shook it in smiling admonition. "That is," she added, "if you call on her, as she requested."

Claire looked grave. "I will call on her," she at length said. "I have not felt sure whether I would or no. I did not like her way of asking me, or her manner beforehand. . . . But I will call on her, provided there are two other ladies." Here she paused a moment, and then proceeded with decision. "But of course there are no other two ladies. At least, not yet."

Mrs. Diggs's eyes were sparkling most humorously. "I don't know why it is," she exclaimed, "that you always entertain me so when you talk of Cousin Cornelia. There 's a latent pugnaciousness in the very way that you mention her name. It seems to be fated that you and she shall become dire foes. She 's so big and mighty that I 'm always reminded, when you discuss her, of dauntless little David, with his sling and stone, marching against the doughty old giant. . . . As for our *one* other lady, Claire, how about Mrs. Arcularius?"

"Mrs. Arcularius? Why, we have quarreled."

"Nonsense. You snubbed her mildly. I don't doubt that she will come. Women at her time of life have survived nearly every sentiment except that of appetite. Ten to one that she will scent the odor of a good dinner, and come, as your dear former instructress, and all that, don't you know?"

"Very well," said Claire, with gravity; "I might ask her. But then there would be the fifth lady. I am afraid that she is not to be found."

Mrs. Diggs put one slim hand to one pale temple, and drooped her bright eyes. "I have it!" she presently exclaimed. "There is my other cousin, Jane Van Corlear. We won't ask Jane until we are sure of the others. Then we shall be certain of getting her to fill the vacant place. You remember her at Coney Island, don't you? No? Well, in a certain sense nobody ever remembers poor Jane, and nobody ever forgets her. She has been a widow for years, like Cornelia. But she never asserts herself. She is tallowy, obese, complaisant. She rarely goes anywhere, and yet she leaves a sort of aristocratic trail wherever she has been. She will accept if I tell her to; she always gives in to me, though in her sluggish way I know she thinks me objectionable. Poor Jane is a perfect goose, and yet I dote on her. She is such a dear, consistent, inoffensive, companionable goose, don't you know? Claire, your dinner-party is entirely arranged."

"I am afraid not," said Claire, dubiously.

The next day she and Mrs. Diggs concocted the invitations together. On the day following, the two ladies whom they had asked each sent a courteous, conventional refusal.

Mrs. Van Horn gave no reason for her refusal. Mrs. Arcularius mentioned a previous engagement as the reason of her non-acceptance.

"You see," said Claire, to her fallacious counselor, "our ladies are not obtainable, after all."

She was secretly chagrined; but Mrs. Diggs showed herself openly so. "It is too bad!" declared the latter. "I 've a lurking belief in the authenticity of Mrs. Arcularius's 'previous engagement.' As for Cornelia, I suspect pique at your not having been to visit her. But we shall see what we shall see, regarding Mrs. Van Horn. Of course our little dinner is ruined. You must preside as the only woman, Claire, and I don't doubt you will do it charmingly. But I shall drop in upon Cornelia to-morrow, and try to sound the unfathomable."

Mrs. Diggs did so, and on the afternoon of the same day she sought out Claire, filled with her recent exploring skirmish.

"She received me, my dear Claire, with a great deal of high-nosed graciousness. I had n't been three minutes in her presence before I felt that her cold, serene eyes were reading me through and through. She mentioned you herself; she made it a point to do so. She spoke of you as that pretty young woman whom Beverley used to know. Then she recollected that you had asked her to dinner. 'But of course I could not accept,' she said, with her best sort of ducal look. 'I do not really *know* your friend. I have met her only once, and then for a few minutes.' She wanted to change the conversation, after that; she has vast tact in the way of changing conversations; great leaders like herself always have. But I would n't put up with that at all. I am usually a good deal awed by Cornelia. But I made up my mind not to be awed to-day at any hazard. I reminded her that she had sought to know you and asked you to visit her. I showed her that I would n't stand her delicate rapier-thrusts. I swung a bludgeon, and I flatter myself that I swung it rather well. I told her that she had given you a perfect right to invite her. I told her that you had treated her with unusual courtesy, and that instead of leaving a slip of meaningless pasteboard with her footman, you had resolved on the more honest and significant civility of asking her to dinner. Moreover, I added, the fact of her brother having been your most intimate friend had rendered, to my thinking, the civility a still more kindly and genuine one."

"You must have made her very angry," said Claire, with a peculiar fleeting smile.

"Angry? She was in a white heat. She could never be in a red one, don't you know, she is so constitutionally placid and chill. She replied that you had actually attempted to offer her patronage, and that your effort had amused her not a little."

"Did she say that?" questioned Claire, with a certain quick eagerness. "Then I was right at first. She had some unpleasant purpose in wanting me to visit her."

"Good gracious!" exclaimed Mrs. Diggs; "you never suggested such a thing before!"

Claire had grown very grave and calm again. "Did I not?" she said. "Well, I had supposed it. It was a sort of fancy."

Mrs. Diggs took one of Claire's hands and held it, at the same time giving her an intent look.

"You're keeping something from me," she said. "Yes, Claire, I know you are. . . . Did Beverley Thurston ever ask you to marry him?"

Claire colored to the roots of her rich-tinted tresses. She tried to draw her hand away, but Mrs. Diggs still retained it.

"He did!" exclaimed her friend. "Your complexion tells me so! Everything is explained now.

You refused Beverley. Yes, my dear, you refused him. And she somehow got wind of it. Perhaps Beverley told, or perhaps his complexion, like yours, divulged secrets, don't you know? . . . And yet, on second thought, Beverley's complexion could do nothing so expressive; it is too battered and world-worn; its capability for blushing is entirely null. . . . No, *he* told her. And she has not forgiven you, and never will. Her monstrous pride would not permit her to do so. I understand everything, now. You remember what I told you about her clannish feeling —how she loves to quietly exalt her family name? . . . Ah, my dear Claire, you have committed, in her eyes, the great unpardonable sin. I was right; I felt it to be in the air that you and she would prove enemies. I begin to think myself a sort of haphazard sibyl; I divined what would happen, and it has happened. You have presumed to refuse her brother, and Cornelia knows it. Prepare to be crushed."

Claire lightly tossed her graceful head, and her lip curled a little as she did so.

"I am not at all prepared to be crushed," she said. "Mrs. Van Horn has spoiled our prospective dinner-party, as regards ladies, but she has not spoiled *me*."

"Delightful!" declared Mrs. Diggs, softly clapping her hands. "That's the spirit I like to see. The fight has begun; it's going to be serious. But remember that I am always your devoted auxiliary!" . . .

The dinner took place. There were no ladies present except Claire herself. It was an extremely elegant dinner. Claire rose when coffee was being served, and left the gentlemen together. She performed, so to speak, her unaided office of hostess with

singular charm and dignity. And during the progress of the dinner she made a friend.

This was Mr. Stuart Goldwin. Everybody in
Wall Street knew Stuart Goldwin. He had drifted
into that stormy region of risk about four years ago.
He had so drifted from a remote New England town,
and his speculative successes had been phenomenal.
He was reputed to be worth, at present, a good many
millions of dollars. He had acquired an enormous
influence among his constituents; he was the reigning Wall Street King. But he had none of the vulgarity which had marked a few of his immediate
predecessors; he had always shown a full apprecia-
tion of his royalty and the duties resultant from it.
He had been admitted, with singular promptness, into
the social holy of holies; he was hand in glove with
what are termed the best people; he belonged to
three or four of the most select clubs; his circle of
acquaintances had rapidly become huge. Women
liked him as much as men. He was personally the
type of man whom women like. His frame was tall
and imposing; he wore a large tawny mustache,
which drooped with silky abundance below a deli-
cately-cut nostril. His eyes were large, and of a soft,
glistening hazel. His manners were full of a fascinating frankness. His age was about forty years, but
he might have passed for considerably younger.
Books had not fed his rapid and distinctive intelligence, for he had no time to read them; and yet he
had caught the reverberation, as it were, of the best
and newest ideas announced by the best and newest
writers.

Claire thought him delightful. He, in turn,
thought her even more than this. She was a dis-

covery to him. He had never married, and he was
fond of saying, in his blithe, epigrammatic way, that
half womankind was so enchanting to him as to have
made, in his own case, anything except the most
Oriental polygamy quite out of the question. He
had wit in no small store, but when he liked a woman
greatly it was his most deft of arts to keep this in
very judicious reserve, and employ it only as a means
of subtly wooing forth the mental sparkle of her to
whom he paid court.

Claire found herself vain, in a covert way, of her
own conversational gifts, before she had talked with
Goldwin more than twenty minutes. She would
have liked to talk with him exclusively during the
dinner, but her two other guests were persons of importance who ought not to receive her impolitic neglect. She managed matters with tact and skill.
Everybody thought her charming when she glided
from the dining-room, in decorous retreat before that
little anti-feminine bayonet, the after-dinner cigar.
She had made a distinct success. She felt it as she
sat in the drawing-room, waiting for the gentlemen
to ascend and join her.

Goldwin had not deceived her. She read him with
lucid insight. She saw him to be imposingly superficial; she perceived him to be a man whose polished
filigrees would ring hollow at so much as one sincere
tap of the finger-nail. He was agreeable to her, but
not admirable; he captivated, but he did not dazzle
her. She compared him with Beverley Thurston
(never thinking to compare him with her husband),
and noted all the more clearly his lack of genuine
and manly magnitude. He came and joined her before any of the other gentlemen. His face was a

little flushed from the wine he had taken, but with no unbecoming suggestion of excess.

"I couldn't stay away from you," he said, sinking into a happy, half-lounging posture on the sofa at her side. He was faultlessly dressed, in garments that seemed to accept every bend of his fine moulded figure without a wrinkle of their dark, flexible surface. "Your husband smokes the nicest sort of cigar, but he has another possession that seems to me vastly superior." Then he broke into a mellow laugh, and waved one hand hither and thither, with an air of mock explanation. "I allude to this beautiful little drawing-room," he continued.

His mirthful sidelong look made Claire echo his laugh. "I will tell Herbert how much you like it," she said; "he will be so pleased to know."

"Pray do nothing of the sort!" he expostulated, with a good deal of comic seriousness. "I should never forgive you if you did. Husbands are such oddly jealous fellows. There is no telling what innocent little outburst of esteem may sometimes offend them."

Claire thought the time had come for a decisive parry, in the parlance of fencers. "Oh, Herbert is not at all jealous," she said, measuring the words just enough not to make them seem out of accord with her bright smile. "He has never had the least occasion to be, I assure you."

He fixed his eyes with soft intentness on her sweet, blooming face. "Never?" he questioned, quite low of tone.

"Never," she answered, gently laconic.

"But he might take some stupid pretext . . . who knows?"

"Oh, if he did I would soon show him the stupidity of it. We understand each other excellently."

They talked on for at least a half hour. The other gentlemen remained below. Goldwin made no more daring complimentary hazards. He listened quite as much as he talked. Their converse turned upon social matters — upon what sort of a season it would be — upon the coming opera — upon the nature of New York entertainments — upon the men and women who were to give them. Claire made it very plain to him that she wanted to enter the gay lists. She at length said : —

"Do you know Mrs. Van Horn ? "

Goldwin laughed. "Why don't you ask me if I know the City Hall," he said, "or the Stock Exchange ? Of course I know her."

"Do you like her ? "

"Nobody ever likes her. Who likes statues ? "

"People sometimes worship them."

"Oh, she is a good deal worshiped, if you mean that."

Hollister and his two remaining guests now appeared. Claire re-welcomed both the latter gentlemen with beaming suavity. They were both important personages, as it has been recorded. They both had important wives, to whom they repaired, a little later, and to whom they loudly sang praises of Claire's loveliness. The remarks of each took substantially the same form, and the following might be given as their connubial and somewhat florid average : —

"That fellow Hollister's wife, you know. The man I dined with to-night. Didn't know he had a

wife? Well, you'd have known it if you'd been
there. She's a splendid young creature. Handsome
as a picture, and good style, too. By the way,
Stuart Goldwin was there; you know how hard it is
to get *him*. I shouldn't wonder if these Hollisters
were going to make a dash for society, soon. Now,
don't repeat it, my dear, but the fact is, this Hollister can be of considerable service to me in a business
way. There's no use of going into particulars, for
women never understand business. But . . . if anything *should* occur — any card be left, I mean, you
may be sure what my wishes are. . . . Oh, of course;
look sour, and refuse point blank. Bless my soul,
when did you ever do anything to help along *my*
interests? You'll spend the money fast enough, but
you won't turn a hand to help me make it. All
right; do as you please. Hollister is to-day the most
rising young man on the Street. There's a regular
boom on him. He's got Goldwin for a friend. You
must know what *that* means."

Both ladies did know what it meant. Both ladies
had looked sour, but both in due time entertained
their afterthoughts. They were ladies of high fashion, each prominent within an exclusive clique.
They were not powerful enough to indorse any new
struggler for position; their own right of tenure was
not unassailable. They dreaded this Mrs. Hollister,
as it were, but they secretly resolved that it would
be folly to ignore her. Meanwhile a certain interview, held by Stuart Goldwin with a certain lady
of his acquaintance, was of quite different character.
Goldwin did not reach the house of Mrs. Ridgeway
Lee until some time after ten o'clock. It was an exceedingly pretty house. Its drawing-room, though
18

as small as Claire's, must by comparison have put
the latter completely into the shade. It was an
exquisite artistic commingling of all that was rare
and fine in upholstery and general embellishment.
Mrs. Ridgeway Lee, too, was in a manner rare and
fine. She rose from a deep cachemire lounge to
receive Goldwin. She was dressed in crimson, with
a great cluster of white and crimson roses at her
breast. She pretended to be annoyed that he should
have presumed to come so late. She had the last
French novel in her hand, pressed against her heart,
as though she loved its allurements and disliked
being thus drawn from them. Goldwin knew perfectly well that she had expected him, that she was
very glad he had come. He often wondered to himself why he did not ask her to be his wife. She was
passionately in love with him ; she had been a widow
almost since girlhood. She had a great deal of
money, for which he cared nothing, and a great deal
of beauty, for which he could not help but care. She
had almost seriously compromised herself by permitting him to show her attentions whose intimacy, in
the judgment of the world, should long ago either
have ceased entirely or else have assumed matrimonial permanence.

Yet she was a woman who could, to a certain degree, compromise herself with impunity. Her connections were all people of high place. She was distantly
related to Mrs. Diggs and nearly related to Mrs. Van
Horn, who felt toward her that fondness which may
exist between a queen and a lady-in-waiting. Apart
from this, she was a social dignitary. Her artificiality
was more plainly manifest than that of Goldwin, and
it had become a commonplace among her friends to

say that she was affected. But she had made her affectation a kind of fashion; other women had so liked the peculiar flutter of her lids, the drawl of her voice, the erratic movements and extraordinary poses of her body, that they had imitated these with disastrous fidelity. She said clever, daring, insolent, or amiable things all in the same slow, measured way, and generally managed to leave an impression that a fund of unuttered experience or observation lay behind them. She was prodigiously pious for one of her pleasure-loving nature. Her charity was liberal and incessant. She trailed her Parisian robes through the wards of hospitals, or lifted them in the ill-smelling haunts of dying paupers. Her religion and her charity went hand in hand. For some people they were both shams; for others they were ostentation, half founded upon sincerity; for others they implied a feverish craving to drown the remorse born of persistent indiscretions; and still for others they were an intoxication, indulged in by one who did nothing half-way, and resorted to as some women drug themselves with opium, chloral, or alcohol. She denounced the new intellectual tendency among social equals of her own sex, as something wholly terrible; she frowned upon it no less darkly than her kinswoman, Mrs. Van Horn, but for a different reason. Its occasional lapses into rationalistic and unorthodox thought roused her dismay and ire.

"Science," she would say, in her grave, loitering manner, "is perfectly splendid. I adore it. I read books about it all the time." (There were those who roundly asserted that she did not know protoplasm from evolution.) "But this confusing it with religion is simply blasphemous and awful. I have the profoundest pity for all who do not believe devoutly. I wish I could build asylums for them, and visit them, as I do my sick and my poor!"

Goldwin always listened to these melancholy outbursts with a twinkling eye. She had long since ceased to try and convert him to her High Church ritualisms. He would never go to church with her and witness, in the edifice which she attended, the Episcopal ceremonial imitate, as he said, the Roman Catholic ceremonial just as far as it dared and no further. But he would never have gone to any church with her, and she knew it, and mourned him as ungodly. That was the way, some of her foes asserted, in which she made love to him : she mourned him as ungodly.

But she showed no signs of making love to him tonight. She received him, as was already stated, with a shocked air.

"It is dreadfully late," she said, giving him her hand. "You ought not to do it. You know that you ought not to do it."

He kept her hand until she had again seated herself on the cachemire lounge. Then he sat down beside her.

Her type of beauty had been called that of a serpent. It was true that her present posture on the lounge oddly resembled a sort of coil. Her face wore at nearly all times a warm paleness; its color, or rather its lack of color, had little variation. Her hair was black as night; her eyes luminous, large, and very dark; her head small, her figure lissome and extremely slender, her shoulders narrow and falling. She could not be ungraceful, and her grace was always what in another woman would have been called

unique awkwardness. She appeared, now, to be gaz-
ing at Goldwin across one shoulder. Her crimson
dress was in a tight whorl about her feet. She had
a twisted look, which in any one else would have suggested an imperiled anatomy. But you somehow accepted her at first sight as capable of a picturesque
elasticity denied to commoner *physiques.*

"I dropped in only for a minute," said Goldwin.
"I wanted to tell you about the dinner."

"Well? Was it nice?"

"Immensely. There was only one woman, but a
marvelous woman. She is Hollister's wife. I feel
as if I'd been hearing a new opera by Gounod.
Don't ask me to describe her."

Mrs. Lee was watching the speaker's face with
great intentness. It was a face that she knew very
well; she had given it several years of close study.

"She is handsome, then?"

"She's exquisite. She is going to take things by
storm this winter. She wants to do it, too. And I
mean to help her."

"Who was she?"

"I don't know. And I don't care. I'm her devoted friend. I hope you will be. I want you to
call on her."

"Are you crazy?" said Mrs. Lee. She said it so
quietly and slowly, as was her wont to say all things,
that she might have been making the most ordinary
of queries.

"Yes," laughed Goldwin, "quite out of my head."

"Do you think I will go and see a woman I don't
know, merely because you ask me to do it?"

He let his eyes dwell steadily upon her pale, small,
piquant face, lifted above the long, rounded throat,

on which sparkled a slim gorget of rubies, to match her dress.

"You 've done things that I wanted you to do before now," he said softly. "You 'll do this, I am sure."

She put one hand on his arm. The hand was so tiny and white that it seemed to rest there as lightly as a drifted blossom. "Will you tell me all about her?" she said, in her measured way.

"I told you that I could n't describe her. She 's like flowers that I 've seen; she 's like music that I 've heard; she is like perfumes that I have smelt. There 's poetry for you. You 're fond of poetry, you say."

She still kept her hand on his arm. He had very rarely praised a woman in her hearing. He had never before praised one in this fashion.

"Will you tell me one thing more?" she said. "Have you fallen in love with her?"

Goldwin threw back his head and laughed. "Good heavens!" he exclaimed, "she is a married woman, and her husband worships her."

"Will you answer my question?" persisted Mrs. Lee.

"Yes," said Goldwin, suddenly jumping up from the lounge. "She is tremendously fond of her husband. There . . . your question is answered."

XVI.

RATHER early the next morning, Mrs. Diggs dropped in upon Claire, "to hear all about it," as she said, alluding to the dinner-party.

She dismissed two of the gentlemen with two little contemptuous nods. "They are both well enough in point of respectability," she affirmed. "So are their wives. All four are so swathed in dull convention that you even forget to criticise them; they're like animals which resemble the haunts they inhabit to such a degree that you can tell them from the surrounding foliage or furrows only when they move or show life. Whom else did you have?"

"There was Mr. Stuart Goldwin," said Claire.

"Goldwin? You don't mean it, really? *Did* you have Goldwin?" Here Mrs. Diggs looked hard at Claire, and slowly shook her head. "My dear," she went on, "it must indeed be true that your husband is achieving great financial distinction. Pardon my saying it, Claire, but Goldwin would n't have put his limbs under your mahogany if this had not been true. He's an enormous personage. Other Wall Street grandees have been very small pygmies in the social estimate. But Goldwin carries everything before him. You need n't tell me that you like him. It would be something abnormal if you did n't. He is really the most charming of men. You can't trust him, don't you know, further than you can see him; he bristles with all sorts of humbug. And yet you accept him, because it is such well-bred, engaging humbug. He has hosts of adherents, and he deserves them. He gives the most enchanting entertainments. They are never vulgar, and yet they cost vast sums. For example, he will give a Delmonico dinner, at which every lady finds a diamond-studded locket hid modestly in the heart of her bouquet. I need not add that in a matrimonial way he is simply groveled to. But beware of him, my dear Claire; he is dangerous."

" Dangerous ? " repeated Claire.

" Well, not so much in himself. Goldwin, in himself, is a shallow yet clever man, a forcible yet weak man, a man whose pluck has aided him a good deal, and whose luck has aided him still more. He has caught the trick of looking like a prince, and hence of giving his princely amassment of money a superb glamour. He will fade, some day, and leave not a rack behind. Of course he will. They all do. I don't know that he would if he married. And now I come to my previous point. He doesn't marry; therefore, he is dangerous."

" I don't follow you," Claire said.

" He doesn't marry Mrs. Ridgeway Lee. That is what I mean. As it is, she guards his approaches. She is a woman of high position, considerable queer, uncanny beauty, monstrous affectation, and a fondness for *him* that amounts to idolatry. She's the most intense of pietists; she riots in all sorts of religious charities. She has other idolatries besides Goldwin, but he is her foremost. I have never been just able to make her out. She is a sort of cousin of mine. She's wonderfully handsome, but it's the lean, cold beauty of a snake. As I said, she guards Goldwin's approaches. She's a widow, and a rich one, and she wants Goldwin to ask her to marry him. He does n't, however, and hence she coils herself, so to speak, at the threshold of his acquaintance. If any other woman draws near — I mean, too near — she hisses and bites. . . . Oh, don't look incredulous. I've known her to positively do both. She'll do it to you, if Goldwin is too attentive. That is why I warn you; that is why I call that nice, brilliant, headlong, gentlemanly Goldwin a dangerous man."

In a few more days Hollister, of his own accord, proposed to Claire that she should engage a maid. He also told her that he had made purchase of two carriages, a span of horses, and an extra horse for single harness besides.

"You will be able to drive out, either in your coupé or your larger carriage, my dear," he said, "by Wednesday next." Then he broke into one of his most genial laughs, and added: "I hope that is not too long to wait."

Claire took this prophecy of coming splendor with serious quietude. She had talked with her husband regarding his recent plethoric influx of thousands.

"I've an idea, Herbert," she said, using a slow, wise-seeming deliberation. "It is this: why do you not buy our house? We both like it; it is comfortable and agreeable; it fills all our wants. And it is for sale, you know."

Hollister looked grave, then smiled, then affirmatively nodded.

"I'll do it, Claire," he answered. "I'll do it to-morrow, if you wish."

"I do wish, Herbert. And when you have bought the house, I want you to put it in my name. I want you to give it to *me*."

He started, and stared at her. A gleam of distrust appeared to slip coldly into his frank eyes. Claire saw this, but answered his look with firm calm. "Why do you say that?" he murmured.

She went nearer to him, and laid one hand on his shoulder. "Why do I say it?" she softly iterated. "Because I know something of the risks and perils you are daily forced to meet."

He watched her intently and soberly, for a few seconds, after she had thus spoken. Then his characteristic smile broke forth like a burst of sun. He kissed her on the lips. "It shall be just as you say!" he exclaimed, drawing her nearer to him, with a look which they of bids and sales and stock-traffic had never seen on his manly yet winsome face. "You are right. You are always right, Claire. There's a lot of money drifting in; it seems as if the money would never stop drifting in."

"I hope it never will," said Claire, showing her pure teeth in a laugh, as he again kissed her. At the same time she drew back from him while his encircling arm still retained her, in a way to which he had grown wholly familiar, and which, in an unwedded woman, would have readily seemed like the reserve of absolute maidenhood.

A slight further lapse of days brought grand results for Claire. She was legally the owner of the charming little house in which she dwelt; she had her maid, obsequiously attendant on her least wants; she possessed her coupé, drawn by a large, silver-trapped horse; she possessed, also, a glossy, dark-appointed carriage, drawn by two horses of equally smart gear, and supervised by coachman and foot-man in approved and modish livery.

Mrs. Diggs was in ecstasies at the prosperous change. "Now you're indeed *lancée*, don't you know?" she said. "By the way, has Cornelia Van Horn left a card on you, my dear?"

"No," said Claire.

"Can she really mean open warfare?"

"Let her wage it," Claire answered. "That is better than to have it concealed."

The opera-season began the next evening. Hollis-ter had engaged a box, permanently. It was a season that opened with much auspicious brilliancy. Claire appeared in her first really notable toilette. One of the reigning *modistes* had made it, and for the first time in her life she was called upon to stand the test of surpassingly beautiful dressing. It is a test that some very fair women stand ill. They show to best advantage in garments which have no atmosphere of festival; it becomes them to be clad with domesticity or at least moderation. This was by no means true, however, of Claire. The diamond necklace which Hollister had spread on her dressing-table but a few minutes before the hour of departure glittered round her smooth, slender neck with telling saliency. Her gown was of a pale, pink brocaded stuff, and she carried its full-flowing train with a light-stepping and perfect repose. Before she had unclasped her cloak and seated herself in the box at Hollister's side, numerous lorgnettes were leveled upon the lovely, dignified picture that she made. When she had seated herself, the spell continued. The large pink roses in her bosom were not deep or sweet enough of

tint to do more than heighten the fresh, chaste flush
in either cheek. She bore herself with a fine and
delicate majesty. Her dark-blue eyes told of the
quicker pulse that stirred her veins only by a more
humid and dreamy sparkle. She was inwardly glad
to be where she sat, and to be robed as she was robed,
but her pleasure softly exulted in its own outward
repression ; she was wonderfully self-poised and tranquil, considering her strong secret excitement. Nearly
everybody who looked upon her pronounced her to be
very beautiful, and a good many people, before an
hour had passed, had looked at her with the closest
kind of scrutiny.

The opera was a favorite one ; a famed and favorite prima-donna sang in it. Below, where the real
lovers of music mostly thronged. Claire's presence
produced neither comment nor criticism. But up in
the region sacred to fashion, inattention, gossip, and
flirtation, she rapidly became an event which even
the most melodious cavatina was powerless to super-
sede.

It was not all done by her beauty and novel charm.
Hollister, sitting at her side, nonchalant, handsome,
of excellent conventional style in garb and posture,
materially helped to increase the notability which
surrounded her. His success had publicly transpired;
a few of those newspapers which are little save glaring personal placards had of late proclaimed with
graphic zeal his speculative triumphs. He had leapt
into notoriety in a day, almost in an hour. There
was but one man in the house besides her husband
whom Claire knew. This man was Stuart Goldwin,
and he soon dropped into her box, remaining there
through the two final acts. Hollister, meanwhile,

chose to be absent. He had found some friends who
were solicitous of presenting him to certain ladies.
He spent nearly the whole of these two acts in
chatting with these same ladies. They were all
gracious; one or two of them had strong claims to
beauty. It was no less an important evening with
himself than with Claire. Perhaps with him it was
even more so, since he obtained his social acceptance,
as it were, by great dames whom he pleased with his
handsome face, happy manners, and growing repute
as a potential millionaire.

His wife, on the other hand, had gained a different victory. She was pronounced to be charming
and remarkable; she had acquired the prestige of
Goldwin's open attentions. But she was a woman,
and she had not yet received the endorsement of her
own sex. It might possibly soon arrive, or it might
be withheld : there was still no actual certainty.

Claire loved the music, but she would have heard
its cadences in discontent if fate had decreed that she
should sit, this evening, with no attendant devotee.
She knew well that Goldwin's company distinguished
her. Mrs. Diggs had given her points, as the phrase
goes. She was quite aware that the horse-shoe of
boxes in our metropolitan opera-house, and the other
more commodious proscenium boxes which flank its
stage, are at nearly all times occupied by just the
kind of people among whom she wished to win her
coveted lofty place. She understood that they would
note, comment, gauge, admire, or condemn ; and
while her manner bespoke a sweet and placid unconsciousness of their observation, she was alive to the
exact amount of observation which she attracted.

"I am so glad that you came," Goldwin told her.

"For very selfish reasons, I mean. You appear, and you corroborate my statements. Now people can at last see and judge for themselves. The verdict is sure."

He said many more things in this vein, all uttered low, and all accompanied by his smile, that seemed either to mean volumes or to leave his true meaning adroitly ambiguous.

Mrs. Ridgeway Lee was in a somewhat near box. When Goldwin returned to her side, just as the curtain was falling on the last act, she accepted his escort to her carriage with a fine composure. He met Mrs. Van Horn, a little later, in the crush that always occurs along the Fourteenth Street lobby of our Academy when a full house disgorges its throng.

The two ladies talked together. Not far away from them stood Mrs. Diggs and Claire, each waiting for an absent husband to secure her carriage.

"What a contrast there is between them," Claire murmured to her companion. "One is so blonde and peaceful, the other so dark and restless."

"Yes, my dear Claire. Have you caught Cornelia's eye?"

"No. She does not appear to see me."

"She sees you perfectly. She has not yet made up her mind just how to act."

"I think that she means to cut me," said Claire, under her breath.

"Never," came the emphatic answer, so bass and gruff because of its vocal suppression that it produced odd contrast with Mrs. Diggs's bodily thinness. "To cut you would be to burn her ships. She has an object in knowing you. I'm afraid it's a dark one. But be sure that she is only making up her mind just *how* to know you. She will soon decide; she has already delayed too long, and she feels it. Be ready for a prompt change."

If the behavior of Mrs. Van Horn was really to be explained on the theory of her prophetic cousin, then she made up her mind very soon after the delivery of these oracular sentences. A chance turn of the neck seemed to render her conscious of Claire's neighboring presence. She bowed with soft decision the instant that their eyes met; and Claire returned the bow.

The next instant she laid one gloved hand on the arm of Mrs. Ridgeway Lee, and then both ladies moved in Claire's direction. Their progress was of necessity made between the forms of several assembled ladies, who nodded and smiled as the great personage and her companion pushed courteously past them. They were mostly the loyal adherents of Mrs. Van Horn, in the sense that they held it high honor to have the right of occasionally darkening her Washington Square doorway. Two or three of them were perhaps co-regents with her as regarded caste and power.

They all saw and intently watched the little astonishing action that now followed. Mrs. Van Horn glided up to Claire and extended her hand.

" I was so very sorry to have missed your dinner, Mrs. Hollister," said the great lady, with her best affability, " but another engagement forced me to be absent." She again put her hand on the arm of Mrs. Ridgeway Lee; she had thus far wholly ignored Mrs. Diggs; her nose was well in the air, as usual, but her smile was bland, conciliatory, impressive; she glowed with an august amiability.

"I want you to let me present my cousin, Mrs. Lee," she proceeded. "We have both heard so much about you, of late, from Mr. Goldwin. You can't think how devoted a friend you have suddenly made."

Before Claire could answer, Mrs. Lee spoke. She had got herself into her usual extraordinary twist. Her visage, her hands, and her lower limbs, regarded according to their relative disposements, would have made a very sinuous line. Like Mrs. Van Horn, she was wrapped in an opera cloak. But her dark little head rose from the large circlet of swansdown about her slight throat with an effect not unlike the slim crest of a turtle stealing from its shell. She constantly suggested a creature of this lean and chill type, though rarely with any of its repulsive traits.

"Indeed, yes!" she softly exclaimed to Claire. "Mr. Goldwin is a great friend of mine, and he has told me hundreds of charming things about you."

"Our acquaintance has been a very short one," said Claire, looking at Mrs. Diggs. In a certain way, she sought to gain a kind of tacit cue from the latter's face. She failed to perceive just how matters were drifting. Was this patronage on the part of both ladies? Or was it meant for irreproachable courtesy?

Mrs. Diggs gave a laugh. "Goldwin can say a hundred charming things very easily on a brief acquaintance," she declared. "Can't you?" were her next words, delivered to Goldwin himself, who had just then slipped up to the group.

"Oh, no, I can't," he at once replied, "unless I mean every one of them."

"Dear me!" said Mrs. Diggs, "how quickly you

grasp the situation! So you heard what we were talking about, did you? You've found out that we were discussing your last enthusiasm?"

"Ah," said Goldwin, "I have very few of them. Don't cheapen me, please, in the regard of Mrs. Hollister."

"You seem to count upon her regard with singular confidence," said Mrs. Van Horn.

"That's entirely our affair," laughed Goldwin. He looked at Claire, but while he did so Mrs. Van Horn placed her hand within his arm. She took it for granted that her carriage had been properly summoned by the financier, and she was going to permit him to accompany her thither, as she had permitted him to find it; she nearly always put herself in the attitude of permitting favors and not soliciting them, by some deft, secure art, quite her own. The bow of farewell which she gave Claire was handsomely suave. Mrs. Lee moved away at her other side. Mrs. Lee had been her guest, that evening, and they were to ride home together.

"So, Claire, it's settled," presently said Mrs. Diggs. "Cornelia is to know you. So is Sylvia Lee. Be careful of them both. I can't feel certain, yet, of exactly what it all means. . . . Here's that dear Manhattan of mine. He has got our carriage. Shall I remain with you till your husband reappears? . . . Very well; I will. But this is no place in which to talk over the whole odd, interesting thing. I'll try and drop in upon you soon; possibly to-morrow, if I can manage it. . . . Does Manhattan see us? Just observe how stupidly he stares everywhere but here. He's been a little strange and absent-minded all the evening. I really think he's

19

forgotten where he left me. He smokes too many of
those strong, horrid cigars, don't you know? I truly
believe that they cloud his brain half the time . . .
but then it's better he should smoke too much than
drink too much. I don't know what I *should* do if
the dear fellow drank too much!" . . .

Mrs. Diggs did present herself at Claire's house
on the following day. But Claire was not at home.
She had driven out in company with her husband.

It was a momentous drive. They had left home
together at about one o'clock. Claire had no idea
whither they were going, at first. Hollister had
chosen to assume an air of profound mysticism. "I
have a great surprise for you," he said.

There was no characteristic twinkle in his eye as
he made this statement. Claire felt that he was far
from saddened, and yet his gravity looked an un-
doubted fact.

"I will accompany you blindly," she said, just
before they entered the carriage. "I suppose, however, there are some more jewels at Tiffany's which
you want me to see and choose from."

"No," said Hollister, shaking his head. "I
should n't spend nearly a whole day away from Wall
Street for anything of that sort."

The carriage had soon passed Tiffany's by a considerable distance, in what we call the downward direction. As its progress increased, Claire's curiosity
heightened, but for some time she gave no proof of
this. Her talk was of their new attainments, of
their growing pastimes, pleasures, and luxuries. She
spoke often with a slightly unfamiliar speed; it was
a little habit that of late had come upon her; it betrayed gentle excitement in place of previous compos-

ure. To Hollister, when he observed it at all, the effect was filled with charm ; he no more disliked it than he would have disliked to see a very tender breeze lightly agitate some beautiful bloom. But now his gravity by no means lessened under the sp ll of Claire's rather voluble advances. She had plainly seen the change ; on a sudden she herself became serious as he ; then, after an interval of almost complete silence, she placed her hand in his. The carriage was now very near to one of the Brooklyn ferries. No doubt the first real suspicion of the truth had flashed through Claire's mind when she abruptly said : —

" Where *are* we going, Herbert? You really *must* tell me."

He met her intent look ; she had rarely seen his blithe eyes more solemn than now.

" Haven't you guessed by this time ? " he said.

" Perhaps I have," she answered. Her tone was a low murmur ; she had averted her eyes from his, and would have withdrawn from him her hand, had not the clasp of his own softly rebelled against this act. Her cheeks had flushed almost crimson. " Go on," she persisted. " Tell me if I am right."

" I think you are, Claire ; I think you have guessed it, at last." The carriage had just entered the big gateway of the ferry ; wheels and hoofs took a new sound as they struck the planks of the wharf. " Don't you remember that night at the Island, a little while after our engagement, when you told me that it would give you such joy to regain your father's body and to have it decently buried, in a Christian way ? "

" Yes, Herbert . . . I remember." She spoke the words so faintly that he scarcely heard them.

" Well, Claire, I made you a promise, then, and I recollected the promise."

" But *I* forgot it ! " she cried, throwing both arms about his neck, for an instant, and kissing his cheek. Immediately afterward she burst into tears. " Oh, Herbert, you remembered and I forgot ! How wicked of me ! I let other things — things that were trifles and vanities — drive it from my mind ! Poor, dear, dead Father ! He would never have done that to me ! He loved me too well — far too well ! "

The tears were rushing down her face, and her frame was in a miserable tremor. Already he had caught both her hands, and was firmly pressing them while he bent toward her, and while she leaned in a relaxed posture against the back of the carriage. He thought her repentance as exquisite as it was needless ; he held it as only a fresh proof of her sweet, refined spirit. It brought the mist into his sight, and made his voice throb very unwontedly, to see her weep and tremble thus.

" My darling," his next words hurried, " you're not in the least to blame. You would have thought about it a little later, I'm certain. But so much has happened since our marriage, you know. Besides, what you call trifles and vanities are just what he wanted you to think about. He must be glad (if the dead are ever glad or sorry in any way) to see you climb higher, and get the notice and influence you deserve. You never slighted his memory at all. Don't fancy you did, Claire. He was in your mind all the while, only you postponed speaking of him a little longer than you intended. You had told me what to do, don't you see, and you felt a certain security as regarded my doing it. That was all.

Now do cheer up. We've quite a ride to Greenwood after we leave the ferry. Everything has been done, quietly, dear, without your knowing. I thought it would pain you too much to stand beside any open grave of his. The body was not hard to find. You recollected its . . . its number, you know. I'm sure you will like the stone I've had put over him. It is just a plain granite one, with the name, and date of death. The date of birth shall be put there afterward; I didn't want to ask it of you yet; that would have spoiled my surprise."

She grew perfectly calm again, some time before they reached the cemetery. The cessation of her tears deeply relieved Hollister. He had never seen her weep before, and the betrayal of such emotion, feminine though it was, had harshly disturbed him. Once more composed, she returned to him in her proper strength. She became Claire again. It was not that he did not like her to show weakness, but rather that in showing weakness she appeared new and odd to him, and hence not just his own strong, serene, familiar Claire. Any jar, as it were, in the steadfast vibrations of his fealty sent to the heart of this most unswerving loyalist a strange, acute dismay.

The autumn darkness had almost fallen upon the multitudinous tombs of Greenwood before Claire was willing to leave that of her father. His name, cut in the modest gray of the stone, seemed for hours afterward cut into her conscience as well. The grand repose of the place, too, left its haunting thrill in her soul. A great sombre note had been struck through all her being, at a time when brain and nerves had begun to feel the full intoxication of worldly longing.

While she was living intensely, death had come to her in the shape of keen, reproachful reminder. The vast cemetery had now no vernal or summer charm. Above, the sky was soft as a clouded turquoise, but underfoot, and on tree and shrub, the lovely melancholy of waning autumn met the bitter melancholy of a far more woful decay. It was all like one mighty threnody put to mighty yet very tender music. With a certain sinister and piercing eloquence, moreover, this huge, mute city of death addressed Claire. Many noted family names had of late passed into her memory, as those of people whom it would be safe, wise, politic to know ; and not a few of these she now saw, lettered on slabs or shafts, and graven over the portals of vaults. Each one, as her gaze read it, wore a frightful sarcasm. More than once she closed her eyes and shuddered, as the carriage made both exit and entrance here in this sad domain. The perfect culture of the place rendered its doleful pathos even more poignant. The dead were not neglected, here ; others, now alive and of the bright world she had yearned to triumph in, must soon lie down beside them. The narrow beds were kept well tended, perhaps, for just this dreary and hideous reason.

That night she spent almost without sleep. She heard her mother's vindictive voice ring through the stillness ; she had waking visions of her father's face, clad with an angelic rebuke ; she seemed to listen once more while Beverley Thurston spoke those words of remonstrance and chiding which were the last he had uttered in her presence: " I warn you against yourself . . . there is an actual curse hanging over you . . . it will surely fall, unless by the act of your own will you change it into a blessing."

Yes, her aim had been false and worthless. She knew it well, at last. Her father's grave had told her so. She was born for better things than to fling down a dainty gauntlet of social warfare at Mrs. Van Horn. The big world had big work for such a woman as herself to front and do. She realized it now; she had realized it all along. Herbert thought she had been right merely because he loved her. To-morrow she would make Herbert see clearly the folly of his own acquiescence. Now that the money had come, there were great charities possible. She would go back, too, among her books; these should teach her more than they had ever yet taught. It was true enough that in one way she was cold; she could not feel passion like other women. The infatuation of a Mrs. Ridgeway Lee was an enigma to her. But she could love a loftier ideal of life — love it and try to climb thither by the steeper and harsher path. This, surely, was what her father had meant, long ago.

Such were her new reflections and her new resolves. It took just one day, and no more, to dissipate them completely. Mrs. Diggs sent her a note on the following afternoon, saying that a hundred little obstructive matters had prevented her purposed visit that morning, but begging to have the pleasure of her own and her husband's company at dinner on the same evening. Would not Claire drop in very early — say about four o'clock? " It is my visiting day," wrote her correspondent. " Perhaps there will be four or five feminine callers, perhaps none. If there are none, we can have a good three hours' chat, don't you know? I've some new things from Paris that I want to show you. It strikes me that Worth's taste grows more depraved every year, and I want you to give me your advice as to whether I shall throw all these hideous importations over to my maid or no. You can leave a little note at home for that delightful husband of yours, telling him that the Diggses dine at seven. Or you can show him this note, unless you have jealous feelings with regard to my florid adjective."

Claire quitted the house at about four that afternoon, leaving behind her a few lines for Hollister. She chose to go on foot, the day being fair and pleasant. But she had scarcely got twenty yards away from her own stoop, when a carriage rattled past her, stopping suddenly. It was an equipage of great elegance. Claire soon perceived that it had stopped before the door from which she had just made exit. A footman sprang from the box, and immediately afterward what appeared to be more than a single card was handed him by an unseen occupant of the carriage. He then ascended the stoop of the Hollister abode, and sharply rang its bell. When his summons was answered the man held brief converse with Claire's new butler, and then presented, with a little bow, the card or cards intrusted to him. In a trice he was down the stoop again, and again at the carriage door. He did not seem to deliver any spoken message, but merely touched with one raised finger the rim of his cockaded hat. The carriage then started briskly off, without its high-throned driver paying the slightest heed to the fact that his liveried associate must scramble up to his side while the vehicle was in full motion. But this feat was accomplished with great ease; a mannerism of fashion demanded that the footman should so perform it; the approved effect of complete unconcern on the one hand and up-leaping agility on the other was never produced with more complete success.

Claire had soon reëntered the house. She found two cards there, awaiting her inspection. One bore the name of Mrs. Van Horn, and one that of Mrs. Ridgeway Lee.

"Delightful!" exclaimed Mrs. Diggs, on learning this occurrence from Claire herself, about a half hour later. "That visit, from those two women, has an enormous meaning. How sorry I am you were not at home. It would have been two against one, but I'm inclined to pay you the very marked compliment of saying that both your antagonists, deep and clever as they are, would have been no match for you. Well, hostilities are postponed. It's an armistice, not a truce. I insist, you see, on using the terms of warfare. How the battle will be fought is still a mystery, of course ; but two potent truths simply *can't* be overlooked. You refused Cornelia Van Horn's brother. That is one of them."

"And the second?" asked Claire, a little absently, because she felt what answer would come.

"The second? You 've roused pointed admiration in the man whom Sylvia Lee worships."

Claire looked at the speaker, and slowly shook her head. There was doubt, trouble, irresolution in her face ; and now, when she spoke, her voice had a weary, almost plaintive note.

"I — I feel like not engaging in the fight, if you really think there is to be one," she said, hesitantly. "I don't mean because I am afraid," were her next words, delivered with much greater swiftness. "Oh, no, not that. There are other reasons. I can't explain, just now." Here she paused, and her face softly brightened, while she gave a little shrug of the shoulders. " Well," she abruptly went on, " perhaps I shall never explain."

She never did explain. This was her last feeble protest against the slow, sure force of that subtle fascination which was once more steadily reclaiming her. The gloomy remorse and the vital energy of yesterday's mood had, neither of them, quite left her. But they both soon withdrew their last remnant of sway.

Hollister came a little late to Mrs. Diggs's dinner. It had been a great day with him. He had risked a very important sum by retaining a large number of shares in a certain precarious stock. He had his reasons for doing so, and they were clever reasons, judged by the general conditions of the market. He had made a memorable stroke, and all Wall Street knew of it before the usual hour for brokers to seek other than their daily haunts of hazard. He was radiant, if this could be said of one whose spirits were always bright, as his temper was sweet. There were only four at dinner. Mr. Diggs overflowed with congratulations to Hollister. He was quite as tipsy as usual, and to Claire's thinking, quite as tiresome.

But the dinner was not tiresome. Mrs. Diggs was at her loquacious best. The recent brilliant manœuvre of her husband had roused in Claire all the old exultant feeling. Yesterday was now indeed yesterday. She was already plunging an eager look straight onward through a long rosy vista of to-morrows.

" I 'm so glad, Herbert ! " she said, as they were being driven home together. " Perhaps I did n't show that I was, there at dinner. That dreadful Mr. Diggs is made of such explosive material that I was afraid he would want to drink your health standing, or something of that absurd sort, if I ventured to tell you how glad I really was that you 've made another hit, luckier than any you ever made before."

Hollister put his lips to her cheek. " I know just how glad you are," he said, while kissing her. " You need n't tell me another word about it."

Claire had spoken with that little half-excited trip of the tongue, which has been recorded as a late change in her demeanor.

She was silent, not having returned her husband's caress. This was quite like the accustomed Claire. Yesterday, in the carriage which had borne them to Greenwood, she had flung her arms about his neck and kissed him, as any ordinary wife might do.

Hollister was quietly re-accepting her, so to speak, as the extraordinary wife — or, in other terser phrase, as Claire.

He went on speaking before she had a chance to answer him. He was still holding her hand while he spoke. " Oh, by the way, Claire, Goldwin had a good deal to do with my luck. He gave me points, as they say down there. But don't breathe it to a living soul. Goldwin 's an awfully good friend of mine, I find, though we have n't always pulled together in a business way."

" Yes ? " Claire answered.

She had somehow got her hand away from his. She was using it to arrange her wrap about the throat.

XVII

THE gay season had soon set in with full force.
It promised to be a season of especial brilliancy.
Claire rapidly found people gathering about her.
She began to have a little list of her own. The wives
of the two gentlemen who had dined with herself and
husband in Goldwin's company, each asked herself
and husband to dine at their own house. The dinners were both of sumptuous quality, and attended
by numerous other guests. Claire made a deep impression at both places. Her toilettes were rich and
of unique taste; she was by far the most beautiful
woman at either assemblage. The sudden financial
glory of Hollister, whose actual wealth was tripled if
not quadrupled by rumor, cast about her exceptional
grace, beauty, and wit an added halo of distinction.
She was the kind of woman whom women like. In
not a few of her own sex she quickly roused an en-
thusiastic partisanship.

"You are bound to lead, or nothing," Mrs. Diggs
soon said to her. "I see this very clearly, Claire, —
though, for that matter, I have seen it all along."

"I mean to lead, or nothing," answered Claire,
with her superb candor. "Thus far I have not found
it difficult."

Mrs. Diggs put up her thin forefinger.

"Tut, tut," she remonstrated. "Don't be too

confident. Ambition *may* overleap itself. **Remember**
that you are still on the threshold."

"I've crossed it," said Claire, laughing. "I've
got into the drawing-room."

"No, you have n't, my dear. You have yet
achieved nothing secure, absolute, decisive. Now,
I'm not a bit of a snob, myself, as you know. But
I understand how to reason like one; I can measure
the mettle of the foe you've got to fight with. Let
us talk plainly together, as we always do. None of
the very heavy swells have as yet admitted you.
There's no use of denying this. You're being a
great deal talked about. You've broken bread already, and you've received invitations to break more
bread, with some very nice, exclusive women. But
they are not of the first rank; they're not of the
great, proud, select clique. True, Cornelia has called
on you, and Sylvia Lee has called. You've returned
their visits, and have seen neither; neither was at
home. But then neither *is* at home except on her
visiting-day, and that is customarily written with
much legibility on both their cards. But on both the
cards which you received, *no day at all was written.*
I've never mentioned this before, have I? Well, it
never occurred to me until last night. I was nervous,
and could n't sleep; that dear Manhattan was out at
the club, smoking those horrid cigars, which flush his
face so and hurt his poor, dear brain, I'm sure. Perhaps it was that which kept me awake and made my
mind wander toward you, and reflect upon this peculiarly interesting stage of your career. The little
circumstance I have mentioned may mean nothing,
but I'm inclined to think otherwise; everything, no
matter how trivial, about Cornelia, is sure to mean

something. But, however this may be, affairs have now reached a peculiar pass with you. You must make a *coup*, my dear — a grand *coup*."

"Which you have arranged entirely," said Claire, smiling, "I have n't a doubt. And now you await my sanction of it?"

Mrs. Diggs creased her pale forehead, in a reflective frown. "No, not precisely that, my dear; I have n't yet quite decided what it is to be. But I have almost decided. Suppose that you do not make it at all — that is, not in your own person. Suppose that I make it for you."

"You?" inquired Claire.

"Yes. Suppose that I send out cards for a huge reception, and place your card within the same envelope. Then you would receive at my side, don't you know, and everybody who came must henceforth be on your list as well as on mine. I would launch you boldly forth, in other words. I would put you under my wing. I would give you my *cachet*."

A marked intimacy now existed between Claire and Goldwin. He would often drop in of an evening — sometimes of an afternoon. Hollister was not by any means at home every evening, when he and Claire had no mutual engagement. He was getting to have a good many solitary engagements. "Stag" dinners claimed him; there would be nocturnal trysts with certain fellow-financiers on the subject of the morrow's chances. Then, too, he had been made a member of the Metropolitan Club, an institution oddly hard, and in a way oddly easy, to enter; it was the one great reigning club of the continent; none other precisely resembled it; the social leaders who did not belong to it were few, and to cross its doorstep at will was the unfulfilled dream of many a social struggler.

Claire cordially liked Goldwin. If he had been obscure she would still have liked him, though his importance was so knit in with his personality, he exhaled such an atmosphere of pecuniary and patrician celebrity, that one could ill think of him as ever being or ever having been obscure. She was boldly frank with him regarding her ambitious aims. He would throw back his handsome head and laugh most heartily at her ingenuous confidences. He would tell her that she was the most exquisite joke in the world, and yet that he was somehow forced to accept her as quite the opposite of one. " Ah, yes, intensely opposite," he would add, with a fluttered pull at his silken mustache that she felt to be studied in its emotional suggestiveness, with a large sigh that she suspected of being less studied, and with a look in his charming hazel eyes that would nearly always make her avert her own. His homage had become a very substantial fact, and she knew just how much of it the popular standard of wifely discretion would permit her to receive — just how much of it would be her advantage and not her detriment. He was too keen not to have perceived that she had drawn this judicious line of calculation. Now and then he made little semi-jocose attempts to overleap it, but at the worst a word could curb him where a glance failed. She found him, all in all, saltatory but never vicious ; a stout pull of the rein always brought him to terms.

After her converse with Mrs. Diggs, just recorded, she told him of the latter's proposed *coup.* He looked at her sharply for a moment, and then made a very wry grimace.

"Good Heavens!" he exclaimed. "That woman endorse you! It would be complete ruin."

"Mrs. Diggs is my friend, and as such I must insist upon your always speaking with respect of her in my presence," reprimanded Claire, stoutly.

"Respect? Why, of course I respect her. Not physically; she's constructed on too painful a plan of zigzags. But in all other ways I consider her delightful. She's got a big, warm heart in that angular body of hers. She's as liberal as the air. But she isn't good form — she isn't a swell, and no earthly power could make her so. Of course she does n't think she has really lost caste. She may tell you that she does, but privately she has an immense belief in her ability to play the fine lady at a moment's notice. I don't know any woman more flatly disapproved of by her own original set. Shall I tell you what this idea of hers would result in if practically carried out? A distinct injury to yourself. She has a crowd of queer friends whom she would n't slight for the world; she's too consistently goodhearted. She'd invite them all, and they would all come. Her notable relations — the Van Horns and Van Corlears and Amsterdams and Hackensacks, and Heaven knows who else — would yawn and perhaps shudder when they got the tickets for her entertainment. They would mostly come, too, and all their grand friends would no doubt follow them. But they would come with a feeling of deadly rancor toward yourself; they would never forgive you for setting her up to it, and nothing could induce them to believe that you had *not* set her up to it." Here Goldwin crossed his legs with an impatient violence, and stared down at one of his shoes with enough intensity for it to have been concerned in the last caprice of the stock-market. "Oh, no," he went on, "that would never do. Never in the world. It would n't be a *coup* at all; it would be a monstrous *fiasco.* Take my advice, now, and politely but firmly nip any such proceeding in the bud."

Claire did. On his own side, Goldwin was secretly determined that she whom he thought the most fascinating, novel, and beautiful woman he had ever met, should achieve the full extent of her desires. These desires affected him much as they affected Hollister; they were part of Claire's charm for him; they were like the golden craft of scrollwork that framed the picture; they set it off, and made it more precious; there was a lovely imperiousness about them that would have bored him in another woman, like a kind of ugly greed, but that in her were a delight.

He had made up his mind to serve her, brilliantly, conspicuously, and he soon did so. He issued invitations for a dinner at Delmonico's, and gave it on a scale of splendor that eclipsed all his previous hospitalities. Rare music stole to the guests while they feasted; the board was literally pavilioned in flowers; the wines and the viands were marvels of rarity and cost; beside the plate of each lady lay a fan studded with her monogram in precious stones; during dessert a little cake was served to everybody present, which, when broken, contained a ring with the word *bienvenu* embossed in silver along its golden circlet. The host had very carefully chosen his guests from among the autocrats and arbiters of fashion. Claire and Hollister were the only persons who did not represent aristocracy at its sovereign height. But on Claire fell the chief honors. It was she whom

Goldwin conducted into the dining room ; it was she to whom he directed the major share of his attentions, contriving with slight apparent effort that she should know every one else, and making it evident that the affair was held in large luxurious compliment to herself alone, though not thrusting this fact into more than partial prominence.

Goldwin, for certain marked reasons of his own, had been from the first resolved upon the attendance of Mrs. Ridgeway Lee. He sent no invitation to Mrs. Van Horn. He knew that Claire suspected the latter of adverse feelings, and he knew no more than this. But Mrs. Van Horn was not a necessity to the success of his festival; she could easily be replaced by some other leader, and it would be much better not to invite her at all than to invite her without avail. But Mrs. Lee must appear.

He had been prepared for refusal, and it promptly came. On the evening of the day it reached him, he presented himself at Mrs. Lee's residence. He found her alone. She had denied herself to four or five other gentlemen during the previous hour. She had expected Goldwin, though she tried to look decorously surprised when he entered her elegant little drawing-room.

She had chosen to clothe herself in black satin, the shimmer of whose tense-drawn fabric about bust and waist, and of its trailing draperies about the lower portion of her lithe person, gave to her strange beauty an almost startling oddity. An irreverent critic who had recently seen her in this robe had declared that she made him think of a wet eel. Allowing the comparison to have been apt, if ungallant, there is no doubt that she could have suggested only an eel very much humanized, with a face of quite as extraordinary feminine beauty as that possessed by the deadly lady whom Keats so weirdly celebrated.

Her dark eyes seemed to-night lit with the smouldering fires of fever. The moment Goldwin looked well at her he made up his mind that he was to have a hard time of it. She had undoubtedly guessed the purport of his dinner, and she meant to tell him so. He strongly suspected that she meant to tell him so, as well, with considerable verbal embellishment.

He pretended, in a playful way, to be dazzled by her fantastic apparel. He put both hands up to his eyes and rubbed them in a comic imitation of bewilderment.

" I 'm not prepared to tell you whether I like it or not," he said, while he sank into one of the big, yielding chairs. " But I consider it splendidly effective. It makes you appear so beautifully slippery. You look as if you could slide into an indiscretion, and then squirm right out again without being observed by anybody."

Mrs. Lee bit her lip. She had often let him say more saucy things than this to her, and not resented them. But to-night her mood held no such tolerance.

" You once promised me," she said, " that you would never speak rudely about my personal appearance." She seemed to shape with some difficulty this and the sentences that followed it. " I did not make myself. Perhaps if I had been granted that privilege I might have hit on a type more suited to your taste."

Goldwin shrugged his shoulders. " Oh, come," he said, " you 've let me chaff you a hundred times before, and treated it as a joke."

He was still seated, while she stood. He forgot to think this a discourtesy toward her; he would have remembered it as such with almost any other woman; his outward manners were usually blameless; but perhaps he was no more at fault than she herself for the present negligence.

As it was, it did not strike her. She was thinking of other weightier things. A delicate table stood near her, and she half turned toward it, breaking from a massive basket of crimson roses one whose rich petals were heavy-folded and perfect, and fixing it in the bosom of her night-dark dress. Goldwin was watching her covertly but keenly all the while. She seemed to him like an incarnate tempest — he knew her so well. His furtive but sharp gaze saw the tremor in her slim, pale fingers as she dealt with the discompanioned rose.

Finding that she did not answer, he went on: "You're out of sorts to-night. Has anything gone wrong during the day?"

She tossed her head for an instant, and her lip curled so high that it showed the white edge of her teeth. But promptly she seemed to decide upon a mild and not a harsh retort. "I have been at the hospital most of the afternoon," she said. "I prayed for an hour beside a poor old woman who was dying with cancer." She gave a quick, nervous shudder. "It was horrible." She closed her eyes, then slowly unclosed them. "Horrible," she repeated, in her most measured way.

"It must have been simply ghastly," observed Goldwin, with dryness. "For Heaven's sake, why don't you swear off these debauches of charity for at least a month or two? They're completely breaking you up. It's they that put you in these frightful humors."

She came several steps toward him, and sank into a chair quite close at his side. She twisted herself so inordinately, in taking this new posture, that her detractors would have decided the whole performance one of her most aggravating affectations. "What frightful humors?" she asked. This question had the same loitering, somnolent intonation that always belonged to her speech, and contrasted so quaintly with her nervous, volatile turns and poses.

Goldwin saw that the time had come. "Oh, you know what I mean," he said. "You went and refused my dinner. Of course you did n't mean it."

"I did mean it," said Mrs. Lee, very low indeed.

"Nonsense. I'm like an enterprising salesman. I won't take 'no' for an answer."

"I shall give you no other."

He leaned nearer to her. "What on earth is the matter?" he inquired. "I am going to make it a very nice affair. I don't think I've ever done anything quite as pretty as this will be. You used to tell me that no one did these things just as well as I. You used to say that if I ever left you out of one of my state feasts you'd cut my acquaintance."

She had drooped her small, dark head while he spoke, but now, as he finished, she raised it. Her tones were still low, but unwonted speed was in her words.

"I don't doubt you will make it a very nice affair. But you give it because you want to give distinction to a woman who has bewitched you. Don't deny that Mrs. Hollister will be there. I know it—I am certain of it."

"I don't deny it," said Goldwin, crossing his legs quietly, "now that you afford me a chance of stating it."

He saw her control an inward shiver from displaying more overt signs.

"Oh, well," she said, "do not let us discuss the question any more. I sent you my regret to-day. I have another engagement, as I told you."

"Another engagement is easily broken."

"It is a dinner engagement."

"I don't believe you."

"You are grossly rude."

"I know I am. It's perfectly awful. It's the first time I ever insulted a woman. I shall be in the depths of repentance all day to-morrow. I don't know if I shall ever really pardon myself. But . . . I don't believe you, all the same."

He said this with a mournful deliberation that would at any other time have roused her most enjoying laughter; for he had in him the rich fund of true comedy, as many of his friends were wont loudly to attest, and at will he could draw flattering plaudits of mirth from even the gloomiest hearer.

But Mrs. Lee did not show the glimpse of a smile.

"There is no use," she said. "I have given you my answer. I shall not go. I shall not permit you to make of my name and position a mere idle convenience. I shall not lend you either one or the other, that it may serve your purpose in presenting to society any adventuress who may have pleased your fancy."

Goldwin was very angry at this speech. She had no idea how angry it had made him, as he quietly. rose and faced her.

" What right have you to call her an adventuress? " he asked.

Her eyes flashed as she looked up at him. " Of course she is one. Her husband, too, is an adventurer. They 're both trying to push themselves in among the best people. And you are helping them. You are helping him because of her; and you are helping her . . . well, you are helping her because of herself."

Goldwin gave a smile at this. She perceived, then, how very angry he was. She knew his smile so well that when it came, different from any other she had ever seen on the same lips, it struck her by its cold novelty.

" You called upon this adventuress," he said; " you were willing to do that."

" Yes — to please you."

"Allow that as your reason. You called on her in private to please me. You will not meet her in public to please me. Is not that just how the case stands? "

She fixed her eyes on his face. Her feverish look had grown humid. He could plainly note that her lips trembled. She was so alive, now, to a sense of his being very indignant, that this realization frightened her, and she let him see, with pitiable candor, just how much it frightened her.

" You are in love with Mrs. Hollister," she murmured. " And — she is in love with you."

She showed him the full scope of his power by those few words. He walked toward the door, pausing on its threshold.

" I won't remain to hear you insult a woman whom I respect," he said; " you called her an adventuress, which is untrue; you now say something even worse."

" Will you deny it ? " she asked, rising.

Her question had a plaintive, querulous ring, which the circumstances made something more than pathetic.

" Will you reconsider your refusal? " he said, making the interrogation a reply.

She sank back into her seat again.

" No, never ! " she exclaimed.

" Good night," he returned. He went immediately out into the hall, put on his coat and hat, and left the house.

" She will yield," he told himself. " I am sure of it. She showed me that she would if I were only hard enough. I mean to be hard. I can make it up in kindness by and by."

He waited three days. No word came to him from Mrs. Lee. But on the fourth word came to him.

" I knew it," he thought, as he read her note.

Mrs. Lee went to the dinner in a truly marvelous gown. It was some curious blending of crimson and black silks, that made her look sombrely clad in one attitude and luridly clad in the next. Her only jewelry was a thin snake of rubies about her slender throat, and the head of the snake, set directly beneath her chin, was a big gold one, having two large garnets for eyes. All the women pronounced her costume ridiculously overdone. All the men professed to like it. She never appeared in gayer spirits. Next to Claire she was the most notable feminine guest.

But Claire ruled absolute. She had never been more beautiful, perhaps because she had never felt more secretly and victoriously exultant. The delicious music, the piercing yet tender odor of the lavish flowers, the insidious potency of the wines, which she sipped sparingly and felt dangerously tingle through her veins — all these influences wrought upon her a species of stimulating enthrallment which made the whole splendid banquet seem, on the following day, like some enchanted dream. On one side sat Goldwin, the genius who had created this lovely witchery, urbane, devoted, allegiant; on the other side sat a man of deserved eminence, a wit, a scholar, a statesman. She talked with both companions, and it could not be said that she then charmed both, for one was already her loyal devotee. As for the other, though advanced in years and freighted with pungent experiences, he soon tacitly admitted that he had at last found, at the most discriminating period of his career, a woman whose graces of intelligence and beauty met in faultless unison. As all the ladies rose, leaving the gentlemen to their coffee and cigars, he leaned toward Goldwin, even before Claire's draperies had swept the threshold of the dining-room, and significantly murmured : —

" You were right. She is an event."

That dinner was the stepping-stone by which Claire mounted into immediate triumph. All through the next year she was the reigning favorite in just that realm where she had aimed to reign. Her father had died a pauper and been buried as one. She, the mistress of many thousands, having fixedly remembered what a feeble, disappointed, obscure, broken-down man had said to her in early childhood, now stood as the living, actual result of his past counsel. Years ago the seed had been sown in that dingy little basement of One - Hundred - and - Twelfth Street. To-day the flower bloomed, rare and beautiful. The little girl had climbed the hill to its top, after all.

She had not grown tired and gone home before the
top was reached. She had done her father's bidding.
She was sure he would be glad if he knew.

'And yet am I quite sure?' she would sometimes
ask herself. 'Was this what he really meant when
he spoke those words?'

She knew perfectly the folly of the course that she
now pursued. Her occasional self-questionings were
a hypocrisy that she realized while she indulged it.
But they were very occasional. She had slight time
for introspection, for analysis of her own acts.

Flattery and devotion literally poured in upon her,
like the new wealth that continued to pour in upon
her husband. The house in Twenty-Eighth Street
was soon exchanged for a spacious mansion on Fifth
Avenue. Claire ceased to know even the number of
her servants. She had a housekeeper, who superin-
tended their engagements and discharges. She dwelt
in an atmosphere of excessive luxury, and found herself loving it more and more as she yielded to the
spell of its subtle enervation.

Her second winter was the confirmation of her sov-
ereignty. As the phrase goes, she was asked everywhere. Her bright or caustic sayings were ever on
the lips of loyal quoters. Her toilettes were described
with journalistic realism in more than a single newspaper. Cards for her entertainments were eagerly
sought, and often vainly. Foreigners of distinction
drifted into her drawing-rooms as if by a natural
process of attraction. She had scarcely a moment of
time to herself; when she was not entertaining she
was being entertained. Her admirers, women and
men, vied in efforts to secure her presence. She had
acquired, as if by some magic instinct, the last needed

personal touch; she had got the grand air to perfection. Diplomatists who had met and known the most noted beauties of European courts had nothing but praise to pay her serene elegance of deportment, the undulating grace of her step, the nice melody of her voice, the fine wizardry of her smile. She had never seen Europe, yet she might have spent all the years of her youth on its soil with no lovelier results than those which now marked her captivating manner. She was American, past question, to transatlantic eyes; yet these found in her only the original buoyancy and freshness of that nationality, without a gleam of its so-termed coarseness.

Foes, of course, rose up against her. There can be no sun without shadow. She had made herself so distinct a rarity that cheapening comment could not fail to begin its assault. It did so, in hot earnest. Two women had denied their sanction to her sudden popularity. These were Mrs. Van Horn and Mrs. Ridgeway Lee. They were not open enemies; neither, to all appearances, were they covert ones. They were on speaking terms with her. They met her constantly, yet they offered her no deference. Deference was what she now required, and with a widely-admitted right.

The invidious statements that stole into circulation regarding her could not be traced either to the vengeance of Beverley Thurston's sister or the jealousy of Stuart Goldwin's abandoned worshiper. It is possible that the most leal of Claire's defenders never thought of so tracing them. But the statements were made, and took wing. She had been a vulgar girl of the people. Her parentage was of the most plebeian sort. A lucky marriage had given her the chance, now accepted and enlarged. Her maiden name had been this, that, and the other. She was absolutely nobody.

Claire heard none of these scorching comments. She reigned too haughtily for that. Mrs. Diggs heard them, but Mrs. Diggs betrayed no sign of their existence. Goldwin was now devotedly at Claire's side; they were repeatedly seen in public together; the world in which she ruled considered it a splendid subjugation; she had brought the great Wall Street King obsequiously to her feet.

But no breath of slander tainted the relation between them. Claire had been very clever; she had blunted the first arrow, so to speak. She had done so by means of her complete innocence. Goldwin was in love with her; no one doubted this. It was something notable to have said of one. But she was so safely not in love with Goldwin that she could continually, by strokes of frank tact, show the world her own calm recipiency and his entire subservience. A swift yet sure chasm widened between herself and Hollister. The latter had become a man of incessant and imperative engagements. Claire never dreamed of feeling a jealous pang, and yet she knew that her husband, no less than herself, had become a star of fashion. Hollister was assiduously courted. He and Claire would now meet once a day, and sometimes not so often. They had separate apartments; it was so much more convenient for both. The same dinner-engagement frequently claimed them; but on these occasions she would appear in the lower hall to meet him, rustling beneath some new miracle of dressmaking, and they would get into the carriage together and be driven to the appointed place. At the dinner they would be widely separated. He would sit beside some woman glad to have secured him; she would be the companion of some man happy because of her nearness. The dinner would break up; the hour would be somewhat late; they would get into their carriage; Hollister would have an appointment, at the club, or somewhere. He would let Claire into the great new house with his latch-key. "Good night," he would say, and hurry off into the carriage that had waited for him. Claire would ascend and be disrobed by a sleepy maid. To-morrow there would perhaps be another dinner, of the same sort. Or it might be an affair to which she went alone, and from which Goldwin accompanied her home. Goldwin was always prepared to accompany her. He obeyed her nod.

But Hollister was still her devout subject. It was merely that the sundering stress of circumstances divided them. He did not forget Claire; he postponed her. Everything was in a whirl with him, now; he was shooting rapids, so to speak, and by and by he would be in still water again. For the present, he had only time to tell himself that Claire was getting on magnificently well. It was like driving four or six restive horses abreast, with his wife seated at his side. He must attend to the skittish brutes, as it were; her safety, no less than his own, depended on his good driving. But she was there at his side; he felt comfortably sure of this fact, though he could not turn and look at her half often enough.

The January of this second winter had been prolific in heavy snow-storms, and the sleighing had filled town with its jocund tinkles. One afternoon Claire, leaning back in a commodious sleigh, and muffled to the throat in furry robes, stopped at Mrs. Diggs's house, and the two ladies were driven together into the Park. It was a perfect afternoon of its kind. There was no wind; the cold was keen but still; not a hint of thaw showed itself in the banks of powdery snow skirting either edge of the streets, or in those pure, unroughened lapses which clad the spacious Park, beneath the black asperity of winter trees, traced against a sky of steely blueness.

Claire was in high spirits; her laugh had a ring as clear as the weather. Mrs. Diggs shivered under the protective wraps of the sleigh. "My circulation was never meant for this sort of thing," she said, at length. "We 've gone far enough, have n't we, Claire? It 's nearly dark, too."

This was a most glaring fallacy, coined by the desperation of poor Mrs. Diggs's discomfort. But the chilly light was growing a blue gloom above the massed housetops when the two ladies found themselves at Claire's door.

It had been arranged that they should dine quietly together that evening. Hollister would not be at home, and Claire, for a wonder, would. Mrs. Diggs had been complaining, of late, that she never had a moment of privacy with her friend. Claire had agreed, three days ago, to disappoint for one night all who were seeking her society. "We shall have a cosey dinner," she had said, " of just you and me. We will chat of everything — past, present, and future."

Mrs. Diggs recalled that word 'cosey' as she entered Claire's proud dining-room, with its lofty arched ceiling, where little stars of gold gleamed from dark interspaces between massive rafters of walnut. She crouched on a soft rug beside the deep, large fire-place, in which great logs were blazing. And while she basked in the pleasant glow, her eye wandered about the grave grandeurs of the noble room, scanning its dusky traits of wainscot, tapestry, tropic plants, or costly pictures : for all was in sombre shadow except the reddened hearth and the small central table, on whose white cloth two great clusters of wax-lights had been set, stealing their colors from a group of flowers, and its clean sparkle from the glass and silver. The whole table was like a spot of light amid the stately dimness.

"Really, very splendid indeed, Claire," said Mrs. Diggs, in a sort of ruminative ellipsis, letting her eye presently rest on the tips of her own upheld fingers, which the firelight had turned into that milky pink that we often see float through opals. "But I really think I liked the little basement house better, take it all in all."

"Did you ? " murmured Claire, who was standing near her, enjoying the warmth, but not bathing in it like her half-frozen friend. "I did n't."

A very impressive butler soon glided into the room, and told Madame in French that she was served. Mrs. Diggs scrambled to her feet ; the majesty of the butler had something to do with her speed in performing this act, though hunger was perhaps concerned in it.

"That dreadful sleigh-ride has left me my appetite," she said, while seating herself opposite Claire, "so I see it has n't quite killed me."

"I think you will survive it," said Claire, with one of her little musical laughs.

There was not much talk between the two friends while dinner lasted, and what there was took a desultory and aimless turn. The butler waited faultlessly; there were eight courses; Claire had said that it would be a very plain dinner, and Mrs. Diggs secretly smiled as she remembered the words. The cooking was perfect; it had all of what the *gourmets* would call Parisian sentiment, though no undue richness. Claire ate sparingly, yet with apparent relish. She drank a little champagne, which she had poured into a goblet and mixed with water. There were other wines, but she touched none of them. Mrs. Diggs did, however, sipping three or four, until she lost her chalky wanness of tint and almost got a touch of actual color.

"I never take but one wine, as a rule," she said, "and that's claret. But the sleigh-ride chilled me to the bone. I begin to feel quite warm and comfortable, now. Do you always take champagne, Claire?"

"Always. But only a little. It's companionable to touch your lips to, now and then, when you sit through those very long dinners. I suppose the dullness of certain society originally drove me to it. But I am very careful."

'What an air she said that with!' thought Mrs. Diggs. 'And one year ago, at Coney Island, she was unknown, unnoticed.'

The whole repast was exquisite. While it lasted, Claire never once spoke to the butler. He needed no orders; everything was done as well and as silently as it could be done. In his way he was an irreproachable artist, like the invisible *chef* below stairs, who had evoked this blameless dinner from the chaos of the uncooked.

Just at the end of dessert, Claire said to her guest: "Shall you take coffee?"

"Oh, dear, no," replied Mrs. Diggs; "I don't even dare. I'm nervous enough as it is."

But Claire had coffee, black as ink, and served to her in a tiny cup as thin as a rose-leaf. Presently the two friends became aware that they were alone. The butler had gone without seeming to go. Like a mysterious *au revoir* he had left behind him two crystal finger-bowls, with a slim slice of lemon floating in each. Claire had finished her coffee. She rose and leaned toward the flowers in the centre of the table. As her fingers played among them they seemed to break, almost of their own accord, into two separate bunches. She went round to Mrs. Diggs and gave her one of these, retaining the other. Presently each had made for herself an impromptu *corsage*. Mrs. Diggs had not spoken for several minutes; she had indeed been abnormally quiet ever since the butler's departure. The calm, graceful splendor of it all had awed her. It had such a finish, such a choiceness, such gentle dignity of execution.

"Shall we sit near the fire?" asked Claire, as together they moved from the table. "Or would you prefer one of the drawing-rooms?"

"The fire is so lovely," said Mrs. Diggs. "Let's sit here." She dropped into a chair as she spoke. Claire also seated herself, not far from the fire, though a little distance away from her friend.

Suddenly the flood-gates of Mrs. Diggs's enthusiasm burst open. She had considerable silence to make up for. "Oh, Claire," she exclaimed, "it's just *perfect!* I don't see how you do it! I don't see where on earth you got the experience from! If I

21

had seven times your money *I* could n't begin to have my household machinery move in this delightful, well-oiled way. My servants would steal; my *chef* would get drunk; my magnificence would all go awry; I 'm sure it would! "

Claire laughed. " I 'm very composed about it all," she said. " I keep quite cool. I like it, too. There is a great deal in that. I don't mean management so much as the superintendence of others' management. I 'm a sort of born overseer."

" You 're a born leader." Mrs. Diggs was looking at her very attentively now. " And how capably you *are* leading! How you 've carried your point, Claire! I observe you, and absolutely marvel! I can't realize that you are really and truly *my* Coney Island Claire, don't you know? You 've shot up so. You 're so mighty. It 's like a dream."

" It 's a very pleasant dream."

She said this archly and mirthfully. But Mrs. Diggs on a sudden became solemn.

" Claire," she went on, " you remember what I told you in our little confab, the other day, at the Lauderdales' reception? It 's true, my dear. You 're like a person at a gambling-table, who begins to play for pastime and ends by playing for greed. You know I dote on you, and you know I never choose my words when I 'm in downright earnest. Your love for pomp and luxury, my dear, is becoming a vice. Yes, an actual vice. You don't take your triumphs moderately, as you do your champagne-and-water. You drink deep of them, and let them fly to your head. Oh, I can see it well enough. And I tremble for you. I tremble, Claire, because " . . .

" Well? Because? " . . .

She put these questions with a smile, as Mrs. Diggs paused. But it was a smile of the lips only.

"Oh, because affairs might change in a day, almost an hour. You know just what vast risks your husband constantly runs. You know what *might* happen."

Claire rose at this. Her repose was gone; her piquant excitability had seemed abruptly to return. She did not appear in the least angry. Mrs. Diggs would have liked it better if she had shown a wrathful sign or two.

"Don't let us talk of those grim matters, please," she said. She came very close to her companion, and then, taking both the latter's hands, sank down on her knees. Her face was lit with a charming yet restless cheerfulness. "Dear friend, you spoke a minute ago of my triumphs. Do you know, I've never secured just what I wanted until to-day? You thought I had, but you were wrong. Shall I tell you why?" Mrs. Diggs was inwardly thinking, as one ill-favored but generous woman will sometimes think of another, how purely enchanting was her manner, and how richly she deserved to win the social distinction she had attained.

"I suppose you mean, Claire, that Hollister to-day completed the last thousand of his fourth or fifth million, eh?"

"Oh, not at all. I don't mean anything of the sort. I don't know anything about Herbert's affairs, nowadays. He keeps them all to himself."

"Well, then, what is it?"

"You'll laugh when you hear. You recollect the great ladies' luncheon that I am to give next Friday?"

"Of course I do. I'm going to honor it."

"And so are two others. Mrs. Van Horn and Mrs. Ridgeway Lee. They have never honored anything of mine until now. Poor Mrs. Arcularius yielded, and bowed before me, long ago. My old school-enemy, Ada Gerrard, more freckled, more arrogant, more stupid than ever, is one of my most willing allies. I had conquered them all, but I could not conquer those two women. They stood aloof, and their standing aloof was a perpetual distress."

"Claire, Claire," exclaimed Mrs. Diggs, "you make me wonder at you! What was the hostility of these two women, whether open or repressed? You had all the others to pay you court. Why should you have cared? They saw your success. They are powerful, but their power could not keep you from asserting and maintaining yours. I repeat, why should you care?"

"I did care. But it is all over now." She rose to her feet, with a full laugh, as she said these words. "They are coming to my luncheon. They have both accepted. They have acknowledged me. I have forced them to do so."

She uttered that last sentence with a mock fierceness that ended in laughter. But she could not hide from her friend the intense seriousness from which these expressions had sprung.

Before Mrs. Diggs could answer, a servant entered the room by one of the draped doorways leading into the *salons* beyond. He was not the butler, who had so admirably served them at dinner, but a footman, charged with other special offices. He handed Claire a card, which she read and tossed aside. The next moment she dismissed him by a slight motion of the hand.

"Let me see that card," said Mrs. Diggs. "Has anybody called whom I know?"

Claire was looking straight into the tumbled, lurid logs of the hearth.

"Yes, you know him, of course," she said. "It was only Stuart Goldwin. I am not at home to-night. Not to any one except you, I mean. I gave orders."

A silence ensued. Mrs. Diggs presently made one of her plunges. "Claire, they say that Goldwin is madly in love with you."

She gave a sharp turn of the neck, fixing her eyes on her friend's face. "That is *all* they say, I hope. They can't say — well, you understand what they can *not* say." .

"That you care for him? Well, no. . . . You have been very discreet. You have arranged wonderfully. Very few women could have done it with the same nicety."

Claire threw back her head, with a haughty, fleeting smile. "Any woman could have done it who felt safe — perfectly safe, as I feel."

"You mean that this grand Goldwin, who sways the stock-market, can't quicken your pulse by one degree."

She looked steadily at Mrs. Diggs. "I did not say that I meant that. But I do, if you choose to ask me point blank. We're very good friends. He amuses me. I fancy that I amuse him. If I do more he doesn't tell me so. He understands what would happen if he did."

She was staring at the fire again. Its lustres played upon the silken folds of her dress, and made the gold glimmers start and fade in her chestnut hair.

Mrs. Diggs was not reclining in her chair; she was leaning sideways, with both black eyes riveted on Claire's half-averted face.

"Claire," she said, "I 'm so awfully glad to hear you say that. It makes me like you better, if such a thing were possible. Upon my word, to be frank, in the most friendly way, I *did* think there was a little danger, don't you know, of . . . Well, you 've settled all doubts, of course. But then, my dear, you never were enormously fond of Hollister. You let him adore *you*, don't you know? Oh, I 've seen it all. There 's no use in getting angry."

"I 'm not angry," said Claire. She was again looking full at her friend. She had put one dainty-booted foot on the low gilt trellis which rose between the rug and the hearthstone. "We seem to drift upon very unpleasant subjects this evening," she continued. "I am afraid our little intimate reunion is not going to be a success."

"You *are* angry!" exclaimed Mrs. Diggs, reproachfully. "You 've changed, Claire. You 're not the same to me as you were before you became a great lady. Now, don't deny it. You feel your oats, as my dear Manhattan would say. You keep me at a distance. You " —

Here Mrs. Diggs paused, for the same footman who had before appeared now made a second entrance. This time he handed Claire a note. "There is no answer, Madame," he said in French, and at once softly vanished.

"Pardon me," said Claire, as she tore open the envelope. Mrs. Diggs watched her while she read the contents of the note. Her perusal took some time. She read the three written pages once, twice, thrice. Her face had grown very grave in the meanwhile.

Suddenly she crumpled the note in one hand, and flung it into the fire. Her eyes flashed and her lip quivered as she did so.

" For Heaven's sake, Claire," appealed her friend, " what *is* the matter ? I suppose Cornelia or Sylvia Lee sends a regret for luncheon. You are so foolish to mind what they do! You recollect what I used to tell you about Cornelia. But why should you mind her airs and caprices now? You are utterly above her — or rather, you have shown her that two can reign in the same kingdom. You could cut her dead with perfect impunity. That's a good deal to say, don't you know, but you positively could ! "

" No, no," said Claire, with a clouded face and a little wave of the hand, " it has nothing to do with either of those women. It is " . . . here she paused, and her breath came quick. " It is from Beverley Thurston."

" Beverley ! " exclaimed Mrs. Diggs. " Why, he 's in Europe."

" He got back yesterday. He has learned about me. I suppose his sister has told him. . And he writes to me in a tone of impertinence. Yes, it 's nothing else. He writes to me as if I were some sinful creature. He presumes to be sorry for me. He says that he will pay me a visit if I can spare him an hour from the giddy life I am leading. . . . I don't remember the exact words he uses ; it is not so much what he writes as what he seems to write. The whole note breathes of patronage and commiseration. To *me !* — think of it ! What right has he? What right did I ever give him ? "

Mrs. Diggs started up from her chair. "Why, my dear Claire," she said, "you are greatly excited!"

"I am miserable!" cried Claire. She almost staggered toward Mrs. Diggs, and flung both arms about her friend's neck. "I am miserable — miserable!" she went on, with a sudden paroxysm of tears. She leaned her proud young head on Mrs. Diggs's bony shoulder, beginning to sob quite wildly. "Do I deserve reproaches? Have I been so wrong? What evil have I done? Let my conscience trouble me if it will, but *he* is not my conscience. How dare *he* reproach me?"

A violent seizure of sobs made Claire incapable of further speech. Mrs. Diggs let the clinging arms clasp her. She did not know what to answer; she scarcely knew what to think. She only felt, at that unexpected moment, that she loved Claire very much, and would always stay her staunch friend, no matter what bitter ill might overtake her.

XVIII.

As Claire was descending into the lower hall, at about four o'clock the next afternoon, she saw her husband enter the house with his latch-key. She quickened her step a little, and met him at the landing of the stairs. They had not seen each other for twenty-four hours; she had breakfasted in her room, that morning, as was of late almost habitual with her, and by the time that she left it he had been driven away in his brougham. On the previous night he had reached home long after she had retired to bed. All this was no new thing. Its first and second occurrence had shocked them both, as an unforeseen result of their altered existence. But repetition had set it securely among the commonplaces. They accepted it, now, with a matter-of-course placidity.

"I was going to the Vanvelsors' reception," Claire said. "Did you think of dropping in?"

"No," answered Hollister. He had taken her hand, and was holding it while he spoke. The next moment he kissed her cheek, and soon let his eye wander over the complex tastefulness of her attire. He then drew her arm within his own, and led her toward the near drawing-room, whose threshold they crossed. Except his recorded monosyllable, he had said nothing for an appreciable time, and Claire, regarding his face with a sidelong glance, had already detected there marked signs of worriment.

" No," he presently continued, taking a seat on one of the rich-clad sofas, and gently forcing her to sit beside him. "I had no idea of going there. I don't feel like anything gay, Claire. Things are doing horribly on the Street. There's a dreadful squall. I hope it will be only a squall, and soon blow over." He then named a certain stock in which he had very comprehensive interests. "It has dropped in the most furious fashion," he proceeded. "Claire, I've lost seventy thousand dollars to-day, if I've lost a penny."

He talked more technically of his ill-luck after that, and told her what he believed to be the reason of the adverse change. She listened with great attention. She knew so much of Wall Street matters that she scarcely missed a point in all that he explained.

" So Goldwin is on the other side," she said, when he had finished.

" Yes, Goldwin is safe. But you can't tell what to-morrow will bring. No one is really safe. Prices are flying about. It's a shocking state of affairs."

" There is nothing for you to do just now, is there ? " Claire asked, after a little pause.

" Oh, no ; I may get a few telegrams later. But nothing serious will happen till to-morrow."

She laid her hand on his arm. She was more alarmed and perplexed than she chose to show. " Then come with me to the reception," she said; " you might as well, Herbert. It is better than to brood over the state of matters down there."

He shook his head negatively. " I should make a very bad guest," he replied. " Go yourself, Claire. But remember one thing." He was looking at her very fixedly ; his frank blue eyes were full of a soft yet assertive pain. " Our life may alter suddenly for the worse. We may have to give up all this." He waved one hand here and there, as though generalizing the whole luxurious encompassment. " There is no telling what *may* happen. I never felt the insecurity of my career as I feel it now. Do you know, Claire, that a few more such days as this may ruin me ? "

" Ruin you ? " she repeated.

She was pale as those words left her lips. Hollister had proposed to her a terrible possibility.

" Yes, Claire, I mean it. Of course I am looking at the worst that might happen. But I want to prepare you."

She rose, keeping her eyes on his. " I don't know what I should do," she said, " if I lost what I have now. I have grown used to it, Herbert. I won't let myself think that it might pass away — that I should be left without all these good and precious things."

As she spoke the last words he rose also, and caught both her hands, looking eagerly into her face.

" Claire," he exclaimed, " you *must* think of losing it all! You *must* try to reconcile yourself with the idea! If you don't, the ordeal will be all the harder when it comes."

" When it comes ? " she again repeated.

" Yes — you see just how I stand. You have grasped the whole wretched situation. Of course there's a chance that I may right myself, but" . . .

" I 'll take that chance," she broke in, quite forcibly withdrawing her hands. " So will you, Herbert. I prefer to look at it this way. We will both take the chance."

Hollister's face was full of reproach.

"Claire!" he exclaimed. "I see that you love this new life with a positive passion!"

"I love it very much," she answered. "I love it so much that I should suffer fearfully if I were turned adrift from it. . . . Come, we will both go to the Vanvelsors' reception."

"No," replied Hollister. He walked away from her. By her lack of sympathy she had dealt him a cruel sting.

"Very well," responded Claire, as she watched his receding figure. "*I* am going."

His back was turned to her, but he suddenly veered round, facing her, and saying, with a bitter sharpness: "Go, if you please! Go, and leave me to my misery! If you cared for me in the right manner, you would not want to go. You would want to stay with me, and forget, for a while at least, the gay crowds that admire and court you!"

These words were utterly unexpected. He had never before alluded to her lack of fondness. She was embarrassed, ashamed. For a moment she could not speak. Then she simulated an affronted demeanor; it seemed her sole refuge. "I — I care for you as much as I have always cared," she said. "No more and no less."

She moved toward the door at once, after thus speaking. She wondered if he would seek to detain her. He did not. . . . She entered her coupé very soon afterward. During the drive to Mrs. Vanvelsor's reception she had a keen remembrance of just how Hollister had looked when her final gaze had dwelt upon him. She knew that she had stung at last into life the perception of how much he had been

giving and how little he had received. Her conscience
sternly smote her; she was more than once on the
verge of ordering that the vehicle should be driven
home again. But in her then mood any attempt at
amendment seemed wildly futile. What could she
say to her husband? That she deplored his possible
ruin? Yes; but not that such regret sprang from
the sweet sources of a wifely, unselfish love. She
could not regard the possibility of being flung downward from her present high place with any unselfish
feeling. Mrs. Diggs had touched the living and sensitive truth last night: her thirst for luxury had
grown a vice. Soft raiment, obsequious attendance,
a place of supreme social distinction, all these had
become vitally, imperiously needful to her happiness.

It was not the sort of happiness which she believed
high or fine. She could most clearly conceive of
another, less fervid, less material, less intoxicating,
fraught with a spiritual incentive and an intellectual
meaning. But it was too late to dream of that now.
She had taken the bent; she must have power or
nothing. She regarded the idea of being obscure
and with straitened funds as a calamity simply horrible. Hollister must think her cruel as death; that
was inevitable. She did not blame him for blaming
her. She blamed herself for having married him
with loveless apathy. His reproachful words haunted
her — but what could she do? He wanted genuine
tenderness, sympathy, fortifying cheer. But he
wanted these from an impulse of which her heart
had always been incapable. Fate was avenging itself upon her. She had tampered with holy things.
Her marriage oath had been a mockery. Could she
go back and tell him this? Could she go back and

lie to him, feign before him? No; best that she should not go back at all.

The reception was a great crush. But they seemed to make way for her with a sort of obeisance. No one jostled against her; they all appeared to give her a little elbow-room in the throng, while they either bowed or stared. She was secretly agonized. She smiled and spoke as effectively as usual; she held her court among them all, as of late she had invariably held it. But her heart was sick; she was besieged by a portentous dread, and she was pierced with that self-contempt whose length of thrust is measured by a consciousness of how far the being we might have become surpasses the being that we are. While she stood the centre of a small, courtly group, a gentleman softly pushed his way into her notice and held out his hand. She took the hand, and looked well into the face of him who had extended it. The new-comer was Beverley Thurston. As Claire looked she swiftly noted that his familiar face wore marked signs of change. He had distinctly aged. The gray at his temples had grown grayer; the crows'-feet under his hazel eyes were a little more apparent; perhaps, too, his gravity of manner was more clearly suggested by a first glance. At the same time she felt herself regarding him in a new light and by the aid of amplified experience. She silently and fleetly made him stand a test, so to speak, and at once decided that he stood it well. She had met no man since they had parted who bespoke high-breeding and gentility with more immediate directness.

"I thought I should find you here," he said, as their hands dropped apart.

" Did you come on that account ? " she asked.

" Not entirely, because I had great fears of not being able to do more than watch you from a distance."

" Ah," she said, with a pretty graciousness, and loud enough for all the others to hear, " you have an excellent claim upon me — that of old acquaintance."

Her surrounders felt that there was either dismissal or desertion waiting for them. She managed to make it promptly plain that her favoring heed had been wholly transferred to Thurston ; she showed it to them with a cool boldness which they would have resented with resolves of future neglect if indulged in by many another woman present ; for they were all men who put a solid worth upon their courtesies, and had a fastidious reluctance ever to be charged with sowing them broadcast.

But Claire had long ago learned that the security of her reign depended upon an occasional open proof of how she herself trusted its power. She had guessed the peril of continuing monotonously clement. To talk with Thurston now interested her more than any other conversational project. It was not long before she had slipped her hand into his arm, and was saying, as they moved through the crowd : —

" If you care to go into the conservatory, we shall find it much pleasanter there, I think."

The house was one of those new and majestic structures near the Park. It occupied a corner, sweeping far backward from Fifth Avenue into an adjacent street. It had an almost imperial amplitude, and was a building in which no lordly or pleasurable detail seemed to have been overlooked. The conservatory, whose spacious interior wooed through breadths of glass its kindest warmth from the churlish winter sunshine, was of refreshing temperature after the heated rooms beyond, while its masses of leafing or blooming plants loaded the air with delightful odors.

A few people were strolling about the cool courts, as Claire and Thurston now entered them. The entertainment of to-day was a kind of house-warming; the Vanvelsors, in current metropolitan phrase, were old people, but their present mansion was new in a decisive sense ; they had migrated hither from a residence in Bond Street, where they had dwelt for forty years or more. The push of the younger generation, left with inherited millions, had thus architecturally asserted itself. Few of their guests knew the ways of their changed and palatial home. But Claire knew them ; she had dined in this imposing abode not less than a fortnight ago. There were many bearers of precious Dutch names who had known the Vanvelsors for many decades ; but Claire had been preferred to hosts of these nice-lineaged legitimists. She was the fashion ; other people were paying homage to her ; the younger Vanvelsors liked everything that was the fashion ; they had paid homage, too.

" We can find a seat," Claire said to her companion ; " the place is not full, as you see ; we might sit yonder, in those two vacant chairs — that is, if you care to sit ; I do ; I am tired."

It was not until they were both seated, with glossy tropical leaves touching their heads, that Thurston answered : —

" You say you are tired. That might mean a little or a great deal. Which does it mean ? "

Claire responded with a question, looking at him fixedly.

" Why did you write me that letter ? " she said.

" Did it offend you ? " he asked.

" No and yes. You might not have reproached me until you knew more of the real truth."

Thurston stroked his gray mustache. " I think I knew all the truth," he said. " I know it now, at least."

" Your sister has told you," Claire retorted, with speed.

" Yes and no," he responded, not mocking her own recent words, yet leaving a distinct impression that he had half repeated them. " You forget that I have seen you reigning on your new throne."

" Let us be candid," said Claire. " Your note was almost a sneer."

He slowly shook his head. " It was a regret."

" You think I might have done greater things."

" I think you might have done better things."

" You admit that I have achieved success ? "

" A marvelous success. It shows your extraordinary gifts. The town, in a certain way, is ringing with your name. If an ordinary woman had gained your place she would have found in it a splendid gratification. She would have been amply, perfectly satisfied."

" You mean that I am not satisfied. Pray allow it. Your tones and your look both show it me."

Thurston smiled, transiently and sadly. " I mean that you are miserable," he said.

Claire bit her lip, and slightly drooped her head. " You have no cause to tell me that."

He leaned closer to her. " I do tell you. It is

true. I saw it in your face when I first looked at you. There is a change. I can't define it, but it exists. You are more beautiful than when I saw you last. You have an air of ease, dignity, command. But you express a kind of superb weariness, and yet occasional flashes of excitement are in your talk and demeanor. You see, I have watched you from a distance; I have my opinions."

"Yes, you have your opinions," said Claire, lifting her head and directly regarding him. "That is very plain."

"It all makes an exquisite picture," Thurston continued. "I have seen the world, as you know. I have seen many beautiful women. Your personality, as I now encounter it, is an absolute astonishment to me. I don't know where, in these few months, you acquired your repose, your serenity, your magnificence, your air. Do you remember what I told you of the restless American type that you represent? I knew you would strive to rise; it was in you; you pushed to the front, as I was sure you would do. But I had no prescience of this mighty accomplishment."

"You are sneering at me, as your note sneered," said Claire, looking at him steadily. "Acknowledge it. I perceive it with great accuracy. I somehow cannot answer you as I would answer another. You warned me months ago. You knew what I desired, and told me of the danger that lay in my path. I recollect all that you wanted me to try and be. Perhaps I *would* have tried, under differing conditions."

She paused, and Thurston instantly said, "As my wife you would have tried — and succeeded."

"Perhaps," she answered, very low of tone, not

meeting his look. "But all that is past. Don't pull corpses out of graves."

"My love for you is living," he said to her. There was no touch of passion in his voice; there was only a mournful respect. "I don't think I am wrong to speak of it now. There 's a sanctity and chastity about the feeling I bear for you which the fact of your being a wife does not affect. I want to know the man whom you have married; I am curious to meet him and know him well. He has a large publicity, as you are aware. They have heard of him in Europe."

"I understand the question you wish to put yet do not," Claire said, at this point. "You lead up to it very adroitly; I might play the rôle of ignorant innocence, if I chose. But I do not choose. You want to ask me whether I loved the man I married."

Thurston again stroked his mustache, for a moment. "Yes," he presently said, "I should like to know that."

A silence now ensued between them. Claire broke it. "He loved me," she said.

"Which means that you did not care for him?"

"Oh, yes. I cared very much. It was no worldly sale of myself. He was not even rich when I married him. He attracted me — in a manner charmed me. I felt that I should never meet another man who would attract and charm me more. Do you understand?"

"Thoroughly. . . . Since then you have met Stuart Goldwin. I know him well. He is a man of exceptional fascination. They tell me that he is your slave."

"Do they?" said Claire, coloring under this rapid

attack of candor. " Well, if he is my slave — which I, of course, deny — then I am not his. They did not tell you that, I am sure. They did not even hint it."

" No. You have escaped the least breath of scandal."

" Be sure that I have. And I shall continue to escape it. I recollect that you once declared I was cold, and that my coldness would prove a safeguard. ' It is very protective to a woman,' you said."

" Quote me in full or not at all," he corrected, with a grim pleasantry. " I said that it is very protective to a woman — while it lasts."

" True," returned Claire. " And it *has* lasted. I prophesied that it would last, and I was right. . . . By the way, from whom have you learned all these important items ? Perhaps from your sister. She is not my friend."

Thurston started a little. " She is not your enemy ? " he said, putting the words as a distinct question.

" I hope not. But I am by no means sure. Thus far she has held herself aloof from me. She has not openly opposed me, but she has behaved with telling reserve. Everybody else has paid me tribute, so to speak. No, I am wrong. There is one other woman — her cousin, Mrs. Lee."

" Of course you know why poor Sylvia would be your foe. She is madly in love with Goldwin ; she has been for years. You must have cost her dire pangs."

Claire chose to ignore this last statement. " I think your sister dislikes me from pride," she said. " I mean pride of family." Here she paused for a moment, and seemed almost bashfully reluctant to proceed. But her hesitation had in it a gentle, unassuming modesty; it sprang wholly from unwillingness to touch on a subject which she knew that only the most delicate tact should deal with, if to deal with it at all were not folly and rashness. "Your sister found out," she softly continued, "that you had liked me enough to ask me to be your wife. Heaven knows, Beverley Thurston, that *I* did not tell her!"

Thurston looked very grave. "I told her," he said. "Or rather, she drew it from me. I was foolish to let her. Cornelia is so clever. . . . Well," he suddenly went on, with an unusual show of animation, "do you mean that she accused you of having rejected me?"

"She did not put it in the form of an accusation. She stated it. Wait; I will tell you more; I will tell when, where, and how it all happened."

Claire did so. He listened with deep attention. She narrated the whole episode of her well-remembered conversation with his sister in the dining-room at the Coney Island hotel.

"Ah, what a woman that sister of mine is!" he exclaimed, in his subdued way, as Claire finished. "I must talk with her. I dine there to-night. I will find out if this knowledge has been at the root of her late behavior."

Claire laid her gloved hand lightly on his sleeve. "I think it best to say nothing. I feel that you are my friend—always my friend. As such you will more discreetly let matters rest where they are."

"Let matters rest where they are?" he repeated.

"Yes." Her face broke into a smile as she spoke

the next words. " Mrs. Van Horn — the great Mrs. Van Horn — has withdrawn her disapprobation. The day after to-morrow she and Mrs. Lee lunch with me. It is a ladies' lunch. You have no idea how monstrously important an event her attendance is to be. It is my crowning glory. After that I shall have no more worlds to conquer. She is actually coming ; I have it in her own graceful handwriting. Frankly, I am quite serious. If you had followed affairs, if you had n't been off in Europe for months, you would understand the momentous nature of your sister's acceptance."

Claire rose as she ended her last sentence. The conservatory was quite empty of guests ; the waning winter sunlight told of the hour for departure. " It is time to go," she now continued. " Remember, whenever you come to me you will be welcome. I shall be at the opera to-night. Drop into my box if you get away from your sister's dinner before ten, and feel like hearing some music."

Thurston replied that he would certainly do so. But, as it happened, he partially failed to keep his promise. Mrs. Van Horn's dinner was attended by several guests. He wanted to talk with his sister, and it was somewhat late before he found the desired opportunity.

" Did you enjoy it, Beverley?" said his hostess, referring to the dinner. They were in the front drawing-room together. Thurston had seated himself near the fire-place, in a big chair of gilded basket-work with soft plush cushions. He was playing with a small locket at his waistcoat, and his look did not lift itself from the bauble as Mrs. Van Horn spoke. She came near his chair and stood at his side for a

moment. She had been giving her servants a few
orders relative to the morrow. She looked very well
that evening. The color of her gown was a sort of
tea-rose pink, and she wore a collar of large pearls
about her throat, and ornaments of pearls in her
blonde hair. While her brother was answering, she
dropped in a chair quite near his own.

" I thought it about as successful as your dinners
always are," he said. " Everything went off to perfection, of course. . . . No, I forget; there was one
drawback. A serious one."

" What was it ? "

" Sylvia Lee."

" You never could endure Sylvia," said Mrs. Van
Horn, in her grand, cool, suave way.

" I think her abominable," replied Thurston.
" Her affectations irritate and depress me. They
appear to grow with age, too. She behaved more
like a contortionist than ever, to-night. But it is not
only the wretched, sensational bad taste of her poses
and costumes. It is a conviction that she is as treacherous as the serpent she resembles. And then her
religious attitudinizing . . . has she got over that
yet? I suppose not."

Mrs. Van Horn, who would sharply have resented
these biting comments if any lips but her brother's
had delivered them, now answered with only a faint
touch of petulance. " You will never believe any
good of Sylvia, so it is useless to tell you how unjust
I consider your opinions. But she is more passionately absorbed in charities and religious devotion
than ever before. If you could see some of the people whom she goes among, and whom she has constantly visiting her in her own house, you would be

forced to grant that the shallow hypocrisy with which you charge her is a most sincere and active almsgiving."

" Say notorious, too. She's a Pharisee to the tips of her fingers. I should like to know of one good deed that she has ever performed in secret. She parades her piety and her benevolence just as she does her newest fantasies in dressmaking. She thinks them picturesque. She would rather die than not be picturesque, and I believe that when she does die she will make some *ante-mortem* arrangements about an abnormal coffin. It's a marvel to me that Stuart Goldwin should have put up with her nonsense as long as he did. . . . By the way, how does she stand his desertion ? "

" Has he deserted her ? "

" Oh, come, now, Cornelia, you know quite well that he has." Thurston was looking directly at his sister for the first time since their interview had begun.

Mrs. Van Horn gave a light, soft laugh.

" You mean for Mrs. Hollister, Beverley ? "

" Of course I do."

" I see that you have picked up some precious bits of gossip since you got back." He was watching her very closely, and perceived, knowing her as scarcely any one else knew her, that a severe annoyance dwelt beneath those last words. She slightly tossed her delicate head. " You are so relentless with poor Sylvia that I naturally don't want to feed the fuel of your disapprobation. Well, then, let me admit that Goldwin *is* devoted to your former friend."

" Say my present friend, if you please, Cornelia."

He saw a little gleam, like that of lit steel, creep

into her pale-blue eyes. "Oh, then you still call her that?"

"Most certainly. Should I withdraw my friendship because she refused to marry me when I was old enough to be her father? On the contrary, I am liberal enough to applaud her good sense."

"Beverley," exclaimed his sister, in tones of harsh disgust, "how can you show so little self-respect?"

He saw that she had grown pale with anger. He set his eyes upon her face with a fresh intentness of gaze. He had a distinct object in view, and he was determined, if possible, to reach it. He leaned much closer toward her while he said, in slow, deliberative tones: —

"My self-respect, or lack of it, is quite my own affair. Pray understand that. You never forgave Claire Twining for refusing me, Cornelia. You need not attempt to deceive me there. I repeat, you never forgave her. Your pride would not allow you."

Her voice shook as she answered him. She was bitterly distressed and agitated. He had touched an old wound, but one which had not healed. She loved him as she had never loved any other man. He was part of herself; his blood was hers; he belonged to the egotism which was her ruling quality. Her speech now betrayed neither wrath nor disgust; it was full of mournful dismay. The times in her life had been rare when her glacial composure had shown such excessive disturbance.

"I concede, Beverley, that it hurt me very deeply to realize your humiliation. It seemed to me then, as it seems to me now, that a girl of her class should have been glad to marry a man of your place and name. What was she? And what were and are *you?*"

"Pshaw! I was and am an elderly, faded old fellow."

Mrs. Van Horn rose from her chair. She was visibly trembling. "You could have given that adventuress a position far more stable than she holds now, as the wife of a lucky stock-gambler!"

Thurston remained seated. "You call her an adventuress," he said, "and yet you visit her — you put her on a social equality with yourself."

During the vigilant scrutiny with which he accompanied these words, Mrs. Van Horn's brother decided that in all his experience of her he had never seen her show such perturbation as now.

"People acknowledge her," she said, a little hoarsely. "I have never been to her entertainments. I have never accepted her, so to speak. If you inquire, you will find this to be true. It is current talk, my reserve, my disapproval."

He shot his answer with quiet speed, meaning that it should hit and tell. "You are going to the lunch that she gives on Friday. I happen to be certain of this — unless you have had the wanton rudeness to write her that you would go, while meaning to remain away." He rose as he spoke the last word. Brother and sister faced each other. There was a tranquil challenge in Thurston's full and steady gaze.

She recoiled a little. "I — well, yes — I did intend to go," she replied, below her breath, and actually stammering.

"What is your reason for going," he questioned, "if you despise and dislike her so?"

She threw back her head; her self-possession had returned, and with it a stately indignation.

"You are insolent," she said.

Thurston broke into a hard laugh.

"Yes," he exclaimed, "I am insolent to the great lady because I detect her on the verge of some petty revenge! Oh, I know you too well, my dear sister," he went on, with stern irony. "You can't rebuff me in that way. There is something behind this fine condescension. Sylvia Lee and you have been putting your heads together. Your revenge and her jealousy will make a rather dangerous alliance. You are both going to the lunch. You are both employing a new line of tactics. What does it mean? I demand to know. I have a right to know."

He was very impressive, yet his voice was hardly raised above that of ordinary speech. She had always admired his gravity and calm; he had been for years her ideal and model gentleman; she hated excitement of any sort, and to see it in him gave her a positive feeling of awe.

"Beverley," she murmured, half brokenly, "remember that if I had any thought of punishment toward the woman who trifled with you and humbled you, it has been because I am your sister — because I was fond of you — because" . . .

He interrupted her with a quick, waving gesture of the hand. "You talk insanely," he said. "She neither trifled with me nor humbled me. I was a fool even to tell you how sensibly she acted. What you call your fondness is nothing but your miserable pride. I see clearly that you have some detestable plan. Do you refuse to tell me what it is? — me, who have the right to learn it!"

Every trace of color had left her cheeks, and she was biting her lips. There was very little of the great lady remaining in her mien or visage, now.

"You have twice spoken of your right," she faltered. "On what is such a right based? How can you possibly possess it? You are nothing to her. You are neither her husband nor"—

"I am her lover," he broke in. "I am her lover, reverent, devout, loyal, and shall be while we both live! She is the most charming woman I have ever met. I met her too late, or she would be my wife now. It was not her fault that she refused me. She is not a bit to blame. Good Heavens! have I the monstrous arrogance to assume that she should have married an old fossil like myself because I was of a little importance in the world? No, Cornelia, that preposterous assumption belongs to you. It is just like you. And you call it love — sisterly love. I call it the very apex of intolerable pride. But admit for the moment that it is I and not yourself whom you care for. Will you tell me, on that account, what it is you mean or meant to do?"

Before he had finished, Mrs. Van Horn had sunk into a chair and covered her face with both hands. Her sobs presently sounded, violent and rapid. In these brief seconds she was shedding more tears than had left her cold eyes for many years past.

"I mean to do nothing — nothing!" she answered, with a gasp almost like that which leaves us when in straits for breath.

"Do you give me your sacred promise," he said, "that this is true?"

The words appeared to horrify her. She looked at him with streaming eyes, while a positive shudder shook her frame.

"Oh, Beverley, what degradation this seems to me! Degradation of *yourself!* You may call me as

proud as you choose. It is no insult. It is a compliment, even. I am proud of *being* proud. I had
never given up hope that you would marry some
woman of good birth, good antecedents, your equal
and mine — young enough, too, to bear you children.
I am childless, myself — how I would have loved
your children! Their own mother would not have
loved them more. Every penny of my large fortune
should have gone to them. This has been my dream
for years past, and now you shatter it by telling me
that an upstart, a parvenu, a nobody from nowhere,
holds you ensnared beyond escape!"

Thurston was not at all touched. This outburst,
so uncharacteristic and so unexpected, did not bear
for him a grain of pathos. He saw behind it nothing
save an implacable selfishness that chose to misname
itself affection. The ambition of Claire saddened
him to contemplate; it had so rich a potentiality for
its background. He was forever seeing the true and
wise woman that she might have been. Even the
nettles in her soil flourished with a certain beauty of
their own, proving its fertile resources if more wholesome growths had taken root there. But in Cornelia
Van Horn's nature all was barren and arid. The
very genuineness of her present grief was its condem-
nation. Her tears were as chilly to him as the light
of her bravest diamonds; they had something of the
same hard sparkle; she wept them only from her
brain, as it were; her heart did not know that she
was shedding them.

"The bitter epithets which you apply to my *en-
snarer*," he said, with a momentary curve of the lips
too austere to be termed a smile, " make me the
more suspicious that you harbor against her designs

of practical spite. I want your promise that you will refrain from the least active injury — that you will never use the great social power you possess, either by speech or deed, to her disadvantage. Do you give me this promise, or do you refuse it? If the latter, everything is at an end between us. The monetary trusts you have consigned to me shall be at once transferred to whatever lawyer you may appoint as their recipient, and from to-night henceforward we meet as total strangers."

" A quarrel between you and me, Beverley! " said his sister, trying to choke back her sobs, and rising with a cobweb handkerchief pressed in fluttered alternation to either humid eye. " A family quarrel! And I have been so guarded — so careful that the world should hold us and our name in perfect esteem! — Oh, it is horrible! "

" I did not infer that it would be pleasant," he answered. " You yourself have power to avert or bring it about. All remains with yourself."

" I — I must make you a promise," she retorted, in what would have been, if louder, a peevish wail, " just as though I had really intended some — some gross, revengeful act! You — you are ungentlemanly to impose such a condition! You — you are out of your senses! That creature has bewitched you! "

He saw her eye, tearful though it was, quail before his own narrowed and penetrating look. He felt his suspicion strengthen within him.

" I do impose the condition," he said, perhaps more determinedly than he had yet spoken. " I do exact the promise. Now decide, Cornelia. There is no hard threat on my part, remember. You don't like the idea of an open rupture with me, you don't think it would be respectable; it would make a little mark on your ermine — a *défaut de la cuirasse,* so to speak. But your beloved world would possibly side with you and against me; you would not lose a supporter; you would still remain quite the grand personage you are. Only, I should never darken your doors again; that is all. Come, now, be good enough to decide."

She sank into her seat once more; her eyes had drooped themselves; the tears were standing on her pale cheeks. "I did not know you had it in you to be so cruel," she said, uttering the words with apparent difficulty.

"I am afraid I always knew that you had it in you," he returned. "Come, if you please. . . . Your answer."

"You — you mean my promise?"

"Yes. Your faithful and solemn promise. We need not go over its substance again. If you break it after giving it I shall not reproach you; I shall simply act. You understand how; I have told you."

She was silent for some time. She had got her handkerchief so twisted between her fingers that they threatened to tear its frail fabric.

Without raising her eyes, and in a voice that was very sombre but had lost all trace of tremor, she at length murmured: —

"Well, I promise faithfully. I will do nothing — say nothing. My conduct shall be absolutely neutral — null. Are you satisfied?"

"Entirely," he said.

He at once left her. He reached the opera just as it was ending. Claire, in the company of two ladies and two gentlemen, and attended by Goldwin, was leaving her box when he contrived to find her. Hollister had purchased one of the larger proscenium boxes some time ago; he had given a great price for it to an owner who could not resist the princely terms offered.

"You are very late," Claire said, giving him her hand, while Goldwin, standing behind her, dropped a great fur-lined cloak over her shoulders, and hid the regal costliness of her dress, with its laces, flowers, and jewels. "Have you been dining with your sister all this time, or were you here for the last act, but talking with older friends elsewhere?"

"No," replied Thurston, who had already exchanged a nod of greeting with Goldwin. He lowered his voice so that Claire alone could hear it. "I arrived but a few minutes ago. I have been talking seriously with my sister. You were quite right. She has withdrawn her disapprobation. You have conquered her, as you conquer everybody."

He saw the faint yet meaning flash that left her dark-blue eyes, and he read clearly, too, the significance of her bright smile, as she said: —

"Ah, you reassure me. For I had my doubts; I confess it, now."

"So had I," he returned. "But they are at rest forever, as I want yours to be." . . .

At an early hour, the next morning, Mrs. Van Horn surprised her friend and kinswoman, Mrs. Ridgeway Lee, in the latter's pretty and quaint *boudoir*, that was Japanese enough, as regarded hangings and adornments, to have been the sacred retreat of some almond-eyed Yeddo belle.

Mrs. Lee had had her coffee, and was deep in one

of Zola's novels when her friend was announced. Her
coupé would appear at twelve, and take her to a certain small religious hospital of which she was one of
the most assiduous patrons; but she always read
Zola, or some author of a similar Gallic intensity,
while she digested her coffee.

She had concealed the novel, however, by the time
that Mrs. Van Horn had swept her draperies between
the Oriental jars and screens.

"I have come to talk with you about that affair
— that plan, Sylvia," said her visitor, dropping into
a chair.

"You mean . . . to-morrow, Cornelia?"

"Yes. . . . By the way, have you seen the morning papers?"

"I glanced over one of them — the 'Herald,' I
think. It said, in the society column, that I wore
magenta at the Charity Ball last night. As if I
would disgrace myself with that hideous color! These
monsters of the newspapers ought to be suppressed
in some way."

"You did n't think so when they described your
flame-colored plush gown so accurately last Tuesday.
However, you deserve to be ridiculed for going to
those vulgar public balls."

"But this was for charity, and " —

"Yes, I know. Don't let us talk of it. If you had
read the paper more closely you would have seen the
statement, given with a great air of truth, that Herbert Hollister's millions are flowing away from him at
a terrible rate, and that to-night may see him almost
ruined."

"How dreadful!" said Mrs. Lee, in her slow way,
but noticeably changing color.

23

Mrs. Van Horn gave a high, hard laugh. "Of course you are sorry."

"Sorry!" softly echoed Mrs. Lee, uncoiling herself from one peculiar pose on the yellow-and-black lounge where she was seated, and gently writhing into another. "Of course I am sorry, Cornelia. Although you must grant that *she* merits it. To desert her poor, ignorant, miserable mother! To run away and leave her own flesh and blood in starvation!" Here Mrs. Lee heaved an immense sigh. "Ah, Providence finds us all out, sooner or later! If that wicked woman's sin is punished by her husband's ruin, who shall say that she has not richly deserved it? But in spite of this, Cornelia dear, *our* stroke of punishment will not be too severe. With regard to my own share in our coming work, I feel that I am to be merely the instrument — the humble instrument — of Heavenly justice itself!"

"No doubt," replied Mrs. Van Horn, with frigid dryness. "But you must do it all alone to-morrow, Sylvia. I have come to tell you so. I can have no part whatever in the proceeding. However it is carried out — whether you bring Mrs. Hollister face to face with her plebeian parent or no, I shall be absent. It is true, I accepted for the lunch. But I shall be ill at the last moment. I withdraw from the whole ingenious plot. I shan't see the little *coup de théâtre* at all. I wish that I could. You know I have never forgiven the refusal of Beverley any more than you have forgiven . . . well, something else, my dear Sylvia. But I must remain aloof; it is settled; there is no help for it."

Mrs. Lee opened her big black eyes very wide indeed. "Have you lost your senses, Cornelia?" she queried, with her grotesque, unfailing drawl. "What! After my wonderful meeting with Mrs. Twining at the hospital! After your exultant conclusion that we had far better fix the stigma of ingratitude and desertion upon her shameless daughter with as much publicity as possible! After our talks, our arrangements, our anticipations! After all this, you are *not going to-morrow!* I don't understand. I am sure that I *must* be dreaming!"

"Let me explain, then," said Mrs. Van Horn, with a quiver in her usually serene tones that was a residue of last evening's dramatic defeat and surrender. "For once in my life, Sylvia, I — I have found my match, I have failed to hold my own, I have been ignominiously beaten. And the victor is my own brother, Beverley."

She went on speaking for some time longer, with no actual interruption on the part of her companion, though with very decided signs of consternation and disapproval.

"Oh, Cornelia, it is too bad!" exclaimed Mrs. Lee, when the recital was finished. "He couldn't have meant that he would cut his own sister! What *is* to be done? Well, I suppose it must all be given up. And it would have been such a triumph! And she deserves it so — running away from her own mother whom she had always hated and disobeyed! We have that poor, horrid, common, but pitiable Mrs. Twining's own word for it, you know. And she would have been such a magnificent spectre at the banquet! She would have risen up like Banquo, ill-dressed, haggard, rheumatic, pathetic. Everybody would have denounced this unnatural daughter when they saw the meeting. I can't realize that you, *you* could let it all be nipped in the bud!"

"It is n't all nipped in the bud, Sylvia," said Mrs. Van Horn, sharply.

"But it *is!* Why is n't it? You certainly don't expect me to carry it out alone?"

Mrs. Van Horn decisively nodded. "Yes, Sylvia," she answered, "that is just the point. I do expect you to carry it out alone. You are clever enough, quite clever enough, and" . . . Here the speaker paused for a moment, and then crisply, emphatically added: "And after all is said, remember one thing. It is this: You have a much larger debt to pay her than I have."

A malign look stole into Mrs. Lee's black eyes. She was thinking of Stuart Goldwin. She was thinking of the man whom she had passionately loved — whom she passionately loved still.

"I believe you are right, Cornelia," she at length replied, in her usual protracted and lingering style. She had got herself, as she spoke, into one of her most involved and tortuous attitudes; she had never looked more serpentine than now.

XIX.

CLAIRE felt, on this same day, like casting about in her mind for some pretext by which she might postpone her grand luncheon on the morrow. She had passed a sleepless night, having gone to bed without seeing Hollister. In the morning she had avoided meeting him. She had no comfort to administer, no reparation to offer. The mask had been stripped from her face; the comedy had been played to its end. She had a sense of worthlessness, depravity, sin. At the same time she recklessly told herself that no atonement was in her power. A woful weakness, which took the form of a woful strength, overmastered her as the hours grew older. Her thirst for new excitements deepened with her misery and anxiety. But she sat in her dressing-room or paced the floor till past three in the afternoon. There were numberless people whom she might have visited; there were several receptions that afternoon at which her presence would have been held important by their respective givers. Even the known jeopardy of her husband's position would have heightened the value of her appearance, adding to her popularity the spice of curiosity as well.

More than once she said to herself: ' I will go to one of these places. I will show them how quietly I bear the strain. If by to-morrow no crash has come, they will admire my nerve and courage. For if I once went, they should never discover a trace of worriment or suspense. I think the fact of my being closely watched would even make me talk better and smile brighter. The wear and tear of the whole thing might make me forget a little, too. And I want so to forget, if I can!'

But she did not go. The morning papers lay on a near table. She had read every word that they had to tell her of the fierce financial turmoil. Some of the stern figures they quoted made her heart flutter with affright; some of their ominous and snarling editorials wrought an added discomfort.

If Hollister weathered the storm, she decided, all would remain as it had been before. Or, if not precisely that, the general outward effect would continue quite the same. She would shine among her courtiers; she would dazzle and rule. He would feel his wound, now that he knew the pitiless truth of her indifference, but he would make the engrossing ventures of his business-life drown its pain until this had perhaps ceased forever. They would drift further apart than they had ever done in recent months, but to the eye of the world there would be no severance. It was possible that he would vex her with no more reproaches. It was probable that as time passed he would forget that he had ever had any reproaches to offer.

While Claire's reflections, nervous and fitful, took by degrees some such shape as this, she found a desperate, yearning pleasure in the hope that she might still drink the *vin capiteux* of worldly success. She almost felt like flinging herself on her knees and praying that the delicious cup might not forever be dashed from her lips. To this stage had her triumphs brought her. She was the same woman who had made those resolves of abstinence and reformation which her biographer has already duly chronicled. She was the same woman whose conscience had smitten her with a sense of higher and purer things when the farewell of Thurston warned her by such appalling remonstrance, and when she found herself confronting her father's placid tomb amid the solemnities of Greenwood. And yet how abysmal was the difference between then and now! The chance of radical change in heart, aim, and ideal had then been given her; but now all thought of such change woke only a willful, imperious dissent. Her vision turned upon her own soul to-day, and showed her its mighty lapse from grace, its supine and incapable droop. The debasing spell had been woven; what counterspell was potent enough to break it? Occasional flashes of regret and aspiration might well assail her spirit, or of recognition that she had lost a high contentment in gaining a low one. This was natural enough. It has been aptly put into metaphor that the saddest place in Purgatory is that from which the walls of Paradise are visible.

By four o'clock Hollister had not returned. But Mrs. Diggs had made her appearance instead, and Claire welcomed it as a happy relief from the torment of her own thoughts. "My dear," said this lady, "there has been nothing so dreadful in Wall Street since the crisis of the famed Black Friday. My poor Manhattan came home at about three o'clock, utterly jaded out. I made him go to bed. He could scarcely speak to me. I asked him about your husband's affairs, but he gave me only mumbling answers; excitement had put him into a kind of stupor, don't you know?"

"Yes," assented Claire, understanding the nature of the collapse perfectly. "So he told you nothing of Herbert's affairs? Nothing whatever?"

"Nothing that I could really make out. I should be in a wild state, and have a feeling about the soles of my feet as if I were already going barefoot, don't you know, if I had 'nt long ago insisted upon Manhattan's putting a very large and comfortable sum safely away in my name."

Claire thought of the house that had been assigned to her, of her jewels, of her costly apparel. But to remember these merely aggravated her distress. What a meagre wreck they would leave from the largess of her past prosperity!

"I would n't be awfully worried, if I were you," continued Mrs. Diggs. "If the worst *should* come, your husband will be sure to save something handsome. These great speculators always do. Some odd thousands always turn up after the storm has blown over. Perhaps he will begin again, and do grander things than ever before."

"That is cold consolation," said Claire, with a bitter smile.

"I know it is for *you*, Claire, dear, who have been tossing away hundreds to my dimes. I might say horrid things, but I won't. I might talk of retribution for your extravagances, and all that. But I so detest the *je vous l'avais bien dit* style of rebuke. And I don't want to rebuke you a bit. You have your faults. of course. But you 're always my sweet, beautiful Claire. My heart will ache for you if anything frightful *should* happen. I say it to your face,

dear, as I would say it behind your back, that you
are the one woman of all others whom money perfectly adorns. You spent it like a queen, and you
looked like a queen while you spent it. You remember how I used to gush over Cornelia Van Horn's
grand manner? It could never hold a candle to
yours. I'm afraid I abused you like a regular pick-
pocket the other night. Oh, yes, I pitched into you
just as hard as I could. But at the same time I was
thinking how well you carried your worldliness —
what a kind of a *beau rôle* you made of it, don't you
know? And whatever *should* come, Claire, always
recollect that I'll stick to you, my dear, through
thick and thin!"

The vernacular turn taken by Mrs. Diggs during
this eager outburst gave it a spontaneity and natural-
ness that more than once brought the mist to Claire's
eyes. She felt the true ring of friendly sympathy
in every word that was spoken; the touches of slang
pleased her; they were like the angularities of the
lady's physical shape, severe and yet not ungraceful.
She was sorry when her visitor rose to go, and had a
sense of dreary loneliness after she had departed.

It would soon be the hour for dinner. But she
could not dine. She knew that the decorous butler who waited on her would perceive her efforts to
choke down the proffered food. Perhaps he would
tingle with secret dread regarding his next wages.
He read the newspapers, of course; everybody read
them nowadays; and her husband's impending ruin
had been their chief and hideous topic.

As the chill winter light in the room turned blue
before it wholly died, she sat and thought of how
many people would be glad to hear the very worst.

They seemed to her a pitiless legion. Then, as she thought of how many would be sorry, three names rose uppermost in her mind : Mrs. Diggs, Thurston, and Stuart Goldwin. Yes, Goldwin surely would have no exultant feeling. He was full of arts and falsities, but he could not fail to regret any calamity that brought with it her own sharp discomfiture.

'He has lately been Herbert's rival in finance,' she told her own thoughts. 'Circumstance has in a manner pitted them against each other. Herbert rose so quickly. They have not been enemies, but they have stood on opposite sides in not a few matters of speculation. Still, I am sure he will lament the downfall, if it really comes. He will do so for my sake, if for no other reason. I should have questioned him more closely last night at the opera. I am sure he wanted me to speak with more freedom of the threatening disaster. I should have asked him '—

And then Claire's distressed ruminations were cut short by the quiet entrance of her husband. The door of the chamber had been ajar. Hollister simply pushed it a little further open, and crossed the threshold.

The dusk had begun, but it was still far from making his face in any way obscure to her. As she looked at it, while slowly rising from her chair, she saw that it had never, to her knowledge, been so wan and worn as now. He paused before her, and at once spoke.

" Have you heard ? " he said.

She felt herself grow cold. " What ? " she asked.

" I 'm cleaned out. Everything has gone. I thought you might have seen the evening papers. They are full of it. Of course they don't know the real truth. Some of them say that I have five millions hidden away." He laughed here, and the laugh was bleak though low. "But I tell you the plain truth, Claire — there's nothing left. The truth is best; don't you think so?"

He was steadily watching her, as he thus spoke, and the detected irony of his words pierced her like a knife. A wistful distress was in the frank blue of his eyes; they seemed to reflect from her own spirit the wrong that she had done him.

"Yes, Herbert," she answered, still keeping her seat, "I think that the truth is always best."

A great sigh left his lips. He put both hands behind him, and began slowly pacing the floor, with lowered head. While thus engaged, he went on speaking.

"I can't think how I ever shot up as I did. I never was a very bright fellow at Dartmouth. I always had pluck enough, but I never showed any great nerve. Wall Street brought out a new set of faculties, somehow. And then everybody liked me; I was popular; that had a great deal to do with it, I suppose — that and a wonderful run of luck at the start. And then there was one thing more — one very important thing, too. I see now what a tremendous incentive it really was. I mean your wish to rise and rule people. If it had n't been for that, I'd have let many a big chance slip."

He paused now, standing close beside his wife's chair. "I was always weak where you were concerned," he said, regarding her very intently, and with a cloud on his usually clear brow that bespoke suffering rather than sternness. "You know that, Claire. I yielded always; I let you wind me round your finger — I was so fond of the finger. If you had said, 'Herbert, do this or that folly,' I'd have done it, and it wouldn't have seemed half so much a folly because of your loved command. Is not this true?"

He came still closer to her after he had uttered the last sentence. He was so close that his person grazed her dress.

Claire was very pale, and her eyes were shining. "It is perfectly true," she answered him.

Hollister's tones instantly changed. They were broken, hoarse, and of fervid melancholy. "Perfectly true. Yes, you admit it. You know that I am right. I gave you everything — love, interest, energy, respect, obedience. And what did you give me? Your marriage-vows, Claire! — were those falsehoods? Speak and tell me! I never thought so till yesterday. Good God, woman! I never thought about it at all. You were my wife; you were my Claire. You were stronger in nature than I, and I loved your strength. I loved to have you lead, and to follow where you led. But your love — oh, I counted on that as securely as we count on the sun in heaven! And yesterday the truth burst on me! It wasn't I that you had cared for. It was the high place I could put you in, the dresses and diamonds I could buy for you, the " —

He suddenly broke off. A great excitement was now in his visage, his voice, his whole manner. Whether from pain or wrath, it seemed to her that his eyes had taken a much darker tint, and that an unwonted spark, chill and keen, lit them.

"If it all *is* true," he went on, speaking much more slowly, and like a man who breathes hard without openly showing it, " then I thank God that no child has been born of you and me ! "

She sat quite still. She was utterly conscience-stricken. From all the facile vocabulary of feminine self-excuse her bewildered and shamed soul could shape no sentence either of propitiation or denial. At such a time she felt the infamy, even the farce of lying to him. And how could she respond with any sufficiency, any gleam of comforting assurance, unless she did lie?

" You say that I led you into this disaster, Herbert," she presently responded, with an effort, and more than a successful one, to steady her voice. " I don't deny it, but at the same time remember that my forethought provided for us both in a case of just the present sort. I have the other house, you know. Its sale will bring us something. And then there are all my jewels — and " —

His eyes flashed and his lip curled. " You talk in that business-like style," he cried, " when I am asking you if you ever really loved me ! Is your evasion an answer, Claire ? *Were* your marriage-vows falsehoods ? "

His hand grasped her wrist, though not with violence. She rose, unsteadily, and shook the grasp off.

" Oh, Herbert," she said, " I never saw you like this before ! Let us think of what we can do in case all *is* really lost."

He withdrew from her, breaking into a hollow laugh. He stared at her with dilated, accusing eyes.

" You don't dare tell me. But I read it, as I read it yesterday. . . . What can we do ? Ah ! you 're not the woman to live on a thousand or two a year. You want fine things to wear and to eat. You want your jewels, too — don't sell them, for you could n't get along without them, now." He kept silence for a moment, and then hurried with swift steps toward the door, again pausing. A kind of madness, that was born of an agony, possessed him and visibly showed its sway. "Get some one else to put you back into luxury," he went on, lifting one hand toward his throat, as though to make the words less husky that were leaping from his lips. "Get Goldwin to do it. Yes, Goldwin. You 've only to nod and he 'll kneel to you — as I knelt. Perhaps he 's got from you what I never could get. You know what I mean — I 've told you."

He passed at once from the room, flinging the door shut behind him. The room was in dimness by this time. Claire almost staggered to a lounge, and sank within it. His wild insult had dizzied her.

He had not meant a word of it. He was tortured by the thought that she had never cared for him. He had used the first fierce reproach that his sorrow and exasperation could hit upon. He went to his own apartments, dressed, and then left the house. He forgot that he had not dined, but remembered only that there might be some sort of forlorn financial hope discovered by a certain assemblage of men less deeply involved than himself, yet all sufferers in a similar way, which would take place privately that same evening at a popular hotel not far distant. All recollection of having suggested an infidelity to Claire quite escaped from his perturbed and over-wrought brain. The piercing realization that she had never loved him still continued its torment. But he failed to recall that the desperate sarcasm of his mood had ever hurled at her the name of Goldwin.

A knock at the door of the darkened room waked Claire from a kind of stupor. The knock came from her maid, and it acted with decisive arousing force. Lights were soon lit, and dinner, that evening, was ordered to become a canceled ceremony.

"You may bring me some *bouillon*, Marie," Claire directed. "That, and nothing else."

She drank the beverage when it was brought, and changed her dress. The glass showed her a pale but tranquil face.

'I would have clung to him if he would have let me,' incessantly passed through her thoughts. 'But now he tells me that another can give me the luxury that I have lost. He is right. Goldwin will come this evening; I am sure of it.'

Goldwin did come, and she received him with a mien of ice. Underneath her coldness there was fire enough, but she kept its heat well hidden.

"I came to talk intimately with you," he at length said, "and you treat me as if we had once met, somewhere, for about ten minutes."

The smouldering force of Claire's inward excitement started into flame at these words. "I know with what *intimate* feelings you came," she replied, meeting his soft glance with one of cold opposition. "You want to tell me that you can set Herbert right with his creditors."

"Yes," he answered, slowly, averting his eyes, "I did have that desire. Is there anything wrong about it?"

"Yes. You should not have come to me. You should have gone to him."

"Why?" he asked.

"Why?" repeated Claire, breaking into a sharp

laugh. A moment later she tossed her head with a careless disdain. "I'm not going to tell you why. You know well enough. See Herbert. Ask him if he will let you help him."

"You are very much excited."

"I have good reason to be."

"You mean this dreadful change in your husband's affairs?"

"Yes, I mean that, and I mean more. You mustn't question me."

"Very well, I won't."

But he soon did, breaking the silence that ensued between them with gently harmonious voice, and fixing on Claire's half-averted face a look that seemed to brim with sympathy.

"Would Hollister take my help if I offered it? Does he not dislike me? I believe so — I am nearly sure so. You tap the floor with your foot. You are miserable, and I understand your misery. So am I miserable — on your account. I know all the ins and outs of your distress . . . ah, do not fancy that I fail to do so. He has said hard things — undeserved things. He has perhaps mixed my name with his . . . what shall I call them? . . . reproaches, impertinences? You have had a quarrel — a quarrel that has been wholly on his side. He has accused you of not caring enough for him. It may be that he has accused you of not caring at all. Of course he has dilated on your love for the pomp and glitter of things. As if he himself did not love them! As if he himself has not given all of us proof that he loved them very much! Well; let that pass. You are to renounce everything. You are to dine on humble fare, dress in plain clothes, sink into obscurity. This is what he demands. Or, if it is not demanded, it is implied. And for what reason? Because he still sees you are beautiful, attractive, one woman in ten thousand, and that having gambled away every other pleasure in life he can still retain you."

Claire rose from the sofa on which they were both seated. She did not look at Goldwin while she answered him. Her voice was so low that he just caught her words and no more.

"To what does all this tend? Tell me. Tell me at once."

Goldwin in turn slowly rose while he responded: "I will tell you, if you will tell me whether you love your husband well enough to share poverty with him after he has insulted you."

"I did not say that he had insulted me."

"I infer it. Am I right or wrong?"

Still not looking at him, she made an impatient gesture with both hands.

"Allowing you are right. What then?"

He did not reply for several minutes. He was stroking his amber mustache with one white, well-shaped hand; his eyes were now turned from hers, hers from him.

"I shall go abroad in a short time. I shall go in less than a fortnight," he said.

It was a most audacious thing to say, and he knew it thoroughly. It was the bold stroke that must either annul his hopes completely, or feed them with a fresh life.

Claire seemed to answer him only with the edges of her lips.

"How does that concern me?"

24

"In no way. I did not say it did. But you might choose to sail a week or two later. Alone, of course. It would be Paris, with me. You have told me that you wanted very much to see Paris."

She turned and faced him, then, more agitated than angry.

"You speak of my husband having insulted me. What are you doing now?"

"I am trying to save you."

"Good Heavens! from what?"

"From him. Listen. I did not mean for you to go directly to Paris. You would travel. But at a certain date I could meet you there. I could meet you with — well, with a document of importance."

"Explain. I don't understand you at all."

"Suppose I put the case in certain legal hands here. Suppose they worked it up with skill and shrewdness. Suppose they gained it. Suppose they secured a divorce between you and him on — grounds " . . .

"Well? What grounds?"

"Of infidelity. You know the life he has lived. Or rather, you don't know. He has been so gay, so prominent, of late, that almost any well-feed lawyer could " —

Claire interrupted him, there. "Leave me at once," she said, pointing toward the door. "Leave me. I order you to do it!"

He obeyed her, but stopped when he had nearly reached the threshold.

"As my wife," he said, "you would reign more proudly than you have ever reigned yet. The moment you were free I would be so glad to make you mine — you, the loveliest woman I ever knew, and the most finely, strictly pure!"

"Leave me," she repeated; but he had quitted the room before her words were spoken.

She glanced in the direction whence his voice had come to her, and then, seeing that he was gone, she dropped back upon the sofa, and sat there, staring straight ahead at nothing, with tight-locked hands and colorless, alarmed face.

XX

SHE heard Hollister reënter the house that night at a very late hour, and pass to his own apartments. It was only after dawn that she obtained a little restless and broken sleep. By nine o'clock she rang for her coffee, and then, after forcing herself to swallow it, began to dress, with her maid's assistance. Marie was a perfect servant. As she performed with capable exactitude one after another careful duty, the ease and charm of being thus waited upon appealed to Claire with an ironical emphasis. The very softness and tasteful make of her garments took a new and dreary meaning. She had forgotten for weeks the dainty details of her late life, its elegance of tone, smoothness of movement, nicety of balance. These features had grown customary and inconspicuous, as cambric will in time grow familiar to the skin that has brushed against coarser textures. But now the light, so to speak, had altered; it was cloudy and stormful; it brought out in vivid relief what before had been clad with the pleasant haze of habit. The very carpet beneath Claire's tread took a reminding softness; the numberless attractions and comforts of her chamber thrust forward special claims to her heed; even the elaborate or simple utensils of her dressing-table had each its distinct note of souvenir. She must so soon lose so much of it all!

As if by some automatic and involuntary process,

memory slipped images and pictures before her mental vision; she had noted them in the still, dark hours of the previous night, and they remained unbanished now by the glow of the wintry morning. She saw herself a child, cowed and satirized by her coarse and domineering mother; she witnessed the episode of her gentle father's firm and protective revolt; she lived again through the prosperous rise of the family fortunes; she watched herself brave and quell the insolence of Ada Gerrard, and slowly but surely gain rank and recognition among those adverse and disdainful schoolfellows; she endured anew the chagrin of subsequent decadence — the commonness and the disrelish of her public school career, the disappointment and monotony of her Jersey City experience, and then, lastly, the laborious and deathly tedium of Greenpoint. . . . Here the strange panorama would cease; the magic-lantern of reminiscence had no more lenses in its shadowy repository; the actual took the place of dream, and startled her by an aspect more unreal than though wrought merely of recollection.

Had these recent weeks all been true? Had she climbed so high in fact and not in fancy? Was the throne from which fate now gave harsh threat of pushing her a throne not built of air, but material, tangible, solid? The strangeness of her own history affected her in a purely objective way. She seemed to stand apart from it and regard it as though it were some lapse of singular country for which she had gained the sight-seer's best vantage-point. Its acclivities were so sheer, its valleys were so abrupt, it took such headlong plunges and made such unexpected ascents.

The discreet and sedulous Marie divined little of what engrossed her mistress's mind, and withdrew in her wonted humility of courtesy when Claire, no longer needing her service, at last dismissed her.

But before doing so, Claire took pains to learn that Hollister had not yet descended for his breakfast, which of late he had usually eaten alone in the great dining-room. She soon passed into her adjacent boudoir, where fresh treasures and mementos addressed her through a silent prophecy of coming loss.

Here was a writing-table, well supplied with various kinds of note-paper, all bearing her initials in differing intertwisted devices. Not long ago she had questioned her husband on the subject of the Hollister crest; she would have been glad enough to receive from him some clew that might lead to its discovery ; but he had expressed frank and entire ignorance regarding any such heraldic symbol.

Claire took a sheet of note paper, and in a hand that was just unsteady enough to show her how strong an inward excitement was making stealthy attack upon her nervous power, began a brief note to Stuart Goldwin. When finished, the note (which bore no ceremonious prefix whatever, and was unmarked by any date) ran as follows : —

"The words which you chose to address to me last night have permanently ended our acquaintance. As a gentleman to a gentlewoman, you were impolite. As a man to a woman, you were far worse. I desire that you will not answer these few lines, and that when we meet again, if such a meeting should ever occur, you will expect from me no more sign of recognition than that which I would accord any one who had given me an unpardonable insult.   C. H."

Claire sealed and directed this note. She did not send it, however. After its completion she went downstairs into the dining-room.

Hollister was seated there, being served with breakfast. He had already found it impossible to eat; he was sipping a second or third cup of strong tea.

When his wife appeared, he slightly started. Claire went to the fire and stood before it, letting its warmth and glow hold her in thrall for quite a while. Her back was now turned to him; she was waiting for the butler to depart. He presently did so, closing a door behind his exit with just enough accentuation to make the sound convey decisive and final import.

Claire then slowly turned, removing one foot from one of the polished rods that bordered the flame-lit hearthstone. She looked straight at her husband; she did not need to see how pale he was; her first look had told her that. She had chosen to ignore all that he had said last night. It did not cost her much effort to do this; she had too keen a sense of her own wrong toward him not to condone the reckless way in which he had coupled her name with Goldwin's. Besides, had not Goldwin's own words to her, a little later, made that assault seem almost justified? She felt nothing toward him save a great pity. Her pity sprang, too, from remorse. She lacked all tenderness; this, joined with pity, would have meant love. 'And I cannot love him!' she had already reflected. 'If I only could, it would be so different. But I cannot.'

When she spoke, her words were very calm and firm. " I thought you might have something more to tell me," she said. " I came down to see you before you went away, for that reason. You said last night that everything had gone. There will be a day or two left us, I suppose; I mean a day or two of — possession."

He was stirring the tea with his spoon. His eyes were bent on the table as he did so. He spoke without lifting them. "Oh, yes," he answered. "Perhaps four or five days. They will seize the house, after that," he went on, "and all the furniture and valuables. Of course they can't touch what is really yours. I mean your diamonds, your dresses, *et cetera*."

A pause followed. "To-day I have a luncheon-party," said Claire.

"Yes . . . you told me. I remember."

"I hope nothing of . . . of *that sort* will happen to-day."

"No." He had taken his spoon from the cup, and was staring down at it, as though he wanted to make sure of some flaw in its metal. His face was not merely pale; it had the worn look of severe anxiety. "You can have your luncheon-party with impunity. By the way, our own *chef* gets it up, doesn't he? You didn't have Delmonico or any one else in, did you?"

"No," she answered. "Pierre was to do it all. He had his full orders several days ago."

A fleet, bitter smile crossed Hollister's lips. He put his spoon back into the cup, but did not raise his eyes. "Oh, everything is safe enough for to-day," he said.

Claire moved slowly toward him. "Herbert," she said, and put forward one hand . . . "I don't see why we should not be friends at a time like this. You were angry last night, and said things that I am

sure you did n't mean — things that I 've almost forgotten, and want entirely to forget. Let us both forget them. Let us be friends again, and talk matters
over sensibly — as we ought to do."

She herself was not aware of the loveless chill that
touched every word she had just spoken. There was
something absolutely matter-of-fact in her tones; they
rang with a kind of commercial loudness. It was
almost as though she were proposing a mercantile
truce between man and man.

Hollister visibly winced, and slowly rose from the
table. Every sentence that she had uttered had bit-
ten into his very soul. His pride was alive, and
keenly so. But he was not at all angry; he felt too
miserably saddened for that.

" Claire," he said, " we had best not talk of being
friends. If I spoke to you harshly last night, I 'm
sorry. I don't quite recollect just what I did say.
Of course we must have a serious talk about how we
are to live in future. But not now, if you please —
not now. Your luncheon will go off all properly
enough. Things are not so bad as *that.* I shall be
away until evening. Perhaps when I come home
again we can have our talk."

Claire looked at him with hard, bright eyes. She
assured herself that he had causelessly repulsed her.
Even allowing the wrong that she had done him of
marrying him without love, why should he now repel,
by this self-contained austerity, an advance which, in
her egotistic misery, she believed a sincere and spontaneous one? She was wholly unaware of her own
unfortunate demeanor; it seemed to her that she had
done her best; she had tried to conciliate, to appease,
to mollify. Was not her note to Goldwin now in the

pocket of her gown? Was not that note a defense of Herbert's own honor as of hers? She made the distinctly feminine error, while she rapidly surveyed the present contingency, of taking for granted that her husband possessed some obscure and mesmeric intuition regarding this same unseen piece of writing.

"Oh, very well," she replied, with an actually wounded manner; "you may do just as you please. I might have resented the unjust and horrible thing you said to me last evening, but I did not. I did not, because, as I told you, I thought it best for us to be friends once again."

"Friends." He repeated the word with a harsh fragment of laughter. His changed face took another speedy change; it grew sombre and forbidding. "You and I, Claire, can never be friends. While we live together hereafter I'm afraid it must only be as strangers."

"Strangers!" she repeated, haughtily and offendedly.

"Yes! You know why." He walked toward the tapestried door of the dining-room, and flung one of its curtains aside, holding it thus while he stood on the threshold and looked back at her. "You yourself make the reason. I'll do all I can. I don't know of any unjust or horrible thing that I said last evening. I only know that you are and have been my wife in name alone."

He had forgotten his speech regarding Goldwin. He had never had any suspicion, however remote, that she had transgressed her wifely vows. He simply felt that she had never loved him, and that she had married him for place and promotion in a worldly sense; that, and no more.

The draperies of the door at once shrouded his departing figure. Claire stood quite still, watching the agitated folds settle themselves into rest. 'He meant that Goldwin is my lover,' she told herself. 'What else could he possibly have meant?'

She had some half-formed intent of hurrying after him and venting her indignation in no weak terms. Best if she had done so; for he might then have explained away, with surprise and perhaps contrition, the fatal blunder that she had made. But pride soon came, with its vetoing interference. She did not stir until she heard the outer door close after him. Then, knowing that he was gone, she let pride lay its gall on her hurt, and dull her mind to the sense of what wrong she had inflicted on him by the permitted mockery of their marriage.

'He had no reason to judge so vilely of me,' sped her thoughts. 'His approval of that intimacy was clearly implied, however tacit. What must our lives together now become? He has brought a shameful charge against me; if I loved him I could doubtless pardon him; love will pardon so much. But as it is, there must always remain a breach between us. A continuance of our present brilliant affluence might bridge it over. The distractions and pleasures of wealth, fashion, supremacy, would make it less and less apparent to both; but poverty, and perhaps even hardship as well, — how should these fail to mercilessly widen it?'

Everything looked black, threatening, and miserable to Claire as she began to attire herself for the great lunch. Her maid had just finished dressing her hair, when a note was handed her.

It was from Mrs. Van Horn. Very brief and entirely courteous, it expressed regret that a sudden sick headache would prevent her from numbering herself among Claire's favored guests that morning. 'The first token of my altered fortunes,' she thought, with a pang that was like a stab. 'This woman was the last to come under my ensign; she is the first to desert it.'

She recalled Thurston's words to her at the opera on the previous night. Surely there was some grave discrepancy between these and the acts of his sister. As for the headache, that was of course transparent sham. If this lofty lady had wanted to deceive, she might have done so more plausibly. But perhaps she did not care whether or no her excuse looked genuine. Rats leave a falling house. That was all the letter meant. Claire could have thrown it down upon the floor and stamped on it. In reality, she tossed it with seeming unconcern into the fire, and gave a quiet order to Marie which she wished taken directly to the butler, regarding the reduced number of her coming guests.

When Marie reëntered the apartment, she bore a card. It was the card of Thurston. On it were written in pencil these words: "I beg that you will see me for a few moments, if you can possibly manage."

She at once went down and received him. He looked fixedly into her face for a slight while, after they had seated themselves. He knew all that had happened, and he understood just how savage and calamitous must seem to her the blows from which she was now suffering. He read excitement and even despair in every line of her features, though he clearly perceived that both were held under a determined repression.

' She means not to let herself go one inch,' he decided. ' If she did, she would break down altogether. She has wound herself up to a certain pitch. She will keep just this way for hours yet. She will keep so — if nothing strange and unforeseen should happen.'

A deep and vital pity pierced him while he watched her. He loved her, and his love made him unreasonably lenient. A sacred sadness invested her, for his eyes, in this the hour of her misfortune and overthrow. He forgot how blameworthy she had been, and could remember only that destiny would soon hurl in the dust the crown that she had worn with so much grace and grandeur.

" Did you come to speak of my — of our trouble? " she said, her lip quivering for an instant and no more.

" No," he replied. " But since *you* speak of it, is all chance of recovery gone? May not matters right themselves somehow? "

She shook her head in quick negative. " I think not. He has lost everything — or nearly that." She broke into a smile, which had for her companion only the brightness one might see in tears. " I suppose it seems to you like a punishment — a retribution." Her gaze dwelt on him with a mournful kind of pleasantry. It was like the spirit of Comedy slipping her gay mask a little down and showing beneath it a glimpse of pallor and fatigue.

" But do not let us talk of that. You wanted to talk of something else. What was it? your sister's refusal, at the eleventh hour, to come to my lunch? "

" Has she refused? "

" She has a sick headache," returned Claire, with a bit of joyless laughter — the saddest he had ever heard leave her lips. " I don't doubt our disreputable downfall has given it to her. Don't make excuses for her; she is quite right to have her headache. It's a fastidious prerogative, you know. I shan't require a physician's certificate. I only hope that all the others will be cruel in just as civil a manner."

The tragic bitterness of these words, though they were quietly enough uttered, stung Thurston to the quick. When a man loves as he loved, compassion waits the ready vassal of tenderness. He had a momentary feeling of hostility against an elusive, disembodied foe — against circumstance itself, so to speak, for having wrought discord in a life that was meant to hold nothing but melody.

He swiftly decided not to tell the real truth regarding his sister. "I would not concern myself with Cornelia's absence," he said. "Another matter, of much more import, must be brought to your notice. It is then settled that Cornelia remains away. I did not know that she would do so. She made no mention of it during our interview last night."

"Her headache had not arrived. Neither had the morning papers, which said such hard things of my husband."

"As you will. Let all that pass. I wish to speak of a lady who will almost certainly be present at your entertainment to-day. I mean Sylvia Lee. Don't ask me why I warn you against her, for I can't give you any lucid reasons. She intends some mischief. I suspected it last night from something my sister let fall, and I visited Mrs. Lee this morning with a most detective purpose. I gained no clew, and yet my suspicions were by no means lulled. I have never liked Sylvia; we are related, but she has always

struck me as an abhorrent kind of creature, bristling
with artifice, destitute of nearly all *morale*, capable
of the worst cunning, equipped with the most subtle
resources of treachery. Be on your guard against
her to-day. This sounds mysterious — melodramatic,
if you will; but she has some snare laid for you,
some petty but perhaps ugly revenge. You know
why I use that last word. She has wanted to marry
Goldwin for years. She isn't a bit above the gross-
est, most unscrupulous hatred. She told me that she
did n't believe in your husband's ruin, and that a few
more days would see him on his feet again. This
makes me all the more convinced that she will not
put her little sharpened dagger back into its sheath.
She has hatched some sort of horrid plot. Thwart
it if you can. I wish I could be here to help you."

Claire had grown very pale, but her eyes sparkled
vividly. "I am your debtor for these tidings," she
said. She drew a deep breath, and he surmised that
under the soft curve of her joined lips she had for
a brief moment set her teeth closely together. "I
thought the lunch would be a hard ordeal, even as
matters stood," she went on, "and that I would need
my best nerve and courage to get through it all right,
with proper coolness and dignity. But now the task
looks far less easy. Still, I shan't flinch. I wish
you *were* to be here: but that is not possible."

Just then a clock on the opposite mantel gave one
little silver note that told it was half-past twelve.
Claire rose as she heard the sound. "I must leave
you now," she pursued. "I have only an hour left
for my toilette, and I shall need it all." She threw
back her head, and a dreary smile gleamed and fled
along her lips. "I mean to meet all these grand

ladies without one sign of defeat. I shan't wear my
heart on my sleeve. This lunch was to have been
my crowning triumph. It proves a funeral-feast,
in its way, but they shan't find me playing chief-
mourner. I intend to die game, as the phrase is."
She gave a slight shudder, drooping her eyes. "It
will be as though I stood in a house whose walls
might crumble all about me at any moment — as if
I could hear the crack of plaster and the creak of
beams. But I shan't run away; I shall stand my
ground very firmly, depend on it, until the bitter end.
When the crash comes nobody will be buried in the
ruins but myself — that is certain, is it not?"

Here her joyless laugh again sounded, and Thurston, swayed by an irresistible mood, caught one of
her hands, pressing it hard within his own.

"You shall not be buried in the ruins!" he exclaimed. "Take my word for it, you shall not! It
will all only be the beginning of a new and better
life. You shall have learned a hard yet salutary
lesson — that, and nothing more."

She shook her head, meeting his earnest eyes.
"You are my good genius," she said. "It is too
bad you have not had more power over me."

"Who is your evil genius?" he asked, with slower
tones, while she drew her hand from his.

"Myself," she answered. "I am quite willing to
concede it." . . . She appeared to muse for a little
while. "I shall have one true friend here to-day,"
she soon continued. "I mean Mrs. Diggs. She is
very loyal to me; she would do almost anything I
should ask. You don't like her, or so she tells me,
but I hope you will like her better than your other
cousin, Mrs. Lee."

"I respect her far more. I have never doubted her goodness. But she gives me nerves, as the French say. She is at such a perpetual gallop; if she would only break into a trot, sometimes, it would be like anybody else's walk. . . . You think you can trust her as an ally to-day?"

"Implicitly. She has promised to come early, too — before the others, you know." . . . Claire locked the fingers of both hands together, and held them so that the palms were bent downward. The weary smile again touched her lips and vanished. "What a day it is to be! And what a day it *might* have been!" She held out her hand to him, after that. "Good-by. With all my heart I thank you! You have done all that you could do."

He did not promptly reply. He was thinking whether he had really done all that he could do. . . . And this thought followed him hauntingly as he left Claire to meet whatever catastrophe fate had in store for her.

Mrs. Diggs kept her promise, and was shown into Claire's dressing-room a good quarter of an hour before the other guests were due. The lady started on seeing her friend, whose toilette was now completed, and whose robe, worn for the first time, was of a regal and unique beauty. It was chiefly of white velvet, whose trailing heaviness blent with purple lengths of the same lustreless and sculpturesque fabric. The white prevailed, but the purple was richly manifest. In her hair she wore aigrettes of sapphires and amethysts shaped to resemble pansies, and while the sleeves were cut short enough to show either arm from wrist almost to elbow, and permit of bracelets that were two circles of jewels wrought in

25

semblance of the same flower and with the same blue and lilac gems, her bust and throat were clad in one cloud of rare, filmy laces, from which her delicate head rose with a stately yet aerial grace. Excitement had put rosy tints in either cheek; the jewels that she wore had no sweeter splendor than her eyes, and yet both by color and glow in a certain way aptly matched them. A gear of velvet is dangerous to women in whom exuberance of figure has the least assertive rule. Velvet is the sworn enemy of *embonpoint*. But Claire's figure was of such supple and flexile slenderness that the weight and volume of this apparel made her light step and airy contour win a new charm and a new vivacity.

"It is all perfect — quite perfect," said Mrs. Diggs, after taking a rapid survey of Claire's attire. "But, my dear, are you perfectly sure that" . . .

"Sure of what?" Claire asked, as her friend hesitated.

"Well . . . that it is just in good taste, don't you know? I mean, under the circumstances."

"What circumstances?" she exclaimed, putting the question as though she did not wish it answered, and moving a few paces away with an air of great pride. "I intend to fall gloriously. The end has come, the fight is lost; but I shan't make a tame surrender — not I! They shall see me at my best to-day, in looks, in speech, in manner. I'm glad you like my dress; I want it to be something memorable."

"You say that with a kind of bravado, Claire. There's a bitter ring to your mirth. Oh, I'm so sorry for you! That lovely dress hides an aching heart. You will suffer, poor child. This lunch will be a positive torture to you."

A moment after these words were spoken, Claire was close at Mrs. Diggs's side, holding one of her hands with firm pressure.

"You don't know how much of a torture it must be," she said, "and for what reason." She immediately repeated all that Thurston had told her. When she had finished, Mrs. Diggs was in a high state of perturbation.

"I have n't a doubt that Beverley is right!" she exclaimed. "If there *was* any plot, Cornelia Van Horn was in it, too, and her brother has made her throw away her weapons. But Sylvia Lee intends to deal the blow alone. . . . What can it be? I 'm at my wit's end to guess. There 's but one thing to do — keep a continual watch upon her. Claire, can you be, by any chance, in that woman's power?"

"Her power?" faltered Claire. . . . "I hope not," she added. . . . "I *know* not," she then said, as the full sense of Mrs. Diggs's question struck her, and using a tone that was one of surprised affront.

"Now, don't be offended, my dear. I merely meant that Sylvia is n't a bit too good to magnify some slight imprudence, or twist and turn it until she has got it dangerously like an actual crime. . . . But *nous verrons.* After all, Beverley's fears may be groundless. With all my heart I hope they are!"

Not long afterward Claire was receiving her guests. All the great ladies came, except, of course, Mrs. Van Horn. The last arrival was that of Mrs. Lee. She contrived to make her entrance a very conspicuous one. She was dressed with even more fantastic oddity than usual, and she spoke in so shrill and peculiar a voice that she had not been in the drawing-room more than five minutes before marked and universal attention was directed upon her.

"Sylvia is in a very singular state of excitement," Mrs. Diggs murmured to Claire. "I know her well. That slow drawl of hers has entirely gone. She acts to me as if she were on the verge of hysteria. I don't know whether you felt her hand tremble as it shook yours, but I thought that I plainly *saw* it tremble. Just watch her, now, while she talks with Mrs. Vanvelsor. She has a little crimson dot in each of her cheeks, and she is usually quite pale, you know. There's something in the wind — Beverley was right."

"Her place at the table is rather distant from mine," said Claire, with a scornful, transitory curl of the lip. "So there is no danger of her putting a pinch of arsenic into my wine-glass."

"You're not nervous, then? I am. I don't know just why, but I am."

"Nervous?" Claire softly echoed. "No, not at all, now. I've other more important things to think of. What *could* she do, after all? Let her attempt any folly; it would only recoil on herself. . . . Ah, my friend, I am afraid I'm past being injured. This is my *finale*. I want it to prove a grand one."

"It will, Claire. They have all come, as you see. They have met you with perfect cordiality, and you have received them with every bit of your accustomed grace. I dare say that some of them are stunned with amazement; they no doubt expected to find you shivering and colorless."

The repast was magnificent. There were more than thirty ladies present, and these, all brilliantly attired and some of striking personal beauty, made

the prodigal array of flowers, the admirable service
of many delicious viands, and the soft music pealing
from the near hall just loudly enough not to drown
conversation while it filled pauses, produce an effect
where the most unrestrained hospitality was mingled
with a faultless refinement.

Claire's spirits seemed to rise as the decorous yet
lavish banquet proceeded. Her laugh now and then
rang out clear and sweet, while she addressed this or
that lady, at various distances from where she herself
sat. Mrs. Diggs, whose place was next her own, observed it all with secret wonder. She alone knew the
bleeding pride, the balked aspiration, the thwarted
yearning, which this pathetic and fictitious buoyancy
hid. It was a defiance, and yet how skilled and radiant a one! Could you blame the woman who knew
how to bloom and sparkle like this, for loving the
world where such dainty eminence was envied and
prized? Was there not a touch of genius in her pitiable yet dauntless masquerade? Who else could
have played the same part with the same deft security, and in the very teeth of failure and dethrone-
ment?

Claire's gayety and self-possession made more than
one of her guests lose faith in the tale of her husband's ruin. They were all women of the world, and
they all had the tact and breeding to perceive that
their hostess, now if ever, merited their best courtesy.
They could all have staid away at the last moment;
Mrs. Van Horn held no exclusive claim to the possession of her headache; its right of appropriation belonged elsewhere. But they had not availed themselves of it; they had chosen to sit at Claire's board,
to break her delicate bread. Hence they owed her

their allegiance to-day, even if to-morrow they should find expediency in its harshest opposite. But it now appeared to them as if she were refuting the wide-spread rumor of her husband's misfortunes; her own equipoise and scintillance bespoke this no less than the irreproachable *chic* of the entertainment to which she had bidden them.

Mrs. Lee was not very far away from Claire, and yet the latter never addressed or seemed to notice her. But Mrs. Diggs noticed her; she indeed maintained a vigilant, though repressed, watchfulness.

"You have quieted her," she found a chance to murmur in Claire's ear, sure that the indefinite nature of the pronoun would not be misunderstood. "She is still looking excited and queer, but she has almost relapsed into silence. Perhaps she really wanted to poison you, and feels hurt at the lost opportunity." Mrs. Diggs had had several sips of good wine, and felt her anxiety lessened; her jocose ebullition was the result of steadied nerves. "I never saw you so *spirituelle*, Claire," she went on. "You have said at least eight delicious things. I have them all mentally booked, my dear. When we are next alone together I will remind you of them."

"Pray don't," Claire answered, putting the words into a still lower aside than her friend's. "I shall have hard enough work to forget, then. I shall want *only* to forget, too."

She had just finished this faint-spoken sentence when one of the servants handed her a note. As she glanced at its superscription the thought passed through her mind that it might be some dire and alarming message from her husband. But the next instant a flash of recollection assailed her. She remembered the handwriting — or, at least, in this festive and distracting environment, she more than half believed that she did so.

Her hands, while she swiftly tore open the envelope, were dropped upon her lap. She read several lines of a note, and then crushed it, quickly and covertly. As her eyes met those of Mrs. Diggs she had a sense that she was becoming ghastly pale.

"What is it?" whispered her friend.

"Oh, nothing," she afterward remembered saying. The servant was still close at her elbow. She turned her head toward him.

"Let her wait," she said. "Tell her that I will see her quite soon."

The whole affair had been very rapid of occurrence. No one present had given a sign of having observed it.

'If I had only not grown so pale,' she thought.

The paper was still clutched in her left hand, and she had thrust this half-way beneath the table-cover. With her right hand she began to make a play of eating something from the plate before her, as she addressed the lady on her other side. What she said must have been something very gracious and pleasant, for the lady smiled and answered affably, while the servants glided, the music sounded, the delightful feast progressed. Everything had grown dim and whirling to Claire. And yet she had already realized perfectly that Mrs. Lee was striking her blow. It had come, sudden, cruel, direct. Her blurred mind, her weakened and chilling body, did not leave that one fact any the less clear. She understood just what it was, why it was, and whence it was.

The note had been from her mother. It was half illiterate invective, half threatening rebuke. Its writer waited outside and demanded to see her. "If you don't come," the ill-shaped writing ran, "I will come to you." Claire knew that this thing had been Mrs. Lee's work as well as if a thousand witnesses had averred it. The missive contained no mention of Mrs. Lee, but she nevertheless had her certainty.

'I must go,' she told herself. 'I must go and meet her. *Can* I go? Can I walk, feeling as I do? Should I not fall if I tried?'

She always afterward remembered the food that her fork now touched and trifled with. It was a sweetbread croquette, with little black specks of chopped truffle in its creamy yielding oval, and the air that they were playing out in the hall was from a light, valueless opera, then much in vogue. She always afterward remembered that, too. So do slight events often press themselves in upon the dazed and dilated vision of a great distress.

'Can I rise and walk?' she kept thinking. 'Should I not fall if I tried?'

XXI.

IT is doubtful if any guest save Mrs. Diggs and
one other had seen Claire either receive, open, or
read her note. The constant movements of servants
hither and thither, and the little conversational
cliques formed among the ladies at this central stage
of the entertainment, would have made such an escape from general notice both natural and probable.
But Mrs. Diggs, who had thus far kept a furtive
though incessant watch upon Mrs. Lee, soon felt
certain that her cousin had not merely seen what had
passed; she was visibly affected by it as well; she
could not help regarding Claire across the considerable space which intervened between them. Her expression was a most imprudent betrayal; it clearly
told, by its acerbity and exultance, that she held
the present occasion to be one of prodigious and tri-
umphant import. No one except Mrs. Diggs was
watching her, and she was unaware of even that
sidelong but intent gaze. The natural mobility of
her odd face, which repelled some and attracted
others, needed at all times a certain check; but chagrins or satisfactions were both readily imprinted
there. It corresponded to the pliability of her body;
it would have been a face in which some clever ac-
tress might have found a fortune. She usually
restrained it with discretion, but just now the force

of a malign joy swept aside prudent control. Before
Mrs. Diggs's exploring search of it ended, her last
doubt had fled.

'I never saw her look more like the snake that she
is,' Claire's friend had thought. 'The mischief —
the deviltry, it may be — lies in that letter. Claire
has grown as white as its paper; but nobody notices,
thank Heaven! She won't faint — she is n't of the
fainting sort.'

"Claire," she now said aloud, yet in tones which
the most adroit of eavesdroppers could not have more
than just vaguely overheard, "did you get any bad
news a minute ago?"

Claire was no longer addressing the lady at her
side. "Why do you ask?" she responded. "Do I
look pale?"

"Not at all; not the least in the world; I 've
never seen you more composed," returned Mrs. Diggs,
with enormous mendacity, hoping that her charitable
lie would bear reassuring and tranquilizing results.

It did, as soon became apparent. Claire's condition was that in which we grasp at straws. Perhaps she grew several shades less pale on hearing
that she was not so.

"I must leave the room," she said, pronouncing
the words with the edges of her lips. "I must leave
immediately."

"Are you unwell?"

"No — yes — it is n't that. I must go. Could I
do it without — without — ?" She paused here; she
had not enough clearness of thought, just then, to
finish her sentence coherently.

"Without causing remark?" gently broke in Mrs.
Diggs. "Why, of course you could, my dear. Are

you not hostess? A hundred things might call you
away for a little while. No one would dream of
thinking it in the least strange. Why on earth
should one?''

There was a light nonchalance about this answer
that Mrs. Diggs by no means felt. She knew that
something had gone terribly wrong. Her rejoinder
had been a stroke of impromptu tact, just as her recent glib falsehood had been.

Its effect upon Claire was immediate. Her friend
was doing her thinking for her, so to speak, and was
doing it with a rapid, unhesitating *aplomb.*

" You don't know what has happened, do you? "
she now said.

Mrs. Diggs at once felt the helpless disability of
mind and nerves which this last faltered question
implied.

" Give me your note," she said. " Slip it under
the table. You will not be seen."

Claire obeyed. Mrs. Diggs had long ago learned
how and why her friend had left home, before that
episode began of her residence with the Bergemanns.
She read the note like lightning, and digested its contents with an almost equal speed. The sprawl of its
writing was uncouth enough, but not illegible.

For a slight space horrified sympathy kept her
silent. Then she said, with a coolness and placidity
that did her fine credit, considering the cause in
which she employed them : —

" I would go at once. You can keep everything
quiet. Of course you can. I will follow you shortly.
I will make a perfect excuse for you. You are feeling a little unwell — that is all. No one has noticed ; take my word for that ; I am simply *certain*

of it. When you return — which I promise you that you shall do quite soon — scarcely a comment will have been made on your absence. Go, by all means. Go at once, as I said."

'Some of her color has come back,' at the same time passed through poor Mrs. Diggs's anxious and agitated thoughts. 'I knew she would n't faint; it is n't *in* her. She will see that I'm right, in a minute. Her wits will begin to work. She will go.'

Claire did go. She had no after-recollection of how she left the great dining-room. But she had indeed moved from it in so silent and yet so swift a way that her chair had been vacant several seconds, and her skirts were sweeping one of the thresholds of exit, before the fact of her departure became even half perceived among the guests.

Once in the large, empty drawing-room immediately beyond that which she had quitted, she felt her leaping heart grow quiet, and her bewildered brain clear. It took only seconds, now, to restore in a great measure her self-possession and her courage.

She passed into the further drawing-room. Both were as void of human occupant as they were rich and stately in their countless beauties of adornment. Her visitor was evidently not here. Then she remembered the smaller reception-room which opened off from the main hall. She directed her steps thither. They were firm steps; she had grown sensible of this, and of her newly acquired composure as well.

Two breadths of Turkish tapestry hung down over the doorway of the reception-room, thus obscuring its interior. As Claire softly parted them and entered, she saw her mother.

Mrs. Twining stood near a white-and-gilt table that was loaded with choice ornaments. The chamber was one of great elegance and charm. It was all white and gilt and pink; there were cherubs on its ceiling throwing roses at each other; its hangings were of rose-color, and its two or three mirrors were framed in porcelain of rare design. A *connoisseur* who was among Claire's admirers had once assured her that this little room was exquisite enough to stir the dust of Pompadour.

Mrs. Twining did not at all look as though she might have been any such famous ghost. Not that she did not present a ghostly appearance. Her black eyes seemed to be of twice their former size, so lean and haggard was her altered face. Its cheek-bones stood out with a sharp prominence. You saw at once that some serious illness had wrought this wan havoc. Her garments were dark and decent; she did not seem to be a beggar; no rusty and shabby poverty was manifest on her person. She had refused stoutly to wait in the hall, and the servant who had admitted her, being hurried with other matters, had yielded to her insistence, yet deputed an underling to keep watch on the reception-room after showing her thither. Claire had not seen the sentinel, who was stationed at a little distance up the hall, and who joined his fellows when sure that the lady of the house had condescended to meet this troublesome intruder.

Mrs. Twining looked boldly and severely at her daughter. The drapery had fallen behind Claire's advancing figure. The two faced each other in silence for a lapse of time that both no doubt thought longer than it really was. Each, in her different way, had an acute change to confront. Claire scarcely recognized her mother at first. Mrs. Twining, on her own side, had good reasons to be prepared for a difference, and the superb house had in a way told her, too, what she might expect. But still, for all that, this was Claire! This was her Claire, whom she had last seen not far removed from slums and gutters — who had gone forth from the little Greenpoint home, not two years since, to follow her father's charity-buried corpse! And here she stood, clad in her white-and-purple vestments, a shape of more lovely and high-bred elegance than any she had ever looked upon. The face was the same — there could be no doubt of that. But everything else — the figure, the attire, the jewels, the velvets, the laces, the movement, the posture, the mien . . . it was all like some fabulous, incredible enchantment.

Forewarned and forearmed as she had been, Mrs. Twining stood wonder-stricken and confused. The soft strains of the near music seemed to speak to her instead of Claire's own voice, and with a disdain in their melody. She saw no disdain on Claire's face, however, as her eyes scanned it. But it was quite inflexible, though very pale.

Claire broke the silence — if that could be called mere silence which was for both so electric and pregnant an interval.

"You have come at a strange time. And your note shows me that you chose it purposely."

Mrs. Twining gave a sombre laugh. What associations the sound woke in its hearer!

"I was all ready for just this kind of a welcome," she said, knitting her brows. She began to stare about the room. "It's very fine. It's mighty splendid. But I wonder the walls of this house don't fall and crush you, Claire Twining! I wonder I ain't got the power, myself, to strike you dead with a look!" Her voice now became a growl of menace; there was something very genuine in her wrath, which she had persuaded herself to believe an outgrowth of hideous ingratitude. "But I did n't come to show you your own badness," she went on. "You know all about that a'ready. What I've come for is quite another kind of a thing — oh, yes, quite." Here she laughed again, with her mouth curving downward grimly at each corner.

"What have you come for?" inquired Claire.

"To get my rights! — *that's* what I've come for! To let people see who I am, and how you've cast me off — me, your mother. I d'clare I don't believe there ever was so horrible a case before. Perhaps some o' the folks in yonder can tell me if they ever knew one."

Claire kept silent for a moment. Her face was white to the lips, but there was no sign of flinching in it.

"I did not cast you off," she said. "I left you because you outraged and insulted the dead body of my father. I have never regretted the step I took, nor do I regret it now. You say you've come here to get your rights. What rights? Shelter and food? You shall receive these if you want them. I will ring and give orders at once that you shall be taken to a comfortable room and be treated with every care that it is in my power to bestow. In spite of what I said to you on the day when you shocked and tortured me into saying it, I would still have sought you out and rendered you my best aid, if I had known that you were ill. For I see that you have been ill — your appearance makes that very plain. But I had no knowledge of any such fact. You were stronger than I when we parted — stronger, indeed, and better able to work. This is all that I am willing to say at present. In an hour or two I will join you, and hear anything you may choose to tell me."

While Claire was in the midst of this rather prolonged reply, Mrs. Diggs quietly entered the room. The speaker saw her, and did not pause for an instant, but put forth her hand, which Mrs. Diggs took, while she steadily watched the large, gaunt, hollow-cheeked woman whom her friend addressed.

If anything could have intensified the vast sense of accumulated wrong in Mrs. Twining's breast, it was this placid appearance of one who so promptly indicated that she stood toward Claire in a supporting and accessory attitude.

"So, you'll make terms, will you?" said the parent of Claire. "You'll browbeat me — *me*, your mother — with your fine clothes and fine house and fine servants? And where's my satisfaction, if you please, Miss? Hey? Oh, I ain't any saint — you know that, by this time. I ain't going to forget how I laid eight months in Bellevue Hospital, crippled and nearly dying. First it was the typhoid fever, 'n then it was the pneumonia, 'n then it was the inflammatory rheumatism. And where was *you*, all that time? Spending your thousands as fast as the Wall Street stock-gambler you'd married could scrape 'em together. Who's this friend that steps in and looks as if she was going to protect you? Hey? You're both afraid I'll go in among those grand folks you've got eating and drinking somewheres, and speak my mind. You'll send me up to a comf'table room, will you? You'll give orders to your servants about me, will you? And s'pose I object to being treated like a troublesome tenth or 'leventh cousin? S'pose I go straight into where they all are, and just tell 'em the square, plain truth?" The scowl on her wasted face was very black, now. She had made several quick steps nearer to Claire and Mrs. Diggs. Once or twice during this acrid tirade she had waved one hand in front of her, and made its finger and thumb give a contemptuous audible click. But her voice had not noticeably lowered.

Claire had been watching her with great keenness. She had been reading her mood. By the light of the past — the retrospective light flung from weary years lived out at this mother's side, did this daughter now swiftly see and as swiftly understand.

"Claire," said Mrs. Diggs, spurred by an impulse of heroic interference no less than an alarmed one, "let me speak a few words; let me " —

"No," interrupted Claire. Her simple veto seemed to cut the air of the room. She turned and met Mrs. Diggs's gaze for a moment, while dropping her hand. "I thank you, Kate; but please leave all to me."

Then she faced her mother's irate glare. She was still decidedly pale, but in her clear voice there was no hint of tremor.

"Very well," she said, "suppose you *do* go in and find my friends. Suppose you *do* tell them everything. I do not merely invite you to go; I challenge you to go. I will even show you the way myself."

"Claire!" faltered Mrs. Diggs, below her breath.

Claire walked toward the curtained doorway and

slightly parted its draperies. She was looking at her mother across one shoulder.

" Will you come ? " she asked. " I am quite ready."

The enraged look began to die from Mrs. Twining's face. She receded a little. " I can go myself when I choose," she muttered. " I can find the way myself, when I'm ready. I ain't ready yet."

Claire let the draperies fall. She resumed her former position. " You will never be ready," she said, with a melancholy scorn, " and you know it as well as I. You thought to come here and make me cringe with terror before you, while you threatened and stormed. But you had no intention of bringing matters to any crisis. You think me very prosperous, very powerful, and very rich. You are secretly glad that I am. You would not on any account harm me as a person of importance ; but you wanted to keep me, as one, in a state of rule, a state of subjection. By that means you could climb up to a place something like my own . . . so you have argued. You would share what I have secured. You were always a very ambitious woman. Your sickness (which Heaven knows I am sorry enough to hear about) hasn't changed you a particle. I thought at first that it might have turned or clouded your brain — have made you reckless of consequences. But it has done nothing of the sort. You are precisely the same as ever."

Here Claire paused. Her mother had sunk into a chair. In her working lips and the uneasy roll of her eyes a great, abrupt dismay was evident.

" I think I can guess just what has occurred to send you here," Claire soon proceeded. " You became sick; you got into the hospital. While you were there a certain lady now and then visited your bedside. You told this lady who you were. Perhaps she asked you questions, and drew out all your history — perhaps you gave her all of it voluntarily. The lady was an enemy of mine. She put this and that together. She began by suspecting; she finished by being certain. We will say that you described me to her with great accuracy; or we will say that she knew I had once lived with the Bergemann family, and that you easily recalled the fact of Sophia Bergemann having been my friend long ago at Mrs. Arcularius's school. It is of no consequence how the real truth transpired; it *did* transpire. As you grew better, the lady formed a little plot. I think you perceived this; it is like you to have perceived it. You saw that the lady wanted to make you her tool, her cat's-paw."

Here Mrs. Twining rose, and put out both hands. "She did n't do it, though," was her flurried exclamation. "She thought she'd have me come here and get up a scene. I was 'cute enough to see that. I was reading her just like a book, all the time."

"I have no doubt of it," said Claire, with the same melancholy scorn. "But you chose *this time* at which to come. You were willing to be her accomplice *that far*."

"She would n't tell me where you lived nor what was your name," protested Mrs. Twining. "She kept putting me off whenever I asked her. She fixed things at the hospital so 's I only left it to-day; she made 'em keep me there, though I was well enough to quit more 'n a week ago."

"She told you to-day, then, of this entertainment?

She told you that if you came to-day, at a certain hour, you would find me surrounded by friends?"

Mrs. Twining set her eyes on the floor. She had begun to tremble a little. "Well, yes, she said something of that sort. And I knew what she was up to, just as clear as if she'd told me she had a grudge against you and was crazy to pay it. I was going to stay away till the party was all over — but I . . . well, I " . . .

Here the speaker raised her eyes and flashed them confusedly at her daughter. That glance was like the expiring glow of her conquered, treacherous wrath.

"Look here, Claire, I'm weak, and I can't stand this kind of thing much longer. Let me go up to that room and lay down. I'll wait till you come up. We can talk more when all your big friends have gone."

"I will send a woman to you," said Claire. "You can give her what orders you please." . . .

"Do you feel strong enough to go back at once?" asked Mrs. Diggs, when she and Claire stood, presently, in the front drawing-room.

"Oh, yes, perfectly," was Claire's answer.

Mrs. Diggs kissed her. "Claire," she said, "the more I see of you, the more you astonish me. I thought everything was lost, and how splendidly you turned the tables! Ah, my dear, you were born for great things. You ought to have been on a throne. I hate thrones. I'm a Red Republican, as I told you the first time we met. But I'd change my politics in a minute if you represented an absolute monarchy."

Claire smiled. The color was coming back to her cheeks. "I am on a kind of throne now," she said,

"Only it is going to pieces. Kate, you have seen that woman. She is my mother. I wish you had seen and known my father. Whatever strength there is in me comes from *her*. But what little good there is in me comes from *him*."

They went back into the dining-room immediately afterward, and Claire spoke with lightness to a few of the ladies about having felt a temporary indisposition which had now entirely ceased. She at once changed the subject, and throughout the remainder of the repast betrayed not a sign by which the most alert watcher could have detected the least mental disturbance.

A watcher of this sort was Mrs. Lee, and both Claire and Mrs. Diggs were certain of it. "She has n't tasted a morsel for three courses," soon whispered the latter. "Upon my word, I don't think I could be restrained from throwing a glass or a plate at her, if I were sure it would n't hit somebody else. I was always a wretched shot."

But Mrs. Diggs delivered another kind of missile after the banquet had broken up and the ladies had all passed once again into the drawing-rooms.

"I want to speak with you, Sylvia, if you don't object," she said dryly to Mrs. Lee. The latter had opportunely strayed away from her companions; she was pretending to scrutinize a certain painting in the front apartment. This gave Mrs. Diggs precisely her desired chance.

"You know I've never liked you, Sylvia, and I don't think you 've ever liked me," her cousin began. She showed no anger; her voice was so ordinary in tone that she might have been discussing the most commonplace of matters.

Mrs. Lee started, and twisted herself, as usual, into a fresh pose. "I really don't see the occasion, Kate," she murmured, "for this vast amount of candor." She had got back her old drawl. She was concerned with a knot of roses at her bosom, which had or had not become partially unfastened; her gaze was drooped toward the roses, and thus avoided that of her kinswoman.

"You don't see the occasion for candor, Sylvia? I do. You know just what you have tried to do this morning. There is no use of denying."

"Tried to do?" she repeated, raising her eyes.

"Yes," sped Mrs. Diggs, with a kind of snap in every word. "We've never liked each other, as I said, and I preluded my remarks with this statement because I want to show you why, from to-day henceforward, we are open foes. You would have had Claire Hollister's mother rush like a mad woman into that dining-room. You wanted it. You planned, you plotted it. There's no use of asserting that you did n't."

Mrs. Lee quietly threw back her head. "Oh, very well, since the poor woman," she began, "has really betrayed me, I" —

"Betrayed you?" broke in Mrs. Diggs. "She has done nothing of the sort. If you exacted any promise from her, I know nothing of that — nor does Claire. We both understood that you were behind the whole affair, and when Mrs. Twining was taxed with your complicity she did not presume to disavow it."

Mrs. Lee looked at her roses again, and touched some of their petals with a caressing hand.

"If you think me culpable to have told a poor

wretch in a hospital the address of the daughter who had deserted her," she said, " I am only sorry that your code of morals should so materially differ from mine."

" Morals?" replied Mrs. Diggs, with a quick laugh that seemed to crackle. " It's amusing, truly, to hear such a word as that from you to me, Sylvia ! "

Mrs. Lee again lifted her eyes. She was smiling, and her small, dark head, garnished with a tiny crimson bonnet, was set very much sideways. " My dear Kate," she said, " did it ever occur to you how enormously vulgar you can be at a pinch ? "

" I 'd answer that question if I did n't see through the trick of it. We 're not talking of manners, if you please ; we 're talking of morals. Do you consider that there is anything moral in a mean, underhand revenge ? That is exactly what you resorted to. To serve a spiteful hatred, you would have had Mrs. Twining dart like a Fury into yonder diningroom."

" If it were not unladylike, I should tell you that you are uttering a falsehood."

" Bah ! You can tell me so a thousand times, if you want. Why did you never let Claire's mother know her marriage-name or her address until to-day? Why did you keep her in the hospital until to-day ? Why, unless you wanted to unloose her, like a raging lioness ? "

" Really, Kate, you have passed the bounds of impertinence. You are now simply diverting."

Mrs. Diggs laughed a second time. " I intend to divert you still further, Sylvia, before I have done with you."

Mrs. Lee took a step or two in an oblique direction. The lids of her dark eyes had begun to move rapidly. "I have the option of declining to be bored," she answered, in a muffled voice, "unless you intend personal violence. In that case, you know, there are always the footmen."

"Answer me one question, please, if you have a spark of honesty left. What right had you to believe that Claire Hollister ever wronged her mother?"

"You haven't yet become violent. You are still diverting. So I will answer. She left her alone in poverty, neglect, and misery."

"She left her after a life of tyranny and persecution. She left her a strong, hale, able woman. She left her with ten, twenty times as much money in her pocket as Claire herself had — for Claire had scarcely anything, and this persecuted heroine of a mother had enough money to give her dead husband decent Christian burial, yet refused it. Did she tell you that, Sylvia, when you found her sick in the hospital? Did she tell you how her daughter cried out in grief, beside the very body of a dead and beloved father, that if only he were not laid in Potter's Field — if only he might receive holy rites of interment, she would work, even slave, for her mother's support? Did she tell you — this model and deeply wronged parent — that her child got from her nothing but a surly refusal? Did she tell you that Claire then, and only then, resolved to leave her forever? Did she tell you how Claire, faithful till the last, followed her father, on foot or by street-car, to his pauper grave, and saw the clods heaped over him as if he had been a dead dog, while she, his lawful wife, stayed shamelessly at home? No, Sylvia; I will warrant that she made another plausible story, nearly all false, with just a grain of truth. And you readily accepted it, because it suited your malicious ends to do so!"

By this time Mrs. Lee had produced an exquisite fan of dark satin, painted with charming figures of birds and flowers. While she used the fan, slowly and gracefully, she answered: "And is it possible that you credit this theatrical improbability, Kate?"

Mrs. Diggs looked stern. "I don't merely believe it — I know it," she said. "I have seen the woman. To see her — to hear her speak, was enough. You, too, have had both experiences."

Mrs. Lee still slowly fanned herself. "That is quite true. I have. The charity-burial story is the purest nonsense, the most preposterous invention, on your dear friend's part. That is my confident belief; I assure you it is. Do you want me any more, Kate? Or are you going to keep me here with your wild tales an hour or two longer?"

Mrs. Diggs never in her life, with all her personal deficiencies, looked so simply and calmly dignified as when she responded: —

"I shall keep you only a very little while longer, Sylvia. You may or may not have wanted Claire's mother to enter that dining-room. But you had your hour for her coming neatly timed, and any mortification, any distress that you could have inflicted would have been a pleasure to you. But I think that in all this wily and clever performance you quite failed to remember me. I'm very staunch, very loyal to Claire. And I give you my word that your share in the event of to-day shall not go unpunished."

Mrs. Lee stopped fanning herself. "Unpunished?" she repeated, haughtily enough.

" Oh, yes. Are you surprised at the word ? Let me explain it. I merely mean that in as short a time as I can possibly command Stuart Goldwin shall know every detail of your recent behavior. And pray don't have the least fear that he will disbelieve me. He knows how devoted *I* am to Claire Hollister. You know just how devoted to her *he* is. I wonder in what kind of estimation he will hold you after I have narrated my little story, not missing a single particular . . . not one, Sylvia — rest certain of that ! ''

Mrs. Lee began to fan herself again, and at the same time moved away. Mrs. Diggs's eyes followed the slim, retreating figure. She had already seen that her cousin's face wore an expression of pained affright. Claire's guests had begun to make their farewells. Mrs. Lee did not join them in this civility. She slipped from the drawing-room, instead, unnoticed by any one, except her late antagonist, and perhaps Claire herself.

' She will try to meet Goldwin before I do,' thought Mrs. Diggs. ' But she will not succeed. I, too, will leave without saying good-by to Claire, who might not approve my scheme of chastisement if she learned it. But it is no affair of hers. I am doing it entirely on my own account. I propose to make Sylvia Lee remember this day as long as she lives.'

Among the carriages of the departing guests, that of Mrs. Lee was the first one to roll away. The carriage of Mrs. Diggs soon followed it. Both were driven at a rapid rate, and for a certain time in the same direction. But ultimately the courses of the two vehicles diverged.

Each lady sent a telegram to the same destination,

less than ten minutes afterward. And each lady, after so doing, employed the same formula of reflection : ' He will come as soon as he receives it.'

But Mrs. Diggs's summons was the more potent; it contained the name of Claire.

XXII

GOLDWIN was the recipient of the two telegrams. He went first (being driven rapidly in a cab from his Wall Street place of business) to the house of Mrs. Diggs.

He remained with her for at least two hours. It was now somewhat late in the afternoon. He dined at his club, and by eight o'clock in the evening was ringing the bell of Mrs. Lee's residence.

She was alone, and received him with a freezing manner. "At last you are here," she said.

"At last," he replied, with careless ambiguity, throwing himself into an arm-chair, and looking straight at a very comfortable wood-fire that blazed not far off.

"Did you receive my telegram?"

"I did."

"In time to come to me when it entreated you to come?"

"I received it this afternoon. I have been prevented from making my appearance until now."

His voice was quite as cold and distant as her own. She went up to his chair and laid her hand upon its arm.

"Your manner is very abrupt and strange," she said, in greatly softened tones. "Has anything occurred?"

He turned and met her look. He nodded significantly once or twice before answering. " Yes, something has occurred, most decidedly. Can't you guess what it is? If so, you will save me the distress of explaining."

For several moments she was silent. " I suppose you mean that you have seen Kate Diggs," she then hazarded.

He nodded again. " I have," he replied.

" Ah ! " said Mrs. Lee, with an airy satire. " Then she must have made a very strong case against me, as the lawyers phrase it."

" Undoubtedly she has," he answered, rising. " I have heard the prosecution ; do you want me to hear the defense ? "

" Of course I demand that you shall do so," she exclaimed, " although I don't at all like the word you describe it by ! I have no need whatever of defending myself."

Goldwin gave one of his rich, mellow laughs. The twinkle had come back to his eye ; all his wonted geniality seemed to reclothe him. And yet his companion rather felt than saw that it was worn as an ironical disguise.

" Upon my word, I think you have been very hardly treated," he declared. The sting of the real sarcasm pierced her, then, and she sensibly recoiled. " You ought to have been allowed the privilege of witnessing your little scandalous comedy, after you had planned it so cleverly. How you must have suffered when it all went off in so tame and quiet a way ! "

Mrs. Lee, pale and with kindling eyes, slightly stamped one small foot. The sound wrought by this action was faint, though quite audible.

"You believe all that Kate Diggs has told you!" she exclaimed. "You think I wanted a public scene. It is not true. I wanted her to be humiliated by her own conscience at a time when she thought herself most enviable, most lofty. I had no other motive. It was not revenge. It never was anything like revenge."

Goldwin's face had sobered, but he made a little shrug of the shoulders, which was like him at his brisk, mercurial best. He had plainly seen her falsehood. "Why on earth do you use the word?" he asked.

She recoiled once more. "Use the word?" she half stammered, as if thrown off her guard by this unexpected thrust. A moment afterward she went on, with renewed vehemence, all her native drawl flurriedly quickened by excitement. "I used it because Kate Diggs used it — because she presumed to say that I brought that poor, suffering, deserted, outraged mother face to face with her daughter for this reason. I don't doubt that Kate has invented the same nonsense for you that she tried to foist upon me. She is very loyal to her friend. She has most probably told you that Mrs. Twining was always a monster to her daughter, and that she insisted on having her dead husband buried by charity, in spite of prayers, supplications, adjurations from the bereaved offspring. For my own part, I choose utterly to discredit this trumped-up tale. I never heard anything that resembled it from the feeble lips of the wretched woman who had lain for weeks in the hospital. I only heard" —

Goldwin here broke in with a voice more hard and stern than any which Mrs. Lee had known to leave his lips.

"If you will pardon me for saying so, I do not wish to continue your listener. If you think my interruption outrageously rude, then let me admit with frankness that I can not — yes, literally *can* not — endure what you now choose to state."

She gave her small, dark head a passionate toss. "You can't endure it," she cried, "because you think that woman perfection ! You can hear nothing that is not in her praise. You used to tell me that you thought Kate Diggs ridiculous ; you used to laugh at her as a wild, eccentric creature. And now you are willing to credit her fictions."

"They are not fictions," said Goldwin. "All she told me to-day was pure truth. Don't try any longer to shake my credence of it. Your efforts will not avail, I assure you."

Mrs. Lee shivered. She put both hands up to her face, pressing them there for a moment, and then suddenly removed them. She set her dark eyes on Goldwin's face ; they were glittering moistly.

"You think I edged that woman on, to serve purposes of revenge," she faltered. "Well, Stuart, if I did so, what was my real reason ? "

Goldwin was drawing something from an inner side-pocket of his evening-coat. "Truly," he said, in dry, tepid tones, "I have no idea." He fidgeted with the required something while he thus spoke. The next moment he had produced it. It was a slim packet of letters.

"I want to give you these," he said, with a brief, formal bow.

He handed her the packet. She examined it for several minutes.

"My letters," she murmured.

" Your letters," he answered, with a slight repetition of his recent bow.

She thrust the packet into her bosom. "You . . . you have *kept* all these?" she questioned, after hiding them.

" Yes," he said.

"And you give them back to me now," she pursued, " with a meaning? Well, with what meaning?"

Goldwin walked quietly toward the doorway that led into the adjacent hall. "Oh, if you want the meaning put brutally," he said, using a tone and demeanor of much suavity, " I . . . I — well, I am tired."

" Tired?" she repeated. Her next sentence was a sort of gasp. " You — you hate me for what I have done!"

"I did not say that." His foot was almost on the threshold of the door while he spoke.

"Stuart!" she exclaimed, hurrying toward him. The lithe symmetry of her shape was very beautiful now; her worst detractor could not have said otherwise. She felt that the man whom she loved was leaving her forever. She put a hand on either of his shoulders. She tried to look into his eyes while he averted his own.

"Will you leave me like this?" she went on. " You knew me long before you knew *her!* Don't let us quarrel. I — I confess everything. I — I have been very foolish. But you won't be too harsh with me — you will forgive, will you not?"

He did not answer her. He removed her hands. Then he receded from her.

" Stuart!" she still appealed.

"I have given you back your letters," he responded, standing quite near the threshold.

"Tell me one thing — do you love her? Is it because you love her that you want to part from me? I — I have scarcely seen you for weeks. You once said that a day wasn't a day unless you had seen me. Do you remember? I 've been stupid. But you won't mind so much when you 've let me explain more. Don't go quite yet. Stay a moment, and " . . .

He had passed quietly from her sight. She waited until she heard the clang of the outer hall door. Then she understood what a knell it meant. The alienation must now be life-long. She had made him despise her, and she could never win him back. Seated before the fire, that snapped and flashed as if in jeering glee at her own misery, she wept tears that had a real pathos in them — the pathos of a repulsed love. She had never believed herself at fault in her conduct toward Claire. Jealousy had speedily blackened the filial act of her rival, but in any case the story, as Mrs. Twining told it, would have roused her conviction that this desertion had been a most unnatural and cruel one. So esteeming it, she had played the part of castigator. She was not sure that she would have done very differently if Claire had not been at all an object of her hatred. She had not found the least difficulty in persuading herself that it was wholly a moral deed to use with vengeful intent knowledge which she would have been justified in using with an intent merely punitory.

But now she had wrecked all her own future by seeking to destroy Claire's. Mrs. Twining had broken faith and betrayed her. The passion which she felt for Goldwin was an irrecoverable one. Her

27

detestation of the woman who had caused their ceaseless parting grew as she wept over the ruin of her
hopes, and mingled its ferocious heat with the more
human tenderness of her tears. She passed a lurid
hour, there in her little picturesque parlor; she was
in spiritual sympathy, so to speak, with its Oriental
equipments. She could have understood some of
those clandestine assassinations which the poisoned
draught, the stealthy bow-string, and the ambushed
scimitar have bequeathed to history and legend.
Her past pietistic fervors had left her with no memento of consolation. A stormy turbulence had
taken hold of her mental being, and shaken it as a
blast will shake a bough. In her sorrow she was still
a woman; in her hate she was something grossly below it.

She at length remembered the letters that he had
returned to her, and drew them forth from her
bosom. For a moment the anguish of loss gained
mastery in her soul, and she held the packet clasped
between both hands, her eyes blinded to any sight of
them, and her frame convulsed with racking, internal
sobs. She knew that she must read them all over
again, and thus replunge into coverts of memory
whose very charm and fragrance would deepen her
despair. To re-peruse each letter would be like pry-
ing open the slab of a grave.

A sudden impulse assailed her as the violence of
her grief subsided. She rose, and raised the letters
in one hand, meaning to hurl them into the opposite
blaze, and thus spare herself, while the destructive
mood lasted, fresh future pangs. But at this moment her glance lighted on the packet itself. It
was of moderate thickness, and tied together by a

strip of ordinary cord. Inside the cincture so made, and held there insecurely by one sharp corner, a folded paper had caught, which seemed foreign to the remaining contents. Mrs. Lee disengaged this paper, opened it, and cast her tear-blurred eyes, carelessly enough at first, over some written lines which she had immediate certainty were not her own.

But presently a little cry left her lips. She turned the page with a rapid jerk, searching for a signature. She did not find any, but found merely two initials instead. She dropped into her seat again, and with a fire in her dark eyes that seemed to have quickly dried their last trace of moisture, she read, pausing over nearly every word, and pondering every sentence, a letter which ran thus: —

Friday.

DEAR MR. GOLDWIN, — I think that I meant all the harsh treatment I gave you last evening. When I recall what my feelings then were, I am certain that my indignation was quite sincere. But very much has happened since then to change me, and to change my surroundings as well. I suppose I am in a most reckless mood while I write these lines: my head is hot, and my hands are cold, and tremble so that the words I am shaping have a strange, unfamiliar look, as though I myself were not writing them at all. Well, for that matter, the same woman whom you lately parted from is not writing them. Another woman has taken her place. She is a wayward, desperate sort of creature; she is a coward, an ingrate, a worthless and feeble egotist.

But this new identity of mine will last. I have made up my mind to take a bold step, and nothing can now deter me. I shall not be explicit; at some

other time I will send for you and tell you everything. You shall hear my reasons for acting as I
propose to act. I don't claim that they are strong or
good reasons, and yet I feel that they contain a certain propulsion — they push me on. My marriage
has been an irreparable mistake; I can't go back
and live the last year over again; I can't repossess
my yesterdays. Hence, I have become willful and
headstrong about my to-morrows. If I had ever
really loved Herbert, all would now be so different! But I have never loved anybody who is now
living. There you have a frigid confession. You
never roused in me anything but a decided liking;
that other woman — the woman who called herself
by my name a few hours ago — used to disapprove a
good deal that there is about you. But my new self
will doubtless pass over these faults very indulgently;
she will have enough of her own to account for.
Still, she can never do more than think you good
company. I fancy that when I was a very young
child nature locked up a certain cell of my heart,
and then threw away the key where no one can ever
find it.

I mean to go abroad, very secretly, after the sale
of certain property and chattels shall have put me
in possession of the needed funds. It will be a flight
— and a flight from more than you are yet aware of.
If we meet abroad — say in Paris — I may even
stoop to discuss with you that question of a divorce.
It is horrible for me to write these words. It is sin,
and I feel the stab of it. But surely Herbert deserves to be rid of me, and perhaps he will come in
time to value his freedom. I should want him to
have the right of marrying again. Would not that

be a possible arrangement? I know almost nothing of the law on these points.

It does not now seem conceivable that I should ever become your wife after I had ceased to be his. I have had enough of marriage without love. But if you should prevail with me, it would be only because of your great wealth, and the ease and distinction that are now slipping away from me. You see I am hideously candid; I don't mince matters . . . where would be the use?

Do not answer this, but destroy it immediately. In regard to the last request, I count with perfect confidence upon your honor. Were it not that I did so, I should never send you this imprudent, daring, perilous scrawl.

Do not come to me until I send for you. I cannot tell how long that will be. C. H.

Before Mrs. Lee refolded the letter which contained these words, she had read them through certainly five successive times.

Not until then had she made up her mind just what to do. She would put the letter in an envelope, and direct this, very legibly, to Herbert Hollister. Her determination was as fixed as fate. . . .

When her guests had all departed, on the afternoon of this same day, Claire slowly walked the spacious drawing-rooms for at least twenty minutes, with her eyes bent upon the floor.

She felt literally hunted down. The end had come; the clock had struck twelve, and her fineries were rags, her coach-and-four was a pumpkin and mice. She had carried it off well until the very last; she was sure of this, and the surety gave her, even now, a bitter pleasure. She had no doubt that the coming of her mother, with imperative demands of support and countenance, would mean a return of all the old taunts and gibes. If Claire's wealthful life of to-day had been destined to continue, this prospect would have opened a less dreary vista; as it was, she foresaw only a dropping back into the former ruts and sloughs of maternal acrimony and intolerance. The history of her past would in a manner repeat itself. There would be poverty again, or something closely akin to it; there would be the mother's unpardoning disapprobation of her child's ill-favored lot. For one marked difference, Herbert would be present, as a fresh, assertive force. And what a miserably adverse force it must prove! To exist with him would be hard enough, now, under any circumstances. But if he felt perpetually the shadow and weight of this second gloomy and heavy personality, what new hostile traits might not his depression, his impatience, his revolt develop?

Claire tried to take a very calm survey of the whole potential consequence. In so doing she regarded the advent of her mother as one factor that consorted with other untoward agencies; the central knot of the tangle would be wrought of several tough and stubborn threads. There could be no unraveling it. 'But the knot could be cut,' she thought, silently continuing her metaphor, as she paced the stately rooms.

It sent a thrill of actual terror to her when she reflected *how* the knot could be cut. To the feet that have set their tread on slippery ways, evil can do much downward work by a gentle push. Claire felt herself lapsing, now. . . .

What if she wrote to Stuart Goldwin a letter very different from the one she had already written him, and which was then hid under the fleecy laces that clad her bosom? What if she told him that she must fly from it all? — the love that she had outraged by cold hypocrisy, the keen if mute reproaches that would be punishment and torture alike, the thrusts and innuendoes from a tongue whose venom had poisoned her childhood, the tarnish in place of splendor, the dullness in place of brilliance, the obscurity in place of prominence, the service in place of mastery — perhaps even the toil in place of ease?

She tried, in a pitiable way, to rebuff temptation by taking the sole means at hand of ending these desperate reflections. In reality she took the most cogent means of rendering temptation more potent. She tightened its black clutch on her soul; she went upstairs and talked with her mother.

Mrs. Twining had been securely convalescent some time ago. She had passed through a complicated and dangerous illness; she had given Death odds, yet won with him. She was still subject to those attacks of fatigue which are inevitable with one who has proved victor in so grim a wrestle. But she had once more gained a very firm foothold on that solidity which bounds one known side, at least, of the valley of the shadow. She intended, in a physical sense, to live a good many years longer; her freshening vitality was like that of a fire in a forest, which has stretched an arm of flame across a bare space, at the risk of not reaching it, but in the end has caught a mighty supply of woodland fuel.

Claire found her stretched quite luxuriously on a lounge, with a little table beside her, which held the remains of a hearty repast. She had the traditional vast appetite of the recovering invalid. She had devoured enough to have sunk a hearty person of average digestion into abysses of dyspepsia. She had enjoyed her meal very much. It had appeared to her as an earnest of many similar joys.

She promptly began a series of her old characteristic sarcasms and slurs as soon as Claire appeared. Mingled with them was an atmosphere of odious congratulation — a sort of verbal patting on the back — which her daughter found even more baneful than her half-latent sneers. She was thoroughly refreshed; her food (mixed with some admirable claret) had gone straight to the making of bodily repairs. She had never had anything so fine and wholesome in the hospital, though after the patronage of Mrs. Lee she had been supplied with not a few agreeable dainties. The temporary result was that she had become in a great measure her real self.

Claire said very little. She did a large amount of listening. She had never known her mother not to be without a grudge of some sort. It brought back the past with a piercing vividness, now, while she sat and heard. The vision of a pale, refined face, lit by soft, dark-blue eyes, rose before her, and the memory of many a wanton assault, many a surreptitious wound, appealed to her as well. Her father had stood it all so bravely — he had been such a gentleman through it all! *She* had stood it only with a sturdy, rebellious disapproval through many of the years that preceded his death.

She stood it, now, with a weary tranquillity. When she went away from her mother, these were her parting words: —

"I do not think I shall tell my husband, for some few days, that you are here. There are reasons why I should not. He has some very engrossing matters to occupy him. But you will be perfectly comfortable in the meanwhile. Order what you please. The servants will obey you in every particular. If you should need me, I will come immediately. You have only to send me word. I shall be at home for the rest of to-day, and all through the evening."

Claire went into her own private sitting-room, after that. When she had been there a little while, she had torn up her first letter to Goldwin. When she had been there a little while longer, she had written the second letter. Having finished the last, she promptly dispatched it, by messenger, to Goldwin's private address.

Between the hours of ten and eleven that same evening, the following note from Goldwin was brought to Claire : —

Friday Night.

In some unaccountable way I have lost the letter which you sent me to-day. I feel in honor bound to tell you of this loss, after a protracted search through my apartments and numerous inquiries and directions at my club. I cannot sufficiently blame myself for not having at once burned it to a crisp. But I thrust it into my pocket after many readings, with the wish to learn each word by heart before it was finally destroyed. Do not feel needlessly worried. I shall do my best to recover it, and even if it should be read by other eyes than yours and mine, the fact of your mere initials being signed to it is an immense safeguard. S. G.

Claire had grown deathly pale as she finished the perusal of this note. She had prepared herself for a night of wretched unrest, but here was a dagger to murder sleep with even surer poignance.

It was past midnight when she heard Hollister go to his apartments. She fancied that his step was a little unsteady. If this was true, no vinous exhilaration made it so. An excitement of most opposite cause would have explained the altered tread.

A saving hand had interposed between himself and ruin. The chance had been given him of starting again — of meeting all the fiercest of his creditors, and appeasing them. Instead of utter wreck, he had chiefly to think of retrenchment. Perhaps what Claire believed unsteadiness in his step was a brief pause near her own door. But even if an impulse to tell her the good news may for a moment have risen uppermost, there must have swept over him, promptly and sternly, the recollection of a dark and sundering discovery.

Meanwhile Claire, wondering if the lost letter had, through any baleful chance, drifted into his hands, lay pierced by that affrighted remorse which a monition of detected guilt will bring the most hardened criminal, and which of necessity strikes with acuter fang the soul of one yet a neophyte in sin.

XXIII.

HOLLISTER passed downstairs the next morning at a little after nine o'clock. He had obtained some sleep, of which he stood in sad need. The cheerful elasticity of his temperament would have placed him, by natural rebound, well in the sunlight of awakened hope and invigorated energy, and after hours of miserable disquiet he would now have felt relieved and peaceful, but for one leaden and insuperable fact. This had no relation whatever with financial turmoils and embarrassments; it concerned Claire, and the desolate difference with which her image now rose before his spirit.

He had told her that they must henceforth be as strangers, but already the deeps of his unselfish love were stirred by a longing, no less illogical than passionate, to make reality of what had once been illusion, and to verify Claire's indifference through some unknown spell of transformation into that warmth which had thus far proved only lifeless counterfeit. Already Hollister found within him a spacious capacity of pardon toward his wife. Already he had begun to exonerate, to make allowances; and more than all, he had already told himself that to live on without her love would be a hundredfold better than to part with her companionship. Here cropped out the old vein of complaisance and conciliation which had run through his earlier collegiate life, and which later experiences amid all sorts of risk and rivalry had never wholly obscured. It had been his power to concede, his amiable pliancy, wed with a peculiar intellectual shrewdness, that had gone far toward the accomplishment of his phenomenal successes. The man who makes the best of things by instinct is very apt to have the best of things made for him by fortune.

His inalienable love for Claire caused him to regard her long hypocrisy with fondly lenient eyes. The wrong done himself rapidly took a secondary place; it was nearly always thus with Hollister, except in those grosser cases of wanton injury from his own sex; and now, when it became a matter between his heart and the woman that heart devotedly loved, he was ready to forego a most liberal share of the usual human egotism.

He had a hard day before him. Exertion, diplomacy, astuteness, concentration, all were needed. He was still to fall, but no longer with a headlong plunge. He would now fall on his feet, as it were, but it required a certain agile flexibility to make the descent a graceful one. At any other time he would promptly have left the house after breakfasting. As it was, he waited for Claire. She appeared sooner than he had expected her. She had drank her coffee upstairs. He saw her figure, clad in a morning robe of pale-tinted cachemire, enter the front drawing-room. He had lighted a cigarette, and was standing beside the hearth, where a riotous fire flung merry crimson challenge to the sharp weather outside. He at once threw away his cigarette, and went forward to meet her.

She perceived him when he had gained the centre

of the second drawing-room. She stood perfectly still, awaiting his approach. There was more than a chill misgiving at her heart lest some inimical hand had sent him her own fatal letter. She did not know how she would act in case he immediately accused her. Hours of sleepless unrest had not supplied her with a single defensive plea.

The new serenity on Hollister's face struck her at a glance. It gave her a sudden relief ; it was like a reprieve just before execution. When he said "good morning" she answered him with the same words. She wondered if he had already noticed her pallor, or that a dark line lay under either eye. Her dressing-mirror had told her of these changes. . . . Might he not guess at sight the guilty agony that she had been enduring?

Her altered looks were not lost upon him. They were a new intercession in her behalf. " I have good news for you," he said, almost tenderly. He went toward the richly-draped mantel just opposite where she stood, and leaned one arm along its edge. He purposely let his eye wander a little, so that she would suspect in him no intentness of scrutiny.

" Good news ? " she repeated, softly.

" Yes. I thought it was all up with me, yesterday. But a friend of yours has placed funds at my disposal which will enable me, with wise management, to weather the worst of the storm. He dropped into my office at a very critical moment. He used the nicest delicacy and tact. Before I actually realized that he was offering me very substantial aid, he had done so. And yet, with all his graceful method, he did n't beat about the bush. He was frankly straightforward. He said just why he wished to see my affairs righted — or at least creditably mended. That reason was his deep respect and sincere admiration for you. He told me, with a winning mixture of humor and seriousness, that you represented for him the one great repentance of his bachelorhood. And when I looked at his world-worn sort of face and his decidedly gray locks, and began to wonder whether he meant his amazing proposition in any unpleasant sense, he assured me that he had always seen in you the daughter whom he had possibly missed being the father of. . . . Of course you now recognize his portrait; or have I not drawn it clearly enough ? "

" Do you mean Beverley Thurston ? " asked Claire.

"Yes. You see, now, how generous an act of friendship he performed."

" Yes, I see," Claire murmured.

" The funds he proffered — and which I accepted — are by no means all his own. His influence is so great, his standing is so secure, that he has actually been able to associate four well-known capitalists (one of whom, by the way, chanced to be my personal friend) in carrying out this wonderfully benevolent work." Here Hollister paused for a considerable space. " Of course," he at length went on, " I shall not do more than just escape a positive deadlock. The next few years must be full of cautious living and thinking. I have accepted the burden of a huge debt; but I believe firmly in my power to pay it off. And I have learned a lesson that I shall always profit by. They shall never call me a Wall Street king again. I have seen my last of big ventures. I shall want, if I can manage hereafter when every penny of liabilities shall be settled, to drift slowly but safely into a steady banking channel.

I shall have friends enough left on the Street; I shan't have lost caste; I shall still hold my own. At least twenty good men have gone clean down in this flurry, without a chance of ever picking themselves up again. But I am going to pick myself up — that is, thanks to the helping hand of your precious elderly friend; for I could never have done it alone."

Claire knew not what to answer. She was thinking of the sweet, deceitful kindliness that Thurston had employed. She was thinking how little she deserved his timely and inestimable support. She was asking herself whether he would not have shrunk in sorrowful contempt from all such splendid almsgiving if he had known the real truth concerning her recent mad and sinister act.

While she was trying to shape some sort of adequate reply, the entrance of a servant rendered this unnecessary. The man handed Hollister a letter, bowed, and departed.

Claire's heart instantly began to beat hard and fast. A mist obscured her gaze while she watched Hollister tear open the envelope and unfold its contents. There was a sofa quite near; she sank into it: she felt dizzy enough to close her eyes. But she did not. She looked straight at her husband, and saw him begin a perusal of the unfolded sheet. Was it her letter to Goldwin? Why should she even fancy this? Were there not hundreds of other sources whence a letter might come to Herbert?

In a very little while she saw her husband grow exceedingly pale. He left off reading; he looked at her, and said: "Did you write this?" He held the paper out toward her as he spoke.

Claire rose, crossed the room, and cast her eyes over the extended page.

" Yes, it is mine," she answered him.

The voice did not seem his own in which he presently said: " I must read it. I must read it with my full attention. If I leave you for a little while, will you remain here until I return ? "

" Yes," she said.

" You promise this? "

" I promise — yes."

Without another word to her, he walked back into the dining-room. Perhaps twenty good minutes passed before he returned. Claire had meanwhile nerved herself to meet something terrible. She had no idea what her husband's wrath would be like, but she felt that there might almost be death in it.

Hollister had hardly begun to address her before she perceived that he did not reveal a single trace of wrath. His eyes were much brighter than usual; he had not a vestige of color; his voice was low and of an increased unfamiliarity, but it did not contain the slightest sign of indignation.

She had seated herself on the sofa again, and he now came very close to her, standing while he spoke. He held the letter in his hand, which trembled a little.

" You wrote this to Goldwin, and it has been lost by him. Some one else has found it, and sent it to me. The handwriting on the envelope is not his."

Claire looked at him in blank amazement. It did not seem to her that he could possibly be the man whom she had thus far known as Herbert Hollister. He appeared radically and utterly changed. She could not understand just where the change lay, or

in what it consisted. She was too bewildered to analyze it or in any way draw conclusions from it. She
was simply pierced with a pungent sense of its existence.

"He lost it," she said. "He wrote me that he
had lost it. You are right in thinking that some one
else has sent it to you."

She wondered what he would now say. She forgot
even to feel shame in his presence. She was asking
herself what had so completely altered him. Why
was he neither angry nor reproachful? The very
expression of his features looked strangely unusual.
It was almost as if the spirit of some new man had
entered into his body.

"Whoever has sent this," he soon said, "is your
enemy, and wishes you great harm. But thank God
I have it!" He crushed the paper in his hand, immediately afterward, and thrust it within his pocket.
Claire rose from the sofa. Her hands hung at either
side, in a helpless way. Her eyes were still fastened
upon his face.

"Are you acting a part?" she asked, with a sort
of weary desperation. "I realize that I have done
a horrible thing. But tell me at once what course
you mean to take. If I am to leave your house, and
never to be noticed by you again, order me to go, and
I will go. The letter shows you that I care nothing
for that man. I don't make excuses; I have none to
make. But I am not an adulteress even in thought.
Remember what I say. My sin, dark as it is, has not
that one hideous element. I wanted to desert you —
to go abroad — you read the whole story in the letter.
You have only to speak the word, and you shall have
looked on me for the last time. . . . It is your silence

28

that tortures me. . . . Why are you silent? Here I stand before you, without a shadow of right to defend myself, and yet you force from me a certain kind of miserable defense, because you will not either rebuke or denounce me."

He had been looking at her very steadily. He now caught one of her hands in both his own.

"Claire," he said, "I have only one wish — one thought: to save you."

"Save me?" she repeated.

He went on speaking with great speed. His eyes were fixed on her own, and they were filled with a light that was rich and sweet. She had never known him to be like this before; he was just as tender as of old, but beneath his tenderness there was a strength, a decision, a virile assertion, that gave him a new, startling personality.

"Yes," he said, "to save you. There is no great mischief done, as it is. I think some woman sent me your letter. It is just what some envious or spiteful woman would do. But I have it, and can destroy it. You ask me what course I mean to take. You ask me whether I shall bid you to leave my house. My only answer, Claire, is this: if you have no love for me, then I have a very great love for you. I think you knew this long ago. I am your friend, poor child — not only your husband, but your friend. You shan't go wrong while I have the brain and the nerve to stand between you and folly. Other men might take another course. I don't care. You are pure, still; I am certain of it, and you shall remain pure. You are my wife; I will protect you; it's my duty to protect you. You have never loved me; you married me without a spark of love. But I gave you as large a love as man ever gave to woman. It's in my heart still. It can never die. If it were not so large and so true it would not seek to guard and shield you now. But it does — it must . . . Claire, Claire, you have been terribly foolish! A little more, and I could have done nothing to save you. A little more, and I must have cast you off. But as it is, I can and will plant myself between you and disgrace!"

He had been holding her hand all through the utterance of these words. But now he released it, and slightly withdrew from her.

She advanced toward him. There was a look of absolute awe on her face. She recognized how much her own blindness had been hiding from her. His very stature seemed to have risen. His tolerance appealed to her with sublimity. It flashed through her mind : 'What other man would have acted as he has done?'

In a few brief moments she knew him as the noble and high being he really was. The tears besieged her eyes. The enormity of the wrong she had done him horrified her. She stood quivering in his presence. The impulse assailed her literally to kneel before him. She grasped his arm ; her dry, tearless eyes searched his pale face with a madness of contrition in their look.

"Herbert," she faltered . . . "Herbert, I — I never knew till now that you could be so grand and strong! What kept me from loving you was your own love for *me*. It seemed to make you weak ; it seemed to put you below me. You were always yielding to me — always paying me reverence. But *I* should have bowed before *you*. You were worthy

of it, and I did not see . . . I never saw till now!
. . . Herbert, *I love you!* . . . Oh, these are not
idle words! They spring straight from my soul!
If you want the repentance of my future life, it is
yours! Why did you not show me your real self till
so late? What shall I do to prove my love? You
must not pardon me so easily — no, I cannot endure
that! It makes me sick with shame to be treated
so! Such a mercy would be cruelty. You must
punish me, somehow — I must undergo some pen-
ance, the harder the better. You have no right to
trust me again until I have passed through some sort
of cleansing fire — suffered, been mortified, humiliated, taught a stern and fearful lesson! You gave
me everything; there was nothing in the world I
did not owe to you; you lifted me from dependence
into the most brilliant prosperity. And I — Good
Heavens! I was a viper of ingratitude! I might
call it madness; I might say that the lust for riches
and power made me conceive this treacherous and
contemptible idea of deserting you — made me decide that we could not live together when the wealth
had gone. But it was no madness — there was too
clear a method in it for that. It was merely base
and mean — it can have no palliative. . . . Herbert,
don't look at me with any love, any pity in your face.
I can't bear it — I — I want to creep away somewhere and die. I am not fit to have you touch me
— No, no! you *must* not!'" . . .

She had receded from him; she meant to quit the
room, though her limbs felt weak and her head
giddy, and she was not sure whether she could reach
the doorway without falling. But on a sudden his
arms clasped her. How strong they seemed! She

had never till now had so keen a sense of even his bodily strength. When his lips touched her own she burst into tears. She was still struggling to free herself, but he held her too firmly; she could not escape.

"Claire," she heard him say, with a tenderness of tone more exquisite than any he had yet used, "I couldn't help forgiving you, dear, no matter how hard I might try. Oh, darling, let us begin all over again! You say that you do love me at last! Well, I believe you! *I want to believe you, and I will!* How could I ever punish you? You haven't been so greatly to blame — don't torment yourself by thinking you have. People were flattering and courting you; they made you a perfect queen; they turned your head. Now all that is over. I think there is a great happiness in store for us both, my love — a happiness that the money never brought us while it lasted. Perhaps, after all, it is better that I should find you weak. It makes you more human in my sight. I shan't bow down before you any more, as you say that I did; I shall only love you . . . love you forever — love you till death, and beyond it, too, I hope!"

He was kissing her cheek as he uttered these final words; but it had already seemed to take a certain chill, and in another moment he was forced to bear up her form, for it had no power whatever of self-support. She had fainted in his arms. . . .

She found him close beside her when she regained consciousness. She lay upon the lounge in her own dressing-room upstairs. He was bathing her forehead with cologne, and holding to her nostrils a handkerchief drenched with it. He had begun to

be alarmed at her continued swoon. The first thing
that her eyes reopened upon was his smile of glad
relief.

The light of that smile stayed with Claire through
years. It bathed her life in perpetual sunshine.

Everything altered in a few more weeks. They
left the great house and went to live in the smaller
one, which Claire personally owned, and which Hollister would not let her give back to him, though she
pleaded with him more than once on this subject.

"No," he would always say. "It is yours, and
that means it is mine as well. I meant, when the
crash first came, that you should keep it, and I was
glad that the law made it yours. If I let you give
it back to me, this would look as if I had lost faith
in you. And I have lost no faith; I have gained a
new faith — that is all."

'To think that I should ever have known this man
and not have loved him!' she would say to herself
again and again.

Every successive day brought with it a dear surprise. She felt toward her husband as though his
nature were a region through which she had journeyed heedlessly but was now revisiting with sharpened vision, vitalized intelligence. Traits and qualities that she could not but remember him to have
possessed, now assumed a beauty, a harmony, a pro-
portion, an allurement that she had never before
dreamed of recognizing. A fresh light, so to speak,
flooded the beloved landscape of his character. Vale,
grove, wayside, were all preciously different from of
old. Over them sang awakened birds, and still higher
leaned a shining sky, fond, fathomless, prophetic.

Very few of their former fashionable acquaintances

showed the slightest sign of deserting them. Hollister had been one of the many victims of the dire panic, but it soon became generally understood that he was going to make honorable settlement with his creditors — that he was on the list of the seriously wounded, so to speak, and not on that of the killed. In many instances there was even an increase of civility. Cards were left at the door of the small house, just as they had been left at the door of the more spacious one. Society made it a matter of *amour propre* not to drop them. It had taken them up; it could not afford to discountenance them for the single fault of a reduced income. The thorough-paced plutocrat is always very slow to admit his claims founded on anything so vulgar as a purely mercenary basis; and the aristocrat, on the other hand, will very often pay you a kind of proud loyalty when he has once openly ranked you as his equal. Moreover, both Claire and her husband had an ample personal popularity to fall back upon. They had been graceful and charming young figures, felicitously harmonizing with their festal background. Their absence left a sensible void.

But it was an absence, and as such it continued. Claire's love for the superficial glitter and pomp of what she had always inwardly felt to be sham and falsity was no longer even a dumb sensation. It had become the merest memory, and by no means a pleasant one. She had changed for the last time in her life. The change was securely permanent, now. If she looked into the future and asked herself what unfulfilled desire lay there, it was always to thrill with the hope that Herbert might one day be rid of all financial worriment, and that their home, already lit and warmed by a precious mutual love, might receive the blessing of a happy tranquillity as well.

For a long time this hope looked very far from being realized. She was untiringly devoted to his interests, and would hold long talks with him regarding the complicated and distracting nature of his affairs. Her apt mind, her ready and shrewd counsel, no longer surprised him ; but he recognized with an untold joy the different motives that now spurred and animated her. In the end light began to break from darkness. Hollister still kept steady the extraordinary nerve which had before enabled him to set aflame and continue such astonishing pyrotechnics of speculation. It slowly and surely became evident to him that he would soon have steered clear of all disastrous reefs, and bring forth from the final dying rage of the big tempest a ship not so wholly shattered that careful repairs and cautious sailing hereafter might not keep it very seaworthy for many years.

Claire had meanwhile exulted in her economies, and conducted them with that same easy tact and skill which had marked her past supervision of a large and splendid establishment. She still preserved a certain residuum of friends. There was no ascetic renunciation of all worldly pleasures, either on her own or Hollister's part. It amused her to observe just whom she retained as her intimates and allies. The survival of the fittest, in this respect, was something to note and value. It showed her that the gay throng in which she had shone was not all made of worthlessly flippant members. But those, both men and women, whom she now liked to have about her had each stood some pleasant test, had each presented to her some solid or sterling trait of mind or character, which gave them a passport into the gentler, healthier, and wiser conditions of her new life.

Beverley Thurston paid only rare visits to her home. She understood why he did not come oftener; she never pressed him to come. She had thanked him for his great service, with moist eyes and breaking voice. But she had not told him of the sweet ascendancy that her husband had gained. She had tried to let him see this change. Such revelation had been less difficult than spoken words; for all words on a subject that had now become so holy appeared to her impious.

During many days after imparting to her husband the knowledge that he must henceforward receive her mother into his household, she had dreaded the clash of their widely opposite natures, and foreseen trouble that would only lend weight and severity to that which fate had already inflicted. But by degrees she found herself laughing with Herbert at the shadows of her own fears. He treated Mrs. Twining as a kind of grim joke. With her invigorated health, she was prepared to hold him strictly accountable for his altered circumstances. Her sarcasms were more pitiless than Claire had ever remembered them. She took the attitude of a person who has been shut out from a banquet until the viands are all demolished, and then admitted to feed upon the unsatisfactory débris. She had no intention whatever of forgiving Hollister his misfortunes. In all her career of repulsive deportment she had never achieved a more obnoxious triumph. And yet, by the sheer force of good-humored, gallant, conciliatory kindness, Hollister at length succeeded in conquering her. She found it simply impossible to annoy him. He insisted upon not taking her seriously. His amiability was so impenetrable that she finally receded before it, and began to profess toward him a sort of gloomy, reluctant liking.

"I see," Claire said to him one day. "She is my punishment. But why should you share it?"

"Nonsense," he answered. "I think she is immense fun." It seemed to Claire that he was quite in earnest as he thus spoke.

"She really does like you," Claire said. "In all my life, Herbert, I have never known her to like — actually *like* — any one till now."

"That makes it all the funnier," he returned, with a slight, blithe laugh. She knew he was in earnest, then, and felt a deep sense of comfort.

Once Claire had spoken to him of Goldwin. . . . It already seemed far back in the past, now, although it was scarcely a year ago. Her words had been very few; her cheeks had burned while she uttered them.

"Herbert," she had said, "I feel that I must ask you whether you have — have met"— And here she paused. Then, while he saw the pain and shame on her face, she went stammeringly on: "Oh, you know whom I mean — I don't want even to speak his name again — but it is best that I knew on . . . on what terms you are, and all that."

He grew pale while he looked at her. His voice was very grave, but perfectly kind.

"I see him nearly every day, Claire. That is inevitable, you know. I have spoken to him only once since — that time. I did n't quite know whether I was strong enough to keep my temper. But I did keep it. I told him that I had learned everything. And then I told him, very quietly, that if he ever dared to address me again I would find an excuse for cowhiding him."

Claire sprang up from her seat. " Oh, Herbert! did you say that? And did he . . . stand it?"

" Yes, he stood it. I did n't think he would, for a moment or two. It was imprudent of me, perhaps — on your account, I mean. But he walked away, without a word. . . . And now, Claire, promise me that you will never, as long as we both live, refer to this matter again."

She threw her arms about his neck. " Never! " she cried. " I did n't want to speak of it, as it was. I promise you, with all my heart! "

They had been married several years when a child, a boy, was born to them. Claire made the most adoring of mothers. Mrs. Diggs, who was forever dropping in upon her friend, with even more than her former intimacy, said, once, while she watched the baby laugh on its mother's lap, after the bath that Claire had lovingly given it with her own hands: —

" Upon my word, it does seem so odd, don't you know? I can't just quite realize it, even yet, Claire, dear."

" Realize what? " said Claire, looking up from the rosy little treasure on her lap with a smile and two touches of color, for which the joy of her own motherhood was solely responsible.

" Why, that you are the same being I used to know. It 's a perfectly lovely change. You remember how I used to dote on you then. But I dote on you even more, now. Still, where *have* all your grand ambitions flown to?"

Claire looked serious, for a moment. Then she gave a light, sweet laugh. "Oh, I 'm a very ambitious woman yet," she said.

THE END.